THE ROOKS
DIE SCREAMING

"Give me a place to
stand, and I
will move the Earth"
Archimedes

Best wishes,
Sam

ALSO BY CLIVE TUCKETT

The Woman with the Red Hair

THE ROOKS DIE
SCREAMING

CLIVE TUCKETT

The Book Guild Ltd

First published in Great Britain in 2019 by
The Book Guild Ltd
9 Priory Business Park
Wistow Road, Kibworth
Leicestershire, LE8 0RX
Freephone: 0800 999 2982
www.bookguild.co.uk
Email: info@bookguild.co.uk
Twitter: @bookguild

Typeset in Aldine401 BT

Printed and bound in Great Britain by CPI Group (UK) Ltd, Croydon, CR0 4YY

ISBN 978 1912881 536

British Library Cataloguing in Publication Data.
A catalogue record for this book is available from the British Library.

For Min

and to the memory of Ernest Kempthorne,
who answered his country's call and made the ultimate sacrifice.

Prologue

"Dear God, forgive me for what I have done…"

London, 1916…

They always maintained the utmost discretion and secrecy when they met.

London society, always gripped by an endless stream of gossip and rumour, never batted an eyelid as their affair gestated, flourished and finally blossomed under the noses of the rich and powerful.

From the decadent cocktail bars that adorned Mayfair and Park Lane, to the seedy world of basement clubs where a world of lecherous and depraved debauchery echoed to the sound of ecstatic moans and the lustful cries of the wicked and immoral, the two lovers gave themselves first to each other, then to the mass of twisted and grotesque bodies that drew them into their infernal orgy.

Their world was one of deceit and subterfuge amongst the respectable middle classes. She, a fashionable and beautiful woman of means, wife of an eminent officer serving on the Western Front, received praise and adulation from the many charities she supported. Whilst he, tall, distinguished, drew praise from the highest levels of both society and government for his war record, along with the scars he bore from past battles.

And by night, whether it be in the privacy of her home in Grosvenor Square, whilst her children slept upstairs, or in his flat in Kensington, they would meet, each encounter breaking new taboos and sexual desires as their affair, like some sordid tale, unfolded and played itself out. As it did so, both knew they were being drawn inexorably towards a final act that neither could prevent or control.

And so that night, whilst war and savagery erupted across the killing fields of Europe, these two lovers met at his flat. She hurried to him by cab, fearful of the inquisitive eyes of the many London policemen and the prospect of being stopped and questioned as to why a woman such as herself might be walking out without a male companion at that time of night.

She alighted from the cab on the opposite side of his street, aware of the connecting alleyway that ran between houses and backyards, and paid the exact fare before adding a generous, but not ostentatious, tip. The driver was an elderly man and she was aware of his eyes boring deep into hers.

Accusingly? Knowingly?

She decided he'd probably driven many such passengers like herself to discreet and intimate rendezvous; maybe a lovers' tryst, a scandalous encounter or an assignation that might one day topple someone from the highest echelons of society.

But this man's eyes, though deep and thoughtful, were tired. It was as though he'd seen so many of her kind that he now felt empty of judgement and only wished that she might pay him and leave before the very aura of shame that surrounded her eventually tarnished him.

The darkness around her was enhanced by a thick smog that hung oppressively over the streets and houses. At times it might threaten to stifle the lungs of those who breathed its foul odour too deeply. Or it might simply swirl lightly, almost ghost-like, at low level, presenting itself as a sea of mist, broken only by the racing figures of those who dared to venture out.

His outer door had been left open, so there was no need to ring the buzzer.

For some reason there was no porter on duty.

The building was Victorian in design, with curtains drawn across all the windows, the same as every other building in a place fearful of another Zeppelin raid. There were only four flats in the building, something she always found troubling, knowing that such a small community would pry and question, snoop and condemn.

But his was on the ground floor, with a door that nestled conveniently within a small alcove, secretive and away from inquisitive eyes.

He'd taken a risk opening the front door for her; light from the hallway spilled out into the street and could certainly attract the attention of a passing policeman. He'd been clumsy, and she would find a way to tell him so, at the right moment, when she felt his hand probing, caressing…

But she was glad of the comforting ray of light. Even within the cab she'd felt the chill November air numb her to the bone. When she'd stepped out onto the pavement, the cold had become intolerable.

Now the light guided her, teased her… and somehow comforted her…

She immediately closed the outer door, briefly pausing to look back along the pavement and into the fog, fearful of the appearance of a policeman. But all she saw was the smog swirling like some clammy, deathly shroud.

He was waiting for her at the door and she paused, momentarily, whilst voices from the flat directly above his called out. Though muffled, they sounded an accusing tone, and she bit her lip in nervous expectation of some reproachful resident descending the stairs and casting a distrustful eye upon her standing on the cold marble floor.

Why was she there at this late hour?

Where were her children?

Yes, where are my children…?

It was the nanny's night off. She'd made no prior arrangement for a replacement and so put them to bed herself, reading their favourite story, Alice in Wonderland.

His telegram arrived just as she settled down herself.

He wanted her… needed her.

The thought of her children on their own racked her conscience and filled her with a guilt she worryingly felt able to restrain, flicking from one side of her mind to the other, seeking moral justification but finding none.

Before she left, she gazed through the half-opened door into their bedroom, immediately noticing her eldest, wrapped within his sheets, one arm draped across his favourite toy, a metal boat, with full sails and rigging. The paint on the metal reflected slightly from the glimmering light behind her, and she just managed to catch a glimpse of his face buried within the pillow beneath him.

Her youngest son lay opposite and, unlike his elder brother, had pushed his blankets far enough down to reveal his face in all its innocent charm. His eyes twitched, and his hand moved instinctively to a cavalry officer perched upon a horse that lay nestled within his arm.

Their beauty was beyond all bounds, her love for them beyond reproach. She believed there could be no greater love in this world and blessed the age they were, so young and innocent of the horrors that were tearing the world apart.

She was thankful the thought passed quickly and didn't linger to add substance to any guilty thoughts that might emerge from the slurry of twisted and contorted demons that threatened to arise from her subconscious and roar their disapproval at what she was doing.

Now, as she closed the outer door to her lover's apartment, she was vaguely aware of the smell of burning. It was a smell like no other, that swept across the city rooftops, and certainly didn't have the familiar stench of burning coal. It had followed her along the final part of her journey and she'd chosen to ignore it. As her heart quickened at the prospect of what the next few hours held in store, she was momentarily halted in her desires as she recoiled at a terrible thought that rose up and grasped her very soul.

And then the moment passed, like a distant memory finally laid to rest... but with the awful lingering sound of children screaming.

As the outer door closed, so unrestrained animal passion filled her, gripping her and holding her fast. She tried to breathe but could only pant like some base creature demanding to be fed. And as she drove the terrible sounds of those childish screams from her mind, a hand was already pulling her into another world.

The curtains of his room were drawn, save for a couple of inches between the two drapes. She'd noticed that he always pulled them thus but had never thought to enquire as to why. They both knew the consequences of shining a light during a blackout, but he'd always been careful to keep any interior lights to a minimum. Within her she felt the excitement of possible discovery, or of being the simple attraction of some voyeuristic neighbour.

The room was small and dark, and she was aware of the faint odour of tobacco. It was a room she was familiar with, and she glanced nervously around her.

She was surrounded by books, and as she twisted her head, feeling his lips upon her throat, her world became one of darkened outlines of large and small volumes sitting neatly from floor to ceiling. For some strange reason she felt compelled to read the spines but couldn't do so in such diminished light. Maybe they could shed more light on the man, help her understand his life beyond his naked lust.

She knew she was in his library, and remembered the first time she'd entered the room, so long ago. As his lips brushed across her face, she leaned her head back and rocked it from side to side, feeling his tongue dart across her neck, moving inexorably downwards.

Images flashed around her.

Books filled her world, with characters that called to her, reaching out from beyond their closed pages to plead for her salvation. She desperately tried to parry their advances, trying to mentally envisage him sitting quietly, either reading or penning a letter to his commanding officer.

But there was no room for such thoughts.

As his hands pulled and tugged at her clothing, tearing undergarments at will, she responded in kind, ripping his shirt from his chest and digging her nails into his skin as she felt him drive her against the wall and hoist her slightly above him, before finally easing himself into her.

With each thrust her body responded with a more determined and savage fury of its own. Pinned against the wall and seemingly helpless to his intentions, she stared deep into his eyes and knew he commanded her emotions. As she manoeuvred her body, working her pelvis against his, controlling her building orgasm, she moaned with pleasure and peered across the room at the gap between the curtains.

The outside world, shrouded in the familiar yellow smog, seemed illuminated by a distant light. As she gazed with bemused interest, she saw the light flickering more brightly across the rooftops, now lighting up the surrounding area and bathing the two of them in a strange glow.

As his thrusts became more powerful and determined, she closed her eyes and felt the growing might of her orgasm spread through her body. When it finally exploded within her, she gave herself up to its electrifying embrace, unable to contain the screams that poured from her lips.

And as that strange light burned with a terrible intensity, consuming her house and cremating her screaming children, she felt his hands slowly removing the rest of her clothing.

1

The county town of Bodmin lay nestled deep within the embrace of the wild and desolate moors that bound it close to its dark and melancholy heart. Its very breath swept across the surrounding countryside and chilled to the bone any who dared to venture forth among its grey and ancient streets.

Many years ago, the place had found favour amongst the smugglers and cut-throats who roamed the county looking for suitable hideouts and bases from which to ply their trade, beyond that of the occasional farmhouse out on the moors. The town's isolation enabled both illicit and legitimate businesses to flourish side by side, with both turning a blind eye to the other's activities. But where isolation allowed mutual trade from the good and the bad, it offered nothing but hostility and suspicion to the unwary traveller who found themselves walking its streets and footways.

Even the county court and gaol did nothing to distract the attentions of the footpads and smugglers. The regular crowds that came from afar to observe the public hangings brought with them both business and a morbid fascination for a place where those who walked its streets did so with a hurried step and a frequent glance over their shoulder.

Tales were still told of bodies lying buried and forgotten out on Bodmin Moor, their unmarked graves testament to the terrible fate that might await the uninvited. As the man the locals called Old Solomon had once said, nobody had any purpose in coming to Bodmin other than to trade goods or watch a hanging.

But that had been a long time ago, more than a lifetime for many who had fought through the carnage of a war that was said to have been the 'war to end all wars'. The broken homes and families that had once flourished within the town now fought a different conflict – one of loss and grief. As with many communities throughout the country, Bodmin tried to settle back into a routine of life that had, at the turn of the century, promised so much.

Its youth, once the proud and arrogant blood pulsating through the town's veins, had been decimated. The men and women who lived their lives, and had raised those children, themselves the very heart of this ancient town, now stared blankly into empty chairs and bedrooms, and asked for what purpose they should draw their next breath.

It was particularly worse on certain days, when the sun shone and a warming breeze swept through the town, cruelly teasing those unfortunate enough to still feel the dull ache in their hearts – a feeling of loss that all the pomp and grandeur of celebratory bands and monuments could never erase. When children chased each other through the streets and the gentle cry of a new-born baby heralded the passing of war, people still walked with shoulders hunched and eyes empty and sad.

The day had dawned brightly, promising a change from the seemingly relentless showers that had swept across the south-west peninsula for the past week. A breeze, fresh and vibrant, had lifted the spirits of those who'd risen early, either to begin their labours for the day, or to simply enjoy the fine weather.

The arguments and conjectures as to who had first seen Captain Wilbur Grant would rumble and reverberate throughout Bodmin for a long time to come. Suspicious characters were usually met with closed doors and turned faces; at best they might receive a polite and cordial refusal of lodgings or a meal.

The strangest thing, a woman reflected years later, was that she'd risen early to clean her doorstep and had wondered why – being a chore she usually did at the end of the day. For some reason she'd felt inclined to complete it early, and so claimed she was the first to see him, striding purposively by, his eyes set deep and staring blankly ahead.

She'd felt a tremor of excitement race briefly through her body at the sight of him and had wondered why she didn't feel ashamed at the thoughts that came to her as she held the scrubbing brush in her hand, aware of the warm and soapy lather splashing her face.

When she'd wiped it away, she'd looked above and noticed a lone rook circling her house, and the thought of his body next to hers was replaced by something dark and troubling.

A farmer later speculated that he'd caught sight of him walking down the hill adjacent to the Berryfields Estate, heading towards the gaol, but then couldn't be sure. He'd been struck by the immaculate army uniform, and his military bearing, which made the farmer feel inclined to stand to attention and respectfully watch him march past.

But the general talk in pubs between local folk was of the opinion that he'd appeared from nowhere, his image just emerging from a strange heat haze that had settled upon the town. Others, more apt at keeping a firm grip on rationale and logic, convinced themselves that he'd appeared from the direction of the small railway terminus opposite the army barracks. Whatever their opinion, all stood in awe of his noble bearing, his worn-down officer's boots, tanned and highly polished, and his immaculate uniform.

That Captain Grant appeared that morning to the townsfolk is beyond all doubt. The fresh breeze that had washed the town's sleepiness away had seemed to give way to a warm breeze that brought with it those circling rooks.

He was a tall man, with a pale complexion made strangely all the more apparent by a thick moustache that added several years to the thirty-two he'd recently celebrated. He strode confidently through the town, as though he'd lived there all his life, his blue eyes gazing vacantly ahead and not once acknowledging the passing look of a local resident. His luggage was a single kitbag slung over his shoulder, which he steadied with his left hand whilst regimentally tapping the ground with a thin and battered walking cane held tightly within his right.

If he'd cared to look, he would have seen and heard curtains closing and doors slamming shut. Children were called indoors, and worried faces peered anxiously after him as he passed by. Though seemingly oblivious to those around him, there was a feeling of mutual pain, shared between himself and the entire town. It was a recognition that war had, like a terrible pestilence, visited, stayed awhile and left, carrying with it any last vestige of life – or, more importantly, any *interest* in life.

It was when he reached the bottom of Fore Street that he paused outside of a small office set back a little from the road. The front door sat between two large windows, both of which were grimy and nearly rotten. The building itself looked quite dilapidated, and Captain Grant would probably have continued his journey if he hadn't noticed a small wooden sign attached to the wall.

Mabel Tregunnel
House and Room Rentals
Enquire Within

He didn't bother to pull out his pocket watch; the sound of bolts being pulled back from the other side of the door announced that, whoever this Mabel Tregunnel was, they were now opening for business.

As though anticipating his presence outside, the door swung open, and Grant was surprised to notice an elderly lady wearing a black dress with a white shawl, her grey hair tied neatly back. Her craggy face and stooped back made him feel compelled to step forward and help her as she tried to push the door far enough back so she could secure it to a latch on a rickety old post.

A glancing look from eyes reflecting a lifetime of business acumen, and a mind that was deadly sharp, caused him to step momentarily back.

She looked up at the circling rooks.

"Rooks will always bring bad luck to whoever lives in the house they settle on." She gazed high above the roofs of the surrounding buildings, baring teeth that were tobacco-stained. "Rooks shouldn't settle on a house…" She turned to Grant. "Rooks circling overhead, and a stranger like you walks into town." Her gaze turned to one of suspicion.

Grant lowered his kitbag and leant gently upon his stick.

"I'm looking for a cottage to rent. Somewhere in town, preferably."

Glancing around, he noticed the granite and brick buildings, with dreary alleyways disappearing into darkened recesses. Walls that were once whitewashed were now green with dampness or discoloured by the smoke that belched from the numerous chimneys around them.

"Well, you'd better come in, though I don't have much available here in town." The old lady beckoned him in and into a small office crammed on all sides with box folders and ledgers piled high from floor to ceiling. The musty smell reminded him of an old second-hand book shop he'd once visited in London on the Charing Cross Road. Due to the position of the terraced building, being set back several feet from the line of shops and houses, and the deep-set grime upon the windows, the room was uncommonly dark and dreary. "Only have one property here in town, though people don't usually want to stay there."

Grant studied the woman speculatively before replying, "I really don't care. As long as it's a small cottage, private and in the middle of town." Concluding that she was the proprietor, he would have felt the urge to inwardly chuckle at her appearance and the world in which she obviously existed, but something about her told him not to.

He couldn't be sure what.

Maybe it was the look in her eyes. Maybe it was the ease with which she glided between the rows of shelves and the desk that creaked under the weight of documents. To say he was fearful of her might have been an exaggeration, but he was certainly wary, believing that stronger men than himself had probably found themselves on the wrong side of her, much to their detriment.

"Well, there's 13 Creek Lane. And I'm guessing it's exactly what you're looking for, young man. Of course, I can arrange lodgings for you…"

Mabel Tregunnel had pulled an old box file from the top shelf and was blowing dust from its cover.

"No, a private cottage will suit me just fine." Grant coughed and sneezed as the dust assailed his senses. Observing the endless rows of old keys behind her desk, he added, "Can you take me there now?"

"I don't take anyone anywhere, young man," Mabel Tregunnel scowled; "I have a husband for that." She turned her head slightly, though didn't lose eye contact with him. "Horace!!" Her voice cut like lightning through the room and reverberated throughout the house. "Horace!! Come down here!!"

Grant shrank back a little as she glared at him.

"Horace is younger than me. Moves faster than I do. Horace!!"

From a distant part of the building came a faint reply, "Coming, dear."

Mabel Tregunnel opened the file before her. "13 Creek Lane. Two bedrooms. I'll take one month in advance."

"Do you want me to sign anything?" Grant asked nervously. "How long is the lease?"

"You pay me one month now, and we'll see." For once the old lady actually forced a smile; but it was what it was, contrived and without warmth.

From a door to Grant's left appeared a small man, bald and haggard, his face ashen, with eyes that appeared to vanish within their sockets. Though he struggled for breath, he did manage to extend a rickety old hand that Grant immediately shook.

"Good morning to you, young fella." The voice was terribly hoarse, with a disconcerting rattle.

"Good morning... Mr Tregunnel?" Grant smiled.

Horace Tregunnel stared across at his wife and meekly nodded.

"Horace is younger than me." The old woman had lost that beguiling smile and was returning her husband's gaze. "Mother said I should never have married him. Sixty years and neither chick nor child..." She paused before winking at Grant. "Weren't through lack of trying, though."

"I'm sure," he replied.

"Anyway, why don't you lodge over at the barracks?" the old lady asked suspiciously, eyeing his uniform.

"Because I'm here on private business that has nothing to do with the garrison in Bodmin," he quickly countered, before taking a deep breath and adding, "How far is Frobisher Hall from here?"

"Now, why would you be wanting to visit that place?" Mabel Tregunnel leaned forward on her desk, her visage now one of deep concentration.

"I have business with Captain Harry Frobisher," he replied guardedly.

"Frobisher Hall is about five miles yonder out upon the moors, young fella," Horace Tregunnel croaked weakly.

"Bad place, Frobisher Hall... Murders there last year," his wife hissed. "And that Scottish woman. They said she was mad... Locked her up over at the asylum. They say she's cursed... a witch with red hair, and so beautiful that no man can resist her—"

"Now, dear, I think—" her husband tried to intervene.

"Think what you like, Horace Tregunnel," Mabel interrupted; "you must be the only man in Bodmin not to fall under her spell."

"I'm sorry, I don't think I follow you." Grant observed the husband and wife before him and tried to ascertain some kind of grounding in his mind before proceeding with the discussion. "Harry Frobisher is an old colleague of mine from the war. Who is this woman you refer to?"

"She killed his parents and shot his poor brother William."

"You can't say—" The old man began.

"You be quiet!" Mabel Tregunnel's eyes blazed with an intensity and passion Grant thought might put her in danger of bursting an artery. "You mark my words... They call her the 'woman with the red hair'... They say she's the most beautiful woman a man will ever see in this life or the next."

★★★

Though the morning had dawned brightly in Cornwall, London was struggling to clear the remnants of a front that had drifted eastwards and was now stagnated over the city. The rain had eased in its intensity, but a fine veil of drizzle fell with an annoying persistency as people peered out into the gloom and weighed the odds for and against the use of an umbrella.

Still feeling the effects of the short walk from Scotland Yard over to Whitehall, Inspector Cyril Edwards sat back in a soft leather chair and puffed nonchalantly on the Cuban cigar he'd just lit. Dressed in his usual three-piece pinstriped suit, with gold watch chain, he removed his favourite Fedora hat and placed it on his knee.

His features seemed more deeply set than they had been six months before. The lines on his forehead hinted at a man carrying a weight of responsibility he could never hope to shed. His moustache, though, bristled with style and panache, with silver streaks that matched the threads of grey that ran through his hair. When he brushed it with his fingers, he did so first to the right, then to the left, majestically flicking up the ends.

His usual guilty pleasures came in the way of a glass of decent whisky, accompanied by his favourite pipe. But when a Cuban cigar was offered his way, and with no immediate connotations, he really thought it might be too rude to refuse the offer.

He was, though, sitting in an office in the bowels of Whitehall, cocooned within the plush décor and fighting the urge to frown disrespectfully at such authoritative surroundings. Yes, he'd visited different departments in the building over the past few years in the line of duty, but it wasn't until he was in this particular office that he realised just how cold and empty they actually were in comparison.

The furniture surrounding him was Georgian, very sleek and highly polished. Mahogany cases with huge glass fronts adorned the walls and were filled with beautifully crafted ornaments the likes of which he'd never seen before. The windows, large and stately, gleamed with crystal clarity and were partially covered by huge velvet drapes. The floor was covered in the most intricately patterned and plush carpet, and Edwards more than once chanced a slight glance at the underside of his boots, fearful that he might have stepped in something unsavoury before mounting the stairs and entering the room. He was of the mind to associate the origins of the carpet with the name Persia. This was simply because, somewhere in the midst of time, during an investigation on some remote country estate, he'd stood on a similar carpet and was told by an indifferent butler of its make and value.

But he declined the urge to suggest as such to the man standing before him.

"Inspector Edwards." A man in his early fifties, with eyes that narrowed so deeply and intently that the police inspector thought they might be lost forever, stepped forward from behind his desk and crossed the room to a drinks' cabinet tucked discreetly out of sight behind two small mahogany doors fronting a large cabinet. "I hope you like whisky, Inspector. There was a time we couldn't find a decent malt anywhere." He was of average height, portly, with a flushed face that gave Edwards the impression of a Father Christmas, without the white beard, and dressed smartly in the uniform of a very high-ranking British officer. "Now things have certainly changed." He drew forth two glasses, followed by a bottle.

Edwards drew on his cigar, held the smoke briefly, then exhaled slowly, watching the smoke drift towards the finely crafted ceiling.

"Inspector, do forgive the drama, inviting you here without any explanation." He advanced towards Edwards and held out a glass containing a single measure of whisky.

Edwards noticed his own moderate measure, before spying, with unrestrained envy, his host's double measure.

"I suppose after many years working in this department, I've developed a taste for the melodramatic... The cigar and whisky." He nodded at the décor before returning to his desk. "All this, and not your normal Whitehall office."

Edwards followed his movement and now felt slightly irritated at the fact that he held a glass of whisky in one hand, a rather ostentatious cigar in the other, and yet knew absolutely nothing as to the purpose of his visit. Though happy to keep a box of cheap cigars and an equally cheap bottle of rum in his desk drawer across the road at Scotland Yard, he usually produced them at the successful conclusion of a case, or maybe when he was working late and knew he had nothing more to look forward to at home than a cold bed and the memory of his wife.

He eyed the man before him suspiciously.

"My name—"

"Is Colonel Standish... Charles Standish," Edwards interrupted.

"Yes, of course, you already know that part..." Charles Standish glanced nervously around the room.

"It was you who summoned me, Colonel." Edwards drew on his cigar before deciding it was a convenient moment to lean forward and rest it upon the side of an ashtray situated on the desk in front of him. Staring at the glass in his other hand, and reflecting upon the stunningly beautiful taste of its contents, he decided to keep it firmly in his grasp. "I do find it a rather annoying distraction that I be pulled away from the two investigations I'm currently leading to attend this meeting." Edwards sipped his whisky, resisting the urge to drain the remnants in one gulp. He was sitting in a rather low soft chair and finding it difficult to decide what to do with his legs. Though the room was large, it was warm and quickly becoming heavy with cigar smoke. "I do realise that such a high-ranking officer as yourself does not invite a simple police inspector over to share his cigars and malt whisky..."

"Ah, yes, your investigations..." Standish spoke with a twinge of mocking arrogance. "Still chasing after that woman who poisoned her family?"

"Her family, before going on to poison two other men," Edwards corrected.

"Good grief," Standish stiffened.

"Yes, that's what I said when we exhumed the third victim." Edwards sipped his whisky. "Anyway, a colonel in Whitehall doesn't invite me over here because of a morbid interest in murder... or maybe he does."

"You're obviously familiar with the name Captain Harry Frobisher, Inspector?"

This time there was no tentative sip; Standish gulped a mouthful of his whisky and licked his lips, replacing the glass upon the desk.

The statement carried the same impact as someone yielding an emotional sledgehammer.

Edwards leaned back in his chair and eyed the colonel speculatively. Running a hand across his chin he said calmly, "Just about everyone in Scotland Yard read my report, even though the Assistant Commissioner tried to hush it up. I have no doubt that what you just asked me was a rhetorical statement."

"Yes, Inspector, I also read your report," Standish smiled. "Quite remarkable, really. Also very unorthodox..."

Edwards remained silent, though lightly brushed a finger over his moustache. Surveying the man before him, he felt as though a dam were about to burst, and time was running out for him to decide on what to do.

Of all the things he could have said, he heard himself say, "So, what's your interest, then?"

"And you, Inspector Edwards..." Ignoring the question, Standish opened a drawer to his left and pulled out a file. Opening it, he perused the contents, smiling and shaking his head as he did so. "You have quite a record... Very impressive... Decorated several times whilst serving in the army. The last..." he flipped over several pages, "was during the Siege of Mafeking... where you were wounded twice... Honourable discharge from the army, and within a year you'd joined the

Metropolitan Police… quickly rising through the ranks to make inspector within twelve years… Fascinating… Decorated again for your undercover work against Irish Nationalists…" Standish glanced up and eyed Edwards intently. "Do you still box?"

"No," Edwards replied flatly.

"Your record shows you boxed for the regiment and the police?"

"That was a long time ago." Edwards sniffed and tried to focus on the opened file on the desk.

"Quite so…" As though aware of Edwards' attention, Standish pulled the file closer to himself. "Married Elisha Donaldson, sister of Morag Donaldson. I see your wife died of Spanish flu." Without looking up, Standish said blankly, "I'm sorry."

The words fell flat, and Edwards sighed deeply.

"You're quite the individual, aren't you?" Standish's voice had taken on a colder edge, as though the factual background of Edwards had been covered and now it was time for personal opinions to be aired. "You've refused three invitations to join the Freemasons and have openly spoken of your support for women suffragettes. You allegedly struck the King's cousin whilst serving as his bodyguard and have, on several occasions, ignored protocol and orders…" He paused, flicking over several sheets before leaning back in his chair. "Yet you've never been disciplined or made to answer for what I can see have been flagrant abuses of your position." He leaned forward and picked up his glass of whisky. "Have I missed anything out?"

"Cricket," Edwards replied nonchalantly.

"What?" Standish was about to take a sip before he paused.

"I love cricket… When I'm not turning down invites to dubious organisations, and thumping arrogant members of the Royal Family, I love nothing more than to relax at Lord's and watch a game of cricket." Edwards stretched and picked up his Fedora hat, contemplating getting up and walking out of the room. "I'm hoping to see the Second Test at Lord's next month, against Australia."

Standish nodded, his eyes appraising, his face cold. "Since your return from Cornwall last year, you've visited several spiritualists… Did something happen down there to prompt this sudden interest?"

Inspector Edwards gazed into his glass before swallowing the contents in one gulp. "This meeting is over," he said, more to himself than Standish. He made to stand up.

"On the contrary, Inspector, it is only just beginning… Please, sit down…"

Edwards returned the colonel's stare. "Quite frankly, Colonel, I wish you would just get to the point. You mentioned Lord Frobisher… It seems that after the events of last year everybody wants to know about Lord and Lady—"

"How well do you know him?" Standish interrupted.

"Well, considering he's now my brother-in-law, that I dined with him when his own brother was trying to poison him, and nearly froze to death trying to rescue him and my sister-in-law, I would say I know him quite well."

"No faults or flaws you can think of, Inspector?"

"We all have faults, Colonel." Edwards' irritation had given way to intrigue, which soon threatened to give way to further irritated impatience.

"Quite so, Inspector. Quite so. And I'm probably not making sense to you." Standish gulped the rest of his whisky down and crossed the room to the cabinet. As he lifted out the whisky decanter he paused, staring down at the solid crystal glass in his hand. "Did Captain Frobisher talk much about his time in the army?"

"Only his experience after losing his sight," Edwards responded, trying to recall if there had actually been any other references made.

"He never spoke to you about his time in France before he lost his sight?"

"No…" Edwards said firmly. "Look, can I ask exactly why you've summoned me here, Colonel?"

Ignoring Edwards' remark, Standish continued, "Captain Frobisher—"

"Lord Frobisher I believe now, Colonel." Edwards made no attempt to blunt the acerbic thrust of his comment.

"Hmmm, yes. I stand corrected." Standish grinned, pouring himself another large measure. "You met Lord Frobisher last year for the first time. Was that the case with his brother William?"

"Yes, I'd never met either of them before last year." Edwards pulled himself out of his chair. In one continuous movement he skirted round to the rear of the chair and leant on the headrest.

The chair now made a suitable barrier.

As if sensing the policeman's rapidly dwindling patience, Standish placed his glass on the table and said, "Okay, Inspector, what we discuss in this room goes no further. The consequences for all of us are dreadfully severe if you repeat anything I am about to say. As you know, Military Intelligence is still hunting down enemy agents across the world, even though we're officially at peace with Germany. These people remain a dangerous threat to the national interest, and the security and defence of the realm. We know they're still operating in this country. Sleepers, whose role is to awaken when activated, and create God knows what damage, still remain among us. We don't know their exact identity as many of them worked outside of the spy networks supposedly under our control. When we penetrated these cells, we found no trace of them…"

"Seems like you've had your hands full," Edwards reflected sardonically.

"Oh, we have, Inspector, we certainly have. Because now our problems have taken a rather nasty turn. Enemy agents were known to have infiltrated our own cells during the war and, by doing so, left themselves vulnerable to discovery. But at the end of the war, they slipped back into society… Our society…"

Edwards remained silent.

Though he felt the dam had burst, he feared the main deluge was yet to sweep over him. Colonel Standish looked as though an immense weight had been lifted from his shoulders; yet even within those deep and concentrated eyes, Edwards saw the rising of something dark and troubling.

His concerns were deepened as he observed Standish reach nervously for his glass of whisky and drain the contents in one gulp.

Men, he thought, *who drink whisky like that usually have a problem or two in their lives.* It was an idle thought, one that didn't prepare him for what came next.

"Ha-Have you met with Lord Frobisher since the incident last year?" Standish stuttered slightly.

"Why do you ask?"

"Please, Inspector. Before we go any further…"

"Yes, if you need to know. I met with Lord and Lady Frobisher in London a couple of days ago. We dined at The Ritz." Edwards smiled inwardly as he recalled the evening.

Morag had been beautifully attired in a woollen dress that hung to a level just above her knees. He'd kissed her lightly upon each cheek and felt his eyes well up as he saw the reflection of her sister in her eyes.

Harry had shaken his hand in a grasp he thought might never end.

The bond of love and trust had enfolded the three of them within its wings, as it had done so one terrible night not so long ago…

"And before then?" Standish's voice echoed from a darkened place.

"Their wedding in Cornwall." Edwards felt his patience finally fall apart at the man's persistent questioning. "And if you

16

don't get to the point soon, Colonel, I'll leave you to enjoy your next glass of whisky alone."

"Military Intelligence has a dossier on Lord Frobisher," Standish sighed heavily, "pertaining to his activities when not serving with his regiment."

Edwards tried to digest the words.

"We suspect he was involved with a network of spies during the latter part of the war…" It was as though Standish was using short, thrusting statements to bring about some form of response from the policeman.

Thinking this was the case, Edwards stared back with a cold indifference.

"After losing his sight, he disappeared from our attentions… Possibly due to the fact that—"

"He had a nervous breakdown…" Edwards interrupted, his mind struggling to cope with the torrent of emotions that threatened to drown him.

"Hmmm… Yes, quite…" Standish scratched his head before adding, "And then he returns home and walks into one of the strangest tales of murder and false imprisonment I've ever read about."

It was at this point that Edwards noticed the strange walking stick lying across the desk. He hadn't noticed it before. But now Standish instinctively reached out and grasped it by the handle. He thought it strange, due to the rather sinister shape of a silver serpent that coiled itself around the handle.

"You think he was a spy?" he asked indignantly.

Standish pulled the stick towards him and held it against his chest, as though ready to protect himself from some assailant.

"You say he had a nervous breakdown after his injury. Military records here in London record him as receiving medical treatment for his wounds, but with a diagnosis of complete blindness. The doctors wanted to remove his eyes and replace them with false ones, or leave them closed. He refused…"

"Because he believed he might seek a second opinion," Edwards proffered.

"Blind is blind, Inspector."

"That's quite an arrogant statement, even from such a high-ranking officer as yourself," Edwards sneered, shaking his head. He observed Standish swallow hard and lick his lips, trying to ignore the slight.

"Arrogant or not, Inspector, the truth is, Military Intelligence lost trace of his movements for a whole year until he returned to Frobisher Hall."

"He was ill. Good God, the man fought in just about every battle there was." Edwards scanned the colonel's chest, where he counted three ribbons stitched onto his tunic. "And I can tell you, he holds more medals than you'll ever receive."

Standish shrugged. "Personal insults against me are not going to help Lord Frobisher, Inspector. Thousands of men fought and earned their country's recognition, but they didn't commit treason against their country."

"You must be insane if you think Lord Frobisher was a traitor."

Standish sighed and peered over towards the window. "I understand your loyalty to the man, Inspector, but Lord Frobisher needs to account for his actions during those months he was away—"

"I've told you," Edwards tried to interrupt but stopped at the raised hand of the man before him.

"Speculation, Inspector, from a man who, if we are to believe your accounts of those events last year in Bodmin, nearly froze to death trekking across Bodmin Moor in thick snow to rescue him and your sister-in-law." Standish eased himself forward and walked across to the window, finally to stand, eerily silhouetted within its frame.

"Speculation, Colonel." Edwards composed himself. "But that is all you have. Because, so far, you've provided not a shred of evidence."

"Yes, Inspector, that is where you come in. I have it all arranged." Standish stayed as he was, like some ghostly apparition hovering, threatening…

Edwards felt uneasy, as though a black pit were opening up before him. The real purpose of his summons was about to become clear, and he began to mentally prepare himself, annoyed that he could be duped into accepting a cigar and whisky with such ease. He also became aware of just how much he disliked and distrusted this man before him.

"We need you to travel down to Bodmin under some pretence of tying up loose ends from your investigation last year," Standish spoke carefully, as though issuing an order to a subordinate.

"You want me to find the evidence you quite obviously don't have…" Edwards stepped closer to Standish.

"If you want to put it that way, yes."

"But why me? Like you said, I have a rather biased opinion to start with."

"Because Lord Frobisher trusts you. Because you are now related. If we send in another officer to investigate, he'll become suspicious."

"And if I refuse?" Edwards moved closer to Standish, who subsequently lost that blurred and ghostly image.

"You can't, Inspector. I could make life very difficult for you." Again, Standish pulled his stick up close to his chest. He twirled the handle round until the serpent's head was facing the policeman. "What you did last year, though very heroic, was completely unorthodox and quite without any authorisation. You endangered the life of a serving policeman who subsequently resigned from the force. I read, with interest, your statement about losing your notebook up on the moor during your trek through the snow. Quite frankly, Inspector, I think truth and fabrication have become so intertwined with local folklore and legend that nobody will ever know for certain what happened over those few days you were down there... In short, if you refuse this request," Standish grinned, revealing nicotine-stained teeth, "I will ensure you're dismissed from the police force."

"And the Assistant Commissioner?"

"Informed last night. We have his full cooperation..." The grin took on a more contemptable sneer. "Like yourself, Inspector, he had no choice."

"And if I find nothing? If Lord Frobisher is innocent of these suspicions? What then?" Edwards reflected, "Are you simply going to accept my word?"

"It may interest you to know that a former colleague of Captain Frobisher's has already made his way down to Bodmin... Someone we know was an agent working in France and Belgium."

"Answer my question, Colonel." Edwards remained unmoved.

"In answer to your question, Inspector, I think Lord Frobisher was involved in something, but to what extent, I need you to ascertain. How you do so, I'll leave to your... shall we say... indomitable skills of following your own lines of investigation."

Edwards felt the room grow colder.

Where once it had radiated charm and comfort, it now mocked and sneered. The once aromatic smell of cigar smoke now left a stagnant and almost repulsive odour in his nostrils. He moved a little closer to Standish, his feelings of hostility now dissipated. There was now only sadness and melancholy in his heart.

He spoke softly, "Okay, I'll do this for you."

"Good!" Colonel Standish stepped forward with a noticeably lighter step. "How about another drink, Inspector?"

Edwards shook his head.

"Really?" Standish made his way back to the drinks cabinet, collecting his empty glass on the way. Once he'd poured himself another drink he made his way back to his desk, opened a drawer and pulled out a large file, held together by string, with the words 'Top Secret' set ominously on the front. "You might want to pour yourself another drink before we discuss this matter further."

"What do you mean?" Edwards eyed him suspiciously.

"Tell me, Inspector," asked Colonel Standish, flipping open the file, "what do you know of an organisation called The Nest of Rooks?"

★★★

"Can you tell me something of the place?" Captain Grant dropped his kitbag down on the kitchen floor and laid his walking stick across the table, immediately noticing a pair of reading glasses positioned in the middle.

"What do you want to know?" replied Horace Tregunnel as he fiddled with the keys that jangled in his hand.

"How long has it been empty?" Grant peered around the kitchen. It was fairly small, but then so was the cottage, nestled within the middle of a group of terraced houses along a dirt road that led down from the main Bodmin high street.

"I can't remember, myself," the old man replied.

Grant had interviewed enough people in the line of duty over the years to know when someone was lying to him.

"Who were the previous occupants?" Grant persisted, sniffing slightly at the musty atmosphere around him.

"I think you might want to ask my wife that question, sir. She keeps all the records."

"Why did they leave?"

The old man's blank face did little to belie his uneasiness. "Do you want me to show you upstairs?" His voice rattled.

"No, it'll suit me perfectly." Grant gazed up the small stairway, before turning his attention to the small room at the end of the hallway. "The lounge, I suppose?"

"This business of yours…" Horace Tregunnel began, apparently oblivious to Grant's question. "If you don't mind me saying, young fella, I see a troubled look in your eyes. Frobisher Hall has had its fair share of trouble this past year—"

"And you think I'm here to add to it?"

The old man fell silent and shifted awkwardly.

"I have come to settle an old score. I'm telling you this as I think you are a man of discretion." Grant looked into the kitchen and caught sight again of the reading glasses. "If anyone has trouble coming their way, then believe me it's because they deserve it…" He was tempted to say more but found he couldn't draw his attention away from the glasses. They seemed in such stark contrast to the rest of the building. Where the kitchen was musty, with a layer of dust upon the surfaces, the glasses sparkled as though they'd just been taken off and cleaned. "Whoever last lived here seems to have left their reading glasses…" His voice became low and inquisitive. "Have they never returned here to collect them?"

The old man stood in the hallway, a little ahead of him and entirely out of view of anything residing within the kitchen. His blank face had shrunk to something resembling a death mask, and Grant was concerned enough to discontinue his line of questioning.

"As I said, I'll take it," he said, before adding, "though I could do with some local advice."

"I'll try and help if I can, young fella." Horace Tregunnel's features lightened a little, and Grant detected an enormous weight lifting from the old man's shoulders, along with the thought that he might be allowed to scurry off back to his wife.

"What is the post like for local deliveries?"

"Why, there be normal collections and deliveries. But if you want a letter posted locally and quickly, then there's young Dennis over yonder garage. He'll take it for you for half a crown." The old man started to make his way to the door. "Anything else?"

"Who is your most trusted solicitor in town?" Grant followed him to the door.

"Why, that would be Peran Freeman. He's been our legal adviser for as long as I can remember." Horace Tregunnel paused at the door. It had been left open, and the sun radiated through into the hall, giving the illusion of passing from a world of dark melancholy into one of light as they drew nearer to the front door. "You'll find his office just along Fore Street."

"Thank you, Mr Tregunnel." Grant held the door open and watched the elderly man step slowly down onto the top of three steps. "Oh, and one more thing…"

The old man continued his descent towards the dirt road. When he finally reached the bottom, he turned and looked back up at the cottage. His face saddened, and Grant thought that whatever life there was in his heart seemed to dissipate as 13 Creek Lane bid him farewell. "What is it, young fella?" He sounded tired.

"Could you possibly tell me where Rose Cottage is?" Grant smiled.

"Rose Cottage?" replied Horace Tregunnel. "Now, why would you want to visit Rose Cottage?"

★★★

The room in which Inspector Edwards sat later that evening was in total contrast to the one in Whitehall earlier that morning. His fingers tapped restlessly on the mahogany table and his eyes darted around the room. A dull glow from a single lightbulb overhead did little to illuminate his surroundings; and if it hadn't been for the fact that he'd sat in this very chair on several prior occasions, he would have struggled to make out the dimensions of the room. He knew the wallpaper was dark red, with gold trimming, a style that matched the tablecloth, adding to the general gloom embracing him. The furniture was sparse, save for some small tables and a strange cabinet that seemed foreign in design. Its curves and angles, carefully carved by someone obviously skilled in Gothic design, appeared to fan out into eerie demonic images that stared mockingly at him.

The atmosphere in the room was oppressive. Shadows flickered and danced around the table, and to his left he thought he caught sight of something emerging from the darkness.

Across the table sat a woman of similar age to himself, though looking younger than his fifty-three years. She eyed him speculatively, and grasped both her hands together, before resting them on the table. The grey dress she wore was plain and unassuming, and Edwards recognised it as the one she'd worn on their first meeting.

How long they sat there he couldn't surmise. He was aware of the ticking of a grandfather clock somewhere in the house, it's gentle tick... tick... counting the seconds by with unremitting monotony. He noted the fact that it didn't chime, and that had troubled him on his first visit, as the lack of regular quarter-hour chimes seemed to herald the death of something deep within the house...

As though something crucial were missing...

All that was left was the gentle tick... tick...

Haunting, relentless, hypnotic...

Edwards tapped his fingers in unison...

A faint smell of incense aroused his senses, making him feel a little light-headed; its fragrance drifted from a small burning stick on one of the tables. On his first visit, the smell had annoyed him, but now it soothed, caressed and helped to lift the claustrophobic feeling that had descended upon him.

"Tell me about your wife." The woman's voice was soft and engaging.

"We met just after I joined the police force." He spoke clearly, losing himself within the memories that came flooding back. "She was visiting London with her sister, Morag... I fell in love with her as soon as we met."

"What made her so special?" The woman leaned forward, moving from the shadows into the light. Her eyes bore deep into his, probing, searching...

"Elisha was the eldest of the two. Where Morag was wild, Elisha had a calming effect on anyone she met. I remember they were both lost, searching for a hotel in which they were staying... I walked with them, saw them safely to their hotel and never forgot the look in Elisha's eyes as I turned to walk away..." Edwards stopped tapping his fingers and paused, feeling his heart grow heavier with every word that tumbled from his lips. "The next day I was off-duty, so went straight to the hotel and left a message for her to meet me in one of the local cafes..." He smiled. "I thought she might come, and if she did she'd bring Morag as a kind of chaperone... Well, she did come, and Morag wasn't with her... We were never apart after that... She stayed in London and we were married the following month..."

"Happily married?"

"She was the rock in my life, the only person ever to stay the anger and hurt in my heart... We lived in a simple house over in Islington. She played the piano and wrote the most beautiful poetry I ever read. She was so different to her sister."

"How so?" The woman narrowed her eyes.

"Morag was always the wild one..." Edwards closed his eyes and let his thoughts float peacefully away on the melodic sounds of the clock, so distant yet so near... Tick... tick... To let his thoughts drift, to ease the ache in his heart... "All Morag wanted was adventure, to travel... Sometimes she'd stay with us, before moving on somewhere. Elisha didn't have Morag's beauty. She would sometimes say that Morag was the red-haired ice-maiden, wild and reckless, immune to the charms of men. Elisha once teased her, telling her she would one day meet

25

an Englishman, someone who would melt her heart… I'm glad she met Harry Frobisher…"

"Why do you seek her now she's passed over?" The woman's voice took on a deeper tone.

"I told you on my previous visit…" Edwards sighed. "My experience in Cornwall last year…" He ran a hand nervously across his face. "I'd never experienced anything like that before…"

"Your meeting with Old Solomon?"

Edwards nodded. "In all my years, serving over in Africa, and then in the police force, I saw more dead bodies than any man ought ever to see… I saw things I couldn't explain. I suppose the mind will do that when it's broken and without hope…" He looked down at his hands and realised why he'd been tapping the table in the first place.

They were now shaking.

"Old Solomon was as real as you are in front of me… He saved my life when I should have frozen to death on Bodmin Moor… yet the man had been dead for years…" Edwards shook his head despairingly.

"And by having this encounter with Old Solomon, you believe you might be able to reach your wife?" The woman's voice moved from one of deep intensity to one of sympathetic warmth.

Edwards took several deep breaths and briefly stared at his hands.

He said, "I lost everything when Elisha died – the will to breathe… to get up in the morning… to ever live my life again… The occurrences down at Frobisher Hall last year, and what happened to my sister-in-law, gave me a reason to live… The decision to make that journey through the snow was based purely on the desire to ensure that Morag lived… Nothing else mattered."

"My dear man…" The woman ungripped her hands and reached out, resting her fingertips upon his hand. "In all my years as a spiritualist, I have never encountered a person so open to psychic phenomena; it positively glows around you. These years since the Great War have seen so many people looking to the spirit world, trying to find a peace and consolation with those they have lost. The spirit of Old Solomon came to you for a reason, to help you make that journey to save the lives of your sister-in-law and Captain Frobisher. He may never appear to you again... Unless, of course, you face a similar journey?"

Edwards nodded, unable to speak.

She grasped his hand. "There is something else... something you haven't spoken of yet... You carry a terrible weight, Inspector... a dreadful weight..."

"I have a job to do, and it breaks my heart even to consider it." He stared into her eyes and smiled wearily. Within her eyes he saw his own reflection, a sad and mournful reminder of happier days.

She returned his smile. "I believe you will draw strength for this task, Inspector. I also know that you are a genuinely courageous man and will do the right thing, however good or bad it might be..." Squeezing his hand, she continued, "Did you and Elisha ever have children...?"

Edwards gazed vacantly ahead before gently removing his hand from her grasp. He whispered, "Elisha was carrying our first child when she died."

2

The following day dawned brightly; and, with the prospect of a sunny day for travelling, most of the passengers who scurried along the platforms of Paddington Railway Station carried with them a light and breezy countenance. Men tipped their hats with a more genial smile than normal, and women felt compelled to return friendly acknowledgments as the heart of London beat with a decidedly more affable pulse.

However, these happy and carefree manners were lost on Platform One, as the ticket inspector stood before a man and woman who, in turn, stood at the front of a fairly long queue.

"Now, please, madam, don't think I'm being rude, but these tickets are not dated for today. You should have checked when you bought them."

The man with the grey moustache and hair to match stared down at the tickets in his hand and took a deep breath when he looked up and saw the growing look of anger begin to flare up in the eyes of the woman in front of him.

"They were ordered by telegram two days ago," a man's voice, crisp, polite, yet authoritative, replied. "A clerk from the hotel picked them up for us yesterday."

The ticket inspector continued to glance down at the tickets, shuffling his weight from one foot to another before rubbing his chin reflectively. At first sight his appearance suggested an elderly man, slightly stooped and with a rattle that emanated from his chest with every breath he drew. He wore rounded spectacles that sat neatly on the bridge of his nose and were hooked to a small chain that drooped down before disappearing into his tunic pocket.

"I'm sorry," he continued, still staring down at the tickets, "but these are what they are – tickets not valid for travel on this train." He peered up at the huge station clock proudly set above the platform.

"You won't find the answer there!" The voice, feminine and with a strong Scottish accent, was both defiant yet somehow smooth and engaging.

It arrested his attention and enticed him to lower his head.

She was beautiful, breathtakingly so... And with a passion in her eyes that...

"Well, you can't travel on this train today. Not in First Class, anyway. Either you travel Second Class, or you don't travel at all, and there's an end to it. I'm getting a little fed up with you suffragette lot..." His voice thundered above the general roar of a London terminus station at the height of the mid-morning arrivals and departures.

Her facial expression didn't change. But then it didn't need to... Her eyes were hypnotic, beguiling, sensuous... They burned with fire that could empower and inspire a man to greatness, or bring him to his knees...

Behind her, a man reached out his hand, and she felt it tenderly touch her waist. Fingers rested against the base of her back, and she felt the familiar surge of energy at his touch. She

29

resisted the urge to reach out and draw him closer, and instead coughed a little, cleared her throat and said to the man in front of her, "My dear man, in all probability you've seen the world pass you by whilst standing on this very platform. I expect you've never moved from this spot in the entire time you've worked on the railways."

"And what do you mean by that, young lady?"

"Two things…" The voice, resonating with a repressed Celtic temper, didn't need to rise above the platform noise. It cut through the steam and noise with equal ease and alacrity. "That when the tide of suffragettes sweeps along this platform, it will carry you and every other pompous arse with it."

Again, those fingers caressed her back before sliding around her waist.

"And the second thing… We have purchased First Class tickets and that entitles us, my husband and I, to travel First Class. If you keep us standing here and persist in talking to me in that patronising voice, the rising tide of the suffragette movement will be the least of your worries."

"Madam, please—" Surprise, mixed with a little uncertainty crept into the man's voice.

"Please nothing. This train is due to leave shortly. That man over there…" a gloved hand pointed in the direction of a small, smartly-dressed platform porter standing patiently with several boxes and a large trunk, "is waiting to load our luggage. We are getting on this train and taking our seats in the First Class coach marked on these tickets. Just because one of your clerks put the wrong date on them is nothing to do with us."

The fingers resting against her back drifted down and she was aware of their touch as they gently squeezed her thigh. She responded by arching her back and gently nestling herself backwards until she felt the whole of his body against her back.

She noticed, with a little thankfulness, that her actions had been lost on the man before her. Though, with a brief glance to either side of her, she wasn't so sure of the waiting passengers, who were viewing the confrontation with a mixture of amusement and impatience.

"Now, are you going to stand aside?" she continued

He responded by eyeing her intently, and she reacted by hardening her features until she felt as though one of them might turn to stone.

"I think you should do what I tell you to do, madam." He drew himself up a little and stared into the eyes of the woman in front of him, his own eyes cold and lifeless.

Lady Morag Frobisher saw his look and felt the icy sting of his words. Up until now she'd been content to try and reason with this man on a pleasant, though frustrated, level. But his last sentence had been delivered with a tone that dripped with menace, and she had slightly recoiled at their impact.

Maybe it was the look in her eyes, she couldn't decide, but his manner took on a more calm and convivial tone. "You must understand, I'm just doing my job, madam." His words were eventually drowned under the roar of steam whistles and the rumble of voices along the platform. "You see…"

"Aye, I do see. I see right through you. Don't think for one minute that you can bully me with your pompous attitude…"

Mumblings that were, up until that moment, inaudible, now became discernible as voices from the queue behind them called for them to "hurry up" and "get a move on".

"Don't think we're not getting on that train…" Morag thundered.

"Okay… Okay… Please… Just get onboard and stop making a scene, madam. If there's a problem, the guard can sort it out." The man took a step back and opened the gate for Lord and Lady Frobisher to walk through.

Before she did so, she turned and looked at the man, who had drawn himself so close behind her she could feel his warm breath upon her neck.

"Yes, madam," he spoke in mock resemblance to the ticket inspector, "please don't make a scene."

"And you, Harry Frobisher, enough of your cheek." Morag smiled at her husband as a tidal wave of love and devotion swept through her heart.

***

At the same time that morning, as Lord and Lady Frobisher climbed aboard the Cornish Riviera Express, Susan Matthews opened the main doors of Frobisher Hall and stared ahead, her gaze distracted only by the movement of her husband behind her.

"When are they due back, Larry?" She glanced along the gravel drive that swept majestically down past the main gates and away towards the main road that cut through the massive forest that ran along the valley and towards the main railway line.

"Their last telegram asked for me to pick them up from Bodmin Road at 4.30pm." Lawrence Matthews had just walked down the main staircase before pausing at the bottom. He'd paused there for a while, deep in thought. Where once his tall and wiry frame had stood erect, with fair hair that had naturally swept back upon his head, he now stood slightly bowed, with a paleness of colour and a worn-down look to his demeanour.

Susan heard his voice and turned her attention away from the sweeping panoramic views from the door and towards her husband. He'd paused for a few seconds, to gaze thoughtfully at the floor at the foot of the staircase, before moving across the hall. As he stood beside her, he gazed down the long driveway and pulled her close.

"How is your shoulder today?"

Susan leant her head against his chest.

"It's fine; just aches a little. If I do too much out on the estate, it tends to flare up." Lawrence spoke softly as he continued to stare ahead.

"Well, we have two men joining us next week; surely that will make life easier for you."

"The fact they're experienced gardeners will help," Lawrence replied, a little flippantly. "Remember, I was a policeman, not a groundsman or gardener. I can help out, but the estate needs good men with experience."

"It's going to take time, Larry. Up until last year I was a maid, too scared to even look anyone in the eyes. Now I'm the housekeeper."

She wore a pleated skirt, pink blouse and loose cardigan. Her shoes were light and comfortable, enabling her to move quickly and nimbly around Frobisher Hall, directing staff, responding to tradesmen and organising the general daily routines of those around her.

Upon her cardigan she wore a small brooch, a Cornish chough, a gift to her from Lawrence on her twentieth birthday. Two days later, when they'd married, she'd wanted to wear it on her dress, so deeply did she feel about it.

Lawrence had taken to wearing tweed jacket and trousers when working on the estate, and Susan thought he looked the better for it. The transition from waiter and general footman had been quite breath-taking, as the man she'd fallen in love with now embraced the position of Estate Manager with elegance and, dare she say it, a certain style.

Morag and Harry had formally asked them to consider the roles vacated with the deaths of Edith and Reginald Travers only a few days before their wedding. Although somewhat mystified, they'd both finally accepted when Morag took them to one side and said, "You both stood beside us when we needed you most. It would be an honour to have you both run the estate for us."

"I suppose," Lawrence said as he pulled himself away from Susan, "I'd better check the Daimler is clean and ready to pick them up. What are your plans today?"

"I still need to complete the staff register. After everything that happened last year, many of the staff just upped and left. They didn't even wait for references. Apart from the two of us, we have the wonderful Mrs Chambers in the kitchen and two new house staff, plus a young scullery maid who cycles in from Bodmin twice a day."

"And Gregson?" Lawrence prompted.

"Ah, yes. Gregson. Taking over my old job, though how anyone thinks they have the right to step into the shoes of a shy and frightened young girl, I'll never know."

"What's her background?"

"I don't really know. There was some confusion as to her employment. I thought Lady Frobisher had interviewed her... She just seemed to appear. She works hard and is polite. But she does have a habit of getting lost around the house."

"Lost?" Lawrence looked at her, a little bewildered. "I know it's a big house, but it's not too hard to find your way around."

"Well, I've found her in rooms she shouldn't be in. She just says she's still getting used to the place."

"Well," he said, moving away from her and heading towards the kitchen, "it might be best to keep an eye on her, all things considered."

Susan watched him disappear out of sight. Turning to close the door, she hesitated. At the bottom of the driveway, alone and quite still in the main gateway, a woman stood, staring at the house. From that distance Susan couldn't recognise who she was and thought it strange that one of the estate workers might decide to stand there gazing at the house. She thought she might call out to her but decided against that, as the woman was standing outside the main gate and could quite easily be a local person taking a shortcut into Bodmin.

There was no reason to either feel alarmed or call out to her.

But there was something in the woman's countenance, even from that distance, that was both troubling and intriguing. She felt strangely drawn to her, as though she could have stood there for ages just staring at her. As she looked, the woman opened a bag, drew out what looked like a notebook, and started to either write or… Susan strained her eyes… Or was she drawing, or sketching…?

Susan narrowed her eyes and instinctively stepped back a little, as though to draw nearer into the protective embrace of Frobisher Hall. Turning around, she was of a mind to call after Lawrence.

But when she returned her gaze to the driveway, the woman had vanished.

★★★

"You're just in time for a cup of tea," the voice of Mrs Chambers called out from the other side of the kitchen, and Susan was pleased to find her there.

"Anything I can do to help?" Susan responded.

"No, the kettle's just boiled. Take a seat." Mrs Chambers emerged from a veil of tea towels that hung from a line above their heads.

Susan slumped somewhat thoughtfully into her favourite chair, the one furthest from the ovens.

"I've some freshly baked biscuits." Mrs Chambers had already picked up the teapot and was walking around the enormous oak kitchen table that sat, with room to spare on all four sides, within the great kitchen of Frobisher Hall.

At the far end of the kitchen stood a huge oven range, with two large ovens, warming shelves and roasting spits. Upon more shelves sat copper pots and pans, highly polished and gleaming with the morning sun that shone through the huge windows. Around the room, doors led off into numerous pantries storing just about everything, from game to butter and a vast array of cheeses.

Susan frowned and tried to vanquish the image of the woman by the gates. Breathing deeply, she let her senses delight in the unmistakeable smell of gingerbread. The room always smelt of something delectable, and today was no different. Since Harry and Morag had been away on their honeymoon, it seemed as though Mrs Chambers had made an extra effort to treat both Susan and Lawrence and the new members of staff, letting her natural flair for the exuberant and the lavish fill the stomachs of colleagues who usually ate heartily but never to the extent of the family they served.

"Well, today is the big day. Our very own Lord and Lady Frobisher returning from their honeymoon. I hear they spent time in Rome?" Mrs Chambers asked.

"Rome, Paris and then some time in London. They stayed at The Ritz..." Susan felt her authoritative visage falter and her girlish envy take over as she imagined the life they must have led during the past month. "Can you imagine that, Mrs Chambers?" She instinctively glanced around the kitchen and remembered her family home at the back of the grocers in town. The last time she'd seen her family was the day she'd married Lawrence. "Maybe Lawrence will whisk me away to London for a holiday." She smiled. "I met his parents at our wedding. He was an only child, with no aunts or uncles. He said he'd take me to London someday..." She pondered further, "But that will have to be after we've sorted out Frobisher Hall."

"Well, it's not for you to take on all the responsibility, Susan." Mrs Chambers brushed some flour off her apron. "Lord Frobisher will know the workings of this estate better than anyone, and I don't think Lady Frobisher will be one to sit on her backside all day playing the role of Lady of The Manor..." She paused and gazed across at the teapot. "Anyway, I thought they were going to Scotland. Lord Frobisher did say how much he was looking forward to meeting Her Ladyship's family in Edinburgh."

"I'm not sure as to the exact reason they didn't go to Scotland," replied Susan; "I overheard…" She paused.

"Go on, Susan…" the cook prompted.

"Well…" continued Susan, hesitantly, "I think they want to choose the right moment. I'm not sure just how close Her Ladyship is to her parents…" She paused again, this time closing her mouth resolutely.

"Well, my honeymoon was a couple of days in Torquay," reflected the cook. "Sidney and I were both in service in Plymouth. We were allowed two days, with strict instructions to be back for the masked ball at the weekend." She picked up the teapot and drew a tray of cups towards her.

"Well, Larry and I were back at work here after our visit to the registry office in Bodmin," Susan smiled, eagerly anticipating the tea and cakes.

From the hallway the grandfather clock chimed out a quarter to eleven, the noise reverberating around the house. From somewhere along one of the wings, a door slammed, and from somewhere else, muffled voices spoke words that Susan thought might be reproachful but couldn't be sure.

"Well, I expect they'll have much to talk about when they return." Mrs Chambers poured the tea and pushed a cup across to Susan.

"Well, everything is ready for them. They have a mountain of post and telegrams. I've managed to settle all outstanding accounts from people in town. It was amazing just how much the estate owed and how the debts had piled up during that time, when…" She sighed and looked apologetically at the cook.

"The past is finished, Susan. We all contributed to its demise. When Lord and Lady Frobisher step through that front door, it will be a completely new start for them." As if to lighten the moment, Mrs Chambers eased her hand across the table and pulled a plate of scones and gingerbread biscuits towards the two of them. "How are the new members of staff shaping up?"

"Oh, they're fine; maybe a little daunted by everything. I think they applied to work here more out of curiosity. The place doesn't exactly have a bubbling reputation with the local population, yet some probably thought it a little intriguing." Susan took a bite from her scone. It was buttered heavily, with a thick layer of jam. She eased herself back into her chair, all thoughts of the strange figure at the main gates vanquished from her mind. "But I think they'll cope. Lord and Lady Frobisher have two guests tonight."

"Yes, Canon Trebarwith and Doctor Mitchell." Mrs Chambers leaned back in her chair, a warm and inviting scone nestled within her plump hand.

"Doctor Mitchell?"

"Yes, I know Doctor Mitchell well enough," retorted the cook. "He lives alone over in Temple. It's a small hamlet five miles or so across the moors. He was once the family doctor, until he retired. Before that, he was a very important surgeon in London before moving down here. I do know that he volunteered for the army as a specialist surgeon in London during the war."

"And what about Canon Trebarwith?" asked Susan.

"Oh, he's the vicar in Bodmin. Came down here just before the end of the war. They say he was a padre during the war. Suffered with his nerves and was given a position down here. Other than that, I don't know too much about him." Mrs Chambers sipped her tea.

"They both sound like very nice people."

"Well, it will be good company for Lord and Lady Frobisher." Mrs Chambers took a large bite form her scone, then quickly wiped away the resulting jam that was smeared across her lips. "Lord Frobisher did tell me before he went off on his honeymoon that he wanted to use the summer to start inviting old friends and family to stay. His parents were very keen on socialising and held the most wonderful dances here when I was a young assistant cook. I was once invited to accompany them to London, to their second home in Knightsbridge. I remember Lady Margaret looking so beautiful in her gown, utterly stunning…"

"I think Morag will sweep London society off its feet," Susan added thoughtfully.

"Yes, I think she will," Mrs Chambers agreed, before adding; "I think she could sweep just about anyone off their feet."

★★★

Morag stared intently at her husband before reaching across the carriage seat and grasping his hand. The day had been fraught with all kinds of mixed emotions and irritating occurrences that seemed to sap her energy and self-restraint. And, as usual, when these trials and tribulations confronted them, it was Morag who stepped forward and either allayed the growing anger of the moment or turned the full wrath of her temper upon the person who had mistakenly thought it wise to bring disruption into their lives.

Though the incident with the ticket inspector had been resolved, and certainly to her satisfaction, she was troubled by a nagging doubt as to what had happened during the confrontation. She couldn't put her finger on it as they'd settled into their seats, and it surfaced again during a light lunch taken in the restaurant carriage. Afterwards, she'd been tempted by a small sip of whisky from Harry's hip flask, but had decided upon a cup of tea.

She smiled, casting aside such thoughts, and stretched out her hands above her head. The coat she wore was Scottish tweed and sat lightly upon her blouse. Her skirt complemented the overall style of the jacket and hung comfortably to a point in line with her knees. She'd decided upon a light make-up for the journey down to Cornwall and so a brief glance at her face revealed delicate freckles that radiated out across her cheeks and forehead. Her high cheekbones and penetrating blue eyes added to the alluring charm and magnetism that burned deep within her, and made any attempt to understand the world she'd seen through her thirty-five years almost impossible.

Though not beyond the man who now sat beside her.

As the train meandered its way towards the West Country, they'd taken to their seats and snuggled up together, both seemingly happy to enjoy the journey and relax with the gentle swaying of the carriage.

Harry's voice, thoughtful and heavy, broke the relaxed mood, "That man back in Paddington…"

"What about him?" Morag replied, resisting the urge to let her own thoughts and speculations tumble forth.

"I got the strangest feeling he was hiding something."

"Something about him has been troubling me as well." Morag pulled herself back and stretched her arm. The fact they were alone in their compartment gave her the impetus to open up. "I was sure we had the right dates on the tickets. I checked them myself. He must have been mistaken. Besides—"

"The train, especially this carriage, isn't that busy," Harry interrupted.

"That's right, it isn't…" Morag eyed Harry and touched the side of his face. Though the scarring continued to heal, she often worried about the deeper scars, and she shuddered to think of the day when that grenade had taken his sight.

Harry smiled. "It's my senses, darling. I'm aware of things a sighted person might miss… I just haven't heard that many people around us."

"Hmmm… Harry Frobisher, you are a clever man." Morag looked around the compartment. "So, you think he was lying?"

"Not sure." Harry reached out his hand. "There was something in his voice, an uncertainty… I couldn't quite make him out."

"Well, he nearly made me lose my temper, right enough."
Morag took his hand and held it to her lips.

"Then we wouldn't have got on the train at all," Harry
laughed, his facial expression moving from one of concern to
that of mischievousness. "Knowing your temper, my dear, we'd
probably be seeing out the last day of our honeymoon residing
in one of His Majesty's prisons."

"Aye, and that's a fact." Morag leaned into his side and
nestled her head into his neck, grimacing as her hair, pinned
and tied back, caught in his collar. "I wish I could take these
pins out... You know how much I hate tying my hair back..."

"Here... Let me..." Harry swung around and Morag leaned
her head towards him.

His fingers brushed against her face, sending tingling
sensations through her body.

She closed her eyes.

And in that sudden world of darkness, with the rhythmic
sway of the train, she saw her husband before her, his eyes wide
open, seeing her face and marvelling at her beauty. Keeping
her eyes closed, she filtered out any background noise, the
rattle of wheels upon the tracks, the distant roar of the engine
and the occasional sound of someone coughing in the next
compartment.

He unclipped her hat from one of the pins with such tender
dexterity, she didn't even feel it fall away, and certainly didn't
hear it roll onto the carriage floor. As her mind's eye gazed
lovingly into his, she felt ugly and jagged pins gently pulling
away from her head and the wonderful smoothness of her
husband's fingers gently massage her long beautiful red hair
away from its confines, slowly to fall about her shoulders.

"My darling..." he whispered.

She sighed, feeling his hand slide across her lap, gently
pulling her towards him. He was the only man in this world
who could ever convey a lifetime of emotions in the simplest of

words, and such warmth with the touch of his hands. Moving towards him, she pulled her knee up onto the seat, causing her skirt to rise. If there had been anyone else in that compartment, discretion and modesty would have been instantly compromised.

The thought made Morag pause and glance nervously towards the compartment door; the blinds were drawn, and nobody had passed along the corridor in ages.

His hands pulled her undergarments to one side and she hastily unbuttoned his trousers. Though the train lurched and clattered, he gently countered the awkward swaying of the carriage, tenderly probing, before easing himself into her.

"Stop now. Behave…" She feigned innocence before adding, "You're just a hopeless romantic, Harry Frobisher." Holding his head in her hands, she kissed him with a passion that threatened to overwhelm her. Through her closed eyes, she saw him staring at her, his eyes beautifully set and so full of love.

Feeling him inside her, she marvelled at the way he seemed to read every minor orgasmic tremor that gripped her. As the train pitched and swayed, she felt the growing tide of her orgasm and knew she was losing all self-control. When it finally exploded within her, she arched her body, feeling waves of ecstasy pulsate through her. Waiting for the tide to ebb and for the fire that was consuming her to release its hold, she felt him pull her close and cry out, feeling his warmth spread through her, electrifying and oh so beautiful…

Sliding to one side, she collapsed onto the seat beside him, pulled her dress down and lay breathless with her head on his lap. He ran his hand tenderly through her hair and, as the memory of her climax lingered teasingly in her body, she felt a sleepiness descend and envelop her in its embrace.

★★★

The woman pushed her hair away from her face and stared up at the circling rook, watching it closely as it circled above the rooftops of Frobisher Hall. She'd moved away from the main gates, knowing that she'd been foolish to have stood there for so long.

She had no right – not now.

Her face, like her clothes, was rugged and bore the look of one who had suffered the trials and tribulations of life with a weary, yet stoic, countenance. Her eyes reflected the deep pain of a lifetime of hardship, whose brief interlude of happiness had been taken so coldly and dispassionately from her.

Staring at a page in her sketchbook, she felt her heart grow heavy, knowing that even here, within these rough drawings, she was still able to capture the beauty and romance of such a house set so deep within her heart.

She'd seen the young girl at the door, and knew that she wasn't the woman with the red hair; that encounter was yet to come, and she thought about that eventual day with a troubled smile as she closed her book and pushed it back into the small canvas bag beside her.

As she did so, she stared at the glass jar in her bag marked 'Poison'.

***

… How long Morag had been sleeping, she couldn't tell.

All she knew was that she had stretched out on the seat and slept with her head upon Harry's lap. She felt warm and loved. Her nerves had settled somewhat after the thrill of what they'd done and the risk of being discovered. It was as if all her girlish fantasises had come true in the arms of the man beside her – along with all her wild imaginings, now kept safe within his heart.

She flickered her eyes.

Someone was sitting opposite.

Panic and embarrassment pushed each other aside for control of her immediate reactions, and she wondered why Harry hadn't woken her when this passenger had entered.

It was a man; well, she assumed it was. Whoever it was held a newspaper rigidly in front of them and so the only clue to their identity was a pair of black trousers and gleaming shoes so highly polished she thought she caught the reflection of someone standing in the doorway to the corridor.

Though she tried to move, her body felt heavy, as though she were drugged and only slowly emerging from the twilight world of sleep. Knowing that Harry was beside her provided some comfort…

But there was something familiar, strangely familiar, about the sinewy and bony knuckles that clenched the newspaper…

Why familiar?

And why hadn't Harry nudged her awake when he'd entered?

She noticed a ring, gold and really quite unobtrusive, upon the man's little finger. It bore the initials '*MT*'.

Morag wanted to say something, wanted to tell Harry that she was sorry. Raising her head from his lap, she pulled herself into a leaning position and tried to swallow. But her mouth had gone dry, and when she tried to speak she could only gurgle an intermittent gasp… Just like that first night at Amble Lodge, when he'd come to her and sat on her bed.

The paper began to fall slowly away, like a grey veil descending from a chapel of rest…

That hand… the ring on his little finger… glinted in the candlelight as his hand explored her naked body that first night… that terrible night… when she was held… restrained… and finally stripped…

If only Harry could stop him…

The paper fell completely away, revealing the figure of Morgan Treave, grinning, with a face so hideously disfigured she couldn't comprehend his true identity until she stared into his one remaining eye and saw the reflection of herself standing above him in the East Tower, a broken bottle in her hand and a lifetime of hatred in her heart.

As she raised herself completely, she noticed Harry asleep beside her.

Pulling desperately at his arm, she looked up at a figure hovering within the doorway. Feeling her heart miss a beat and a cold, icy hand caress her face, she stifled a scream as she saw Nurse Edwina Baker standing there, smiling with evil intent, straitjacket in one hand, hypodermic syringe in the other...

The train rattled as it changed tracks, approaching the Brunel Bridge and the crossing into Cornwall.

Morag awoke, startled and shaking.

"My dear, are you okay?" Harry soothed.

She sat bolt upright, staring intently at the empty carriage before gazing fearfully at the closed door.

"I think you must have had a bad dream." He reached out blindly and she grasped his hand, desperately thankful to feel his touch. She held it to her cheek and closed her eyes, vaguely aware of the sound of raised voices in the next compartment and luggage falling onto the floor.

3

Susan Matthews sat in the study at Frobisher Hall and stared at the numerous accounts' ledgers, box files and envelopes piled upon the main desk. She congratulated herself on the fact that she could now see part of the desk beneath the mountain of paperwork, though this had not been the case the night before Morag and Harry had left for their honeymoon.

In the interim period between the night William had died and the day Morag had married Harry, Susan had worked meticulously on the accounts, balancing figures, questioning discrepancies and digging deeper into the family finances, desperately looking to clear a path through the financial quagmire that lay before her.

She realised Harry had many attributes, but he certainly didn't have a head for figures.

It had been Morag who had sat beside her, patiently working through outstanding bills, cross-checking and then re-checking endless lines of figures. The Frobisher Estate held interests in many businesses across the county and had even branched out into neighbouring Devon. New industries had seen financial backing from the family pay dividends at the turn of the century; yet the Great War had brought with it such an immense economic and social upheaval, many estates were feeling the effects of business interests now consigned to a distant past.

A new economic dawn was rising and it didn't take long for Susan and Morag to realise that they had to first settle old debts before they could look to move forward.

She turned slightly and gazed at Harry's favourite chair.

Several nights before Harry and Morag's wedding, whilst herself and Morag had totalled up figures, they'd asked Harry the occasional question concerning the Frobisher Estate and its finances, whilst he'd sat peacefully smoking his pipe. His vague and credulous answers, delivered with a wry smile, were accepted by the two women, but with a hesitant glance at one another. There had been both a strength and a resolve within Morag to grasp the challenges that confronted them, whilst shielding him from some of the stark realities that became clearer with every receipt they checked.

Bank statements were out of date.

Quotes for maintenance work throughout the Hall remained unopened, let alone read. And those tradespeople who'd been employed to carry out work had remained unpaid. Monies available to pay the workmen had seemed to go unheeded by William.

The family share portfolio had not been reviewed, and Harry had listened as Morag had read the most recent letters from his brokers in London, a sullen grimace settling upon his face at the realisation that many investments had dwindled to nothing and they would have to either realise their losses or sit tight and pray the new decade would herald a new dawn of positive market return.

Susan pushed some of the box files away from her so that she could lean on the desk. She gazed at the prints and photographs upon the walls. The wallpaper, a deep purple flock with a *fleur-de-lis* pattern, gave the room such a cosy appearance she felt it could easily become her favourite room in the Hall. But that would conflict with her growing sense of attachment to the lounge, with its vast portraits of the former lord and lady and the strange painting of the Hall perched above the fireplace.

She decided her attachment to the study was due to the fact that it mirrored her own personality and mannerisms. It was small, as small as any room might be in such a vast house. Yet it was practical and hospitable; it was also ordered, yet able to warm to anyone who might find themselves standing within it.

"Mrs Matthews?" The voice was formal and heavily accented.

Susan jumped sharply in her seat.

"Mrs Matthews, I'm sorry to disturb you." It was the footman, Dodson. A recent acquirement, he'd come from as far as Launceston and had spent the last ten years in service since leaving school at fourteen. There had been some issue with his hearing that had precluded him from war service.

Morag thought him too cocky, but Susan liked both his ten years' experience and the references he presented.

"Yes, Dodson?" She ran her hand across her forehead, trying to flick back her fringe, and scolding herself at the same time for doing so.

"Mrs Matthews, a couple of things. Cook would like to speak to you about dinner tonight. Also, I'd like to talk to you about the wine that'll be served. As you know, I've only recently taken up employment here and have not had the pleasure of waiting on Lord and Lady Frobisher. I have taken some time to peruse the wine cellar but cannot, for the life of me, fathom which vintage—"

"Frobisher Hall used to make its own wine," Susan said nonchalantly, wondering what it was Mrs Chambers wanted to speak to her about.

"Really?" Dodson was of average height, with thick brownish hair that was heavily oiled to allow a dubiously fashionable parting in the middle.

Susan had noticed this on several occasions and felt it her duty to say something to him; but, for the life of her, she couldn't think of what to suggest. Providing fashion advice to a male member of staff was not something she'd envisaged when taking on the role of housekeeper. She made a mental note to take him to one side later. Forcing a smile, she continued, "The bottles in the wine cellar date back to the beginning of the century. From there the production of wine seems to have been interrupted and certainly was so during the war. If I were you, I'd bring a couple of random bottles up, but don't open them. You'll find Lord Frobisher will stick to his whisky whilst Lady Frobisher will drink rum."

"What, all evening?"

Susan nodded. "All evening. I'm not sure about Doctor Mitchell or Canon Trebarwith. Just wait and see what they ask for. Don't open bottles when you don't need to."

Dodson was about to leave when Susan added, "Oh, and, by the way, you might want to talk to Kenick about helping to wait at table tonight. I know it will just be the four for dinner, but I think the experience will do him good, before they start entertaining on a larger scale."

"But Kenick is only a houseboy," Dodson said disdainfully.

"And I was a simple maid only six months ago," Susan retorted. "Frobisher Hall is still finding its feet after the events of last year. I am acutely aware of staff shortages, so we will all have to pull our weight."

"But surely you have a butler to help wait table." There was a confused tone to Dodson's voice that Susan didn't quite register.

"No, Dodson. No head butler at present. We have advertised… even as far afield as Plymouth, but nothing yet."

"Then who is the chap I've seen around the house?" Dodson frowned, genuinely confused.

"What do you mean?" Susan leant slightly against the desk.

"I've seen him a couple of times. Kenick saw him yesterday. Tall man, grey beard. I saw him briefly over in the west wing. He disappeared down some back stairs. Kenick says he called out to him but the man didn't hear him. That was by the door leading into the lounge."

Susan took a deep breath before answering, "I think you must be mistaken."

"Mrs Matthews, I know when I see someone." Dodson stepped forward. "And I don't think I'd forget this chap's face… Especially with that patch over his eye…"

***

"Bodmin Road! Bodmin Road." The cry echoed along the carriage. It was followed by the screech of brakes, the shrill of a whistle and an eruption of steam that permeated all around them. At the sound of this sudden commotion, Morag moved away from Harry, stood up and momentarily had to counter the swaying motion of the train.

She saw her husband attempt to struggle to his feet and called out to him, "My dear, wait until we have stopped."

He relaxed back into the seat and smiled in her direction. She knelt slightly and retrieved his stick to place in his hand.

As the train glided into the station, finally coming to a halt with their window facing the wooden structure of the footbridge, Morag swung open the door and immediately called for a porter.

With a smile, she recognised the face of Lawrence Matthews as he moved swiftly along the platform gazing intently at the passengers as they disembarked from the train.

"Over here, Lawrence," she called.

"My dear woman, you now refer to Lawrence merely as Matthews," Harry muttered behind her.

"Now, Harry Frobisher, don't you be starting with all that pompous rubbish," Morag replied, waving at Matthews as he searched for her voice through the throng of passengers and steam.

"Lawrence!" she called across the platform, her strong Scottish accent diverting the looks of some of the passengers. When she realised she had his attention, she added, "Over here…"

At the sound of her voice, he dashed towards her.

"Welcome home, Your Ladyship." Lawrence climbed into the compartment and glanced down at Harry. "And you, Lord Frobisher. It's good to see you both again."

Morag stepped to one side as he perused the luggage above him and glanced briefly around the carriage, before finally stepping onto one of the seats to reach up and grasp the first of the bags – a task easily completed due to his height.

But Morag noticed, painfully for herself, and more importantly for Lawrence, that his weaker arm could still not take such heavy weights. "Lawrence, please, I can call for a porter."

"No need, Lady Frobisher. I can manage." He smiled. Within a matter of seconds, he'd pulled the trunks and bags down and settled them upon the opposite seat.

When the cases and trunks were finally stacked on the platform, Morag helped her husband alight from the train. The day seemed rather like London had earlier, with clear skies overhead and the faint sound of birdsong emanating from the trees around them. She felt happy to be away from city life and felt herself noticeably relax as a cool Cornish breeze enveloped her and whispered welcoming words in her ears.

"Good to be home?" Harry whispered.

"To be home and with you," Morag replied and squeezed her husband's arm. In front of them, Matthews was scratching his head and looking around the platform. Morag guessed he was searching for a trolley.

"Knew I forgot something. Back in a moment." He walked briskly back towards the ticket office where there were several trolleys stacked against the brick building.

"You know, my dear? This is a new life for us both..." She was standing close to Harry, to his left, knowing that he always held his stick in his right hand and would feel gently, respectfully, for her arm with his left. He'd said, not so long ago, that he would always reach out for her, hoping, but not expecting, that she would be there to support him.

Now it was simply a habit with her that she would instinctively drift towards his left side, and at the most appropriate moments. Understanding and anticipating his next move was actually easier to work out than she'd initially thought. She didn't want to step instinctively to his side whenever he made a move himself; realising, if she relaxed, she could fathom his next move and decide if he felt confident enough to make it on his own.

This had been a little difficult over the past couple of weeks, as they'd both found themselves in strange and unfamiliar places. Yet, for Morag, the idea was simple wherever they were. If she felt Harry had mentally grown accustomed to his surroundings, then she would hold back and let him perform whatever task he had set himself. She might discreetly manoeuvre herself into a more accessible position where she could quickly, yet tactfully, act if he needed her. Or, if he seemed disorientated or unsteady on his feet, she would carefully and unobtrusively make her way to his side and whisper, "I'm here..."

Maybe it was the simplistic nature of those words, or the soothing yet resilient way she uttered them, but Harry would nearly always reach for her and grasp her arm with a grip that was always light.

And so it was, on the platform of that quaint and romantic railway station tucked away deep within the Cornish countryside, that Harry held onto Morag's arm, whilst raising his other hand to shield her face as steam and smoke erupted from the engine and was swept down the platform by the swirling breeze.

As the station porter waved late arrivals onboard and slammed shut any remaining open doors, Morag gazed at the train and realised that the last link to their honeymoon was about to depart. Life was going to be a lot different from now on.

The scream that erupted from the compartment just to her left was so ear-splitting and nerve-shattering that it momentarily drowned out the roar of the engine and the shriek of a whistle.

Morag instinctively grasped Harry's arm, forgetting that he already had his other hand resting on her waist. Realisation quickly dawned upon her that a late arrival, a young woman with a small handbag, had quickly opened the door to the compartment next to their own and had then staggered back down the one wooden step and back onto the platform. She was holding her hand to her mouth and was staring intently at something within the compartment.

"What is it, Morag?" Harry asked, and Morag heard the deep concern within his voice.

"I don't know. A young girl..." Morag tried to peer into the open compartment but could not do so without taking her supporting hand away from Harry. But when she saw that the young woman's face had turned to a deathly ashen complexion, she decided to quickly rush forward and assist her. "Harry, my dear. Wait here." She muttered.

"Yes, of course," Harry replied, before adding, "be careful."

Morag quickly reached the woman and caught her just as her legs began to buckle and she sank to a crumpled heap on the platform.

"What's going on here?" The stationmaster, a short and wiry figure of a man, came skidding to a halt beside the two women. He was joined by a rather panic-stricken guard.

"I don't know. We heard her scream and then she staggered back out of the compartment." Morag knelt beside the woman and was gently supporting her head. She stared back at Harry and called, "Harry, have you got your hip flask?"

"Yes, of course." Harry fumbled in his jacket pocket and pulled out his hip flask. It was small and displayed the regimental crest of the Duke of Cornwall's Light Infantry. He tentatively moved forward and held it out.

"I have it, sir." The guard walked round to Harry and prised it unceremoniously from his grip before passing it down to Morag.

The smoke and steam were now beginning to thin out along the platform. So taken were those who stood around the prostrate woman and the kneeling figure of Morag Frobisher that nobody thought to peer through the open door and into the compartment.

Finally, it was an elderly gentleman, a local man from Bodmin who was hoping to catch the train into St Austell, who turned his attention from the commotion on the platform and peered into the compartment.

"My dear God…" he muttered and recoiled back.

"Good heavens above." The stationmaster glanced through the clearing smoke and narrowed his eyes.

When Morag also turned her gaze into the open compartment, she saw the figure of a man slumped on his side upon the carriage floor, his head horribly twisted round on his neck, his eyes staring blankly, his tongue swollen and protruding.

Even from outside of the compartment and standing on the station platform, anyone who cared to look upon that scene of death could not fail to see the rope that was still tightly wrapped around his throat.

Morag overcame her initial shock with surprising ease. Though the dreadful look of death staring out at the gathering crowd might have caused many to turn away in horror, something about the man intrigued her and compelled her to leave the young woman in the safe hands of another passenger and draw closer to the carriage door.

"Mother of God," she whispered, and instinctively held out her hand for Harry. Unaware that he was not beside her, she approached the opening and stared in.

"Morag?" Harry's voice carried along the platform. He was tapping with his stick and probing with his free hand. The crowd that had gathered behind Morag parted and respectfully stepped back.

"Over here, Harry." Morag glanced over her shoulder, saw her husband groping blindly for her, and stepped back, immediately feeling the grasp of his hand. It was clammy and shaky.

"What is it, Morag?" Harry sounded apprehensive.

"A man lying dead on the carriage floor," she replied, her voice drained of emotion.

"What… one of the passengers?" Harry drew her close.

"No, Harry. It's a ticket inspector; the one who told us we couldn't board the train back in London."

4

Captain Grant sat alone and deep in thought in the bay window of the St Petroc Hotel dining room. From the latticed window he could see the road winding its way up towards the small railway halt and, if he looked the other way, the reassuring outline of the parish church.

The few crumbs that remained on his plate paid testimony to the delicious pasty he'd just consumed. When the young waitress had come to refill his glass of brandy, she'd giggled and promptly told him that the landlord had them delivered freshly baked from the bakers just along the high street.

Looking at his pocket watch, he casually noted just how late the time was. But it had been a busy morning. Waking early, he'd lain quietly in bed, aware of a heavy atmosphere in the house and certain he'd opened several windows before retiring to bed the previous evening.

He'd been more curious than alarmed to find them closed.

His breakfast had been a plate of bacon and eggs in the very hotel in which he now sat; from there he'd walked the short distance back to 13 Creek Lane to sit and write two letters.

He stared out of the window, feeling his heart warm to the sight of local townsfolk going about their daily business. From the courthouse, well-dressed men scurried back and forth through the main doors; along Fore Street, horses pulled carts that carried everything from fruit and vegetables to coal and beer barrels from St Austell. Occasionally, the peace and quiet was interrupted by the sound of a car or small lorry, harbingers of a progress that was snapping relentlessly at the heels of this tranquil and ancient town.

Most of the morning, he reflected, had been taken up with his visit to the solicitor, Peran Freeman, whose office lay only a short walk further along Fore Street past the bakers who had prepared his lunch.

He'd formulated a high opinion of Peran Freeman, admiring the fact that he seemed to know everything about everyone, yet always kept on the professional side of discretion. His knowledge of local history was astounding, and Grant had been especially impressed with the significance of the name of the hotel in which he now sat.

Whilst sitting in his office, he'd warmed to the short, immaculately dressed solicitor who was completely bald, with no facial hair at all. His looks had been beguiling, in terms of gauging his age. He may have been well into his seventies, or still only a man enjoying middle age. Either way, Peran Freeman had been brisk and professional, though utterly friendly and welcoming. He'd talked about his love of Bodmin and of the fact that he'd once travelled, even reaching as far as Plymouth during his younger days as a solicitor's clerk.

Grant liked the print behind Mr Freeman's desk.

It was old, probably late nineteenth century, and one similar to many he'd seen amongst the shops in London. Not a great lover of that form of art, he had at first given it a cursory glance, before studying it with a growing interest. It was of a towering monument, well over one hundred feet, with a plaque upon the front. He soon realised he'd seen the actual structure, high upon a nearby hill, overlooking the town.

Peran Freeman had explained that it was the Walter Raleigh Gilbert Monument and of its significance to the town of Bodmin. Grant hadn't been able to take his eyes off it, especially when he'd leant forward to discuss the purpose of his visit.

Now, with the time pushing on towards two o'clock, Captain Grant felt the moment had come to explore this strange and enchanting town a little further than the small roads and dirt tracks around his cottage.

He also wondered where Annette Myers might be at this time of the day.

After complimenting the landlord upon his cuisine, and promising to visit in the not too distant future, Wilbur Grant stepped out onto the street and felt compelled to turn to his right and walk at a leisurely pace up the main high street.

Around him, the town drew a deep breath as he began to make his way up the road, nervous of his presence and eager to know the true purpose of his visit. As he passed the grocers, Susan's father paused as he weighed potatoes for old Mrs Nancarrow, deep wrinkles appearing on his brow as he eyed the uniformed stranger suspiciously.

Following his sense of direction, Grant breathed a sigh of relief when he eventually turned off the main high street and began to climb an even steeper hill, knowing in his heart that he was heading for the Walter Raleigh Gilbert Monument. Small cottages lined his progress, curtains fluttered, and an old woman stood silently in a doorway watching him closely.

As he reached the boundary of the field in which the monument stood, he glanced to his right, noticing a small school, with a group of children silently watching him. A teacher appeared, a young man in an ill-fitting suit that reflected the disharmony of the moment. Grant spared him a cursory glance but felt no compulsion to acknowledge his presence.

He'd first noticed the huge obelisk whilst walking down the main street into Bodmin on his earlier arrival into town. Now, as he approached the massive structure, he found it strangely overwhelming, and certainly distracting as he tried to enjoy the panoramic views around him. He thought it both majestic and terrifying; a huge sentinel standing guard above the town.

Standing before it, he felt compelled to touch the stone base. It was cold and dank, even on a warm day such as this. The thought struck him that it might be so deeply set within the ground, it could easily have roots that fanned and radiated out under the entire town; that if some great hand were to appear from above and pull the whole thing clear, it might rip the very heart out of Bodmin.

But these were idle thoughts and speculations.

He thought about Rose Cottage.

It was already five o'clock when he made the decision to return down the small road back towards the main high street. The day had gone from one of planned tasks and an itinerary he had pondered over for many days prior to his arrival, to one of passing fancy as he'd felt compelled to visit the monument after his visit to Peran Freeman.

When he finally descended the hill running back into town, the sun was still fairly high, and the town of Bodmin shimmered beneath a strange warmth that made people pause for breath, wipe the sweat from their brows and turn towards this stranger who had suddenly appeared in their community.

He decided to cut down one of the many alleyways that led to the lower road, calculating that it would take him back towards the gaol – as indeed it did. The black and ominous tower of Bodmin Gaol loomed up in the distance across the rooftops. Though such a dreadful sight might strike a feeling of melancholy into the hearts of most men, Captain Grant felt quite happy as he stared across towards the opposite side of the lower road and the magnificent outline of the Berryfields Villa, beautifully set in the lush green fields that swept away to the north of the town.

He found Rose Cottage quite by chance, knowing he'd not followed any deliberate route, trusting to his sense of direction to find his way back to Creek Lane. The small wooden sign looked as though it had just been painted:

Rose Cottage

It was a simple four-bedroomed abode constructed out of flint, with small latticed windows and a fine-looking roof of Cornish slate. The small garden, leading down to where he stood, boasted a beautiful display of rhododendrons and narcissi, and he felt his heart swell at the thought of her tending to her plants, tidying her path and engaging in passing conversation with the locals.

The cottage seemed in such stark contrast to his apartment back in London; the quaintness and rustic charm toyed with his emotions, and he needed to recall the cold and unassuming city streets and bombed-out houses to check himself as he drifted into her world...

He tried to take a step along the path.

His fortitude failed him miserably.

As he tried to take another step, something caught his eye. Turning round, he noticed two young boys staring at him from across the road. Though quite clear in many respects, Grant struggled to define their features, as though his eyes had become blurred and watery. Their images shimmered, as though they were mere reflections.

And then they were gone.

He drew out a pencil and an old empty envelope from his inside pocket. As he scribbled down his name and the address of his cottage on Creek Lane, he stared up at the windows of Rose Cottage. They returned his gaze, defiant and protective. He wrote a few words before signing the note with his initials, WRG. After making the decision not to knock on the door, the process of walking down the path and posting the note through the letterbox became easier.

And so he did, without once looking up at any of the windows.

With a heavy heart he posted the note through the letterbox, turned and walked away from Rose Cottage.

He felt inclined to cut along an alleyway and make his way back towards his lodgings another way. His general sense of direction was pretty good, and he knew that if he kept moving in this particular direction he would dissect the road that ultimately ran down towards Creek Lane. He hadn't walked too far when he realised he was trekking back into town and away from his house. When he decided to follow a small road that ran down towards the bottom road which would lead him back to Creek Lane, he paused alongside a large red-brick Victorian wall.

There was a gate which enabled him to glance into the garden and towards a fairly large cottage. Initially he chose not to look, so involved was he in finding his way home. But the inclination to look through the gate and towards the cottage was somehow overpowering, even if it caused consternation from the occupant and embarrassment for himself.

Though he couldn't see anyone, he was immediately aware that someone was staring back, and a feeling of unease crept over him.

★★★

Canon Roderick Trebarwith eased himself into his large leather chair and gazed reflectively out of his study window. He had lately wondered how his chair was ever going to continue to support his massive frame, so frequent had been the squeaks and shudders that greeted him every time he sat down upon the thing. But it was his favourite chair within the study; indeed, probably his favourite chair within the vicarage, and the one in which he liked to greet guests and visitors on parish business.

Upon the desk before him sat an array of paraphernalia, from ink pens to paperwork, from ornaments to rare and dusty books that were heaped upon each other in several disjointed piles. He'd cleared a space in front of him, seemingly with the intention to write letters, but his attention was drawn towards a letter, gilt-edged and headed with the Frobisher coat of arms:

Requesting the pleasure of Canon Roderick Trebarwith
to dine with Lord and Lady Frobisher.
8pm
Thursday 21st May, 1921
Frobisher Hall

By pushing all other paperwork to one side, he'd created a frame around the letter, so his attention was continually drawn to its contents. He'd not been invited to Frobisher Hall before and had only met the new lord and lady when he'd presided over the burial of William Frobisher and then their eventual wedding.

He sat perusing it intently before looking up at the woman sitting to his left.

"Mrs Myers, I really do think we need to start thinking about embracing works by German composers... I mean, the war has been over for a few years now." He drew his gaze towards the window and the rhododendrons that bordered the vicarage lawn on both sides, their spring blossom a pleasure to observe whenever he beheld their beautiful colours.

"All I'm saying, Canon Trebarwith, is that an afternoon of piano recitals by solely German composers is a little too much to take... Many of your parishioners still bear the scars of having lost loved ones, and I think this programme you've suggested weighs too heavily on the likes of Beethoven and Shubert." Annette Myers placed her cup of tea back onto the small table beside her and discreetly ironed out a small crease in her corduroy skirt. "Why not patronise some of our French composers, like Poulenc? At least they fought on the same side as us."

"Because, my dear Mrs Myers…" Canon Trebarwith glanced back out of the window, holding his words, as though on a knife edge. His focus of attention: the red-brick Victorian wall that enclosed the entire garden, that was only accessed by an iron gate to his right, had suddenly made him feel quite claustrophobic. Usually it provided him with a feeling of protectiveness. "… Peran Freeman probably doesn't like playing Poulenc, and I can't say I blame him. Love him or hate him, everyone recognises Beethoven. And besides…" he turned again to her and this time let his usual dour features break into a broad and appealing grin, "maybe it's time for the Bodmin community to finally lay the past firmly in its place and look to the future. No matter what the pain, God does tell us to forgive our enemies."

"If you say so, Canon," Annette Myers replied, and Canon Trebarwith heard the strained emotions in her voice.

Turning fully to her, he leaned forward and changed his broad grin into one of sincere warmth, "You know my feelings for you, Mrs Myers… As my wife, maybe we could both finally consign the past to history…"

Annette Myers blushed slightly and smiled. "I know… I just need a little time… Things to sort out…" Her words became hushed. "I think of my husband every day, as do most people who lost loved ones. But that's the trouble with war. No matter how many letters they write, no matter how many times you say goodbye when they leave, there's still a sense of things left outstanding, of words that should have been spoken. I thought that moving to Bodmin might have helped… A new start, new people." She sighed and looked past the clergyman opposite her to gaze dreamily at the garden beyond.

"There is still time for your wounds to heal. It was an immense struggle and a great sacrifice for many." Trebarwith tried to speak with a dignified and refined strength that might lift her spirits. Melancholy reflection would simply harbour a deeper pain, and maybe now was the time for a more jingoistic perception. "Sometimes mankind is called upon to stand up against the aggressor, to draw a line in the sand and do what is morally right, no matter what the cost." He leaned back in his chair and eyed her reflectively. Since her arrival in the town, she'd thrown herself into supporting his predecessor, and then himself, in the immense challenges of running a parish church and providing pastoral support for a community desperately coming to terms with the consequences of conflict.

"Yes, Canon. But that won't bring my husband back." She shifted forward in her seat and reached across for her cup of tea.

From the hallway a grandfather clock chimed the hour of 5pm, and she confirmed this by reaching down, opening her handbag and pulling out an old pocket watch without the chain. On the reverse was engraved 'To Annette, Love From W'. She noticed, as always, that the time was accurate, and she ran her thumb lovingly over the glass face.

The chimes of the grandfather clock had stimulated them into action and both went to say something at the same time.

Canon Trebarwith politely acceded to Annette Myers' embarrassed look and said, "Please, Mrs Myers, you go first and I'll sip my tea." He smiled encouragingly.

"I really wanted to ask about numbers to the recital on Saturday, as some of us will be providing tea and cakes." Her voice had taken on a more formal tone which had the effect of relaxing the atmosphere in the study by driving away any potentially ambiguous conversations that might arise out of idle chat.

It also gave a purpose to the meeting, albeit a little later than Canon Trebarwith would have preferred, as the blank page of his sermon looked up at him with a reproachful reprimand.

"Well," he answered, "how many tickets have you sold?"

"Canon, there are no tickets, just voluntary contributions on the day, along with the raffle and tombola. I just worry that we might not have enough cakes."

The large clergyman nodded his head and thought carefully about what he was going to say next. "My dear woman, considering what the community has been through, I don't think we should worry too much about baking too many cakes—"

"It's not that, Canon…" Annette Myers interrupted.

Trebarwith noticed the concerned look upon her face and remained silent.

"Lord and Lady Frobisher will be arriving back at the Hall today."

"Yes, I happen to be dining with them tonight." He tapped the invite gently with his finger.

"I sent a personal invite for them over to Frobisher Hall. I saw their housekeeper, Susan, in town the other day and she said they would love to come along."

"Well, that's a good thing, isn't it?" Trebarwith struggled to contain his impatience.

"I want so much…" she said, "I want so much to try and make Lady Frobisher welcome here."

"I think we all do, Mrs Myers, especially after what the poor woman has gone through." He felt his impatience dissipate and a feeling of sad resignation sweep over him. "I think it's very brave of them both to come back to Frobisher Hall. But then it is their ancestral home and, like it or not, the estate has a deep-rooted connection with the town."

"But after—"

"But after nothing, Mrs Myers." Trebarwith's voice took on a more authoritative tone. "What has happened cannot be undone. We can only pray for His Lord and Ladyship, for their life together as man and wife…" He paused, aware of the sermon he feared he might be lapsing into. "We might also," he continued a little more contritely, "pray for those who died, whatever the cause of their deaths; no matter if it was good or evil that burnt in their hearts last year, we must pray for their souls." Again he looked back at the envelope.

His words resonated not only through the little study but also through the house. The atmosphere lifted and any tension that had threatened to invade their exchange of words silently dissipated through the gaps in the windows and door. Trebarwith noticed for the first time exactly what she was wearing.

Her grey flannel jacket, blouse and pink scarf brought out her natural beauty and also added a touch of middle-aged dignity to her countenance. She hadn't removed her hat during her visit, and he thought that she'd probably feared not being able to pin it back in place. As these thoughts threatened to draw him into a world he thought he'd better avoid, he coughed, turned his body round in his chair and stared out at his garden.

His attention was distracted a little by the brief glance of a soldier, an officer, tall and of noble stature, who'd paused just along the path that ran parallel to his garden and was only glimpsed through the gate in the outer wall.

He was staring into the garden and towards the cottage.

Trebarwith's position within the room would have hidden his presence to the man, due to the shadows cast from the wall and the small latticed windows that separated the two men.

But Canon Trebarwith had no such trouble observing the stranger.

And in those couple of seconds, a cold hand reached into his heart and planted a seed that threatened to germinate into doubt, before growing like a vine through his body to eventually enshroud him in a terrible—

"Canon? Are you okay?" Annette Myers' voice cut through the room.

Even before she'd finished her sentence, he'd quickly turned his head towards her before turning it back again towards the garden and that gap...

The man was gone.

"You look as though you've seen—"

"It's nothing, Mrs Myers. Honestly. I get tired. My eyes play tricks. It's been a long day," Trebarwith replied quickly. "I think it's a wonderful idea of yours to formally invite Lord and Lady Frobisher."

"Do you think she'll like the music?" Annette Myers placed her empty cup and saucer on the nearest table and was making a move to stand up.

"I don't follow you, Mrs Myers."

"She is Scottish, isn't she?"

"What's that got to do with it?" Trebarwith mirrored her actions and also made to stand up.

"Well, it might be a little above her." Annette Myers coughed and glanced anxiously towards the door.

"Mrs Myers, I was once invited to attend a lecture by a prominent professor in theology at the University of Dundee. I was privileged to be welcomed by my friend, who is a clergyman in the Church of Scotland, and spent two weeks engrossed in the most uplifting spiritual and cultural learning I have ever known. Morag Donaldson came to this place and suffered a completely different experience." Trebarwith was now standing, his large frame towering over the slight woman before him. "I think it would be nice for us to welcome her into our town and maybe atone for our lack of judgement and spiritual guidance when she suffered most."

"I… eh… agree…" Annette Myers tried to straighten her hat that was already in place, before looking around for her handbag. She had settled it against the side of her chair, nearest to the study desk and in plain sight of the clergyman.

Though he could see it, the angle of the chair meant she could not. Noticing her uncomfortable glance around the room, and the sudden look of panic that spread across her face, Canon Trebarwith quickly reached down to retrieve her bag, ignoring her protestations when she realised what he was doing.

"It's okay, Mrs Myers." Trebarwith laughed, scooping up the bag in his hand.

The top had not been clipped shut properly.

The first thing to catch his eye was a glint, as the afternoon sun, though muted through the cottage windows, reflected off something metallic tucked within the bag. With one continuous movement he swept up the bag and stood upright, momentarily using his height to counter her initial move to take the bag from him.

The moment lasted seconds, but it was long enough for him to notice the small revolver tucked innocently between some tissues and a small address book.

5

"You know, Harry, I truly wished to God that that man had been Morgan Treave," Morag whispered, as though the staff might hear them from the far reaches of Frobisher Hall. As it was, her muted words were immediately lost in the spacious and decadent master bedroom that looked out onto the main driveway. She was fiddling with his necktie and cursing under her breath as her normally supple hands struggled to tie his knot.

"I remember the night you undressed me, starting with my necktie…" Harry smiled reassuringly.

From downstairs the grandfather clock chimed the half hour past 7pm.

Morag carefully eased the knot into place before leaning forward and kissing him lightly on the cheek. "Aye, Harry Frobisher, and I remember what happened next…" She was completely naked, with her evening gown laid out on the bed. She felt his fingers drift down her body before gently massaging her thighs.

"Behave," she smiled, before drawing away from him and sitting down on the edge of the bed. She slipped her stockings over her legs, clipped her suspender into place and delicately fastened them together. Drawing the evening gown from behind her, she stood up and slipped it over her shoulders, running the palms of her hands along and over the curves of her body. Sitting back down on the bed, she shook her hair, feeling it tumble around her. Turning to Harry she asked, "Shall I tie my hair back or leave it as it is?"

He sat down beside her. "Canon Trebarwith will be one of our guests," he said frowning.

"So, tied back?" Morag pulled her hair back, cringing as she did so.

"Hmm…" Harry reached over.

Morag inclined her head towards him.

Running his fingers through her hair he muttered, "Considering you're not wearing anything under this dress, I really think the question is irrelevant."

"Nothing gets past you, does it, Harry Frobisher?" Morag leaned over and kissed him. "What time does Sergeant Cadan wish to see us tomorrow?" She shook her hair loose.

"He's asked us to visit him around 11am," Harry sighed. "He suggested coming over here to take our statements, but I thought it might be nice to drive over into town." He stretched out his hand, which Morag immediately grasped. "Susan rang through to the police station shortly after we arrived back."

"Do you think Morgan Treave had anything to do with that body on the train?" Morag squeezed his hand. The softness of the carpet cushioned her feet, making her feel safe and warm.

"I'm not sure," Harry commented. "All I know is the feeling I had when we said goodbye to Inspector Edwards at the station last year. I've never felt anything like it in my life… Treave was on that train, I was sure of it…"

"Well," Morag said rising from the bed, "he'd better stay away from here."

"Why do you say that?" Harry ran his hand over the bed, searching for his jacket.

"Darling, your coat is over the back of the chair... Here, let me..." Morag pulled the dinner jacket from the chair and walked over to her husband. Instinctively she moved behind him and slipped it over his shoulders, brushing the fabric as she did so.

"You didn't answer my question," he prompted.

Morag glanced around the room, holding her breath at the décor. The most beautifully designed wallpaper she had ever seen adorned the four walls; vast wardrobes and dressing tables were positioned around the sides; and above them the ceiling shimmered in the lowering light, as artistic patterns and figures reached downwards in all their splendour.

"Harry," she began, "when I was hiding out in Frobisher Hall last year, I would sometimes walk the rooms and corridors at night. I felt safe here, and when I finally saw you come home I knew I'd found the man I wanted to be with for the rest of my life. I would dream of our children running along these corridors, and of us walking hand in hand through the gardens..."

"I feel the same, darling," Harry murmured.

"I know, Harry. But after what happened last year, I also made myself a promise that if ever that man came near this house again, I'd kill him."

"I know how you feel." Harry nervously fiddled with his cufflinks.

Morag could see they were already attached, and smiled at his apparent uncomfortable reaction to her words. "You married a fiery red-headed Scot, Harry Frobisher. If I ever get near him he'll wish he did bleed to death in that tower."

Harry coughed and turned his head away.

"I'm sorry, Harry."

"No... It should be me who's sorry. I'm not much use to you in this state. If Morgan Treave walked into this room right now, I'd be completely useless." Harry found his way to the bedside table and the glass of whisky he'd brought up with him earlier. "When you speak like that I feel at a loss as to what to say. You are the most brave and resolute woman I've ever met, Morag. And I suppose that that is one of the many reasons why I love you so. But I feel so conscious of my inability to…" He paused, desperately trying to find the right words.

"To protect me?" Morag whispered.

"Yes," Harry hesitantly lowered his voice. "In my world, you see, I was taught to always stand up when a lady walked into the room. My father was quite old-fashioned in his approach to women… but…"

"But what?" She moved around the bed and sat down beside him, taking the glass from his hand and draining the last of the whisky.

"I know how much I am dependant on you now, especially at this time. This afternoon on that platform, when you left me to tend to that woman…"

She replaced the glass on the table and held his hand to her lips.

"I felt so alone," he continued, his breaths coming in short gasps, "Alone… and scared…"

Morag went to say something, but Harry anticipated her and raised his free hand slightly.

"Knowing I can't be the man who cares for you, protects you… Stands up when you walk in the room… Oh God… These bloody eyes…" He sighed heavily.

"Harry Frobisher, you listen to me." Morag tightened her grip on his hand. "I draw as much strength from you as you do from me. Do you think I could ever face this world without you beside me? My father taught me never to back down when I was right; he also taught me how to be a crack shot with a rifle and to ride a horse without a side saddle. Yes, I know I'm strong; it's a strength that got me through those months locked up in Amble Lodge. But all that means nothing without you,

Harry. When I knelt beside that woman and stared into that compartment, I also felt alone, and I desperately needed you there beside me… Now…" She stood up and ran her hand under his chin. Lifting his face, she kissed him on the lips and felt him respond. "Let's not be late for our guests."

★★★

"Lady Frobisher, may I congratulate you on a beautiful bottle of wine." Doctor Mitchell held his glass up towards the shimmering chandelier that hung impressively above the dining room table and marvelled at the flickering light through the crystal glass. "May I ask what vintage it is?"

Morag glanced at her guest and then across at her husband, who was already smiling into his glass of whisky.

"I wouldn't have a clue, Doctor Mitchell," she also smiled, "it's from the Frobisher Estate…"

"You mean…?" Mitchell pulled the monocle from his right eye and stared at his two hosts.

"Oh, yes," Harry responded. "We did grow our own wine here on the estate. The bottles here on the table were brought up from the cellar, but I wouldn't have a clue as to what year they are…"

"We asked for a couple of bottles to be brought up but didn't check the labels," Morag added nonchalantly.

"Good Lord…" mumbled Mitchell as he lowered his glass.

"Good Lord indeed," Canon Trebarwith, seated opposite, confirmed. He also held a glass of the same wine in his hand, his third that evening, but this one he analysed with deep intent, and Morag was finding it increasingly amusing to observe their interest.

"I'd say quite sweet… and very fruity…" Mitchell took another sip and sloshed it around his mouth. "Carries a punch, by Jove…"

"Like someone I know," Harry muttered loud enough for everyone to hear but only one person to comprehend.

Morag gazed across at him and smiled.

"I say…" Canon Trebarwith followed his fellow guest's example, taking a small sip.

Morag looked at her glass of lemonade and at the empty plates now being cleared by one of the kitchen staff, a young girl whom she'd never seen before and assumed Susan had taken on. Later, she knew that Doctor Mitchell would ride his horse the five miles or so back to Temple and, by the look of him, guessed that his horse would probably canter back to his home, oblivious of Mitchell dozing on his back.

Of an average build with a dark complexion, she marvelled at his thick white hair. His hazel eyes sparkled with a genuine warmth that had drawn her to him from the moment he'd walked into the house. Though now long retired from his profession, and well into his seventies, Morag had several times seen a mischievous glint in his eyes.

But it was Canon Trebarwith she was more concerned about.

He'd driven over in a rather stylish Austin Twenty that he'd left outside the front door. By the amount of wine he'd already consumed, she wondered if he was ever going to be in a fit state to drive back. In contrast to Doctor Mitchell, Roderick Trebarwith was much taller, in a way that could be quite intimidating, and probably some fifteen years younger. He emanated an aura of vulnerability, as of one who'd viewed the world through naïve eyes and now carried the pain of what he'd seen.

She wondered if one of the guest rooms had been aired.

"I say, Lord Frobisher," Doctor Mitchell had placed the monocle back into place, squinting his eye as he did so and grasping one of the bottles, "how many bottles of this stuff do you actually have?"

"I wouldn't have a clue, Doctor," replied Harry, draining his whisky. Deftly, he filled his pipe, before striking a match and drawing heavily.

Morag noted that this was his third glass of the evening and wondered if he might take a fourth.

Harry continued, "The Frobisher Estate has its own vineyard on the southern slopes. You can see them behind you as you turn into the main driveway. My parents loved their wine and so decided to produce their own. That was probably just before William and I were born. I'm afraid it was left abandoned somewhat during the war years as many of the staff left to join up. Then, of course, after what happened last year…" His voice trailed off.

"Well," reflected Mitchell, "it's a damn shame."

"I think it would make a nice Holy Communion wine, myself." The clergyman eyed the glass in his hand before taking another sip.

"Rubbish, Canon, this stuff is too good to waste on parishioners," Doctor Mitchell roared. He turned to Harry and added calmly, "That would probably explain why your parents never mentioned it to me when I used to visit."

"We'll have to visit the cellar and make a list of everything down there," Morag reflected.

"We need to make a list of a lot of things," added Harry solemnly. "We're still not too sure of who exactly lives out on the estate. We had groundsmen living in tied cottages who went off to war, and William drove their families out of their homes if they didn't come back. We had a blacksmith who lived with his family down by Meadow Creek, his father and grandfather had done so for years. Morag and I took a stroll down there at the beginning of the year. Their cottage was empty, as were many we inspected."

"Does anyone still live on the estate?" Canon Trebarwith enquired.

"Oh yes, the estate still employs many people. Susan and Lawrence live over in the Housekeepers' Cottage," replied Morag. "After what happened to Edith and Reginald Travers, they kindly agreed to take over as Housekeeper and Estate Manager." From the corner of her eye she noticed Doctor Mitchell pull a small leather pouch from his breast pocket and from it a small cigar. When he glanced across at her, she smiled approvingly, before turning to the clergyman. "Canon Trebarwith, please feel free to smoke if you wish."

"Here, Canon, try one of these…" Mitchell offered his pouch across the table.

"No, thank you." Roderick Trebarwith raised his hand in a friendly, but firm manner. "I've never felt the urge to smoke. It's one vice I've managed to resist."

Doctor Mitchell smiled and shrugged his shoulders.

Morag was about to ring the buzzer under the table to her right and ask for the brandy and cognac, when she gazed at the clergyman across from her. With a dexterity of movement, he subtly pulled out a small tin of snuff, flicked open the lid and removed a tiny amount which he spread across the back of his hand. Without seemingly a care in the world as to who might be watching, he lowered his head and sniffed twice, filling both nostrils, before closing the little tin and depositing it back into his pocket.

"I… er…" Morag noticed a deep glow spread across Trebarwith's pale face. His eyes had taken on a distant lustre, as though the world in which he found himself was a million miles from Frobisher Hall. "I think," she added, recovering her composure, "it might be nice to take drinks in—"

"Have you visited Ellen Carfax over in Sunrise Cottage?" Doctor Mitchell asked, his voice cutting through the smoky atmosphere.

"Ellen Carfax?" Harry's words were as leaden as the frown that spread across his face. He had, up until this moment, been drawing happily on his favourite pipe.

"I expect she still lives there?"

"I… er… expect she does, yes," Harry replied stiffly, his fingers nervously reaching for his whisky glass. When he found it, his frown deepened when he realised it was empty.

"You never told me of her, Harry?" Morag eyed her husband speculatively.

"To be honest, my dear, with everything that's happened since my homecoming last year, I'd not given her any thought." Harry smiled reassuringly.

"Maybe we should ride out there and visit her." Morag took a sip of her lemonade. "I mean, if she's living on the estate, I want to know why. If she's a member of staff then we have an obligation with regards to her welfare…"

"Oh, I don't think she's a member of staff, Lady Frobisher," Doctor Mitchell countered, staring at the table.

"Then, who is she?" Morag looked across at her three companions in turn.

The blank look on Canon Trebarwith's face omitted any hope of information from him. The unassuming manner of her husband gave slight cause for concern. But it was the knowing and wry smile upon Doctor Mitchell's face that intrigued her the most.

From the hallway, the grandfather clock chimed the hour of ten. As always, its echoes reverberated heavily in the dining hall; something that always led Morag to feel as though the house were reminding the dinner guests of the lateness of the evening.

Sounding as though he had awoken from a dream and needed to contribute quickly to the conversation, Canon Trebarwith blurted out, "I heard about the body you discovered on the train this afternoon."

Morag couldn't decide if the statement was a mere reflection on what everyone in and around Bodmin seemed to already know, or was a prompt for her to say something. She was strangely aware that, during the exchanges regarding the Frobisher wine, and this strange woman living out on the estate, she had completely forgotten about their encounter on Bodmin Road Station.

And that concerned her.

Since that night out in the hallway when she'd ended the life of William Frobisher, though she'd talked quite freely about it to Harry, she'd been troubled by her rather cold and indifferent reaction to his death. During the months that followed, she'd occasionally lapsed into quiet contemplation, had even stood at the top of the stairs and stared down towards the spot where William had fallen, but she'd never felt compelled to succumb to emotional outbursts.

Why should I? she'd once thought. *He was about to kill the man I love.*

"Well, that's not quite right, Canon," Harry corrected. "It was a young girl climbing into that compartment who found him. Morag responded to her screams."

"A shock for you, Lady Frobisher." Canon Trebarwith smiled.

"I've experienced worse." Morag felt the coldness of her words and desperately wanted to add something a little more warming.

"And you've no idea who he was?" Doctor Mitchell drew on his cigar and exhaled a cloud of bluish smoke up towards the huge family standards that were held suspended above their heads.

The wry smile had gone.

Morag observed a deeper level of interest, something way beyond mere curiosity. The evening was turning out to be hotter than she had at first anticipated, with a feeling of stifled mugginess hanging about the room that complemented the smoke that was starting to float like a fog over the table. Rising to her feet, she smiled before walking over to the large glass doors that opened out onto the vast Roman terrace. As she did so, a gust of warm air swept through the dining room, and she stood, momentarily happy to breath the clean air and listen to the occasional forest sounds that echoed in the darkness.

"He was the ticket inspector with whom we'd a small disagreement in Paddington." Harry turned his head towards Morag. "He tried to tell us we had the wrong dates on our tickets. We're going into Bodmin tomorrow morning to give a statement to Sergeant Cadan."

"And you found him in the compartment next to yours?"

"As I said, Doctor, we didn't find him—" Harry corrected.

"Quite so, Lord Frobisher."

"Yes," Morag gazed out into the darkness, catching the distant sound of a fox, "it was the compartment next to ours…"

"And you never heard anything?"

"We both heard a slight commotion."

Harry slid his chair back and rose to his feet. Leaving his stick beside his chair, he moved his hand along the side of the table, before shuffling his way over towards the sound of Morag's voice. He hesitantly crossed the short space between the table and the open doors, his face creased in deep concentration.

Morag moved herself a couple of steps to her right to ensure Harry would find her outstretched hand.

"And you saw nobody?" Mitchell took short, deep puffs on his cigar, as though afraid it might go out.

"The blinds in our compartment were pulled down," Morag explained thoughtfully, her mind recalling the events with an ease and clarity she thought quite strange considering what they'd done and the terrible dream she'd experienced.

"How very strange." Canon Trebarwith's voice, restrained and emotionless, drifted across from the other side of the table. "Whoever the poor fellow was, it must have been a terrible way to die. I shall certainly pray for his soul."

The room fell silent.

From the distant corners of Frobisher Hall came sounds, warming and familiar, echoing and resonating. Footsteps, probably Susan's, tip-tapped their way down one of the corridors; a muffled voice, probably Mrs Chambers', barked orders to her kitchen staff.

Morag stared out into the darkness, aware of the closeness of Harry and the fragrant smell of cherry tobacco. Frobisher Hall was enveloping her within its tender embrace, as Harry would do later, entwining her naked body next to his.

★★★

Five miles away, Captain Grant sat in the kitchen of 13 Creek Lane and solemnly reflected on the day's events. When he pulled the watch from his jacket pocket, he struggled to read the time, so darkened had the room become. By angling it slightly to the window, he managed to read a couple of minutes past ten. How long he'd sat there he couldn't deduce; if he'd eaten dinner, he certainly didn't remember. Glancing around the room, he smiled to himself, before turning his attention to the reading glasses sitting in the middle of the table.

He may have drifted off, so tired had he been since his exertions during the day. Thinking about it, Grant was sure he had, for he'd awoken to an incessant sound of something swinging, or creaking, echoing around the house. And there was something else, something that made him feel more uncomfortable than he'd ever been since his arrival in 13 Creek Lane. The cottage seemed to be invested with flies.

Quickly shaking off such sombre thoughts, he turned his mind to Rose Cottage and the only woman he'd ever loved. He thought about the last time he'd seen her face. It had been during the early hours of a day that he'd managed to eradicate from his mind. Until now, that was.

Captain Grant pulled out a small hip flask from his tunic pocket and poured several shots of whisky into his mouth, swallowing as he did so. Though warming, there was no relief from the pain that tugged relentlessly at his heart.

The last time he'd seen her face…

The moon had shone through the gap in his curtains and illuminated her face, pale and innocent. She'd looked up at him with such a look of need and desire he had sworn never to let her go. Her marble skin, reflected in the moonlight, had been so incredibly soft he'd just wanted to kiss her and never stop.

He imagined her reading his note and the look upon her face. She might be scornful of the fact he'd only written his words on an old envelope. Maybe he should have knocked on the door, instead of losing heart and scurrying off, leaving her to contact him. His mind juggled different scenarios, but to no avail. Each one concluded with her falling into his arms; and that was the worst part, knowing his mind could be so relentless in its brutality. As much as he tried, he couldn't ignore the terrible reality he knew he had to confront.

Around him, the cottage echoed to the familiar sound of something swinging back and forth… creak… creak… creak…

Even now, as he sat smoking a cigarette and flicking the ash into the fire grate, he heard it, echoing in the furthest recesses of his mind. It could have emanated from anywhere in the house, or absolutely nowhere. When he'd earlier tried to follow the sound, he'd simply found himself wandering aimlessly from one room to another.

And those reading glasses.

Several times he'd reached out to them, with every intention of picking them up and disposing of them in one of the many drawers that surrounded him.

So now, as the darkness of night and 13 Creek Lane wrapped him within their shroud-like embrace, Captain Grant felt a chill run through him. Looking at the reading glasses neatly sat in the centre of the table, and with a heart full of a sadness that threatened to overwhelm him, he reached into his jacket pocket and pulled out his service revolver.

6

Morag awoke with a thin shaft of morning sunshine piercing through a gap in the bedroom curtains and warming her face. The bedcovers had been pushed aside during the night, as the evening warmth hadn't lifted as anticipated but had settled across the county bringing a heavy, muggy feeling in its wake.

Harry lay naked on his side, still sleeping deeply, his breathing low and rhythmic.

She'd been nestled within his embrace, feeling the softness of his breath upon her neck and his arms around her. Staring down at the ray of light as it shimmered across her own naked body, she watched fascinated as small dust particles danced and swirled over little drafts of air that permeated through the open windows. Her skin, pale and freckled, dazzled as the light danced across the surface.

Easing herself from his embrace, she moved to the side of the bed and sat quietly for a couple of minutes, waiting for his whispered words or the touch of his hand upon her back.

When neither of these things happened, she turned her head and smiled as she watched him sleeping peacefully.

His nightmares, thankfully, were starting to ease.

Rising from the bed, she made her way to the bathroom, gasping slightly at the sudden coldness of the marble floor. There was no need to turn on the light, as there was enough sunlight bursting through the gap in the curtains. Besides, she'd taken to bathing with Harry with the lights either turned down or extinguished completely, trying to imagine his world of darkness.

She turned the taps on and secured the plug.

Crystal-framed mirrors surrounded her, sweeping stylishly down to marbled tops. Patterned tiles, decoratively carved and painted, bordered the marble surfaces, and above, secured upon the ceiling, a gold-rimmed mirror reflected her image as she sat beside the bath, feeling the water cascade through her fingers.

Her slender figure, as seen from the reflection above, gave the impression of a model lying naked within a room, being drawn by a group of artists. The perspective fascinated her, and she angled her head to one side and brushed her hair away from her face. As she eased herself round, she caught sight of her breasts and recalled the touch of Harry's tongue as it had flicked and rolled across her nipples sometime during the night when she'd dreamily felt his hands fondling and caressing her, drawing her to him – her sleep, along with any inhibitions, tumbling away with each kiss she felt upon her body.

Positioned as she was, sat upon the marble floor, she felt a sense of vulnerability, and waited impatiently for the bath to fill so she could slide into its warm embrace and wait for him to slip in behind her. When he did so, she would lie back against him.

When, finally, the bath was filled to her liking, she closed the taps and lifted and tied her hair back. Climbing in, she gasped slightly, feeling her skin dance with a tingling sensation that made her all the more desirous of his presence.

Sliding down, she let the water cover her until it lapped against her neck and shoulders.

Closing her eyes, she breathed deeply, waiting to hear the softness of his steps, the feel of his body…

A hand brushed gently against her cheek, before fingers spread down towards her mouth.

"My darling…" she moaned.

The tip of a finger flicked against her lips, before drifting down her neck. Gently it caressed her neck before moving below the surface.

"Oh, God…" She felt the familiar flame stirring deep within her and sighed heavily.

The hand gently massaged her breasts, that same fingertip drawing circles around her nipples…

"Oh, Harry… Oh, God…" Her words were mere whispers, spoken lightly and carried away upon a mist that swirled around her as she floated dreamily upon a boat, lost within the pages of some romantic novel…

She opened her eyes.

Blinking several times, realisation soon dawned on her that she was alone. Startled and slightly disorientated, she sat up in the bath and turned her head towards the door. It was closed; yet she knew she'd left it open, knowing that Harry might stumble into it when he entered the bathroom.

Emerging quickly from the bath, she didn't wait to grasp a towel but hurried quickly towards the door. When she opened it she peered around the bedroom.

Harry was still sleeping soundly upon their bed.

★★★

Sergeant Cadan removed his helmet and tunic and laid them neatly on the wooden, and extremely old, table that stood in the mortuary within Bodmin Hospital. The room, though encased in thick stone, with whitewashed walls that were immaculately clean, still carried with it an oppressive atmosphere, heightened by the early morning warmth that had permeated throughout the building and was not alleviated by any number of opened windows.

Such a beautiful morning, with an uncommonly warm breeze upon his face, he pondered the unfairness of it all; that Bodmin should be awakening to such a glorious day, and yet here he stood, accompanying the dead as they awaited the scrutinising eye of a pathologist.

He'd been hoping to spend some time before the weekend catching up on general reports and writing out the new duty rosters for the approaching summer months. By completing these tasks beforehand, he'd be able to spend a relaxing Saturday with his wife and hopefully attend the piano recital in the afternoon. Since the discovery of the body on the Cornish Riviera Express the previous day, procedures had been followed, telegrams sent and numerous reports made out recording all statements taken and possible witnesses to the event. It reminded him of the colossal amount of work involved the previous year when the body of that poor girl was found strangled up on the moor.

To think that Death had once again visited his beloved town filled him with both sadness and foreboding.

No, it was certainly not a time to be examining corpses.

He pushed his helmet and tunic against the wall, as far as he could from the edge of the table. From the smell that assailed his senses he guessed that the floors had only recently been disinfected, and the last thing he wanted was such a smell to linger on his clothes if he were clumsy enough to let his tunic fall onto the floor.

The marble slab, built upon a decorative arch of stone and brick, gave the impression of an altar, with the body laid out ready for some grisly sacrifice. The sides were slightly raised and, at the foot of the structure, a large hole opened up to a metal bucket that sat expectantly on the stone floor. How many years it had stood like this, a sad and pitiful resting place for the dead to pause on their melancholy journey to the grave, he could hardly guess; a brief respite, he decided, whilst they were unceremoniously cut open for inquisitive eyes to peer and analyse.

And today was no exception.

For under a linen cover lay the figure of a man, naked, with a tag, the same that one might find attached to a parcel in a postal office, tied to his big toe. Both feet protruded from under the cover, the result of some assistant hastily ensuring the face was covered up at the expense of the feet.

Cadan walked around the body and stared at the writing in ink on the tag.

21ˢᵗ May 1921 – Name unknown

The first thing to strike him was how clean the feet were, with the nails neatly clipped. He assessed the size of the man at around six feet, quite athletic in build, though he was only surmising this as the outline of the body under the cover suggested as much. All this would be confirmed by the pathologist when he finally arrived from Plymouth.

He cast his mind back to the previous year and the moment he'd stood in one of the hospital rooms over at Bodmin Gaol…

It hadn't been a marble top, but a couple of tables hastily pulled together. Where this morning carried with it an air of cold formality, then it had been a far different affair; one that was as haunting as the dank and musty walls surrounding him.

He remembered the first time he'd pulled the cover back.

A beautiful face bruised and so sorrowful in death…

This body had been stripped but not cleaned, as there'd been no blood that needed to be cleared prior to examination. In fact, the body was as clean as any he'd ever seen in this place.

Vagabonds and drifters, thick with the grime and dirt of the moors upon which they lived, usually found their way to this resting place, unwanted and despised by those who'd carried them here. Cursory examinations by disinterested doctors assumed death by liver poisoning, or as a result of some knife attack. Either way, with one less beggar to concern itself with, the authorities usually marked the deceased's record appropriately and they were buried within a pauper's grave in the furthest reaches of the parish cemetery.

No, there would be no such disinterest in this chap, he thought as he scratched his bald head.

He pulled the sheet back and away to reveal the body, nonchalantly folding it before laying it neatly upon the window ledge.

He averaged the man's age at mid to late fifties, maybe early sixties. The grey hair and moustache contrasted with the athletic body and made any accurate attempt at establishing age quite difficult.

Turning to the table upon which he'd laid his own jacket, he perused the victim's clothes, recognising the uniform of a ticket collector for the Great Western Railway. It was set neatly in order, alongside personal possessions discovered when he'd made his initial search. Scrutinising them carefully, he decided which item to pick up and examine first.

He decided upon a length of rope that lay coiled like a snake, of a small diameter and probably around two feet in length. When he picked it up he held it to a small window that looked out to a level just above the stone pavement outside. Though usually left open in such hot weather, it was expected to be kept closed when a corpse was laid out in the room.

It offered vague and dismal illumination for analysis of the rope or anything else.

Cadan approached the body, quickly locating what he was looking for. A red line, the same thickness as the rope, cut deep within the victim's throat, with the obvious result of violently crushing the windpipe. He'd seen similar marks before, mainly during his time as a young officer working in Plymouth; but it didn't take a professional examination to determine that this was the cause of death.

The face had still retained its grotesque distortion, with mouth open and tongue still protruding. The eyes had become somewhat diluted from the previous afternoon, though the general look of utter dread as the victim had breathed his last, fighting for air that could not be drawn through a crushed windpipe, was a dreadful scene, and one that held Cadan momentarily transfixed.

There were no other major marks upon the body that he could see, other than slight bruising on the arms and face, along with some minor scarring to the hands.

Holding the rope out before him with both hands, he slid them along from the centre, eventually pulling it taut. He couldn't move them any further as the ends were tied neatly in a small knot. Twisting the ends around his hands, he held the rope up, smiling as he realised that he now had within his hands a very dangerous and effective means of choking the life out of someone.

He gazed at the corpse.

So far so good.

Establishing some idea of the cause of death was a start.

Sergeant Cadan turned back to the table and replaced the rope. His next item of interest was a dagger, approximately seven inches in length, with the most beautifully decorative handle he'd ever seen. Engraved upon the handle was the letter: L.

He felt this might give some indication as to the deceased's name, and he carefully picked it up by the hilt, holding it with his handkerchief and trying to ascertain if there were any further identification marks. Confusing clouds of miasma started to clog his thought patterns as he tried to comprehend why a ticket collector, of late middle age, might be carrying such a weapon.

Noticing that there was no obvious blood on the blade or handle, he quickly deduced that it had not contributed to the man's death.

He laid it back on the table next to its sheath.

The only other items of immediate interest were a pair of white gloves, again with the same letter stitched decoratively on the back, some five-pound notes and some loose change. There were also two railway tickets, both dated for the previous day and scrunched up together.

A leather wallet was empty. There was nothing to indicate the man's identity.

He held up one of the gloves, considering both the beautiful and delicate stitching and the burning question as to why a ticket inspector for the Great Western Railway might be wearing them. Scratching his head, he pondered the fact that the victim wasn't wearing them when he was found; they'd been discovered stuffed into his jacket pocket.

His mind drifted to the phone call he'd made to Scotland Yard the previous evening, reporting the crime and requesting assistance. Replacing the glove on the table he smiled and wondered…

And it was then that he saw the slip of paper, folded once and partially covered by the man's trousers and braces. He hadn't noticed it before when he'd emptied the pockets. Scooping it up he turned to the window, unfolded it and read the one line of writing, hurriedly written in pencil:

Lord & Lady Frobisher, train leaves Paddington 10.30am

Sergeant Cadan stood silently reading the words for several minutes, a deep frown settling upon his already worried face. The message was simple, though its implications were not so easy to deduce. At the sight of Lord and Lady Frobisher's names, a heavy feeling of dread settled upon his shoulders, and he sighed heavily, uncertainty now rising out of that cloud drifting in his mind.

After quickly throwing the cover back across the body, he turned and walked out of the mortuary. Like a man in a dream he climbed the stairs from the basement, leaving behind the oppressive atmosphere of the mortuary but finding scant relief with the clear and fresher air of the ground floor.

Unaware of anyone passing him, he found the administrative office and the small telephone exchange that served the main hospital.

A young girl sat knitting and looked slightly alarmed as he entered the room.

"Please put a call through to Frobisher Hall," he muttered. "I need to speak to Lord and Lady Frobisher."

★★★

Lawrence Matthews was finding that his longer walks into the forest on the Frobisher Estate weren't sapping his energy as they once had. From the moment he'd been asked to take on the role of Estate Manager, he'd felt compelled to familiarise himself with his new environment, and that had meant long excursions out into the surrounding fields and forests. It had been his way of coming to terms with the rather daunting prospect that now confronted him: that he was stepping into the shoes of a dead man and taking on a role for which he knew practically nothing.

But then it had been Lord Frobisher who'd said that five years' service in the Metropolitan Police Force would be enough to prepare and sustain anyone through the task of managing such an enormous estate. He found the accounts and general administrative duties quite easy, being used to working through the intricacies of arrest reports and the understanding and implementing of countless law manuals that had filled just about every shelf in his lodgings in London.

Sitting in the estate office, adjacent to the stables, he'd quickly familiarised himself with the different ledgers and box files containing receipts that went back before the Great War. Although he'd only met his predecessor on a couple of occasions, he'd known him to be meticulous in his work and dutiful in his relationship to the Frobisher family.

Lawrence had felt these attributes merge seamlessly with his own as he'd sat in Reginald Travers' chair and shuffled through the last sheets of paper he'd been working on before the snow arrived the November before...

The thought always chilled him to the bone.

But time had also given his shoulder an opportunity to heal, something that had taken a lot of patience. The bullet had been removed by a surgeon who'd been summoned from Plymouth, though the delay had caused significant nerve damage that had given both him and Susan cause for concern. But being able to spend time in the estate office, going through the files and receipts, accounts and order books and, most interestingly, the huge estate maps that adorned the walls, had enabled Lawrence to shed the feeling of guilt that he should be out on the estate.

It had also kept him away from the severe winter storms that had savaged the Frobisher Estate in the aftermath of William Frobisher's death. Susan had said it was as though the house were finally ridding itself of a terrible curse and seeking atonement for the crimes committed within the confines of its walls.

And while Frobisher Hall bore the brunt of those winter storms, desperate to heal wounds that had lain open too long, Lawrence Matthews had sat engrossed in the numerous papers and maps within the solitude and comfort of the Estate Office.

But even now, as winter turned to spring, he felt the dull ache of his wound.

He still found it extremely sore if he slept heavily on that side, and would wake in the middle of the night in excruciating pain.

But now, with the warmer days and milder climate, he felt compelled to step forth from his office and begin the arduous task of exploring the estate, visiting places that were mere reference points upon a map. He wanted to complete the puzzle, to finally embrace his new role as Estate Manager.

And so, as dawn broke that morning, spreading a dazzling explosion of sunlight across the Hall and surrounding forests, and whilst Morag Frobisher stood staring at Harry asleep in their bed, her mind racing with thoughts too dreadful to contemplate, Lawrence Matthews finished the final mouthful of his bacon sandwich, drained the last of his tea and unfolded one of several estate maps.

The Frobisher Estate was vast.

The grounds spread down through the valley towards the main railway track, that acted as a natural boundary, and also reached out across the moors. Lush farming land flanked the estate and stretched as far as the outskirts of Bodmin. Farms, carefully marked by Reginald Travers on several maps, lay situated around the estate. Tied cottages and small agricultural workshops, meticulously recorded, bore testament to the thriving business that had once blossomed and prospered.

Lawrence knew his role as Estate Manager was one that would encompass just about every job there was in and around the house. He would need to visit the families that worked the farms and win the trust and respect of estate workers who would know more about the running of the place than he ever would.

He'd smiled when Lord Frobisher had told him that he'd won their respect the night he'd lit the Frobisher Beacon.

Sitting in the Estate Office, he felt the warmth of the fire raging in the fireplace and wondered if the time had come whereby he might not need to light it. The winter had been harsh, and a dampness still clung to the outbuildings and offices. Susan had told him to work through the estate documents inside the Hall, but he'd wanted to be in the office, even if the dampness did aggravate his shoulder.

He sat staring at an old map.

He'd found it earlier that morning just after one of the servants, a young woman he thought might be the new maid, Gregson, had brought his bacon sandwich and mug of tea out to him. She'd asked him about his shoulder and commented on the warm weather. When she'd left, he'd realised he hadn't actually established her name; and even now couldn't remember what she looked like.

Now, looking at the old map before him, he noticed it was more worn and frayed than the others, having been stuffed behind some old box files. It had fallen onto the stone floor when he'd pulled them out. It was dated 1870 and covered an area of the estate he'd not seen on the other maps.

At least he initially thought so.

He was surprised to see just how far across and into the valley the estate actually reached. Though the area was covered in thick forest, with very minor dirt tracks, Lawrence noticed a small square symbol denoting one of the estate cottages. It was faded and nearly beyond recognition, but it was there. He reached across the desk and pulled towards him another, more recently dated, map. Scanning the area marked out, he traced his finger across the different symbols and markings, scrutinising the contours and elevation levels, along with the streams and pathways. It didn't take him long to orientate himself as he swivelled the map round and located the same area as marked on the older map.

He pulled the two maps together so they were overlapping, with the same two areas positioned side by side. Leaning forward, he stared intently at the older map and the thin outline of the cottage; but when he turned his attention to the more recent edition, there was no cottage.

Initial thoughts tumbled around in his mind and settled on the assumption that maybe the place had been knocked down, or been left to grow derelict, and so played no further part in the estate. He might have accepted that explanation had it not been for the fact that the area on the more recent map was now covered with trees, with no faint borders or anything to suggest there might once have been a clearing.

He checked the date on the recent map: 1900.

There was also associated notes pertaining to the surveys that were carried out on the estate that year. Dates and the company that had performed the work were detailed, along with scales and reference points.

He glanced again at the older map, squinting his eyes and lowering his head as he tried to decipher the minutest of two handwritten words... A name... He strained his eyes and angled the map towards the window... The name of a house... Sunrise Cottage.

Considering it a mystery he would try and resolve at a later date, he eased himself out of his chair and stretched his long arms and legs until his fingertips brushed lightly against one of the cross beams.

The twinge in his shoulder threatened to turn into a sharp pain, so he quickly lowered his arm, rubbing the offending area with his other hand.

Deciding that he would take one of the horses out onto the dirt track that led to the first of the estate farms, he pulled his tweed jacket from the back of the chair and his hat from the stand near the door. Pulling his jacket on, he moved resolutely out onto the path that led from the Estate Office to the stables.

Something caught his eye.

A figure moved swiftly away from the Hall, skirting the walls as if a shadow flitting silently and unobtrusively and only partially seen out of the corner of an eye. That Lawrence was not expecting to see, or half see, such an image made it all the more difficult to determine who it might be.

He was certain that the figure had come from the direction of the house, but was less certain as to where it might be heading; he thought maybe the path that led down to the family chapel and beyond into the forest.

His attempt to call out ground to a halt before he could articulate the words, his breath stilled by a menacing hand that reached into his stomach and became a clenched fist.

Whoever it might be, and wherever they were heading, Lawrence Matthews felt a chill run through his body.

★★★

Harry shuffled the newspaper before laying it down on the breakfast table. Running his fingers around the edge, he tried to ascertain if he'd correctly positioned it for reading; a task he had no realistic chance of completing successfully. He did, however, deduce from memory that his father would always leave a newspaper folded over at the front page, once telling him that it was a habit adopted by most people. He remembered a time when the papers would be laid out flat on the dining room table, recently delivered and all creases ironed out by a member of staff.

And so, after breakfast, while Morag walked across to the study to retrieve the letters Susan had deemed prudent to leave unopened until their return, Harry tentatively brushed his fingers across the table, his face set deep in concentration as he remembered his wife bringing the local newspaper into the dining room and depositing it somewhere on the table.

When his finger caught the edge of the newspaper, he pulled it towards him, caressing the sheets, and relieved to find it had been folded over. Deciding that the fold would open up with the spine to his left, he swivelled the newspaper round, flicked it opened and pulled it up before him, shuffling it as he did so.

Though he couldn't read the headlines, he always found great pleasure in Morag reading the main stories to him.

Hearing someone enter the room, he confidently guessed it was his wife, as he'd become accustomed to the sound of her footsteps, recognising the tap and echo of her shoes compared to Susan's or other members of staff.

"Well, my dear," Harry smiled triumphantly, "I've opened the newspaper for you, front page ready for your perusal…"

"Harry, my dear, it's upside down and the wrong way up," Morag's voice was distant, as she had been all morning. Though they'd breakfasted together, she'd been quiet and distracted, any conversation muted and reserved.

Harry might have felt inclined to feel a little hurt by his apparent failure to correctly position the newspaper, a feeling made even more obtuse by his wife's apparent lack of interest, but something was bothering her and that made him uncomfortable.

"Susan dealt with most of the letters whilst we were away." Morag pulled out the chair next to his from under the table. "I thought we'd go through them together before consulting with her about our plans for the next couple of days."

"Morag—" Harry whispered, closing the newspaper and pushing it away towards the middle of the table.

"I think Sergeant Cadan wishes to see us around 11am," she continued unabated.

"Morag." Harry's voice cut through the dining room. Though not loud, its tone carried an air of sharp authority.

Silence descended.

He reached out his hand across the table and felt her grasp it and immediately tighten her grip.

"What is it? You've been quiet all morning. Has something happened?"

He slid gently off his chair, hearing the clang as his stick fell to the floor. She was so near to him that he found himself quickly beside her, and so knelt by her side, gazing sightlessly towards her face.

"Harry," Morag's voice quivered, "after what happened last year, Lawrence nailed shut all of the entrances to the secret passages around the house." It was a statement, not a question.

"The ones we knew about," replied Harry. "Or should I say the ones you told us about. You were the one and only person who was brave enough to use them."

Morag smiled and squeezed his hand.

"Why do you ask?"

Harry stood up, feeling the familiar twinge in his upper leg. He was once told by the family doctor that shrapnel wounds never truly healed.

"It's nothing, dear. Really. It's just me being silly, that's all." Morag smiled, reaching down to pick up Harry's stick. "I'll read these letters and then we can take coffee in the lounge and I'll read the newspaper headlines to you." The sparkle in her voice had returned, but it was a dull glow compared to her usual vibrant and confident tone.

Harry settled himself back into his chair and rummaged in his jacket pocket for his pipe. When he found it, he lit a match and puffed gently, enjoying the sweet taste of cherry tobacco as it filled the air around them.

"This first letter is an invitation." Morag's voice had lost its discerning edge and was now tinged with an air of inquisitiveness.

"Really?" replied Harry with genuine interest. "Our first invite to a party as man and wife."

"Hmm, not quite. It's an invitation card. It seems Bodmin Town Hall is holding a piano recital on Saturday afternoon. 'Saturday 23rd May. The Bodmin Women's Institute requests the pleasure of Lord and Lady Frobisher. Two thirty. Tea and cakes during the interval.'" Morag read the invitation card several times, falling silent as she did so.

"Does it worry you?" Harry could feel Morag's uneasiness.

"They'll obviously be watching me," she replied. "The woman who escaped from Amble Lodge and won the heart of the future Lord Frobisher…"

"Who *saved the life* of the future Lord Frobisher," Harry corrected.

"Aye, but they'll be watching me…"

"You knew this moment would eventually come, my dear." Harry stretched himself back in the chair. "As Lord and Lady Frobisher, we'll be expected to perform public duties. My parents did so on many occasions, even attending the Royal Court in London."

"Aye, Harry. I suppose that, up until now, it's just been you and me and Frobisher Hall. Everything that happened last year did so *here*, after I escaped. The people of Bodmin only ever knew me as the woman who was locked up in a mental asylum."

"I think you do the people of Bodmin an injustice, Morag. My family has ties with the town and surrounding moors dating back centuries. And it's not just one of people doffing their caps when we pass by because they feel they have to; the bond between my family and Bodmin goes much deeper. When the truth about William and our parents finally became clear, and when they realised the injustice of your imprisonment, I heard they ripped this town apart looking for Morgan Treave."

Morag sighed. "I know. Just before our wedding, when we had lunch in the St Petroc Hotel, an elderly couple came up to me whilst you were talking to the landlord. They shook my hand. The old lady had tears in her eyes and actually apologised for what I'd been through…" She read through the invitation again. "I suppose it's time for me to make my peace with the people of Bodmin."

Harry drew on his pipe, frowning as he discovered it had gone out.

Morag laid the card on the table and picked up the remining letters. "Looks like belated wedding cards."

Harry heard her sifting slowly through the letters and was gripped with the notion that she was searching for one with her father's handwriting on the envelope.

"This one looks different," Morag said with interest.

"In what way?" Harry re-lit his pipe.

"It just looks different from the rest."

She held it up, for no other reason than that the colour of the envelope was a deep cream, the paper thick within her grasp. She'd only encountered envelopes of this quality occasionally in the past, mainly when her father had written his letters to 10 Downing Street, usually to air his views about Government meddling in Scottish affairs.

What really caught her eye was the fact that someone had gone to all the trouble of writing a letter, and using an exquisite envelope, then only written the name 'Harry Frobisher' on the front. There was no address.

Not waiting for Harry to say anything, she slid her fingernail along the fold and opened it. The actual letter, like the envelope, was of the highest quality paper, with a distinct watermark that she quickly noted before allowing her concentration to become totally wrapped up in its contents.

She read it through twice, silently, before gazing across at Harry.

"Who's it from?" Harry asked, a little impatiently. He'd heard her open the envelope before distinctly hearing the sound of paper being unfolded. The following pause had simply told him she was reading its contents.

"I'm not sure, Harry," Morag replied hesitantly.

What she initially read made no sense, and Harry sensed her trepidation.

Maybe it was the black ink, common enough, but quite chilling in its style upon the page. The flow of the pen, its accentuated curves and dips, the lines that crossed the letter 't', and the elongated flick that completed a word or sentence; the essence of the writing style suggested something quite Gothic, belonging to a world long since dead and forgotten, though closer scrutiny of the script suggested just a simple, well-crafted letter.

Harry resisted the urge to tell her to read it, knowing she would do so eventually. He did, though, say, "Is it good news or bad?"

Morag replied, "It doesn't quite make sense to me, Harry, but it might to you. It says:

'My dear Harry

How fortunate our paths come so close to crossing yet again.

I remember how you twice saved my life. The first from that madam in that café in Paris, and the second during the Somme Offensive. Well, old boy, it might be that I need you to save my life again.

If I tell you now that the rooks have flown, you'll understand what I mean. Or maybe you won't.

You see, time has erased so many memories for all of us and, though I dare to hope I might feel your handshake again, a part of me wishes you have no memory of me or the organisation that brought us together all those years ago.

I am in Bodmin for a few days, renting a cottage at 13 Creek Lane.

If the mists of time ease enough for you to remember, then please come soonest. If not, I pray that you live a long and happy life with your new wife and that the nightmares leave you well alone.

I pray also that I may yet still find absolution for something that has haunted me for too long.

If this rook should be found dead upon the ground, look for the fourth rook behind the…
WRG'

Morag repeated the last line again, followed by the letters. Looking at Harry she commented, "It ends rather abruptly… Who is WRG?"

"My God," Harry muttered.

"What, Harry? Who is it?"

"Wilbur Grant. It must be him. But here in Bodmin?"

Morag glanced back at the letter. "What does the 'R' stand for?"

"I'm not sure," replied Harry thoughtfully. "He did tell me once. I think it was Richard."

"You obviously know him."

"Yes… Captain Grant… Captain Wilbur Grant…" Harry laid his pipe on the table and shook his head. "I haven't heard that name in a long time. What was that he said about the rooks?"

Morag glanced down at the letter, searching. When she found what she was looking for she repeated aloud, "The rooks have flown…" She skimmed further down the page. "And then says 'If this rook should be found dead…'"

Harry digested the words, as if in a dream.

He knew if he let his emotions run away with him, this could quite easily turn into a nightmare. He also knew that a part of him had become numb, as though his body had instinctively drawn down barriers at the mention of those words. Though he knew his pipe would bring him temporary comfort, he chose not to reach for it, knowing that his hands were visibly shaking.

"What does it mean, Harry?" Morag's voice was surprisingly calm, considering the sullen and reflective shroud that had descended upon her husband.

It was her composed and level response that gave Harry the strength to turn his head in her direction and say, "It means that something in my past has finally caught up with me."

7

Lawrence Matthews eased himself into the saddle and inwardly moaned as his shoulder cried out in agony, sending a shuddering jolt down his arm and a tingling sensation along his fingertips. He paused momentarily, expecting to hear Susan's voice call across from one of the rear doors of the main house, concerned and reproachful. She'd told him on several occasions not to go riding too far out onto the estate, insisting that one of the new gardeners accompany him.

The pain eased, as did his apprehension at the prospect of hearing his wife's voice, as he settled his tall frame into the saddle, ignoring the ache in his backside, a reminder of previous excursions on what was now his favourite horse. The notion of asking Reynolds, the Head Gardener, to ride with him this morning was instantly rebuked as he felt the estate map ruffle inside his jacket pocket and a warm breeze run its beguiling fingers across his face.

Sunrise Cottage had been marked on every map up until the most recent edition published at the end of the last century. He had accounted for every dwelling and barn on the estate since taking over the role of Estate Manager, visiting them all either in the company of Morag and Harry, or with Reynolds.

Today, though, would be different.

Today he would find the confidence and courage to venture forth deep into the estate alone.

Lightly digging his heels and speaking words of encouragement, he steered the grey mare around and headed towards the old track that led towards Templers Copse, glancing back one last time towards the Hall. He wondered as to the identity of the figure that had flitted swiftly past the cottage, moving with ghostly ease and heading in the same direction as he was now. It must have been one of the gardeners or local farmhands; though when he tried to recall what they were wearing the image merely blurred within his subconscious.

That they were headed in this direction was no great surprise; the track leading down to Templers Copse was popular with the estate workers, as it linked several paths and wagon tracks that dissected the estate, connecting many of the old cottages and farms on the outer extremities. It was also a picturesque route favoured by Harry and Morag, and even some of the staff, when looking to spend a relaxing afternoon taking a quiet stroll in the grounds.

The main house quickly faded from view as he took a familiar route, easing his horse along the rugged and uneven track. "Easy, girl," he called, reigning her in and looking for the small gate he'd seen in the past but not given any attention to until he'd studied the map that now resided in his pocket.

Cantering forward, he felt the ground dip slightly, and saw the rolling fields spread out to his right, revealing lush farmland that had recently been sown and would eventually bear a rich harvest of barley and wheat. Above him, oak and ash trees spread their canopies far, sheltering him from the morning sun and bordering the forest to his left.

Descending even further into the huge valley, that eventually swung round to meet the main Great Western Railway line, Lawrence felt the morning warmth dissipate and a damp chill set in as he realised he was now riding towards Templers Copse.

There was a dampness in the ground and in the undergrowth that brushed against his trousers and boots. Mud splattered up from puddles that would probably never dry out, even in the height of summer.

He was moving further into the forest, leaving the fields behind him, feeling the embrace of trees, centuries old. Though he'd travelled this way before, it had been in the company of someone who knew the estate, and he shuddered slightly as he felt the cold hand of solitude run its fingers down his neck.

Finally, he found the gate. It was as he'd seen it before: wooden and decrepit. The strange thing about it was, there didn't seem to be any fence either side. It was as though the forest undergrowth had just parted enough for an old gate to reside there, marking an entrance to some obsolete trail.

But now it was open, and Lawrence Matthews pulled his horse to a halt and reflected on why this was so, certain that it had always been shut when he'd passed this way before.

Beyond, the path vanished into a maze of undergrowth and trees, so thick and overgrown it seemed as though someone on foot would struggle to follow it. Around him echoed the forest sounds, birds calling, animals screeching. He reached into his pocket and pulled out the map, locating his position immediately and scanning the area beyond the gate.

Though hard to distinguish, if he scrutinised the area in front of him he could vaguely discern the outline of a path.

Pushing the map back into his pocket he glanced quickly at his watch and read the time: 10.30am. His shoulder was beginning to ache, and he assumed the damp atmosphere had penetrated into his wound, aggravating the still-tender muscles.

He kicked his heels and moved forward, aware of a lone rook calling out from one of the branches above him. Looking up, he saw it flutter from the green foliage and descend awkwardly, finally landing on one of the decayed old posts supporting the gate. It eyed him mischievously, screeching and turning its head, as though intrigued as to the purpose of this strange visitor.

Moving forward, Lawrence felt the forest reach out and enfold him within its damp and clammy embrace. Foliage opened and closed around him, brushing watery fingers across his face and flicking arms across his back, welcoming him into a strange fairy-tale world he'd once read about when he was a boy.

Looking around, he noticed the rook had disappeared.

So engrossed was he with this collage of colours surrounding him, blurred yet somehow defined, and shadows that darted mysteriously around him, pausing, staring, that he lost track of all time and distance. He felt the forest swallow him, digesting him with every step his horse took.

Lawrence also noticed the forest had quietened, stilled almost to a hushed whisper, with creatures no longer eager to follow his journey.

He patted his hand down the neck of his horse and muttered something encouraging – more for himself, he inwardly acknowledged. For some time he'd been conscious of a dampness down his back and a shortness of breath, but it wasn't until now that he realised just how anxious he was. Even the pain in his shoulder had reduced to a dull ache.

Finally, the density of the forest receded, revealing a small glade, with rays of light breaking through the green canopy of leaves and branches. A low mist had settled upon wild grass and drifted like some ghostly miasma, swirling its tentacles around his horse.

Lawrence held his breath, aware of a twig snapping behind him. He grasped the reins tightly and turned slightly in the saddle, conscious of his inability to yet master the art of balancing himself whilst looking round.

The shadow that rose up before him was one he instantly recognised, with the mutilated face and eye patch terrifyingly clear. With a mouth opened in hateful spite, the figure threw up its hands and roared at the horse with a voice that raged with demonic anger.

Lawrence felt the horse rear up, and he tried desperately to realign himself in the saddle.

He failed miserably.

Fighting to cling hold of anything, he saw his flailing arms wave strangely before him, flitting in and out of the rays of sunlight that seemed to shine on him like an actor on stage. As if in slow motion, Lawrence saw his world twist and turn upside down as he pitched back and fell heavily onto the ground, instantly knocking the wind from his lungs and sending a terrible, searing pain from his shoulder to just about every other part of his body.

Though he fought to stay awake, he felt the warm hand of unconsciousness close his eyes.

★★★

The lounge at Frobisher Hall always radiated a profound sense of family history and status. Decorated with beautiful flock wallpaper, with huge concrete pillars forming part of the walls, the paintings that hung within this room reflected the most intimate and personal traits of the Frobisher family, each one bearing a remarkable story that touched the very soul of the building.

Positioned around the room, oil paintings depicted family members, now consigned to distant memory and stories told and retold to become eventually entwined within local folklore and legend. A lush carpet lay majestically across the floor, and the most decorative and comfortable chairs and lounge sofa were positioned before a huge fireplace that swept upwards through the heart of Frobisher Hall. To the left of this fireplace hung a large oil painting of Harry's father, the former viscount, resplendent in his heraldic robes, his dark brown eyes piercing the room, his features firm and unflinching. The resemblance to his son was, though, tenuous to say the least. His cold and unassuming poise was in stark contrast to Harry's, though an observer would have found certain peculiar similarities: the slight angle of the head, the wry smile that seemed to materialise the longer you stared at the portrait, as though a family secret laid hidden, about to be exposed.

No such similarities were shared with the portrait of his wife, the former Lady Frobisher, to the right of the fireplace. Dressed in a long flannel coat, unbuttoned to reveal a simple woollen top and tweed skirt, she leant against a large wooden table, her eyes alert and engaging, though tinged with a sadness that some might interpret as melancholy. Her long flowing hair was tied back and set to one side, to cascade down over her right shoulder. Though painted at the turn of the century, and with herself approaching middle age, the artist had captured the essence of her youth and beautifully interwoven it with the harshness of the advancing years.

Morag moved her gaze from Harry's mother, turning as she did so to watch Harry fill his pipe before striking a match. As he exhaled clouds of aromatic smoke, his facial expression changed from one of deep concern to that of relaxed calm.

"They say the lounge is the heart and soul of Frobisher Hall, that my parents still live and breathe within those two portraits." Harry sat back in one of the large lounge chairs.

"I loved them both very much, Harry." Morag glanced back at the portraits, her mind a whirlpool of emotions. "I don't actually think these portraits do them justice. Your father looks so cold, yet I remember him so friendly. And your mother looks so sad."

"She refused to be painted in her robes and finery. She wanted something simple, something to reflect her personality. People would ask why she looked so sad, but she never spoke about it. I remember she always seemed to carry a worry or a concern about something. I never questioned her too deeply, but it was always there." Harry sighed heavily. "What I would give to have them with me now in this room… the four of us…"

Morag moved to the lounge sofa. She'd decided upon a light skirt with a silk blouse, and her favourite tartan scarf around her neck, which was practically hidden by her long red hair which had not been, as yet, tied back for the day. Her feet were bare, having kicked off her shoes the moment they'd walked into the lounge, so desirous was she to feel the lush carpet beneath her. She sat down on the sofa nearest to Harry and held out her hand, resting it lightly on his arm.

"I served with Captain Grant over in France. Our battalions came into contact with each other on several occasions, and we would meet up, sometimes with William, whilst on short leave pass in Paris. That was where we…" Harry coughed and fiddled with his pipe. "The madam in question was…"

"I think I can work that one out for myself, Harry dear." Morag said reassuringly.

"Yes, quite…" Harry paused to gather his thoughts before continuing. "He often spoke about an organisation called The Nest of Rooks. I say an organisation; they were a group of four agents working closely with French and British Intelligence, delivering communiqués to agents working behind enemy lines across Europe. They worked in small cells and were controlled by a commander called the Fourth Rook who they never got to meet."

"He told you this?" Morag whispered.

"Yes; it was during a stay over in Paris that Grant first confided in us one night. He had grown to trust us, you see."

"But why? I would have thought it was not something one would babble about, surely?" Morag stared at her husband, reading every line that creased his face, his every movement and the way he held his head – slightly forward and lost in deep concentration.

"Something had scared him. Something he wanted to confide in us but knew could possibly put us in danger."

"What was it?"

Harry breathed deeply. "You've got to understand, Morag; spies, agents, call them what you will, from both sides, were infiltrating each other's staff on a regular basis. Grant even had friends working for and against the Russians. If they were caught, they were shot. And those who weren't shot were usually found in some Paris backstreet with their throats cut. Grant had found something out about the cell he was working with. Someone had turned bad, was feeding false information to British Intelligence, and feeding information about troop movements and planned advances to the Germans. Nobody knew who it was. He'd written his suspicions down in a letter that he sealed in an envelope and gave to me, asking me not to open it unless I heard of his death."

Harry stood up, pulling his hand away from Morag's and momentarily steadying himself, tapping the floor a little with his stick and feeling with the back of his free hand for the outer rim of a lampshade that sat upon a small table. Using this as a guide to pivot himself slightly to his right, he walked a couple of paces before standing directly before the drinks' cabinet to one side of his mother's portrait. He was standing just within reach, exactly where a sighted person might also position themselves.

Morag was momentarily taken aback at her husband's confidence in navigating himself around the room.

Though he stood before the whisky decanter, Harry made no move to open the lid and reach for a glass. Standing with his back to the main room, he drew on his pipe and gazed sightlessly at the wall.

"I kept it in the top pocket of my tunic. It was the safest place I could think of, as we were always on the move, and if I left personal belongings anywhere, I might never see them again. I even thought about sending it back to my parents here at the Hall, but I was worried it might somehow implicate them in something they were best to stay clear of."

"What happened, Harry?" Morag prompted.

"It was in my tunic pocket on the day the grenade blew up in my face. The day when…" He fell silent, seemingly lost within his memories.

"Good God," mumbled Morag.

"Yes, my sweetheart. Those were my words as well." Harry had hooked his stick over his arm and turned, now somewhat hesitant of where he should go. His hand shook slightly as he reached out. Grasping his stick, he tapped lightly to his front and then to his right. "My dear, could you say something; I seemed to have become a little disorientated…"

"Harry, I'm here, darling." Morag swiftly rose from the sofa and moved towards her husband. "Would you like me to pour you a drink?"

"No… it's fine… I think we'll both need clear heads today." Harry reached out and visibly relaxed as he felt Morag grasp his hand and lead him back to the sofa.

When he was finally settled beside her, he continued, "By the time I was in any fit state to know what was happening, my belongings had been gathered into a bag. Sergeant Benson checked through it, but there was no letter."

"What happened then?" Morag prompted.

"That was it, really. I never heard from Captain Grant again," Harry continued. "By that time, I was busy trying to sort out my life as a blind man. The rest you know."

"There's something you're not telling me, Harry Frobisher." Morag narrowed her eyes and watched the change in Harry's expression as he absorbed what she'd just said.

"You see right through me, Lady Frobisher." Harry smiled.

From the hallway the grandfather clock pealed the hour of 10.30am, its chimes ringing out across the hallway, echoing along corridors and reverberating from one room to another.

"Grant once said that if the cell was in danger, if they needed help, then one of them would pass a message saying 'The rooks have flown'. But why he's down here, or writing this letter to me, with everything it implies, I have no idea. Remember, we're talking about something that happened a long time ago, with people who might already be dead."

Morag eyed Harry closely and asked, "Were you one of these Rooks?"

"No, Morag. My only link to this organisation is by association. If Captain Grant had never spoken of them, or written that letter, then I would have been none the wiser."

"Do you think this might be connected to that body on the train yesterday?" she prompted solemnly.

"I don't know. It does seem quite a coincidence."

"Are we in danger, Harry?" Morag's words fell like a leaden weight upon the room. Even the house seemed to breathe deeply and hold its breath.

"*I* might be," Harry sighed.

"Well, if *you* are, then, going by past events, so am I. We need to drive into Bodmin and see this Captain Grant as quickly as possible. We have an appointment with Sergeant Cadan, so I think it would be wise to visit Captain Grant beforehand; it might shed some light on that body yesterday." She could feel the rising tide of anxiety, like a cold hand caressing her, but managed to suppress it. Recalling the chimes of the grandfather clock, she added, "Though we did agree to meet Sergeant Cadan at 11am."

"Come to think of it…" Harry blurted out, his forehead narrowing into a frown as he desperately probed the recesses of his mind, searching for the spark that had ignited a glow that burned distantly in his subconscious. He turned round. "Over in the study there's a photograph of me and Captain Grant – unless it's been moved. I sent several back from the Front and Father had them framed and positioned in the study. There are several of me and William with our fellow officers. I'm sure it's in there…"

"Give me a minute to look." Morag rose from the sofa and walked briskly towards the door.

Harry called after her, "If it's there, you'll see me standing next to Captain Grant. It was taken on the steps of a chateau somewhere just outside Paris. William took it."

Morag hurried across the main hallway and into the study, quickly adjusting her eyes to the numerous photographs and regimental awards and crests that adorned the walls. Faded photographs, distant memories and lost comrades welcomed her, their fixed smiles and stalwart features causing her to pause in sudden and heartfelt admiration. Each one told a story, and each story tugged mournfully at her heart.

She scanned the images, looking for Harry standing next to another man.

It was there, lost amongst several old regimental photographs of Harry standing beside his fellow officers. Morag stared at it for a couple of seconds before running her fingers over his image. To see him, eyes wide with youthful expectation, maybe not as handsome as his comrades, filled her with sadness.

"Is it there?" Harry's voice startled her. He was standing just behind her, having made his own way over to the study.

"Yes," she replied, "I think so." Lifting the photograph from the wall she observed Harry standing on some rather elegant steps and leaning against a stone pillar. Beside him stood a taller man, in uniform, more erect in stature than Harry, with a moustache that curled up at the ends. Where Harry's pipe was gripped firmly in his mouth, the man she assumed was Captain Grant held a cigarette firmly in his left hand. "It's here, Harry." She held the photograph nearer, again running her fingers over the glass. "Yes, looks like a stately building of some sort."

"I'd forgotten all about it until now," Harry reflected, his body turned in her direction. "Tall chap, if I remember."

"Yes, looks quite tall."

"Moustache waxed at the ends?"

"Yes."

"Hmm, must be him," Harry reflected. "I remember he was tall. I once told him he'd live a longer life as a spy; if he tried to cross no-man's-land with his height, he'd be a sitting target."

"Okay, at least I know what he looks like. We need—"

The phone in the main hallway began to ring with a high-pitched repetitive tone that reverberated across the ground floor. Morag was initially tempted to wait for one of the staff to answer it, before shaking off the thought and picking up the extension line in the study. Listening intently, she spoke only twice: once to confirm her name and once more to say yes. As she replaced the receiver, she turned to Harry.

"That was Sergeant Cadan. He wants to see us over at Bodmin Hospital as soon as possible." Her voice sounded concerned. "We can drive over to Creek Lane after we see him."

"We need to find someone who'll drive us into Bodmin." Harry gripped the doorframe. "Lawrence Matthews is probably out on the estate, or in the estate office—"

"I can drive, Harry," Morag interrupted.

"Can you? What, the Daimler?" He couldn't contain his surprise and scepticism.

"Don't sound so surprised, Harry dear. Your father taught me to drive when I was here working as his secretary."

"Why didn't you say?" Harry's brief moment of scepticism turned to one of admiration.

"You didn't ask, my darling," Morag replied.

★★★

Susan eased herself into the lounge chair, moaning with relaxed delight as she kicked off her shoes, feeling the softness of the chair enfold and comfort her. The cottage felt warm, though its position, sat amongst the shadow of Frobisher Hall and the shade of the forest edge, usually meant there was always a chill in the air and a dampness that required a fire to burn continually in the both the oven range and the main fireplace in the lounge.

But today was different.

The morning had seen both herself and Lawrence rise early and take a light breakfast before chatting through the plans for the day. His shoulder had been causing him some discomfort in the night and he'd slept fitfully, tossing one way and the other before finding relief sitting in the opposite chair as the darkness lifted and the early rays of light flickered through the trees. It was the chair in which he usually sat when they shared an evening together, talking, reading, or just reflecting on the hand of fate that had brought them together the previous November.

The walls, still whitewashed, looked homelier, with decorative wall hangings and prints depicting the local landscape – not wild and desolate images of the moors, but coastal panoramic scenes of local towns such as Padstow and Newquay. On the beaches there were, invariably, crowds – mainly children. The sands were golden and the sea exceptionally blue. The rolling waves were gentle, the whiteness of their foam a tender outline of the approaching tide.

The paintings and prints brought with them an extra dimension, one of life where there had only once been death. It had been important for her to eliminate all traces of Edith and Reginald Travers. Some might have thought it strange that they wanted to begin their new life together in a house that carried such a dreadful past, but she had drawn strength from Morag and Harry, who had defied all talk of moving away and of escaping the terrible nightmare that had once gripped Frobisher Hall...

"This is Harry's birth right," Morag had commented to Susan one day.

Well, the cottage was never my birth right, she reflected, *but it is a place we can call home*.

The paintings were vibrant and had immediately breathed new life into the place; it was from these images that Susan drew her strength, helping her to quickly come to terms with the fate of the cottage's previous owners. The very chair she now relaxed in was the one in which she'd sat that night with Lawrence resting his head in her lap, both fearful of what the night might bring.

The revolver he'd left with her that night now resided in one of the drawers in the Welsh dresser behind her. She knew Lawrence would occasionally take it out and clean it, endeavouring to keep it from her, but she could always smell the gun oil. When she'd been alone, she'd taken it out and held it, balancing it within her grasp. At first, she'd been happy enough to break it open and load the chambers.

But Morag had shown her how to fire it.

Twice the two of them had stood behind the cottage, aiming at six empty cans perched on a tree stump. Morag had taken careful aim and knocked each one from the stump; all six were dispatched with grim professional coldness.

Once Susan had learnt to balance herself, breathe properly and allow for the natural pull of her arm as she squeezed the trigger, she'd quickly grown in confidence. On the second occasion they'd developed a natural competition between the two of them, one that Morag had won, though she was quick to compliment Susan on her natural ability.

When she'd told Lawrence of her achievement, he'd smiled and nodded his head; but there had been a sadness in his eyes, tinged with a glow of admiration and respect.

Now the revolver sat out of sight, but within easy reach.

She was all too aware of their vulnerability out in the cottage, and of the fact that Morgan Treave and his accomplice Nurse Baker were still at large. She'd been reminded of this when she'd watched Morag take aim at the cans – the focussed glint, the cold and empty look in her eyes as she'd squeezed the trigger.

Morag had suggested that both she and Lawrence reside for the time being within the relative safety of Frobisher Hall; and though Lawrence had felt it was an excellent idea, Susan had been adamant that they weren't going to be driven from their home. Her decisiveness had earned the admiration of Morag and Harry, though Lawrence had taken to sleeping in the lounge, blaming his shoulder for keeping him up at night.

On the occasions she'd wandered down to sit with him, she'd always felt the cold muzzle of his revolver under the blanket he had wrapped around him. He'd tried to hide it, pushing it down and out of sight. But the alertness in his eyes and the way he'd put his arm protectively around her always made her strain her ears, listening for any sound that might emanate from the darkened recesses of the immense forest that made up so much of the Frobisher Estate.

But that had been during those long winter nights, when his wound had struggled to heal and the nightmares of that early snowstorm still found their way into their dreams. And when the wind blew through the forest, it was as if the souls of Edith and Reginald Travers were calling to them, warning them, fearful of the danger they faced and mournful of their own lives taken so violently from them.

Now, sitting in her chair and feeling the warmth of early summer caress and embrace her, Susan could forget such thoughts. Snuggling her small frame into the chair, she felt herself begin to drift, conscious only of the distant sound of a horse clip-clopping on the cobblestones in the rear courtyard.

Dreamily she imagined Lawrence awkwardly riding the old mare back along the dirt track from the direction of the lower glades and into the courtyard. He'd chosen her simply for the serene way she'd stared at him, telling Susan, "She understands what a complete chump I am on horses, and will look after me…"

She heard the horse come to a halt.

With the windows and kitchen door open, she could hear every sound and echo permeate through the cottage, outbuildings and stables. She guessed he would be trying to climb down, that his shoulder would probably be aching, and that it wouldn't be long before he took the saddle off and led his horse to the water trough.

Silence greeted her anticipation.

She opened her eyes and stretched her arms out in front of her. The small carriage clock on the mantelpiece struck 11am. Stifling a yawn, Susan climbed out of the chair, her skin tingling with the sudden chill that descended upon her. Walking into the kitchen, she expected to see Lawrence approaching the door.

From where she stood, there was nobody to be seen within the immediate vicinity of the courtyard. Moving swiftly, and with a heart that was beginning to beat with a frantic resonance, Susan stepped out through the kitchen door, feeling the cobbled stones dig into her stockinged feet. He should have been calling to her by now; even though she might be anywhere within the Hall, he always called to her. Promising herself she would chastise him for worrying her so, she drew a deep breath, ready to say something guarded and stinging…

Lawrence's horse was standing by the fountain, head hung low, as though saddened by the news its arrival now heralded.

Lawrence was nowhere to be seen.

8

Annette Myers entered the small parish church situated on the Launceston road by the side door. One of the oldest buildings in town, its beautiful structure, a lasting monument, stood bold and magnificent, nestled within the houses and cottages – a beating heart that fed the community's spiritual needs.

She had paused, before entering, to glance nervously around her, worried that she might be seen, prompting questions to be asked as to why she chose to enter the building so secretively. It was whilst she did this, initially pleased at the lack of morning townsfolk busily going about their business, that she spied the shiny and rather decadent Daimler sweep past her. She'd seen the car before, whilst out shopping in town on several occasions, so had immediately recognised it as belonging to the Frobisher Estate. Even though she'd been too far away to be seen by its occupants, she'd slid closer into the shadows, nestling herself into one of the darkened recesses, fearing discovery. She'd watched with intrigue as it meandered its way up towards the town hall, the sun sparkling off its beautiful bodywork.

Inside the church, she neither saw nor heard anyone. Usually there might be some kind of choir practice, a meeting of sorts, or fellow parishioners sitting in silent prayer or contemplation.

Today it was different.

Today the church seemed to have anticipated the purpose of her visit and solemnly warned off anyone who might interrupt her. There was a coldness within the building; the rows of pews, with hymn books neatly settled on wooden seats, smelt of polish. From darkened corners, gargoyles stared down at her; but where they'd once twisted their faces in sinister contortions, warding off evil spirits, now they peered down at Annette Myers with a look of dreadful judgement.

She found herself looking up at these faces and resisting a sudden urge to flee from this supposed place of quiet sanctuary. Reflecting on the fact that she'd visited this place many times, both to worship and to help with general parish duties, she found herself slightly bewildered as to the aura that seemed to surround her.

Not only was it the twisted faces above her that caused the consternation that threatened to erupt within her, but the massive structural pillars, so symbolic of the building's spiritual support, now stood like sinister phantoms, cold and oblique, accusing and reproachful. From darkened shadows she thought she saw figures flit suddenly from a side chapel, before moving quickly between a row of pews, silently, stealthily.

Something caught her eye and she glanced across towards the All Saints Chapel. This side chapel was smaller than most and contained, within the heart of its three main walls, a beautifully painted image of Christ holding the hand of a little boy. Annette Myers recalled a sermon, given by Canon Trebarwith not so long ago, wherein he'd referred to all the children that now suffered through the loss of a father during the war and subsequently faced an uncertain future. He'd gone on to say how the community might hold out a hand, both spiritually and morally, that those children might have their grief eased somewhat by the actions of those sitting before him.

She stood staring, blinking heavily as she tried to focus on the little boy in the picture. The image had initially seemed a little blurred a moment ago. But as that blurriness cleared, when the little boy's face emerged from the mental fog that had enveloped Annette Myers' mind, she moaned deeply and instinctively reached for her handkerchief.

"Oh, please, God... No..." she whispered, staring at the boy's radiant features, blessed even more by the Holy figure standing beside him. "I'm so sorry... God, forgive me for what I have done."

It was when she stared into the eyes of Christ, and saw his cold and accusing eyes, reprimanding and oh so judgemental, that she pulled herself away.

With both a heavy heart and a growing feeling of fear never felt before, especially within this place of worship, she scurried quickly down towards the main altar and the first line of pews situated under the huge lectern with a brass eagle holding a large leather-bound Bible within its wings.

When she reached the front, she looked for a space midway along the second line of pews on the right. This was her seat, unofficially, but still the place she sought every Sunday morning and, indeed, any other time she attended a service. Slowly, and with infinite care, she slid along the pew until instinct told her she was hovering over her place. She hardly had time to pause before she fell to her knees and burst into uncontrollable sobs.

"Mrs Myers?" The voice soothed. It came from a long distance, as though carried by the breeze from another place and time.

"Dear... God..." She grappled with the handkerchief in her hand. Her knees had missed the cushion on the stone floor and were screaming in agony as the harshness of the cold slabs penetrated her skin. "Forgive me my sins..." The words blurted out between sobs, her body heaved, and if it were not for the back of the pew in front of her, she would have collapsed in a heap on the ground.

"Mrs Myers, can I help?" The words came from someone close by, and the voice was comforting and familiar.

She paused and raised her head. Through puffed and swollen eyes she saw the figure of Canon Trebarwith, sitting on the front pew a little to her left. His face held a look of acute concern, and his hand hovered, respectfully, inches from the side of her face.

Her first thought was to quickly apologise and hastily start cleaning the pews or dusting the altar; but when she saw the look in his eyes, she knew he was looking deep into her soul and grappling with the dreadful torment that burned within her. His usual dour expression relaxed somewhat as he tried to force a smile.

Hastily she dabbed her eyes before pulling herself into a more upright position. Her knees still screamed in agony, but for some curious reason Annette Myers thought it was all part of God's plan to help her achieve some kind of atonement. The presence of Canon Trebarwith was a blessed relief for her, and she started to feel herself being drawn into his world of confession and absolution.

"Is there something you wish to tell me?" Trebarwith hesitantly reached forward and brushed her hair away from her eyes. "Or is it something between God and yourself?"

"I don't know where to start…" She felt her voice falter at the realisation that she'd finally come to a place, a place she'd visited many times before, to confess something to which she had no hope of achieving forgiveness.

"I can hear your confession, Mrs Myers. All you need to do is open your heart…" Trebarwith let his hand move down and rest lightly on her clenched fist as it gripped the back of the pew.

"I've done something terrible, Canon. No law in this world or the next will ever forgive me." She drew strength from her own words. A calm resignation descended upon her, though the walls of the church threatened to move in, and the general air within the building appeared oppressive and heavy with expectation.

"Whatever sin you've committed, Mrs Myers, God will forgive you if you truly repent." Trebarwith smiled.

"And then what?"

"What do you mean?"

"I live my life in this town, amongst people I've grown so fond of since I came down here…" Her voice trailed off as she stared past Trebarwith and towards the cross that sat majestically upon the altar. She breathed deeply, knowing that she was going to accede to his suggestion but searching her heart for the right words.

She imagined a light shining through the stained-glass window behind the altar, a warmth engulfing her, releasing the spiritual restraints that bound her tightly to her world of suppressed torment and anguish. She remembered happier times as a child, attending church with her parents and older brother; she thought maybe forgiveness might herald a return to those years, so innocent, so warm.

But there was no such light, no Heavenly guidance or inner peace at the thought of what she was about to do.

She thought of Captain Grant and sighed deeply.

Trebarwith reached forward and grasped her free hand, shuffling forward slightly so he could lower his head and hear her whispered words. He said nothing, but Annette Myers saw a look of sereneness spread across his face, the likes of which she'd never seen before.

Drawing herself closer to Canon Roderick Trebarwith, she whispered, "Please hear my confession…"

★★★

"Lord and Lady Frobisher." Sergeant Cadan stepped forward to greet Morag and Harry as they closed the doors of the Daimler. "I'm sorry to drag you both over here. I know we agreed to meet in the police station, but events have taken a certain turn, and I thought it best to meet here."

The huge stone façade of Bodmin Hospital, damp and grey even in the brightness of that early summer morning, stood imposing and intimidating, as though ready to wrap its cold embrace around the three of them.

Morag shivered, wishing she'd put on a thicker coat than the light flannel jacket she now wore. Shaking the hand of the burly policeman before her, she said affectionately, "My dear Sergeant, I am so pleased to see you again." Glancing around, she caught sight of Harry, tapping his stick and inching his way around the front of the car. He'd thrown on a light-brown jacket and was wearing a flat cap, his head angled forward so his face was hidden from view. He seemed ill at ease and hesitant in his step. Reaching forward she said softly, "Take my hand, Harry, there are steps just over here."

"As I said, Lord and Lady Frobisher, this request might sound a little strange." Sergeant Cadan guided Morag and Harry through the maze of hospital corridors, moving slowly as he patiently waited for Morag to chaperone Harry beside her. "It's to do with the body…" He paused as a nurse passed the three of them before disappearing into one of the offices. "It's to do with the body you discovered on the train…"

They'd reached the top of the stairs leading down to the mortuary.

"Why does everyone think we discovered the body?" Harry muttered irritably.

The light had visibly dimmed and the whitewashed walls had now taken on a greyer, gloomier shade, one that was complemented by the heavy feeling of dread as they began to slowly descend the old stairway.

"Harry dear, I don't think the sergeant meant anything by it." Morag felt her husband make his way shakily down the steps. Twice he stopped, as though waiting to catch his breath, and she paused, trying to ascertain the reason for his hesitation.

"He's just through here, Lady Frobisher." Sergeant Cadan directed them into a small room that led ultimately into a larger room containing a marble slab.

"I'm a little confused, Sergeant." Morag gazed into the other room, aware of a body lying upon the marble slab covered by a large sheet. "I can't tell you anything more than what I told the constable yesterday at Bodmin Station. I'd never seen the man before, other than he was the ticket inspector who queried our tickets back in Paddington." The sight of the outline of a dead body under the grey sheet made her feel slightly nauseous, and she took a couple of deep breaths.

Sergeant Cadan reached into his pocket and pulled out the note he'd retrieved earlier from the body. "He had this note upon his person, Your Ladyship." He proffered it to Morag, who received it suspiciously. "I asked you to come to this place to look again at the man's face and try and recollect whether you'd seen him at any time before you boarded the train at Paddington."

"This is nonsense, Sergeant Cadan." Harry removed his hat and ran his hand through his hair.

"After what happened down here last year, Lord Frobisher, I think I would just about believe anything…" Sergeant Cadan moved towards the covered body and eyed it speculatively. "I just want to find out who he was and who killed…" He paused and turned his head towards the outer door that led back into the hallway and the stairs.

Morag glanced up from the letter and Harry turned his head.

The unmistakeable sound of footsteps descending the stairs echoed around the lower floor, accentuated by the stone walls and floor. With a slow yet deliberate tap, they grew louder as they reached the bottom, paused slightly, then began to move towards the room in which the three of them stood.

Morag drew nearer to Harry and instinctively moved in front of him.

Footsteps approached the open door before pausing. A voice spoke, familiar and reassuring, "Finding out who lies under that sheet and who killed him is going to be the easy part of this investigation, Sergeant Cadan."

Inspector Edwards stepped into the room.

Morag and Harry were momentarily taken aback, and settled into stunned silence.

It was Sergeant Cadan who muttered under his breath, "Good Heavens. Who would have thought it?"

Morag fought the urge to cross the room and hug her brother-in-law. She gazed, with a smile that overflowed with love and gratefulness, recognising his familiar beige Fedora hat, pinstripe three-piece suit and two-tone shoes of cream and light brown. He had one hand thrust deep in his pocket, whilst holding his pipe in the other. Though it had been only a few days since their last meeting in London, the time seemed an eternity. He looked tired, yet alert. His blue eyes pierced the gloom around them, sizing up the room, before settling upon hers.

"Hello, Morag." He drew his hand from his pocket and held it out towards her.

"Oh, Cyril... thank God..." Morag held out her hand and stepped a little away from Harry, conscious of not letting go of her husband's hand.

Edwards stepped forward, embracing her warmly.

"I say," Harry beamed, "we weren't expecting you, Inspector."

"Well," repeated Sergeant Cadan, "who would have thought?" He shook his head.

"When did you get here?" Morag couldn't contain her excitement. "I mean... Did someone send a telegram?"

Edwards turned towards the door, and Morag saw the familiar inquisitive look in his eyes as he searched for anyone else who might overhear them. Closing the door, he turned round to face them, eyeing the scene before him with his usual detached style, which left those around him speculating as to what he was thinking. With the door now closed, an oppressive atmosphere settled upon them, along with a murkiness that seemed to plunge the temperature to new levels.

"Lord Frobisher, it's good to see you again." He stepped forward and received Harry's outstretched hand.

"It's damned good of you to be here, Inspector," Harry replied.

"Thank you, Lord Frobisher. It seems one mystery follows another in this place." He turned to Sergeant Cadan. "How are you, Sergeant?"

"Glad now to see you, Inspector." The big policeman held out his hand. "Though I am confused as to how you managed to get down here so quickly; I sent a telegram to Scotland Yard only last night."

"Which I'm sure has been conveniently intercepted and put to one side." Inspector Edwards brushed his finger along his moustache, left side, then right, before pushing the tip of his Fedora up and back a little. "I'm afraid we don't have much time for any prolonged greetings." He moved towards the body, placing his pipe in his jacket pocket before extending both hands to grasp the sheet.

Morag followed him towards the marble slab, then turned to Harry. He'd withdrawn a little to the side and was standing patiently, leaning on his stick and fiddling with his pipe. Glancing back to the body, she watched as Edwards drew the sheet back, slowly, revealing the face down to the chest. Taking a step forward, she found herself beside her brother-in-law and staring down at the body, now deathly white and with eyes half closed that stared blankly towards the ceiling.

"You want to know who this chap was and how he was killed, Sergeant?" Edwards smiled.

"Well, Inspector, it would be a start," Cadan replied.

"His name is Archie Cummings... Well, that's his official name, though I could rattle off several aliases he used in the past." Edwards moved to the head and leaned forward, so close that Morag wondered if he might be looking for signs of life. "He was one of the top hired assassins working in London but had been responsible for a string of murders further afield." He reached into his inside pocket and drew out the small penknife he used to clean his pipe. Opening the blade, he flicked it across the eyebrows, drawing back a little as tiny particles of white dust flickered up. "He was a member of a gang called 'The Laggers', a rather nasty and vicious group of individuals known for their professionalism and skill in killing people." He stood back, observing the face intently. "And believe me when I say how ruthless these people are. I've had the unfortunate duty of investigating several of their murders and can vouch for their handiwork... That's what makes them so sought after in the criminal underworld." Reaching forward, he gripped the end of the white moustache and gently tugged at it, stifling a chuckle as it pulled away from the upper lip. "There was probably a dagger on his person, inscribed with the letter 'L', and a pair of white gloves with the same letter... Ah yes..." Edwards turned and acknowledged the items on the table where Cadan had left them. "You do have to hand it to these people, they can carry a disguise better than any actor. He fooled the pair of you at Paddington Station, though I can't say I blame you. A ticket inspector for the Great Western Railway... That is impressive." He nodded his admiration at the corpse before reaching across to the hair.

"Why was he on the train?" Morag shook her head and gazed into the lifeless eyes. She was now following Edwards as he flicked his knife through the hair, sending more particles of white dust into the air.

"Oh, that bit's easy... To kill the two of you, my dear Morag, before catching the return train to London." Edwards turned to his sister-in-law and smiled gently.

Morag staggered back, feeling the weight of his statement literally drain the colour from her face and the air from her lungs. Her mind spiralled in a kaleidoscope of threatening images that made her feel suddenly isolated and vulnerable. With the shock of his words came the inevitable cold shiver she'd felt many times before. Groping with her hand she mumbled, "Harry…?"

"I'm here," Harry answered, his voice heavy with concern.

She inched back until she felt his hand. Grasping it, she felt the panic ease and the initial wave of shock dissipate a little. But it was the look on Inspector Edwards' face that provided her with the rock to which she clung. His smile was neither mocking nor humorous, neither mischievous nor malevolent. It was the smile of someone lifting a terrible burden from them – easing it gently, aware of the fear and doubt and the awful realisation that they'd come so close to a violent death.

"He told us the dates on our tickets were incorrect," Morag heard herself mumble.

"There were tickets on his person when we searched his pockets." Sergeant Cadan walked towards the table and picked up two small pieces of paper. He handed them to Edwards.

"These are dated the 21st of May." Edwards reflected.

"But the ones he checked and gave back to us were dated the 22nd." Morag had managed to regain some composure.

"That would make sense. He followed you for several days prior to your journey; probably planning in his mind the most appropriate time to strike. Your trip to Cornwall must have scuppered his plans; he wanted to murder you both in London."

"Why so, Inspector?" Harry asked.

"Because a murder in a city like London is harder to investigate. Potential witnesses can be lost amongst the thousands that go about their daily lives. If he'd waited until you were both back in Cornwall, it would have been a lot more difficult for him. Strangers are often easily remembered by the locals. Also, he wouldn't feel as comfortable in strange surroundings. He'd want to blend in with the community, and that would be impossible down here. He probably falsified these tickets to delay your departure, keeping you in London for one further day so he could strike. Knowing you, Morag, you insisted upon travelling down on the 21st..."

Morag smiled.

"And then he saw any opportunity of completing his task dwindle away. Although you were alone in your compartment, there were people milling around the corridor, walking through to other compartments, or stretching their legs. He knew that, as the train moved into Cornwall, his chance was slipping away. He managed to evade the attention of the real ticket inspector, but as each station stop came and went he became more desperate..."

"But why us, Inspector?" Harry tapped lightly with his stick and positioned himself beside Morag.

"As I said, Lord Frobisher, these men are hired killers. And they don't come cheap. Most have seen action during the Great War, and seen death so many times it means absolutely nothing to them. The question is, who would pay this gang enough money to see the two of you dead?" Edwards placed his pipe in his mouth and slipped both hands into his waistcoat pockets.

"Oh, God," Morag whispered.

Edwards nodded, his smile now faded. His face was cold and blank.

Morag held her hand over her mouth and turned away from the body. The oppressive atmosphere in the room now bore heavily upon her, more so than before, as the rank smell of death permeated through her clothes, finally to settle, like some terrible stain, upon her body. She glanced at Harry, searching his expression for any signs of what he might be thinking. But his face was devoid of any emotion, as though he were lost in some distant world, one which she could never hope to enter.

"Morgan Treave," she spoke, hearing her words fill the room and wondering if they might have been spoken by another. She actually wished they had been because speaking them, in the context of these terrible surroundings, almost invited the man into her life, to live and breathe within her world...

To somehow reach out and touch her...

"It might not be his doing, Morag..." Harry's voice came from somewhere distant.

"Lord Frobisher?" Edwards turned his attention to Harry.

"This man's death might be tied in with something wholly different to what you might be assuming." Harry inched forward, poking his stick until it rattled against the brick side of the mortuary slab. Reaching with his other hand, he shuffled past Edwards, moving tentatively towards the head of Archie Cummings.

"Harry?" Morag whispered.

"It's okay, Morag." Harry paused and reached his hand across, his fingers shaking and his breath coming in short gasps.

Morag watched as he laid them on the victim's face, sliding them across the chin and up over the lips, pausing slightly as he ran them over the bridge of the nose. Taking a deep breath, he pushed the palm of his hand down, sliding it across the left cheek then the right, before finally letting the fingertips sweep across the forehead.

Behind him, an air of expectation hung heavier than the smell of death, as Morag, Edwards and Cadan watched closely.

When he'd completed his examination, Harry stepped back, retrieving a handkerchief from his pocket and wiping his hands. "I thought he might have been..." he said to himself.

Inspector Edwards narrowed his eyes. "Yes, Lord Frobisher?"

"Someone who wrote to me asking for my help. Someone I was acquainted with many years ago; someone, I think, is in trouble." Harry sighed heavily.

"It's not Captain Grant, Harry." Morag's voice was quite sullen. "He doesn't look like the man in your photograph."

"Captain Grant?" prompted Edwards.

"A man who needs our help, Inspector. A man we were planning to visit over in Creek Lane this morning."

"Creek Lane?" Sergeant Cadan blurted out, before adding a little more succinctly, "Whereabouts in Creek Lane?"

"Number thirteen, Sergeant." Morag confirmed, noticing the frown spreading across his face.

"Why did you think this man might be Captain Grant, Lord Frobisher?" Edwards asked, his voice brisk and official.

"Because the letter he wrote to us implied he was in trouble and needed my help…" Harry's voice was equally blunt. "Even if it isn't Captain Grant, he might well be connected to him."

"Which does bring us to the most obvious question." Though softly spoken, Sergeant Cadan's voice cut through the room, silencing all others.

Morag nodded, the realisation of what he was about to ask dawning on her.

In a similar vein, Harry moved across to stand at her side.

Sergeant Cadan continued, "Do we know who killed this man?"

Inspector Edwards stared back at the body and nodded his head. Turning to his companions he said, "I can easily answer that question. I killed him."

9

Lawrence Matthews felt sick and disorientated.

His shoulder seemed detached from his body, and every effort he made to move sent juddering shockwaves through his body that made him cry out in agony with what little air he had left in his lungs. The only relief he found was the damp wild grass upon his face that helped ease the relentless waves of feverish spasms that threatened intermittent bouts of unconsciousness.

His world, through glazed and semi-conscious eyes, was one of hazy green and brown interspersed with flashes of blue, as he tried to comprehend the rays of sunlight that sparkled through the gaps in the branches that shaded him from above. He found himself wondering if this might be Heaven; he immediately dismissed the idea as his body convulsed in unrestrained agony as he clumsily shifted his weight slightly onto his dislocated shoulder.

He sighed heavily and groaned at the irony that his dislocated shoulder was also the one that bore his old gunshot wound.

Clenching his fists, he tried to reduce the pain by counteracting the weight onto the other shoulder, which brought slight relief, but very little. Raising his head, he peered across the glade in which he now lay, realising quickly that he was certainly far from Frobisher Hall and any of the other cottages and farms on the estate. The dense undergrowth around him hampered any realistic attempt to try and peer beyond and into the surrounding forest. It was when he realised his horse was nowhere to be seen that Lawrence Matthews laid his head back onto the cold and damp grass and moaned with despair.

He moved his legs and was relieved to find them working perfectly.

Moving his other hand, he pulled his arm across his chest, trying to feel the extent of the damage to his shoulder. That it was dislocated was beyond any doubt. There was a tingling sensation in his hand, and any attempt to try and raise that arm was met by the worst pain he'd ever experienced.

His first thought was of Susan and what she would say if she found him here. He resisted the urge to call her, stupidly thinking she might suddenly appear.

Unconsciousness swept over him like an approaching tide, before ebbing away.

He didn't want to upset her... Not now... Not after they'd made their home in the cottage...

The sounds of the forest seemed to come alive with his predicament. Something scurried behind him; to his left, a fox cried out. It was as if creatures around him had woken up and now wanted to examine this strange man who lay so helplessly amongst them...

Confusing thoughts resounded in his mind...

Lucky I fell here in the forest and not on some cobbled road in London... Should have told Susan where I was going... God... There'll be Hell to pay from Susan and Morag... Would be nice if Lord Frobisher found me here... He'd understand... Wouldn't get annoyed...

The sound of something approaching snapped him out of his reverie, causing him to hold his breath and widen his eyes attentively.

Maybe I'll die out here and be found one day by a passing woodsman.
He couldn't understand why he'd fallen.

The more he tried to recollect what had happened, the more his mind was consumed by the grey mist of semi-consciousness. He also couldn't understand why he'd ended up in this place. The area around him seemed unfamiliar... not that he knew the Frobisher Estate well...

The noises in the forest grew louder.

As they drew closer he could distinguish the different sounds, though they seemed to be coming at him from different directions. Something was running, plunging through the undergrowth, first from just in front of him, then to his right. Raising his head, he caught sight of a large black dog breaking through the greenery and coming to a halt in the glade, barking as it saw Lawrence splayed out on the grass.

To his right, he caught sight of something racing towards him, and he closed his eyes, waiting for the inevitable pain that would come as both dogs bit and tore at his exposed face. Laughing, he clenched his fists tightly, wondering feebly if he even had the strength to raise them at all.

His strange and demented laughter was short-lived, quickly turning to groans of confusion as the two dogs leapt and chased each other around him, pausing to bark excitedly before lapping their tongues across his face.

From a distance he heard a voice call out, but he couldn't make out from which direction it came, or if it were a man or woman. Flashes came to him...

A figure, dark and menacing, rose out of the ground before him... A familiar face... horribly scarred...

The voice drew near and the dogs raced off in another direction, their barking resonating throughout the forest, sending birds fluttering for safety.

"Help..." Lawrence Matthews whispered, his voice drifting aimlessly towards the sky.

With the realisation that someone was indeed here to assist him, the desire to stay awake, absorb the pain and cling hold to consciousness began to fade. He could feel the warming hand of sleep sweep over him, making his eyelids so heavy it seemed almost ridiculous to keep them open, for the more he succumbed to the desire to sleep, the more the pain in his shoulder sailed happily away on a leaf floating into the night...

"That shoulder needs to be re-set... and quick." The voice was female, of that Lawrence was sure. There was also a toughness that reverberated deep within its tone, arresting his attention and expecting him to listen. "You've taken a tumble, young man..." A hand, grimy and coarse, brushed his hair back from his eyes. It smelt of moss and dirt, and he tried to focus his eyes.

"Susan..." he muttered, watching the canopy of branches and leaves above start to spin like some strange maelstrom.

"I don't think any bones are broken, but that shoulder of yours doesn't look so good..." Again, that resilient echo, that rasping and deeply accented Cornish tone that came from someone capable of helping him and probably saving his life. It held no sympathy, only an abrupt harshness of one who'd lived a life in the forest and had no interest in aimless talk. "Young man... your shoulder's been dislocated in the fall. I'm just unbuttoning your jacket and the top of your shirt to feel..."

Lawrence felt the same hand that had touched his face slowly push his jacket to one side and open his shirt. Dreamily he thought maybe Susan was undressing him, and he was of a mind to reach out and kiss her; but the hand, like sandpaper against his skin, made him flinch away.

"Best if I cut the sleeve..."

Lawrence saw the sparkle of sunlight reflect from a blade before he heard the distinct sound of material ripping.

"There... that's better... Here, Branok... help me move him over, and hold onto him tightly..."

Lawrence tried to whisper Susan's name again but the word was lost in a coughing fit as a stabbing pain shot violently through his body.

"Okay… nearly there now; it'll be easier once…" The voice hesitated, and for the first time a hint of shock stifled the once confident tone. "My God… that looks like a gunshot wound…"

Lawrence rolled his eyes and tried to lick his lips.

"Okay… hold him tight now, Branok…"

Hands so large that Lawrence thought they might enclose the whole of his body held him in a vice-like grip, with arms that resembled tree trunks restraining him in a half-seated position.

The click of his shoulder joint snapping back into place rung out like a branch breaking in two. Lawrence was vaguely aware of screaming, before that familiar feeling of sleep finally found its way into his body and he gave himself up to the grey mist that enfolded him.

★★★

"Believe me, I don't get up in the morning with the sole intention of killing people on trains."

Inspector Edwards ignored the dumbfounded looks upon the faces of Morag and Harry and riffled through the clothing laid out on the table awaiting further inspection. He noticed that the look on Sergeant Cadan's face hadn't altered, that his burly physique hadn't diminished in stature as his story unfolded. His reliability as both a friend and a fellow policeman had been sealed one stormy night when they'd both set out for Frobisher Hall through the worst snowstorm to hit Cornwall in a lifetime.

"Why did you kill him?" Morag asked dumbly.

"I think, Morag, the answer to that is quite simple. To stop him from killing the two of you." Edwards turned over the items laid out on the table before placing them back and turning to Sergeant Cadan. "I take it there were no witnesses?"

Sergeant Cadan shook his head, saying nothing.

"Good. When you compare the athletic build of this chap against myself, you might wonder how I actually bested him. Face to face in a dark alley in London, I wouldn't fancy my chances." Edwards turned his back to the body and tipped his Fedora forward a little before brushing his moustache with his finger, left side, then right. "I've been tailing you both ever since you arrived in London on your honeymoon. With no real clues as to the whereabouts of Morgan Treave, I employed the services of... let me say... certain individuals to watch over you... Individuals who could have given this chap a run for his money..." He paused, waiting for a response. When none came, he continued. "You weren't tailed when you were abroad. I felt that Treave wouldn't chance his luck in Europe. But when you returned to London, I followed your every move. At the same time I picked up on Archie Cummings here doing the same. I recognised him immediately from the mugshots we hold back at the Yard. I was limited as to what I could do, as I wasn't carrying any official authorisation or clearance to have you both tailed; so I managed to incorporate it into an existing investigation. I was going to arrest him on several occasions but always changed my mind... I thought that Treave might be close by, and that Mr Cummings here might lead me to him. The day before you travelled down here I was going to send my men into his hotel room and arrest him before he boarded the train with yourselves... but..."

"But what?" Harry prompted.

Inspector Edwards looked at Harry, narrowing one eye and rubbing his chin. "I was distracted by a meeting I was called into..."

"But you did follow him onto the train." Morag stepped across to Harry and slipped her hand around his waist.

"Yes, had no choice really. Time was running out. Like I said, the likes of Archie Cummings only appear on the scene for one thing... And I needed to do something to prevent it. I would have missed the disguise myself if I hadn't broken into his hotel room and found a spare Great Western Railway uniform and theatrical make-up he was obviously using to disguise himself. From then on, I just needed to ensure he didn't recognise me, and that was where I had the edge. Although I've investigated the crimes he's committed, we've never actually come face to face. I only recognised him by chance that day we dined at The Ritz. He was eating alone at a table on the other side of the restaurant—"

"Good God..." Morag sighed.

"Hmmm... indeed." Edwards smiled. "I managed to dodge both yourselves and Archie Cummings whilst the train made its way to Cornwall." The smile faded as the memory of the final stages of the journey became profoundly clear in his mind. "He was in the next compartment to yours and had slipped that throttling noose around his hand." Edwards pointed to the rope on the table. "I expect he would have just burst into your compartment and throttled you first, Morag, before Lord Frobisher... I passed your compartment; luckily the blinds were drawn down. Something had distracted him, as he was looking out of the window... I think he might have been worried about an approaching station... Anyway, I tipped my hat low over my face, entered, and pretended to be a passenger looking for a quiet compartment. The problem with the likes of Archie Cummings is that they're not fooled for long. Something must have alarmed him and he didn't wait for explanations. I guess I was lucky. When he tried to lash out at me, the train lurched to one side and he stumbled, dropping the noose. I caught him a swift punch to the side of the face and he fell badly against the door..." He paused, thinking of how to explain what happened next but also worried that his silence might denote a feeling of guilt or regret, when there wasn't any. "I was of the mind to use the noose to bind his hands, and started to do so, believing him to be unconscious. But he regained consciousness and a fight broke out… one literally to the death… If he'd been in better shape it would have been my body that woman found, but he was weak from the blow to the head… In all my years, I've dispatched a few criminals into the next world, but this is the first I've throttled to death…"

"Well, Inspector… I think we can all live with self-defence," Harry said.

"Self-defence or not, I needed to get away from the train as quickly as possible as soon as it arrived at Bodmin Road Station. Whilst the cry went up when that woman found his body, I slipped off the train and crossed the track to pick up the connecting train to Bodmin. I stayed last night at the military garrison… They sent a telegram to London explaining everything and they also have my full report."

"Well," reflected Sergeant Cadan, breathing a huge sigh of relief, "that explains everything."

"Unfortunately, it doesn't…" Harry pulled himself up and tucked his stick under his arm. "As you know, Inspector, Morag and I received a letter from an old comrade of mine from the war… It was waiting for us upon our return yesterday, though we only read it this morning." He rummaged in his jacket pocket. "Here, please read it." He offered it to Edwards, who received it, glancing curiously at Morag as he opened the envelope.

"There's no address on the envelope, just your name, Lord Frobisher." Edwards scrutinised the handwriting. "Actually, it says 'Captain Frobisher'. Black ink and very flamboyant… Was it hand-delivered?"

"Susan said it was," Morag confirmed.

"By whom?"

"I didn't ask her. I haven't really seen her all morning," Morag replied, peering at the letter.

Edwards pulled the letter out and unfolded it. He read it through several times before looking across at Harry. "How well do you know this Captain Grant, Lord Frobisher?"

"Well enough for him to confide his fears in me," Harry replied. "Well enough for him to write down his suspicions as to the identity of a traitor in Military Intelligence. And, it seems, well enough for him to travel to Bodmin and write that letter to me."

"Hmmm," Edwards glanced at Harry, trying to discern his features in the gloom. "Looks as though he ended the letter abruptly…"

"That's what we thought," Morag added.

"But he still found the time to arrange for it to be delivered," Edwards surmised.

"Do you think he was interrupted, Cyril?" Morag approached Edwards. "Maybe he had to finish the letter quickly?"

Edwards read through the letter again. When he had done so, he folded it and handed it back to Morag, along with the envelope. "And you say you were going there this morning?"

Morag nodded, now staring at the body laid out behind Edwards.

"Then I think you'd better go there now. Do you mind if I join you?" He turned towards the door, not waiting for an answer. "You might want to give me the full details of your association with Captain Grant on the way there…" As he reached the door, he paused and turned round. "Are we able to walk to Creek Lane?"

"Yes, sir." Cadan reached over and pulled the cover back over the face of Archie Cummings. He seemed hesitant; and with a faltering voice he added, "I'll take you over there now."

★★★

Susan flung open the rear door that led into the kitchen at Frobisher Hall and glanced quickly around, realising that for probably the first time since her own arrival at the Hall Mrs Chambers wasn't actually in there happily baking or sitting enjoying a cup of tea. Feeling the rising tide of panic begin to consume her, she raced through the kitchen and into the adjoining corridor. Small pantries, set to one side and used for the storage of food, invited investigation, but she ignored them and ran through into the main hall.

"Mrs Chambers!" Her usual petite voice reverberated around the downstairs.

There was no reply.

"Anyone? Please!" Her voice echoed with fear and frustration. "For God's sake..." She darted up the stairs, climbing several steps at a time. When she reached the top she called again, "Kenick... Dodson...?"

A distant door slammed.

Glancing round, she peered down the corridor, the same corridor where she'd first seen Morag so long ago...

However, this time she caught the unmistakeable sight of Kenick hurrying towards her. He must have been descending the servants' staircase at the other end of the corridor, making his way back into the house, and heard her calling.

"Yes, Mrs Matthews?" he called.

Susan took a deep breath before saying, "I think my husband has had an accident somewhere on the estate grounds. His horse came back without him... Do you know where Dodson is...?"

"He's cleaning his shoes in his room."

"Okay, can you get him and then meet me by the fountain outside?" Susan's face was flushed, and she gasped for breath that was fast becoming hard to find within this morass of fear and desperation that now encircled her.

She watched Dodson race back towards the servants' quarters, before she turned round, facing the stairs. As she did so, she noticed the figure of a woman with her hair tied back move swiftly towards Morag and Harry's bedroom. Initially, she only caught a slight glimpse, as her back was towards Susan. Within a matter of seconds, she'd let herself into the bedroom and silently shut the door.

Susan remained standing, considering her next move.

Lawrence was obviously in trouble, and he needed to be her first priority. She hoped Kenick and Dodson would be making their way to the fountain at the back of the house. The woman entering Morag and Harry's bedroom was obviously one of the maids, probably cleaning or completing some other routine chore.

The strangest feeling began to take hold of her, refusing to let go. She'd only had the briefest of glances at the woman and hadn't recognised her; she always made a point of getting to know new members of staff, feeling it important in light of the Hall's recent history.

Might it be Gregson? Yes, the elusive Gregson; I still can't work out if it was Morag or myself who employed her...

Susan stepped forward towards the master bedroom, resigned to quickly finding out who the woman was and her reason for entering the room. In the distance, she heard footsteps descending stairs and doors slamming. Muffled voices called out, and she knew she had to hurry.

Quickly reaching the door, she paused and listened.

An eerie silence had descended upon the entire house, as if Frobisher Hall had joined her in nervous anticipation of what might be hiding within Morag and Harry's bedroom. She found her breathing becoming heavier and difficult to regulate, remembering the morning she'd seen the ghostly figure of Morag staring at her before disappearing into one of the guest bedrooms. But that seemed a lifetime ago. Morag was real, flesh and blood, and Susan now felt a love and devotion to her that went beyond the mere role of Housekeeper. Grasping the door handle, she gently squeezed it down and silently opened the door.

The bedroom was, as usual, radiant and splendid. Sunlight cascaded through the large latticed windows, bathing everything before her in a lustrous warmth. The bed had been made and the room tidied. To her right, the door to the bathroom was slightly ajar and, more importantly, empty. Susan gazed around the main room, her eyes warming to the beauty and decadence of the place, feeling her heart miss a beat as she glanced at Harry and Morag's bed.

Her feelings of awe and reverence were, however, short-lived.

The bedroom was empty.

★★★

"Touch nothing." Inspector Edwards eyed the scene that confronted him, steeling his nerves and holding his breath, letting his senses absorb the terrible sight. Out of the corner of his eye he saw Morag hold her hand to her mouth and step back, and he resisted the urge to support her.

"What is it?" Harry's voice, concerned and agitated, came from the hallway. He sounded frustrated, as though aware of some dreadful occurrence and desperate to know what it was.

"A man fitting your description of Captain Grant is sitting at the kitchen table looking as though he's been dead for…" Edwards stepped forward slowly, his eyes trying to focus on the body before him. "… for some time, judging by the colour of his skin and the congealed blood around the wound."

"Good grief," Harry muttered. "Are you sure?"

Edwards ignored the question. Step by step, he tiptoed across the kitchen floor, pulling a handkerchief from his pocket to cover his mouth and gagging slightly at the pungent smell and hordes of flies that buzzed around the room.

Earlier, 13 Creek Lane had greeted the three of them with a dark and forlorn countenance, from the moment Sergeant Cadan had pointed it out from the end of the road. Once he'd done so, the big policeman had moved back, explaining that he was needed over at the police station to complete outstanding paperwork relating to the death of Archie Cummings. But there had been a fear in his eyes, deep and brooding. When Edwards had turned to acknowledge his guidance in helping them find the cottage, he'd been struck by just how diminished in stature the police sergeant had become.

As Edwards himself had approached the whitewashed cottage, intrigued as to the reason why the front door might be left half-open, he'd felt a shortness of breath and a fear begin to stir in the pit of his stomach.

If Harry or Morag had felt it, he didn't have time to think.

With the door open as it was, the cottage seemed to be sneering a kind of sinister welcome, with windows each side that stared down upon the three of them with a beguiling warmth that beckoned them to enter.

Now, standing in the kitchen, Edwards began to draw on all his years of experience as a policeman, before inching his way along the side of the kitchen table.

Behind him, Morag spoke with a clarity that made him pause and listen intently. "That is Captain Grant, Cyril. I recognise him from his photograph. God, what an awful place."

"And just when I needed Sergeant Cadan…" Edwards muttered under his breath.

From where he stood he could now observe in more detail Captain Grant slumped in his chair, head lolled to one side and the obvious signs of a gunshot wound to the right-hand side of his temple.

Looking around, he studied the rest of the room, noting the fact that, though it might have been a kitchen many years ago, it now resembled nothing but a cold and empty room, ragged and dirty, with a sink covered in filth and grime. In fact, it might have been only the sink that gave any clue as to the room's former purpose.

On the far side of the room, to his left, cupboards stood empty, coated in a film of dust and mould. Overhead, a beam cut across the ceiling, lined with old hooks, and he imagined they'd once held cooking utensils. The oven range was so covered in soot that he initially couldn't make out what it was.

But it was the beam above his head that caused him the most consternation. Standing directly beneath it, he felt a churning in his stomach coil menacingly out and reach through his body like a serpent, spreading evil and malevolence in its wake. He had felt these sensations before, mainly after the events of last November. But now, standing in this awful place, impressions came to him, flashes within his subconscious, illuminating terrible events that reached out to him from another world.

Edwards shook his head, clearing his mind.

Swallowing hard, he gritted his teeth and resisted the urge to retch at the awful smell. Kneeling down, he stared intently into the lifeless eyes of Captain Grant.

Without taking his eyes off the corpse, he reached into his pocket and pulled out his notebook and pen. Not even aware if Morag was still in the room, he whispered, "Morag, in the absence of Sergeant Cadan, could you please note down my initial findings...?"

"Yes, of course." Morag's voice, clear and stoic, came from just behind him.

"Lord Frobisher..." Edwards called softly, still with his eyes fixed upon those of Grant, "are you okay?"

A hesitant voice that must have been Harry's, though it trembled and stumbled, replied, "Yes, Inspector... I just feel a little useless standing here... How did he die?"

"That is what I intend to find out," Edwards replied in a hushed whisper. He felt Morag take his notebook and pen from his outstretched hand. His knees were beginning to ache and he shuffled slightly to relieve the growing discomfort. "Any ideas yourself, Lord Frobisher?" The words were so muted that he wondered if he'd even spoken them.

"I'm sorry, Inspector?" Harry prompted.

Oblivious to Harry's comment, Edwards followed the line of the head, noting its angle and the general position of the body in the chair. He knew that if he moved to his left, he would probably see a revolver grasped in Grant's right hand.

When he saw it, hanging limply but still within Grant's clenched hand, he nodded his approval. It might have been the fact that he had a look of serene peacefulness upon his face; no stark disjointed terrible spasms held forever by the suddenness of the shot that would have immediately ended his life.

"First impression is one of suicide. A single gunshot to the right side of his temple, close enough to scorch the skin with powder burns... No sign of a struggle, and a look of..." He paused, aware of Morag scribbling behind him. "... a look of contentment upon his face..."

"Why do you say that?" Morag asked.

"In my experience, Morag, people who shoot themselves in the head leave this world with a look of peacefulness upon their face. If he'd been shot by someone else..." He hesitated, a thought coming to mind, one that was important but couldn't quite be identified or registered.

He glanced at the revolver in Grant's hand.

"Why write to us? Ask us to come here?" Harry pondered. "I remember him being a nervous type, but not one to take his own life..." He paused, before adding, "He said to me, the last time we met, that he was living in fear of his life. He also once told me that he'd done something so bad that he'd regretted it ever since, that he often thought about it..."

Edwards reflected, "Maybe his demons finally caught up with him."

"If he was going to kill himself, maybe he chose this place for privacy?" Morag proffered.

"He could have gone anywhere on Bodmin Moor for privacy," Harry replied glibly. "Besides, I would have thought the sound of a gunshot might have brought half of Bodmin out onto the street outside."

"Strange how he took off his reading glasses," she added

"What do you mean?" asked Edwards, his face wet with perspiration.

"It looks like he took them off and sat them neatly in the middle of the kitchen table."

"Those glasses didn't belong to Captain Grant," he replied, looking up at the beam above him. Why he'd felt compelled to say this, he couldn't work out. But there was an overwhelming feeling in the back of his mind, as though a play were being enacted somewhere deep within his subconscious.

Standing up, he turned to Morag and took back his pen and notebook. "Thank you… I need to get Sergeant Cadan down here as quickly as possible. Do you think you could walk over to the police station and ask him to meet me here?"

"Yes, of course, Cyril." Morag stepped back. She glanced across at Harry.

"Lord Frobisher can stay with me, Morag." He mentally chided himself for the bluntness of his words, quickly adding, "It's easier if you go alone… I just need to clarify a few things."

10

Annette Myers sat by the kitchen table in Rose Cottage and stared blankly around the room, endeavouring to find a spiritual peace she knew was ultimately out of reach. The kitchen was spotlessly clean, as she would expect with a local cleaner coming in to tidy up every day. The walls were neatly set with shelves supporting rows of porcelain jugs and plates, copper pans and numerous cups and saucers. Not the largest of kitchens she'd ever kept, but one that suited both her needs and her present state of mind; it was one of compactness and efficiency. There was no room for untidiness; if she picked up a new plate from one of the shops in town, then one of her existing plates would have to go.

The Welsh dresser had been left by the previous occupants, an architect and his wife and daughter, who'd renovated part of the house to allow them to move with ease between the kitchen and the lounge. She'd liked this feature when first viewing the property; she could sit and eat her meals whilst looking through the lounge to the large windows and out onto the most beautiful garden she'd ever seen.

Her cook, Mrs Banks, would serve her dinner and stand idling, also gazing through the lounge and out into the garden beyond. Sometimes she would comment on the weather, other times she might enthral Annette Myers with the local gossip doing the rounds in Bodmin. And Annette Myers would normally welcome these distractions, finding them a small breath of life within her rather dull and conventional life.

Dull and conventional life, she thought, looking across towards the latticed window in the lounge.

Like the kitchen, the garden wasn't the largest she'd ever owned, but it certainly was the best kept, with the most gorgeous perennial plants that loved the mild Cornish weather. Once her front door was shut and the world locked out, she always felt sheltered from the accusing glances of society. Here, amongst her tidy kitchen and beautifully kept garden, her past could never intrude.

Unless, of course, she invited it in…

She shuffled nervously in her chair, reflecting upon the morning's events. She assumed the police would eventually find the body, but couldn't be sure when that might be. Visitors to that loathsome place were always few and far between; in fact, probably non-existent. If that were the case, her best option was to pack her bags and leave Bodmin on the earliest train. But that would then certainly point the finger of suspicion towards her when the authorities eventually found him.

She tried to imagine him visiting Rose Cottage the previous day and what the neighbours might have thought. Her meeting with Canon Trebarwith had overrun and she'd returned home later than intended. The thought of him scribbling his note made her smile. He would have looked so noble and dashing…

My God, what the neighbours might have thought…

The notion evolved and developed in her mind.

They were bound to talk, especially old Mrs Dunning at the end of the close. She spent all of her waking hours peering through her curtains, watching, noting. The police would ask for witnesses.

God, what a mess…

149

She thought of the letter she'd written to him and of her inability to locate it anywhere in his cottage. No doubt the police would find it; if not here, then probably in his London flat. It had been short and to the point.

As requested, he'd brought the items with him, and a quick search of the cottage had led her to them. What other purpose his visit was going to achieve was full of uncertainty and speculation. Was there ever going to be forgiveness? If she was honest with herself, she hadn't really given it that much consideration. He'd summoned her that night and her children had died. There was nothing more to be said.

But she couldn't help but think that if he'd not sent that telegram, or if she had, for once, put the love of her children before her animal desires... No, any attempt to confront the past could only stir painful memories and ignite feelings of retribution that had now, after her visit to Creek Lane, dulled to a dismal glow.

He was still that handsome man she'd fallen in love with...
So many years ago...

Her mind drifted through the years, blocking out the events of the morning and filling her with a sense of guilt and a desire to attain some kind of atonement. But as she did so, the face of Canon Trebarwith came to her, sad and hurt, as she confessed her sins to him in a place in which she'd once worshipped but now felt she could never enter again.

The years rolled by...

That first day she'd met Captain Grant... She remembered it so well, and a smile flashed across her face; though it was a ruse, a mask that covered the wretched feeling of despair and disgust that squirmed within her.

The day was cold and wet, one of those typical winter days in London when the city seemed buried under a blanket of soot and grime, a grim reminder of the endless dark days the country was enduring. The papers were full of the latest news from the Front; soldiers on short-leave passes wandered aimlessly by, their eyes staring blankly ahead. People hurried past her, their grey, mournful figures almost ghostly in a world that stood helplessly by as the slaughter continued.

And then he appeared...

Walking down the steps from his club just off the Mall. The rain came so quickly she was caught unawares and could only stand there like a drowned rat as he swept past her.

He offered her his umbrella.

From then on, her mind was a blur, a collage of words spoken, of afternoon tea taken in a little cafe off Bond Street; talk of their families, his love of books, her charitable work...

He was worried about her catching a chill so offered her the warmth of his flat...

She accepted...

The fire in his lounge had been burning all morning, so the room was bathed in a beautiful warmth that made her long for the touch of his hands. When he undressed her, he did so respectfully, slowly removing her clothes and gently kissing her body as he peeled away her garments; and when she finally stood before him, naked and trembling, he guided her to the rug laid out before the fire, kissing her face and feeling her hands desperately tear the clothes from his body...

As he pushed himself deep into her, she felt a part of her die... and yet become reborn. From that moment, the world in which she now existed, the person she'd become, lying there, locked in his embrace, both scared and fascinated her.

She grimaced, remembering her husband, and the dreadful relief she'd felt when he'd returned to France to join his regiment, his shell-shocked mind broken and tormented. If she'd known at the time that he was never coming back, she might have felt differently.

But that thought was a luxury she knew didn't belong to her.

The endless meetings, the sordid encounters...

What she thought was love was simply manifesting itself into a tumultuous affair that threatened to consume the two of them in some base and tragic scandal.

Yet she felt no shame... no feelings of degradation, as he exploited her animal instincts.

There was a party in the basement of a house just off Green Park, with only specially invited guests. They seemed to know him, and he introduced her as though she were his latest acquisition... Their hands reached out to her, pulling, demanding, dragging her down into their debauched world, consuming her and releasing any final inhibitions that still desperately tried to reason with her...

Men or women, she had no care...

All that mattered was the feel of their bodies as they coiled around and enveloped her, pulling her into their infernal orgy... A man's thrust, a woman's tongue...

All thoughts of her children, at home with the nanny, were consigned to another world, one of a respectable middle-class existence that found no place in her heart. For if there were such a thing as decency, then it belonged to another.

She sighed...

"Dear God, forgive me for what I have done." Her words fell flat around her, spoken in hope, yet heard by nobody.

There were plans to make for Saturday's recital. She was meeting several ladies, her close friends, for tea and coffee; they were to discuss who would be baking cakes and who would make the tea. Husbands needed to be coerced into setting out chairs and tables; she'd used the word 'coerced' at their last meeting, and her friends had laughed, a painful and contrived laugh. One she'd recognised, along with the sympathetic look they carried in their eyes.

Later today, Peran Freeman would be arriving at the town hall to tune the piano. She hoped there wouldn't be too many problems arising out of his visit. It was a little late to be checking the thing, leaving them with no other viable alternative if a major part needed to be found, or if the instrument was deemed too decrepit for a recital of Beethoven.

Of course, there was always the piano over at Frobisher Hall. They were bound to have one.

She longed to meet Lady Frobisher and welcome her to Bodmin; hopefully she might one day sit beside her at a meeting of the local Women's Institute. Like most people in town, she remembered her arrest and incarceration, was aware of the tragedy that had unfolded, yet was unable to rationale why someone might want to do the things they said she had.

Unless, of course, she *was* mad.

Which was now an utterly ridiculous suggestion, and she felt ashamed to have joined the local community in their collective ignorance of Morag's plight as she resided, strapped and constantly under sedation, in the local asylum.

Her suggestion that the piano recital over in the town hall be planned for the Saturday following the return of Lord and Lady Frobisher from their honeymoon was met with rapturous agreement from the other ladies, and plans were drawn up to invite the viscount and his wife and maybe even entice Her Ladyship to stand up and say a few words.

That was met with a muted response, as the look of embarrassment and shame flickered in their eyes. And, to some extent, she was sadly in agreement with them. Maybe it was too soon to ask Her Ladyship to stand up and address those who had so cynically turned their backs on her; maybe certain wounds ran too deep. Maybe she would always harbour resentment, or would simply feel too embarrassed to even make a public appearance, let alone stand up and speak.

Annette Myers did, however, strongly believe that she'd made the right decision in inviting the viscount and his wife to the recital. At least it would be an opportunity for the town to meet them as man and wife on an informal basis.

She thought of the journey she'd taken, that had ultimately brought her to this idyllic town, in comparison to that of Morag Donaldson's. She considered her own soiled and deceitful life, and the terrible burden she now carried, and contrasted it against that of a beautiful red-headed woman who had risen

153

above the evil that had threatened to consume her, to ultimately win the heart of a lord.

It was only then, when her mind finally cleared of these conflicting thoughts, that Annette Myers stood up and glanced behind her at the two photographs of her boys. Smiling, she let her eyes wander, to finally settle on the toys, that now resided each side of the photographs. The soldier on horseback, charred and battered and so very different to how it had once looked, resting within the arms of her youngest son. To the other side, a charred and partially melted metal boat, the same as the one in the photograph of her oldest son.

To have their toys with her now, along with the memory of the man she'd once loved, filled her with something she couldn't define. All she knew was what burnt within her heart, and that was both wretched and pitiful. Wilbur Grant had loved her in a way she'd never thought possible and had taken her to a place where all her sexual inhibitions had been swept away by his touch.

Reaching out, she picked up the revolver from the table and placed it back into her handbag. Her eyes were glazed and unseeing; the world in which she now resided was one of darkened shadows and a society that would always shun her.

The only consolation she might cling to was the look of peace in his eyes when she'd walked away from 13 Creek Lane.

★★★

Lawrence Matthews gently opened his eyes, blinking several times as he tried to make sense of the colours that merged and danced before him. The first thing he was aware of was the diminished level of pain in his shoulder, and for that he was extremely grateful. There was, however, a residual dull ache he feared might explode into something more sinister if he tried to move. He also felt a cool and comforting cloth covering his forehead, and a smell of freshly cut grass, slightly wet, and fragrant with little pockets of herbs that teased his senses.

These sensations alone helped to lift his spirits and dampen down the feeling of vulnerability he'd felt just a moment ago...

Moment ago...?

His mind grappled with the sudden wave of questions that rose up from his subconscious, demanding answers...

Man's face... Know him...

"Ah, good... you're awake." A voice from somewhere set deep within his mind... "You took quite a tumble, young man."

Lawrence's eyes began to focus, recognising outlines of shapes and objects. Colours that only moments earlier were nothing more than blurred images now merged into defined figures. He was aware of someone hovering over him and of a rough hand gently dabbing his face with the cloth that was soothing his forehead. He moved his left hand, the one not affected by his recently dislocated shoulder, and tried to reach out to the face that was becoming clearer with every cooling touch of the cloth.

"Easy... I would imagine you're also concussed... Will be for several days."

"Man..." Lawrence tried to whisper, desperate to verbally describe the flashing images that kept exploding in his mind.

"Don't speak..." It was a woman's voice.

The same woman who had found him.

He mentally knelt down and started to gather the pieces of the shattered picture that represented his journey to this place. And like most puzzles, the hardest part was wondering where to start. The most painful pieces slotted into place with greater ease, and he winced as they jolted his memory.

"I've made you some nettle tea."

Lawrence recognised the authority in her voice and nodded.

"In a minute, Branok will help you into a seated position. We've strapped your shoulder, so there shouldn't be too much pain."

"Who... Who are..." Lawrence struggled to speak and realised his throat was dry and constricted to the point where he felt happy enough to simply draw breath.

"You'll be able speak when you've had something to drink."

He closed his eyes, before blinking them a few times. The image of a woman, middle-aged, with a roughness of hair and skin that made any attempt at establishing a more accurate estimate of her age impossible, materialised before him. Her smile, though, was warm, and there was something about her features...

"Hello, Constable Matthews..." The warmth in her face ran freely through the words she spoke. When she smiled, her lips drew back, accentuating a dimple on her left cheek. "You're a long way from Frobisher Hall..."

Lawrence resisted the urge to agree, deciding instead to let the hint of a smile flash across his face. He was sure he'd never seen her before, but didn't rely too much on that assumption as he was currently struggling to remember anyone he might have met in his life. However, the more he felt he'd never met her, the more familiar she became.

"I imagine you were going to ask my name?"

Again, Lawrence replied with a feeble smile, trying to ease himself up a little.

"My name is Ellen Carfax. It was myself and Branok who found you and brought you here to this cottage."

"How... How did you..."

Lawrence continued to ease himself up, encouraged by the lack of pain in his shoulder. The blurriness was clearing and the room was becoming more distinct and real. He was in a small bedroom with grey walls, with a solitary painting on the wall opposite that immediately caught his attention. It was of Frobisher Hall, beautifully painted in oil, and would not have looked out of place in the house itself. Though the more he scrutinised the painting and marvelled at its beauty, the more he was struck by the strange aspect. He thought a painting of Frobisher Hall, like most paintings of stately homes, would usually be of a conventional perspective, maybe of the front, incorporating the sweeping driveway and lawns, or maybe from a distance, with the towers protruding through a densely thick forest.

The portrayal of the Hall he now considered, as his senses and concentration became a little more receptive, was painted as though by somebody sat in a most awkward position in the estate grounds. It was of the west side of the building, with the tower to the right and the windows to the dining room just visible through ferns and shrubs that hindered a clearer perspective. A line of trees obscured the end of the building towards the garage and…

His mind grew hazy…

"Do you like the painting?" Ellen Carfax asked, again with that warming smile, yet vaguely beguiling as the tone of her voice betrayed something more akin to concern and intrigue.

Lawrence nodded, taking his eyes off the painting and turning his head to the woman sitting on the side of his bed. As he did so, he noticed the figure of a man standing behind her near the door. His first thought was one of panic, as the figure, dressed in dark corduroy trousers and a black cardigan, appeared more like some terrible apparition in Lawrence's mind. He was huge, his frame completely filling the doorway, with a bull neck and bald head and a face so terribly scarred Lawrence found it perversely hard to take his eyes off him.

Ellen Carfax smiled. "Branok is my friend. He has a cup of nettle tea… It'll do you good."

"How do you know my name…?" Lawrence finally settled into a seated position.

"Later, Constable Matthews. First, try my nettle tea."

Lawrence sniffed, finding it hard to conceal his distaste.

"It'll do you better than anything you drink in London… Here…"

Ellen Carfax nodded towards Branok, and Lawrence watched as the huge figure approached, threatening to fill the entire room. With a tenderness that belied his enormous size and the hardened look upon his face, he reached forward and placed the cup in Lawrence's hand.

Though he stared at Lawrence, his face remained impassive and cold.

"Branok is a mute… I found him starving and close to death outside the cottage at the end of the war. He was still in his army uniform, though you wouldn't have recognised it. How long he'd been without food or shelter I couldn't imagine. I think he might have deserted and made his way back here. But he doesn't speak, and I don't ask." Ellen eased herself back and smiled at her companion.

Lawrence took a tentative sip, expecting to gag on the foul liquid as it drained into his stomach. He ran his tongue along his lips, blinking with interest as it both warmed and refreshed him.

"Well, that's one to ask Susan about," he smiled.

"Your new wife." Ellen Carfax leant back and eyed him closely. "It seems everyone is in the mood for getting married over at Frobisher Hall."

Lawrence took several more sips, trying to work the stiffness out of his neck. "My horse threw me… There was a man… Someone I know…"

"Morgan Treave?" Ellen Carfax spoke the words clearly and with no hint of emotion. It was as though she were answering a simple question.

"Yes," he nodded. "He's wanted for murder."

"We know what Morgan Treave has done." Her words were soft and reassuring, as though he didn't have to fear explaining who Morgan Treave was. "Branok here watches over the cottage at night. I know he's on the run from the police. We've seen him on the estate. I would say Harry Frobisher and that young bride of his are in danger."

"Lady Frobisher is quite a formidable lady," Lawrence reflected.

"She'd have to be against that monster." A look of sternness crossed her face. "Folks around here say she gouged out his eye with a broken bottle... That she battered him beyond recognition. But he never died... or maybe he did." She stared out of the window, "Maybe the ghost of Morgan Treave haunts Frobisher Hall..."

"We never found his body. She thought she'd killed him and left him in the tower." Lawrence finished his tea and was tempted to ask for more. Already feeling revitalised, he wanted to swing his legs out and onto the floor, to maybe sit on the side of the bed and contemplate his journey home. "But when the local police searched the secret passageway in the East Tower and then eventually the room in which she'd attacked him, he was gone..."

Ellen breathed deeply, digesting his words. "Constable Matthews—"

"Please... just call me Lawrence... I'm no longer a serving police officer." Lawrence coughed and fiddled nervously with his cup.

"Constable Matthews," Ellen Carfax persisted, "look after Harry Frobisher and his young wife. When you're feeling better, Branok will walk with you back to the main path to Frobisher Hall."

"Why is this place not marked on the map?" Lawrence blurted out. He was eager to swing his legs out but couldn't due to Ellen Carfax still sitting on the edge of the bed. His question reflected his sudden frustration at not being able to move. "This is Sunrise Cottage?"

Finally, Ellen Carfax pulled herself away from the bed and stood up. She was slim, of average height and dressed quite shabbily, as though she might have just come in from a long day out working in the fields. "Yes, this is Sunrise Cottage."

Lawrence eased his legs across, pivoting himself round, before finally sitting and facing Branok standing in the doorway. He took a deep breath, aware of a lightness in his head. When it passed he said, "As I said, I'm no longer a serving police officer. Lord and Lady Frobisher were kind enough to employ me as Estate Manager after—"

"After the deaths of Edith and Reginald Travers. Yes, I remember Reginald Travers... A good man... I was sorry to hear of their murders; it was wrong of William..." Ellen Carfax sighed sadly, a sentiment that spread to Branok, whose bland demeanour became one of concern for the woman now standing beside him.

"I've been checking through every farm and tied cottage on the estate," Lawrence continued, "Checking the records of families and workers, cross-referencing them to the estate maps... It seems—"

"That Sunrise Cottage isn't registered," Ellen Carfax interrupted, her face deep and reflective. "It won't be... And for all intents and purposes, it never will be." She looked out of the window and Lawrence followed her gaze.

Though still light, the sun was obscured behind heavy cloud, making it impossible to assess the time of day, and he was struck by the realisation that he might well have been unconscious for longer than he'd first anticipated. The light-headedness that had initially affected him had settled, and the aches and pains in his body had become manageable. He couldn't use his bad arm due to the heavy strapping, but he could certainly feel a strength in his free arm and his legs, enough to empower him to contemplate standing up and thinking about making his way back to Frobisher Hall.

"Branok will walk with you back to the main path. Just follow the trail back towards Templers Copse; you'll see the towers of Frobisher Hall from there. Don't worry, Branok will look after you."

"And what about you?" Lawrence heaved himself up until he was standing. The room swayed a little, but his senses and balance held.

"What about me?"

"We both know that Morgan Treave has been sighted around here. I'm now certain it was he who scared my horse... What will you do if he ever turns up here when Branok is unable to protect you?"

Lawrence moved to the door, aware that Branok had already made his way through into another room that looked like the kitchen.

Ellen Carfax reached behind the chest of drawers and pulled out an old double-barrelled, flint-lock action shotgun. As she clicked it open to check the two chambers, she smiled at Lawrence.

"Well, Constable Matthews, we live in hope, don't we?"

11

"If it wasn't suicide, Inspector Edwards," asked Harry, "what was it?"

"It was murder, Lord Frobisher. A good old-fashioned murder. The kind of murder that reminds me why I joined the police force and ultimately became an inspector."

Edwards leaned back in his chair and lit his pipe. He thought he might try Harry's choice of vanilla and cherry tobacco, so fragrant was the aroma that drifted across from his direction. He watched as Harry Frobisher reflected upon this for a moment.

"Did you kill him, Inspector?" Harry replied, his mouth breaking into a wry smile.

Edwards watched as Morag turned sharply to stare at her husband.

"No, Lord Frobisher, did you?" Edwards replied coldly.

"Hardly," Harry responded indignantly.

The silence that followed was only broken by the acerbic sound of Morag's Scottish accent as she reflected, "Good... I'm glad we settled that question."

"But someone obviously did," continued Edwards. "And considering the circumstances surrounding Captain Grant's visit to Bodmin and his letter to yourself, Lord Frobisher, I think we need to act quickly."

He looked around the office in which the three of them now sat. It was the same office at Bodmin Police Station in which he'd once sat with Sergeant Cadan, one cold and grey November afternoon, and contemplated a journey that was going to become part of local folklore for many years to come. He noticed the windows were still grimy and the stone floor probably not swept since his last visit. The only real difference, he decided, was the summer warmth that went a little way to brighten up the room.

But with that warmth came an increasing oppressiveness, as though the sudden humidity was heralding an approaching storm. At the insistence of Inspector Edwards, the three of them had taken a light lunch in the St Petroc Hotel, whilst Sergeant Cadan had arranged for a local photographer to take photographs of the kitchen at 13 Creek Lane and the body of Captain Grant prior to its removal to Bodmin Hospital. During lunch, Edwards had discussed the letter in more detail, but had held back on his initial theories when prompted by Morag. Harry had hardly touched the platter of beef and pickles, seemingly happy enough to smoke his pipe and fiddle around with his walking stick.

Now, sitting within the confines of this office in Bodmin Police Station, he surveyed Harry and Morag, choosing the right words and watching intently the look on Harry's face.

"He died from a single gunshot from his own revolver. If I'm not mistaken, it was his own Webley, quite popular with many officers during the war. That, of course, will have to be checked by forensics. It was made to look like suicide, of that I'm certain." Edwards paused, before continuing, "The muzzle was pressed against his right temple…"

"And…?" Harry prompted.

"My God…" Morag whispered.

"Yes, Morag?" Edwards leaned forward towards her.

"The photograph…" Her words hung heavily around the room.

"I've not seen this photograph," Edwards reflected. "But do continue…"

"He was holding a cigarette…" Her eyes narrowed and she bit slightly on her lip. "He was holding it in his left hand…"

"Well, my dear sister-in-law, you're ahead of me there." Edwards smiled. "Did you notice the writing in the letter and the name on the envelope?"

Morag shook her head, her mouth slightly open as if she wanted to say something but couldn't. Edwards noticed her hair was tied back, but not to the point that the removal of a few pins wouldn't let it come tumbling down around her neck. Sometimes her resemblance to Elisha was painful beyond words; and right now, sitting before him with that look of intensity and intrigue upon her face, he was reminded of his wife and that ability she had to help him work out some of his most intricate cases.

"I'm guessing it was written by a left-handed person?" Harry broke the silence.

"Yes, it was, Lord Frobisher," Edwards confirmed. "I'm not an expert, but I can tell the difference between a left and a right-handed person."

"Assuming that Captain Grant wrote that letter in the first place," Harry proffered.

"Good point, Lord Frobisher, and one to take careful note of." Edwards drew thoughtfully on his pipe. "But then the letter does refer to certain personalised events… Your time together in Paris, for example. Would someone else know that? Maybe… But there is, of course, Morag's point about the cigarette in this photograph of Captain Grant."

"Could still be a coincidence," Harry persisted.

"Yes, Lord Frobisher," Edwards replied, a little too curtly for his own liking. He smiled, hoping his next words might come across a little less tersely. "But there's also one other clue as to how your friend met his end…" He stood up and walked around the desk, his thumbs hooked into the pockets of his waistcoat. "It seems that Captain Grant was seated when he was shot. Usually, in such circumstances, the body might tumble to the ground. He may have done so, and then the murderer placed him back into the seat with the misconceived notion that it would look more like suicide. So, how does someone take Captain Grant's revolver, without a struggle, and point it to his head. Why does Grant remain seated?"

"Was it his gun?" Morag asked.

"I'm assuming that, yes."

"Was he drugged?" Harry asked.

"We won't know until a pathologist comes over from Plymouth. I've asked Sergeant Cadan to request someone comes over and examines both bodies," Edwards replied. "As I said, there is another factor to consider. Morag, when you left myself and Lord Frobisher to come here and fetch Sergeant Cadan, I examined the exit wound and the trajectory of the bullet. In my experience, a person sitting down and placing a gun to their head would fire a bullet either level or at an angle pointing slightly upwards. The exit wound was below his left ear."

"Good Heavens," Harry whispered.

"The bullet exited below his left ear and embedded itself in one of the cupboard doors to his left. I'm hoping that Sergeant Cadan has supervised the photographs of these points…"

"So, someone was standing beside him," surmised Harry. "Obviously taller because Captain Grant was seated."

"That's right, Lord Frobisher… Any ideas who might have shot him?" His words punctured the room with an aggressiveness that surprised him.

Harry's response was quite restrained considering the tone of Edwards' question. "Someone who's eager to kill off the Rooks, of which Grant was obviously one."

"But you have no idea who the murderer might be?" Edwards relaxed, but he refused to completely let go. "Think carefully, Lord Frobisher. You spent time with Captain Grant. He confided in you… He even wrote you a letter—"

"Which was taken from me when I was injured."

"Did you read it?"

"No."

"Are you sure?"

"Cyril!" Morag stood up and moved towards her husband, eventually standing between him and Edwards. Her eyes had lost that look of intrigue; they now blazed with unrestrained fury. "Harry's told you he never got to open it. He promised Captain Grant he'd keep it safe, but it was taken from him."

Edwards released his grip. "And if it was taken from him, who took it? There were only two other people in the immediate vicinity of that trench when William threw that grenade: William himself and Sergeant Benson. Both are now dead, which makes my job harder." Scratching his chin, he brushed his moustache, right then left, before moving back to the other side of the desk.

"I didn't read the letter, Inspector. Captain Grant entrusted it to me. I can only assume that William took it when I lay injured." Harry sighed, obviously feeling the weight of a terrible memory.

"Did you tell William about the letter?" Edwards asked.

"Yes, but I'm sure he didn't know where I hid it." Harry reached out his hand. Morag stepped back and moved closer to him. "What if this man on the train was one of the Rooks? We know that Captain Grant was one of a team of four."

"And that would leave two…" Edwards sat down.

"One of whom is our killer," Morag said blankly.

"Hmmm." Edwards rubbed his chin. "Did Grant say anything that might have pointed to the identity of the Rooks?"

"Nothing…" Harry replied. "Only that they were commanded by someone known as the Fourth Rook. This person controlled everything, all their missions, contacts, the lot. They were officially registered as working with their respective regiments or organisations, but would be recalled with a command, always coded and always referring to rooks."

"Captain Grant must have trusted you, Lord Frobisher. You must have struck up a friendship for him to confide all this in you?" Edwards stifled a yawn. Time was moving on and he still had to meet with Sergeant Cadan and hear his report on the door-to-door enquiries currently being conducted by officers around Creek Lane.

It would be nice, he thought, *to have this conversation over at Frobisher Hall. Maybe over a drink...*

Harry replied patiently, "As I said before, something had frightened him... frightened him to the extent that he felt compelled to write down his suspicions in that letter. He said he had proof that one of the team was a mole, a double agent channelling military secrets about troop movements, potential assaults, everything, through German agents working on our side of the lines. I knew he was a clever chap, that he was working for Military Intelligence. I think maybe he was more involved than he let on. Maybe he was hunting the traitor from within the group. I suppose he saw the letter as some kind of insurance against anyone making a move against him. Personally, I always turned my nose up at that kind of game; not really cricket. Load of cloak and dagger stuff... I'd rather stand up and face the enemy head-on."

"Why hide it in your tunic pocket?" Edwards prompted.

"There was nowhere to hide anything in the trenches. Operation posts were manned by different people each day. My bunk could quite easily be slept in by a fellow officer, or even commandeered as a hospital bed for a wounded solider. I had a wicker basket, as most officers did, which contained personal belongings: shaving kit, polish, writing paper, things like that. Last letters home were usually kept in these and normally held well back from the front line. So, anyone could easily rummage through them..." Harry gripped his stick. "The only place I could think of was my tunic pocket." He tapped the left-hand side of his chest. "At least it was always going to be with me."

"Even if you were killed?" Edwards responded delicately.

"It wasn't the most pleasant situation in which to be placed, Inspector. Believe me, there were several times I thought about just opening it, reading the contents and consigning them to memory. I suppose if I had been killed, then Captain Grant's suspicions would have died with me. But to keep the letter in my tunic pocket ran the risk of it falling into enemy hands if I were killed or captured..." Harry fell silent.

Edwards pondered what had been said, before asking, "Were you aware of anyone else with you, other than Sergeant Benson after he carried you back to the hospital tent?"

"I remember voices." Harry held his head forward, shaking it from side to side. "The pain and shock... I kept drifting in and out of consciousness... I remember..." His words drifted off.

"Yes, Lord Frobisher?" Edwards drew nearer, ignoring Morag's reproachful stare.

"Someone... Someone talking... Not Benson..." Harry shook his head vigorously. "I'm sorry."

Edwards contemplated prompting him further before deciding enough was enough. "Okay... I think we've covered enough here. I need to meet with Sergeant Cadan and discuss the results of his door-to-door enquiries." He flicked the pages back and forth in his black notebook and frowned. "Four Rooks... The Fourth Rook potentially a merciless killer looking to bump off the other three before he, or she, is discovered. We know one Rook is dead, and possibly another. Of course, the other Rook, or Rooks, may live in other parts of the country—"

"And in that case," Morag interrupted, "he or she might already be out of Cornwall and possibly out of reach."

"Let's hope not." Edwards tapped the ash from his pipe into a large glass ashtray and added, "Which leads me to the obvious question… What if they are still here in Bodmin? What if they believe Lord Frobisher knows their identity?"

"But I would have already told you if I knew," Harry said quickly.

"Yes, I agree." Edwards scrapped out the remnants of ash with his penknife. "Or maybe they think you're one of the Rooks… And if that's the case, your life is in mortal danger."

Morag drew nearer to Harry.

Edwards pulled out his pocket watch. "The time is nearly 5pm. I can ask Sergeant Cadan to deploy some of his men over to you at Frobisher Hall… or…"

"Or what?" Morag asked, narrowing her eyes.

"Or leave you both without any obvious protection." Edwards licked his lips, as the outline of a plan began to form in his mind. Noticing the startled look on Morag's face, he added, "If we deploy men around the estate, it might drive the killer off and make them lie low. The fact that I've not instigated their arrest will tell them that you, Lord Frobisher, have been unable to divulge their identity; so, they might feel as though there's no need to force the issue. If I stay at Frobisher Hall and keep Sergeant Cadan's men out of the way, maybe we can draw the killer out into the open—"

"I don't want you risking Harry's life," Morag blurted out.

"It might be the only way," Harry whispered.

"What are your plans over the coming weekend?" Edwards began to refill his pipe.

"We have a piano recital to attend at the town hall tomorrow afternoon," Harry replied. "Also, we wanted to ask Canon Trebarwith to hold a short service of remembrance for Edith and Reginald Travers up at the monument on Sunday afternoon. He dined with us last night, and I forgot to ask him. I thought we might visit him over at the vicarage before we drove back to Frobisher Hall." Harry reached out and grasped Morag's hand.

Edwards nodded. "A piano recital… Hmmm…"

"Cyril…" Morag looked at Edwards, "Harry and I would love for you to come and stay with us… In fact, I insist on it."

"You still worried about Morgan Treave?" Edwards had caught the hesitancy in Morag's voice, another family trait he'd grown to recognise in his wife.

"Yes," Morag whispered.

"If it's Morgan Treave we're talking about," Harry cut in, "I think he's too slimy to catch through conventional police methods… No disrespect to you and your colleagues, Inspector."

"None taken, Lord Frobisher. I would actually agree with you. But there is the possibility that he's simply fled the county—" Edwards responded, before Morag interrupted him, cold and distant.

"He's close, Cyril. I feel his presence all the time."

Edwards nodded. "Then I think we need to find him and finally bring him to justice… I'll leave you both to visit Canon Trebarwith to discuss the memorial service for Mr and Mrs Travers. I think of that night often." He glanced around the room, remembering Edith's message and the sight of her body. It was in this very room that he'd pulled her note from his jacket pocket… "I would also like to pay my respects…" He shrugged off the memories, knowing there was immediate work to do. He needed to speak to Sergeant Cadan, and pick up some of his belongings from the military garrison. "I'll get someone to drive me over to Frobisher Hall later."

12

As a warm and heavy late afternoon descended upon the town of Bodmin, Canon Trebarwith sat thoughtfully at his desk in the vicarage study and contemplated the sermon he'd just completed. Running to several pages, he considered its length and feared he'd written something that might overrun his usual fifteen minutes. Though he could afford the time for minor alterations, he was going to be too busy for any major rewrites.

Knowing that the next day, Saturday, would be taken up with preparing for the piano recital, and that he wanted to visit the hospital first thing in the morning to say prayers over the unfortunate individual found dead on the train, left him with very little time to reconsider his sermon for the service on Sunday.

Reaching across his desk, he picked up a small crucifix and held it in the palm of his hand. Closing his eyes, he cleared his mind and began to pray, "Heavenly Father, watch over the souls of those taken from us through the violence of war..."

His mind drifted inexorably back...

The mass funerals after the battles... The bodies wrapped in sheets... The crosses, neatly stacked... The vacant look in the eyes of the gravediggers...

He tightened his grip on the crucifix...

"Forgive us our sins, and those who sin against us…"

The funeral services… so many he couldn't even remember… The rows of bodies… The awful stench of death… and that terrible look of despair in the eyes of the soldiers, standing, heads bowed… dirty and tired…

My God, he thought, releasing his grip and watching the crucifix fall onto the desk, *how many funeral services were there?*

The memories came, uninvited and shocking in their detail. The makeshift hospitals, constantly under bombardment… the screams of the wounded, the last gasping breaths of the dying as he held their hands and forgave them their sins. Feeling his eyes well up and the tears threaten to flow, he fumbled at the drawer to his left and pulled it open. Pulling a hip flask out, he held it to his lips with a hand that shook violently. The rum tasted warm, and the memories eased a little, receding… dwindling… The more he sipped, the more strength he drew. Like taking water from a well after an endless trek across a wilderness of nightmare images, he regained his composure and eyed the crucifix on the desk…

His mind wandered, thankfully away from such thoughts, only to stray into another room, a place where Annette Myers stared at him with saddened eyes. Gathering up the crucifix he again tried to pray, "Heavenly Father, forgive Annette Myers her sins… Help me to know what to do… Guide me…"

He heard the front door to the vicarage open and close. Glancing at the clock, he realised that Mrs West, his housekeeper and cook, had arrived to tidy the place up and cook his evening meal. Sighing heavily, he gently placed the crucifix at the head of his desk beside the ink well and glanced out of the window. The gathering clouds looked heavy and threatening.

There was a knock at the door to his study, so loud it wrenched him out of his quiet contemplation. Without waiting for him to say anything, the door opened and his housekeeper stumbled in, still wearing the dark raincoat she wore every time she visited the vicarage, come rain or shine. Quickly, and with a speed and deftness that belied his large, clumsy hands, he thrust the hip flask back into the drawer.

"Mrs West, please could you try and knock before—"

"Oh, Canon Trebarwith... Have you heard?" Mrs West stood open-mouthed and staring with horror at the clergyman. Her hair was tied back, and with no make-up her usually pale complexion was flushed with beads of sweat that dowsed her forehead.

"Heard what, Mrs West?" Trebarwith swung round to confront this sudden entrance.

"Another murder..." she spluttered. "Another murder... And after what happened on the Bodmin train, that now makes two."

"What do you mean, another murder...? Who...? Where...?"

"13 Creek Lane... You know, that house where..." Mrs West gasped and held her hand to her mouth.

"Yes, I know about 13 Creek Lane... But what do you mean a murder?"

"Today... the police arrived... they carried out a body... a man... said he'd been shot..."

"From 13 Creek Lane...?" Trebarwith's voice echoed with a hint of indignation. "But that place has been empty since..."

Mrs West kept her hand firmly clasped to her mouth, though she nodded meekly.

"I don't understand... Why would anyone want to visit that place?"

She lowered her hand. "One of the constables said it was the body of an army officer... shot in the head... They said it could be suicide, but you never know..."

Canon Trebarwith closed his eyes, momentarily recalling Annette Myers' confession earlier that morning.

Why in God's name did she tell me...?

"I didn't hear about this." Trebarwith shook his head. "When did it happen?"

"I don't know… The place is swarming with police. They're talking to everyone who lives on Creek Lane… They even have that inspector from Scotland Yard here… You know, the one who was here last year and sorted out that murder up at Frobisher Hall."

"Who? Inspector Edwards?"

Mrs West nodded, eyes wide and staring.

Trebarwith sat back in his chair, suddenly oblivious to the presence of his housekeeper. No longer could he repress the memory of his meeting with Annette Myers, and his heart slumped as her face, that beautiful, tortured face, came into view, broken and guilt-ridden.

Relentlessly, his emotions assailed his senses as he thought about his marriage proposal to her, now torn asunder. His eyes glazed over and he sighed deeply.

"Okay, Mrs West, thank you for telling me this…" He smiled. "How are the preparations coming along for tomorrow's piano recital?"

"P-piano recital…?" Mrs West stuttered. "With a murderer stalking the streets of Bodmin?"

"Murderer or not, Mrs West, this town and its community are not going to be bowed and threatened by a murderer on the loose… This country stood against tyranny in the Great War and won through… and we shall do the same."

"Yes… but—" Mrs West stopped abruptly and turned her head to the main hallway.

The sound of someone repeatedly knocking on the front door echoed through the house, plunging the two of them into a stunned silence. As though in a dream, and not waiting to be asked, Mrs West stepped lightly out into the main hallway, disappearing from Canon Trebarwith's line of sight.

Straining his ears, he heard his housekeeper mumbling words and welcoming someone into the house. She reappeared moments later to announce in a low whisper and with a sense of awe, "Lord and Lady Frobisher. Here to see you, Canon Trebarwith…"

Inspector Edwards stood silently staring at the front of 13 Creek Lane. Raising his hand, he stroked his moustache, right, then left, before placing his pipe in his mouth. From his jacket pocket he retrieved a box of matches, removed one and struck it against the side of the box. Cupping it in his hand, he moved it towards the brim of his pipe.

Before he managed to draw breath, a sudden breeze whipped up from nowhere and extinguished the flame.

Waiting for the breeze to die down, he again focussed his attention on the house in front of him. He knew that the body of Captain Grant had been removed, and the only reminder of the tragedy that had occurred was the sight of a sole police constable, standing at the foot of the front steps and regarding him with an inquisitive eye.

He was hoping to catch Sergeant Cadan, knowing he hadn't yet made it back to the police station by the time Harry and Morag had left for the vicarage. There would hopefully be plenty to talk about after the sergeant's door-to-door enquiries, and he'd hoped to meet him at Creek Lane.

The breeze had dissipated.

Edwards removed a second match and struck it against the box. In amazement, he felt a warm breeze whip through the lane, extinguishing the flame in an instant.

A cold chill ran down his back.

It was fast becoming a familiar feeling and he shuddered every time he felt it. It was usually accompanied by a shortness of breath and an overpowering feeling of knowing something he had no right to know. How or why he felt like this he tried to ignore, hoping the feelings would just leave him.

He'd felt it the night Old Solomon had come to him.

Of course, he hadn't recognised it then.

He had, though, recognised it when he'd earlier stood in the kitchen of the house now before him.

He walked towards the building and nodded at the young constable. "Is Sergeant Cadan in there?"

"No, sir," the young man replied, a little in awe.

Edwards looked around, aware of the absence of any discernible breeze in the air. To try and light his pipe a third time might bring the same outcome, and that would be too strange, maybe even…

Keep it professional, Edwards, he reprimanded himself.

"Anything to report?" He eyed the young man.

"No, sir. Local folk tend to stay away from this house."

"Oh, why's that?"

"They say it's haunted." The young man instinctively stepped away from the house. Looking back at Edwards, he said, "I know it sounds daft, sir, but…"

"No, Constable," replied Edwards wearily, "it doesn't sound daft… Believe me, it doesn't sound daft…" He stepped up to the front door and turned the handle.

★★★

Peran Freeman, of Freeman's Solicitors in Bodmin, had never intended to enter into the quagmire of providing legal services to, it sometimes seemed, the whole of Bodmin. Yes, there were other practices in the town, some of whom he knew quite well, especially through the local Masonic lodge. But now, so far into his long and dedicated career as a solicitor, he certainly felt as though he was the person most people in the town turned to when in need of legal advice.

His workload never relented, no matter what time of year or what day of the week. Minor claims, estate conveyancing and other legal advice filled his life. He noted, for the first time since he cared to remember, a recent divorce settlement; but that had been a husband over in Liskeard who'd wanted to keep local gossip to a minimum.

A small, stocky man in his late sixties, his grey hair and inquisitive eyes projected an image of someone finely attuned to the harsher side of his profession. Those clients who sat before him usually did so with an air of trepidation, even though he was usually representing them. The suits he wore were immaculately fitted, double-breasted, and always had a small, red handkerchief situated in the breast pocket. His hands were scrupulously clean, with nails that were clipped neatly every two days.

All he knew was that he'd never planned for this profession; yet when pressed as to why he'd entered it in the first place, he would simply smile and shrug his shoulders.

What alternative career he might have chosen, one could only speculate.

Why he chose the legal profession, his family and friends could never fathom.

Yet he'd conducted himself with the highest level of integrity and professionalism for the past forty years, serving the town of Bodmin and never once having his conduct brought into question or disrepute. His connections, from his lodge meetings to the town council, were deep and ethically entrenched.

Though he could never fully rationalise his decision to enter this profession, the one thing he was clear about was his loyalty to the people of Bodmin and his determination to treat everyone as fairly as he might ever want to be treated himself.

He lived by himself in a small annex to the main office which stretched discreetly to the rear, where he could sit in his lounge of an evening and enjoy a glass of stout and read his books and the local newspaper. A man devoted to his profession and Christian faith, he could be found on a Sunday attending church services both in the morning and the evening; and, when not relaxing in the evening with his favourite books, he might be found trawling through church accounts and providing professional advice to Canon Trebarwith on different legal matters.

Recently he'd taken to spending long periods reflecting upon the beautiful Scottish woman with the red hair who had once visited him, broken and desperate, asking for his assistance.

The fact that he'd made the decision to help her and accede to her request without any hesitation betrayed the fact that he had, on several occasions since that day, concluded that he was a little in love with her. So consumed had he been with his profession that he'd never found the time to meet someone, fall in love and eventually marry.

The previous year, when Morag Donaldson had handed him that letter addressed to Inspector Edwards of Scotland Yard, only months before she was discovered kneeling beside the dead bodies of Lord Alfred and Lady Margaret, he'd felt an acute sense of love and devotion consume him and guide his subsequent actions.

He'd known her from his visits to Frobisher Hall, for both business and pleasure purposes, from talking through revised legal documents pertaining to the Frobisher Estate, to the occasional bridge nights when Morag might partner him. A mutual trust had gestated in the close relationship between himself and Lord and Lady Frobisher, and had eventually grown into a deep sense of friendship and admiration for the beautiful red-headed woman whose smile could literally take his breath away.

Maybe that was why he was always so keen to accept an invitation to dine at the Hall.

Maybe, he thought, as he sat staring out of the window of his office on that Friday afternoon, *she's the most beautiful woman I've ever known... A radiant sparkle of light... Full of kindness and love... Someone who wouldn't play games with a man's love... Someone who wouldn't hurt for the sheer fun of it...*

The room he had conducted his business from for the past forty years was oak-panelled, with solid brass door handles, a single large desk and two chests of drawers. The lighting was sparse, with a dull light that flickered from a solitary light bulb. The office was usually bathed in a world of perpetual darkness and shadow. The decor was meagre to say the least: no flowers or photographs, not a single item of artistic flair that might take the visitor's mind away from the cold and dispassionate legal world that was, quite simply, Freeman's Solicitors.

Nothing... save for the print hanging behind his chair of the Walter Raleigh Gilbert Monument.

As the clouds gathered and the air became oppressive, Peran Freeman sat quietly at his desk, hearing the front door close gently as his secretary finished for the day. As it was Friday, she'd finished early, making him a small cup of tea before gathering her handbag and coat.

She'd never liked the print behind his desk, and had told him so on several occasions. It was bland, imposing, almost intimidating. No, she did not think it celebrated a local man's heroic achievement, suggesting it might even make clients feel uncomfortable. Yes, she agreed it was an iconic landmark... Maybe it was the dark and melancholy shadows within the print that made her feel this way?

He'd always laughed at her scolding remarks.

That was until the only time Morag Donaldson visited his office.

In the aftermath of the terrible murder of Edith Travers at the base of the structure last November as the first flakes of snow began to fall, heralding the approach of one of the worst snowstorms to hit the county in living memory, his secretary had become more adamant in her opinion.

But, by that time, Peran Freeman was impervious to any criticism about the print.

If anything, he became even more ardent in his desire to keep it where it was.

As he sat sipping his tea he contemplated the planned piano recital the next day. He was aware that Lord and Lady Frobisher had been invited, and it would be his first opportunity to meet with them in more sociable surroundings. Hopefully life would return to some form of normality for them both, and he firmly believed that he might one day strike up the same friendship as he had done with Lord Alfred and Lady Margaret.

The small carriage clock above the mantlepiece chimed six times and he pulled out his gold pocket watch: 6pm exactly. He would be heading over to the town hall shortly to tune the piano and spend a little time rehearsing the pieces he had planned for tomorrow. Beethoven had always been his favourite ever since his father had taught him how to play the piano; and he remembered the wonderful piano sonatas he'd learnt, along with other greats such as Shubert and Liszt.

Ahh... the Romantics, he thought, sipping the last of his now tepid tea. The shadows of late afternoon were beginning to cast their familiar eerie feel around his office. Set so far back from the main high street, there was always a darkened sense of isolation and solitude when evening approached and his secretary made her way home.

He felt his eyes grow heavy.

A short nap would do him the world of good – help clear his mind of the day's events. There had been an influx of conveyancing requests, something he never really enjoyed. There were also further meetings planned with the current Lord and Lady Frobisher as he tried to negotiate the emotionally perilous task of tying up legal loose ends concerning William Frobisher... What he'd done last year, the small part he had played in helping Lady Morag clear her name, still brought a smile to his face...

A woman born to be loved, he thought, allowing the beautiful chords of Beethoven's Moonlight Sonata drift into his mind... *A woman who would inspire the love of everyone she ever met... who would bless their lives simply by being in their presence... Where some women were cold and emotionally-detached, Morag knew only love...*

That he loved her in his own small way came as a privilege, one he would cherish for the rest of his life. Maybe she'd known it the day she entered his office... so frightened, yet so resolute in her endeavours.

He remembered her letter to Inspector Edwards, feeling his eyes grow heavier and the desire to sleep descend upon him. As he drifted away, feeling his head roll forward, he felt that wonderful sense of fulfilment, knowing he had hidden her letter and not betrayed her trust...

... He opened his eyes and immediately winced at the sharp pain in his neck. How long he'd been asleep he had no idea, as time seemed to have played tricks with his senses, and for the briefest of moments he completely forgot where he was.

A door opened and closed.

He couldn't quite work out if it was the front or the back door, but there had been the unmistakeable sound of a loud click as a latch fell into place...

Raising his head, he vigorously rubbed his neck and rotated his head left then right. "Hello?" he called, desperately trying to gather his senses. He thought it might be a customer paying a late call, and quickly glanced at the carriage clock. The light had dimmed somewhat, yet he was still able to make out the time and was alarmed to see that he'd slept for nearly an hour.

He was about to call out again when the sound of someone trying to walk softly along the corridor to his office drifted menacingly into his room.

His door was slightly ajar, and he watched, helplessly, as it opened wide and a figure stepped into view.

181

Susan paused and stared for what seemed an eternity, gazing anxiously into the thick foliage of undergrowth and trees, trying to decipher anything that might be moving, desperate to see the face of her husband. The more she strained her eyes, the less she felt she could actually see; the more she called out his name, the more the forest seemed to absorb her cries.

She'd been calling his name for well over an hour, hearing also the distant cries of Dodson and Kenick. The echoes of their calls, sharp and penetrating, resonated between the trees and created distorted reference points around her. Her own desperate wanderings, with no rationale as to direction, had taken her into the heart of the forest, to the point where she feared for her own ability to find her way back to Frobisher Hall.

Wearing the jacket and skirt from that morning, her stockings had become ripped as the nettles and twisted branches from fallen trees had cut into her legs like teeth rearing up from the undergrowth, full of spite and venom. Her shoes, so comfortable around the Hall, now gave little or no resistance to the mud and stones that both soaked and dug relentlessly into her feet.

Pausing for breath, she turned to her left, certain that that was the direction she last heard Dodson calling out.

Silence.

Even the forest seemed to be holding its breath, as though creeping up on her like some assailant ready to strike and not wishing to make a sound.

To her right, a twig snapped…

She spun round, straining both her eyes and ears and resisting the urge to call out Lawrence's name. Her mouth was dry, and a cold sweat was making her feel clammy and uncomfortable as her blouse stuck to her skin. Brushing a hand across her face, she swallowed and tried to listen for the voices of her companions.

It was as though the forest had swallowed them up.

"Oh, Susan…" A voice, deep and quite hoarse, came at her from all directions, immediately causing her to swing violently around.

"Lawrence!" she instinctively cried out. "Is that you…?!"

"Oh, Susan… I see you…" The voice came from a bottomless pit, a place where nothing good or decent might live, a darkness that was full of hate and malice.

"Who are you?" she whispered, finding it hard to speak with a breath that came in short spasmodic jerks. With a dreadful realisation that enclosed her within its terrible grip, she realised she was completely surrounded by undergrowth, with no room to manoeuvre or react if anyone should rise up out of the foliage around her.

"I know you, Susan… I know where you live… Do you love her, Susan?" The voice penetrated deep into her mind… "Would you kill for her, Susan?"

"I know you…" Susan whispered, "your voice…" Like echoes that permeated through her mind, mingling beguilingly with the whispered mutterings of the forest, she clung desperately to past events, faces glimpsed and words spoken… reaching through the mists of time…

"Help me to bring Morag home" The words dripped from the end of a reptilian tongue that reached out and wrapped itself around her. "Help me to bring her home to Amble Lodge, and we can both enjoy her." The words became clearer, more distinct.

Susan became aware of someone standing behind her.

Whoever it was wasn't so close as to be an immediate threat, but close enough for her to feel eyes boring deep within her, mentally undressing her and toying with her sexual desires. What she felt both alarmed and excited her – a feeling that she might abandon all inhibitions and grow to love the woman with the red hair, if only she might listen to the wonderfully hypnotic voice behind her.

Slowly, yet with eager anticipation, she turned round, feeling her legs cry out in agony as they brushed against a mass of nettles. Swallowing hard and trying to keep a hold on her courage, she finally beheld the dark figure of Morgan Treave standing in a clearing only yards behind her.

Though he was smiling, it was impossible for her to distinguish what exactly was a grin or an erupted parting of a mouth, it being so twisted and deformed, with shattered teeth that resembled broken gravestones. The realisation of who he was came from the cold and hateful stare that emanated from his one eye, and she was suddenly there...

That day in Frobisher Hall when the snow came... The shooting... Harry and William out in the forest... Morgan Treave thundering through the house... head bleeding... cursing... swearing revenge...

She tried to look away, but the look in his eye...

Like some horrendous cyclops it held her entranced, as though readying her for some terrible slaughter.

"Help me... Help me, Susan... Help me bring Morag home to Amble Lodge, and we can both enjoy her delights..."

His mouth twisted up in a horrifically contrived smile that closed the black hole that had once been an eye. The full horror of the injuries inflicted upon him by Morag became hideously apparent; the scars were so pronounced they crisscrossed his face like mountain ridges, with deep pitted holes that seemed to carve deep into his blotched skin.

Susan swallowed hard, trying to restrain the churning sensation in her stomach. She was filled with both revulsion and fascination as she marvelled at the results of Morag's attack. Above her the clouds had thickened to a near black-grey and hung so low they threatened to descend down below the tops of the trees to finally envelop her in their twilight world.

A distant rumble of thunder echoed across the Frobisher Estate.

"Feast your eyes upon her handiwork," Morgan Treave

hissed through his broken mouth. "But help me bring her home, let me once again enjoy her body, and I'll forgive her all that she has done."

Susan was aware of a finality about his words that seemed to signal an end to his searching; as though, in her, he'd found the means by which he might bring Morag back to Amble Lodge. Within his one solitary eye she saw the depth of his madness and knew that the people she loved and was devoted to would never be safe from his curse.

Feeling the churning in her stomach ease and the pounding of her heart lessen to something near normality, she calmly reached into her jacket pocket and pulled out the revolver that had sat in their drawer in the cottage, seemingly waiting for this opportunity. As she raised it, she pulled the firing pin back, taking a deep breath and letting it out slowly as she finally took aim at the terrible apparition before her.

As she squeezed the trigger she muttered, "I will never let you hurt her again."

"Susan! Susan!"

Lawrence's desperate cry broke her concentration, causing her to glance sideways towards his general direction, straining her eyes as she caught sight of him through the trees.

"Susan!" Again, his cry… this time closer.

Lowering the revolver Susan replied, "Lawrence… Lawrence… Where are you…?"

She swung round in an arc, before realising her mistake. As she raised the revolver again, this time moving to her left so as not to create an imbalance in her stance, she quickly aimed the barrel directly at the area where Morgan Treave had been standing.

There was nothing to be seen.

13

The storm that had been threatening all afternoon finally broke and erupted across the Bodmin landscape with a savage fury that took many people by surprise. As the skies opened up to the torrential downpour, workers hurrying home on the Frobisher Estate huddled for shelter under trees, staring at the flashes of lightning that split the sky and illuminated their ghostly features. With no sign of easing, it hammered relentlessly at Frobisher Hall and the tiny cottages scattered around the estate.

In Sunrise Cottage Ellen Carfax stirred her nettle tea and settled back in her rocking chair, stoking the fire in her dining room. Branok had seated himself opposite, and she smiled, knowing he'd seen the young policeman safely home and made it back before the deluge. But she was also aware of a strange and troubled look in his eyes, as though his newfound peace and tranquillity was about to end.

***

In Susan's cottage, she'd run a hot bath and slowly undressed her husband, easing his injured arm out of its strapping and wrapping her arms around him as she buried her head into his chest. Helping him into the bath, she'd stood beside him, slowly removing her jacket and skirt before sliding off the tattered remains of her stockings. When she'd finally removed her undergarments, she'd felt his hand reach out and push gently between her legs.

★★★

The fireplace in the lounge at Frobisher Hall had also been lit, as the day's humidity had lifted and a strange coldness had descended with the rain. With the curtains drawn, the fury of the storm outside had been all but shut out, with only the occasional flash of lightning penetrating through a crack in the drapes. With each rumble of thunder Frobisher Hall creaked and moaned, its very walls sighing with the force of the gale. Rafters groaned wearily as the wind rattled through gaps in the eaves, blowing furiously through the servants' rooms situated in the attic.

Seated around the fireplace in the lounge, Morag, Harry and Inspector Edwards eyed the roaring log fire as it spat and crackled, burning its way through several large logs recently added by Morag. Once she'd poured whiskies for her two companions, she returned to the drinks cabinet to pour herself a glass of lemonade before returning to her place beside Harry on the large sofa chair.

"I'd suggest a toast," Morag eyed her glass speculatively, "but considering the situation we seem to be in, I thought we might wait a while."

She sipped her drink and straightened out a small crease in her dress. It was sleeveless, peach in colour and made of silk and chiffon, with tiny beads that accentuated the curve of her waist whilst slightly flattening her bust. She'd bought it in London, in a beautiful shop just off Regent Street and had worn it the night she met Noel Coward. As with every dress she'd tried on, Harry had insisted she let him run his hands delicately over her body, drifting his fingers across every curve, every line where the silken material ended and her bare, freckly skin emerged, goose-bumped and yearning for his touch.

She'd not worn it since that night, and now, though a raging storm roared throughout her home and in her heart, she felt herself momentarily back at that cocktail party, the eyes of everyone in the room upon her and the gentle touch of the man she loved upon her arm.

Knowing Harry would later unclasp it and let it fall from her body thrilled her with excitement...

There was a knock at the door and Dodson appeared.

"Will you be requiring anything else this evening?" He stood erect, with eyes that stared just past Morag's.

"No, Dodson. Please thank Mrs Chambers for a lovely meal." Morag smiled.

"Very good, Your Ladyship." He bowed slightly and took a couple of steps back.

"Oh, by the way, Dodson, thank you for your help today. I believe you and Kenick helped Mrs Matthews in the search for her husband."

"Thank you, Lady Frobisher. Yes, found safe but a little bruised. I shall pass on your thanks to Kenick." Letting the slightest trace of a smile flicker across his face, he again bowed, turned and walked from the room.

"Sounds like an eventful day," Edwards said, sipping his whisky and delivering the words with a heavy hint of inquisitiveness.

"Yes... It seems Lawrence managed to get himself into some difficulty out on the estate today. He says his horse threw him... Was startled by something..."

"Is he okay?" Edwards asked, his inquisitive tone changing to one of concern.

"Yes, but I think he was badly shaken... Dislocated his shoulder... He said a woman helped set it back and looked after him until he was recovered enough to make his way home."

"Lawrence Matthews on horseback..." Edwards chuckled and shook his head. "He does certainly know how to get himself into tight corners."

"It could have been worse," Harry reflected. "Do we know who exactly did help him? I'd like to ride over there and thank her personally."

"I spoke briefly to Susan before dinner. I asked Mrs Chambers to send something over to them; I think Susan just wanted him over at the cottage and for them to spend some time by themselves. I'll talk further with her tomorrow... She did seem anxious about something, but I wasn't sure if it was just the shock of what happened to Lawrence."

Harry squeezed her hand. "At least he's home safe with Susan."

"I'm glad they're both happy and settled. I lost an extremely good constable when he decided to stay here and work for you." Edwards leaned forward and placed his glass on the table. "I must admit there's a certain magical charm about this place; I can see why he settled here."

"Bodmin is a very old and ancient town, Inspector." Harry turned his head slightly towards Edwards. "It can be traced back to the Doomsday Book and probably beyond. Some of its history is very dark and mysterious, and many myths and legends abound about the local area, especially up on Bodmin Moor. When William and I were young, Father would tell us stories of the smugglers who'd plied their trade in the backstreets of the town and hid their illicit cargo out on the moors. Then there were the stories of the spirits that haunt the wilderness out there." He pointed in the general direction of the windows. "They say when the wind turns from a south-westerly on a full moon, the spirits of lost souls out on the moor can be heard calling."

"Hmm, quite so, Lord Frobisher." Edwards eased himself

back and added, "Since my encounter with Old Solomon, I now understand what you mean."

Harry smiled. "We owe Old Solomon a debt of gratitude we can never fully repay. Just after Christmas, Morag and I visited his grave over in Temple. Nobody tends to it, and the headstone is quite plain... Yet I feel him sometimes... watching over us..." Reaching into his pocket, he pulled out his briar pipe and tentatively searched for an ashtray on the table. With a graceful dexterity he found it and tapped the contents of his pipe into it. "Like I said, Bodmin is a very old place, lots of ancient buildings and a wealth of memories. If ever a place could echo and reverberate with ghostly memories from the past, if a town could make someone feel as though they were stepping back in time, then that place is Bodmin. Once, when I was a boy, I stood under the monument looking across the town. I would ride over there for some peace and solitude. I remember thinking what it might be like to write a book about the place, to be able to capture the very essence of the town and the surrounding moors."

"And did you, Lord Frobisher?" Edwards asked.

"Maybe I will someday, Inspector. Maybe I will."

"Well, you should, Harry." Morag nudged his side, startling him.

The ensuing silence hung heavy with unasked questions and reflections upon the day's events. Outside, the storm raged with no indication of a let-up in its ferocity. The three of them sipped their drinks and relaxed, waiting, Morag mused, for the right moment to say what needed to be said...

Finally, she said, "We have a piano recital to attend tomorrow afternoon at the town hall..." She paused as her words, a prelude to the main point of her comment, settled on the room. "I'm worried about placing Harry at risk—"

"Morag—" Harry tried to interrupt.

"No, Harry... If someone is trying to kill you..." Her voice cut across his, drowning out his objection. "I'm not going to lose you, Harry. I'm not letting you take the same risk you took last year." Her voice, though stoic and resolute, trembled slightly.

Edwards scratched his chin. "You know, it might be an ideal opportunity to bring our killer out into the open..." He held up his hand, momentarily silencing Morag. "Like we said, Captain Grant was murdered possibly because he knew the identity of the Fourth Rook... Whatever way you look at that letter, he needed your help and implied there was an answer hidden somewhere."

Morag wanted to reply, was desperate to stop this idiotic idea she saw gestating deep within her brother-in-law's eyes, but reason and common sense, as usual the great restraints that got in her way as she lived her life, each placed a hand on her shoulders and calmed her rising Celtic temper.

"The plain and simple truth is, you have a choice to make concerning tomorrow." Edwards spoke clearly, and Morag wondered if he'd rehearsed what he was about to say. "You either stay here and hide from this killer – and also from the people of Bodmin who are probably desperate to see you both and certainly welcome you, Morag, into their hearts, especially after what you went through last year – or you attend the recital. I know you run the risk, Harry, but I'll have some of Sergeant Cadan's men in plain clothes in attendance." He leaned forward, lifted his glass and eyed it closely. "But most importantly of all, both of you will be meeting the people who are still reeling from what happened here last year and are now trying to come to terms with two murders in the last couple of days... If there was ever a time when they needed the strength of the Frobisher name, it's now." He took a large gulp and drained his glass.

Morag sighed and shook her head, a pointless exercise as the realisation of the sense of what he'd said worked its way through her body, allaying her protestations and arresting the words her heart so desperately wanted her to say.

She felt Harry grasp her hand.

"It makes sense, Morag. We can't hide away," he whispered.

"And I can't lose you, Harry." Morag looked at her husband, willing him to reach out and brush his hand against her face.

As if reading her mind, Harry reached out and placed his hand against her cheek. The spiritual bond between them lit up the room, as though another flash of lightning had erupted.

"I'll never leave you, Morag. You know that…"

"Aye," she muttered, holding her hand up and clasping his. "You'd better not, Harry Frobisher."

Edwards coughed. "So, that's settled, then. I'll arrange for Sergeant Cadan to deploy some of his men in the building… Not sure if I should be there or not… I might end up scaring them off—"

"If they come in the first place," Morag whispered.

"Yes, I know." Edwards looked across at the two huge paintings of Lord Alfred and Lady Margaret. "I'm working on a hunch here, but I can't see any other way around this. Captain Grant came here looking for your help, Harry, and now he's dead. Like I said back at the station, I think they'll want you dead before you act on his letter."

"I know," Harry agreed.

"There is another thing…" Edwards held up his glass and smiled at Morag.

She returned his smile and nodded her head.

"Someone was seen leaving 13 Creek Lane this morning before we got there." He stood up and walked across to the drinks' cabinet. "A local woman called Annette Myers was seen leaving the premises. She was carrying something under her arm, but our witness wasn't too sure what it was." Pouring himself another drink he turned and looked at Harry.

"Harry, dear, Cyril is pouring another drink; your glass is nearly empty…" Morag gently soothed.

"Thank you, Inspector, that would be nice." Harry shuffled

forward, lifted up his glass and drained the remnants. "Does anyone remember hearing a shot?"

"Good question." Edwards refilled Harry's glass. "From all accounts, nobody heard a single shot. Nothing."

"And yet this Annette Myers was seen leaving the house," Morag said vaguely, trying to recall the name.

"It seems, according to Sergeant Cadan, that 13 Creek Lane has a rather dark history." Edwards replaced the whisky bottle and returned to his seat. "It's owned by an elderly couple in Bodmin… Seems they own several small cottages and flats, and let them out to local people and army officers on detachment from the garrison. I intend to pay these two a visit tomorrow morning after I interview Annette Myers."

"You don't think an old couple had anything to do with Captain Grant's death, other than owning the house in which they died, do you?" Harry asked.

"Well, that depends…" Edwards sipped his whisky. "When you consider who the previous occupant was…"

The ensuing silence was broken by the chimes of the grandfather clock ringing out 10pm.

Not being one for melodrama, Edwards continued coldly, "It seems 13 Creek Lane once belonged to one Edwina Baker…"

"My God," Morag whispered. She already had her glass in her hand and was resting it on her lap, but as much as she tried she couldn't lift it to her lips.

"Yes…" continued Edwards. "Edwina Baker, formerly Nurse Baker of Amble Lodge and accomplice of Doctor Morgan Treave."

If it wasn't for the reassuring touch of Harry's hand, she feared she might lose total control over her senses. Her mind filled with memories she thought she'd finally laid to rest.…

Her padded room, the chains, and the straitjacket that almost crushed the air from her lungs… The injections… His visits in the night… The screams around her… And then her… Nurse Baker… sitting beside

*her and touching her... Softly singing... Gently kissing... touching...
probing... pushing...*

"It's okay, Morag..." Harry's voice came to her, as it always
did, soothing, helping. "It's okay to be afraid."

The images receded, as though swept away by the sound of
Harry's voice. Like malevolent creatures they scurried into the
corners of her mind, peering out from darkened recesses.

"Have you found her?" Morag had regained enough
strength to ask the question.

"Well, it seems she was found." Edwards stared into the
fireplace and Morag followed his gaze. "You see, I was told she
lived over in Amble Lodge, and for all intents and purposes she
did. But she also rented 13 Creek Lane, where she spent time
living with her twin sister—"

"Her twin sister?" Harry said abruptly.

"From what I gather. Local people caught the occasional
glimpse of her, but she never left the house. So, I don't have an
accurate description of her—"

"A twin sister?" repeated Morag.

"Yes. And I desperately need to find her." Edwards turned
his attention back to Morag and Harry.

"You said Nurse Baker had been found," Harry prompted
impatiently.

"She was, whilst you both were on honeymoon. It seems
she made her way back to 13 Creek Lane and hanged herself
from the main beam in the kitchen..."

With these words, the storm outside abated, as though the
fury of the tempest had been stayed by this news. With the
sudden calm outside, the atmosphere inside the lounge became
almost unbearable, and Morag struggled to find her breath.

"I wasn't aware of this until today, when—"

Morag looked across and saw a distant gaze in Edwards'
eyes.

"When what?" she asked.

"When I was at 13 Creek Lane with you both and then later with Sergeant Cadan…"

For the first time in all the years she'd known him, Cyril Edwards looked lost and a little bewildered. Taking a sip from her glass, she eyed him closely, trying to read his mind, aware of a dreadful aura surrounding him.

"It was the glasses on the table and an overwhelming feeling of something terrible… something beyond the discovery of Captain Grant… All I knew was that someone had hanged themselves from that beam." Edwards trembled and gulped his whisky. "She took off her reading glasses before…"

"Why didn't Sergeant Cadan explain this to us?" Harry interrupted. "He was with us this morning over at the hospital. Why didn't he tell us?"

"If the truth be known," Edwards replied, "Sergeant Cadan has been shaken by all this. I think his experience last year, and now this… You see, it was he who found the body… Some children were throwing stones at the kitchen window, and one of them peered in and saw her. We don't know how long she'd been there… I think it was his intention to visit here and formally tell you. Then, of course, there was the incident on the train, followed by the death of Captain Grant."

"But why hang herself?" Harry mused.

"Guilt… Remorse…" Edwards shrugged his shoulders. "It does eliminate her from our enquiries… but there does remain the question of her sister…"

"When did she leave the house?" Morag asked.

"We don't know. It could have been anytime in the last few months, since November."

"Do you think this woman, Annette Myers, murdered Captain Grant?" Harry eased himself forward; Morag noticed the familiar pained expression on his face and knew his leg was troubling him.

"I imagine she would have certainly seen his body. If she

didn't kill him, then why didn't she report his death to the police?"

"This isn't going to go away, is it?" Morag whispered.

"No… it's not…" Edwards sighed, before adding, almost reluctantly, "There is another person we need to be aware of… Someone you might already be aware of, Harry."

"Well?" Morag drained her glass.

"I was initially sent down here by a colonel up in Whitehall. It was his idea for me to visit you and investigate Lord Frobisher's apparent involvement with The Nest of Rooks… It is his suspicion that Harry might be the Fourth Rook—"

"Aye," laughed Morag, before adding, "and his father was the bloody Kaiser himself." She glared at Edwards… "Are you completely out of your mind, Cyril?"

Edwards ignored her comment. "Colonel Charles Standish, Harry. Have you ever heard of him?"

Morag glanced at her husband.

"Only through conversations with Grant." Harry ran his hand through his hair, grimacing slightly as he tried to recall. "Grant mentioned his name once… but I can't remember if he referred to him as one of the Rooks."

"You never mentioned him before," Edwards asked.

"Inspector, I met many people during my time in France. After what happened to me it would be a bloody miracle to remember any of them."

Edwards nodded in agreement.

"Why does he suspect Harry?" Morag stood up and made her way over to the drinks' cabinet.

"Because of his association with Captain Grant. From what I gather, Military Intelligence is groping around in the dark desperate to try and find this Fourth Rook. They knew you'd met with Grant, and had you watched. But you were recalled to your regiment, and shortly after that…" Edwards paused. "Anyway, that's really just the start."

"Because?" Morag's voice was cold.

"Because of those months Harry spent in Europe after his treatment in London for his wounds." Edwards turned directly to Harry. "Agents working for Military Intelligence had you followed when you were away from the front line, Harry. When you were injured and brought back to London, they were going to question you. As you know, those months following your discharge from hospital are a bit of a grey area."

"He was ill, Cyril." Morag poured herself another drink and wandered across to the nearest window. Pulling back the drapes, she stared out. The storm had certainly eased, but the rain still fell, and minor flashes could still be seen across the distant moors. "You saw how ill Harry was even when he returned last year." She turned and walked across to the rear of the sofa and leaned against the back, stroking the side of Harry's face.

He reached his hand back to clasp hers.

"Harry," Edwards eyed his friend across the small table, "if I actually believed there was any truth in this story, then, believe me, we would be having a completely different conversation and in different surroundings. I didn't like Colonel Standish from the moment I sat down in his office. There's something about the fellow that doesn't fit. But that is my personal opinion. What's important are the reasons for him to make these suggestions and to demand my personal involvement in the case."

"Could he...?" Morag wanted to say it, but stopped as she saw a brief smile flicker across her brother-in-law's face.

"He might well be," Edwards confirmed. "You see, I had that immediate suspicion the other day in his office – he might have been connected with Archie Cummings on the train."

"Did he employ the services of someone to kill Captain Grant?" Harry asked.

"Did *he* kill Captain Grant?" Edwards added.

"I thought you said he was up in London?" Morag asked hesitantly.

"That's what I thought. But, as I said, I didn't trust the man from the moment we first met. Before I took that train down to Cornwall the other day, I asked a few of my associates who work in Whitehall to keep an eye on him and supply any useful information. All hush, hush, and they were happy to oblige." Edwards flicked his moustache, right then left. "I had two communications reach me here in Bodmin, telegrams that arrived at the military garrison. The first one was just after I arrived. It read: 'Subject is dark horse'... When I'm away from London investigating cases, I'll sometimes send a telegram to Scotland Yard requesting small amounts of information about someone – usually I just want to confirm my suspicions. The phrase 'Subject is dark horse' tells me that information is limited or restricted. And, believe me, for my colleagues in Scotland Yard and Whitehall to send such a message means Standish really is a dark horse..." He sipped his whisky and Morag noticed that familiar confident glow in his eyes. "The second one was more troubling. After I informed Scotland Yard of the death of Archie Cummings, I received a telegram confirming my message... The telegram then went on to say 'Subject has not been seen since yesterday'."

"So, where is he?" Harry asked, squeezing Morag's hand.

"I've no idea. Although my contacts at Scotland Yard would have handled this carefully and not aroused suspicion in the corridors of Whitehall, they would have been thorough. If Standish chose to stay at home or visit friends, I would have known about it. If he'd chosen to disappear for a few days fishing or painting, I would have known about it. But to give my colleagues the slip like that..." Edwards reflected, and Morag noticed that glow in his eyes burn brighter as he contemplated the turn of events.

"So, he could be down here." Morag moved away from the back of the sofa and made her way round to finally sit back down beside Harry. "But why send you down here if he was coming down here as well?"

"I don't know that he is. He might well be one of the Rooks and has gone into hiding." Edwards held his glass to his lips and eyed the last few drops of whisky. He smiled. "You know, in a strange way, Colonel Standish and maybe Annette Myers are my only two viable suspects... I think..." He swallowed the last of his drink but held his gaze on a painting, situated between the two giant portraits of Lord Alfred and Lady Margaret, hanging directly above the huge fireplace.

Though it was smaller, it seemed to naturally fill the space above the fireplace. It was in oils, of Frobisher Hall, beautifully set, with the twin towers and battlements silhouetted against a dark and brooding sky.

Morag followed his gaze and noticed the troubled look on his face.

She'd felt it the very first time she'd come to the house and set eyes on the artwork.

Framed by a simple wooden mount, the image appeared to change perspective when viewed from different positions within the lounge. Each time she looked at it, she was overwhelmed by the love that seemed to emanate from it, yet always felt as though the position of the painter was never quite right; as though they'd chosen to paint the house whilst sitting out of sight of anyone looking out from a window. Move to the right, or left, and the perspective changed...

Yet, did it?

She stared intently at her brother-in-law's face, searching for any signs of an emotional response.

Edwards was studying it with a professional interest, as though he were scrutinising a piece of evidence. Still seated, he drew slightly away, then moved closer. "That's a rather interesting painting," he muttered.

"The famous painting of Frobisher Hall, Cyril," Morag announced.

"Oh, not that thing," Harry laughed.

Feeling it was time to lighten the conversation, Morag said, "Harry, tell Cyril about its history."

"Not tonight, Morag," Harry sighed.

"No, please do… I can't make up my mind." Edwards held his gaze upon the painting.

"There's nothing really to tell." Harry settled back in the sofa. "A few years before the outbreak of war, before William and I were shipped off to France, the thing just appeared, here in this room and above the fireplace. Nobody knew where it had come from."

"That's not quite true, Harry," Morag corrected.

"I know… but the inspector's probably tired, and it's getting late." Harry shook his head.

"I think what my husband is reluctant to say," Morag announced with a mischievous grin, "is that, although it suddenly appeared out of nowhere, his father, Lord Alfred, seemed to know where it might have come from."

"Yes," agreed Harry, "but he never said."

"Strange how it just appeared." Edwards stood up and approached the fireplace, moving his body to accommodate his critical eye. "It's beautiful… Whoever painted it must have loved the place immensely… Yet it seems—"

"As though they were an outcast and couldn't be seen painting it?" Harry held his head forward.

Morag noticed he was in danger of letting his glass slide off his lap. She reached forward and quickly lifted it away.

Edwards frowned, drawing closer to the painting. "Hmm, something like that."

"Mother hated it." Harry raised his head. "She wanted to get rid of it. But Father wanted to keep it. She was furious to think someone had actually found their way into the house, taken down the old painting and hung this one up in its place."

"What was the old painting?" Edwards asked.

"That's the point, Inspector," Harry chuckled, though it was neither humorous nor sincere, "nobody can remember."

"Well…" Edwards shook off the hypnotic effect of the painting. Still standing, he turned to Harry and Morag. "We all have a busy day tomorrow. I'll be in Bodmin in the morning conducting interviews and meeting with Sergeant Cadan. I propose we meet over breakfast and I'll take you through what I want you both to do during the piano recital. May I borrow one of your cars for the morning?"

"Certainly, Inspector," Harry climbed a little unsteadily to his feet, "take the Austin… Drive straight out of the front gate and turn left. Just follow the main road into Bodmin."

"Thank you, both." Edwards moved towards Morag and took her hand. "My dear Morag, the both of you are the only family I have left in this world. Since Elisha died… Well, I've…" He sighed deeply.

Morag squeezed his hand and drew him close. Reaching forward she kissed him lightly on the cheek and said, "Cyril, we owe you everything… Our lives… Our love… No man will ever be more welcome than you at Frobisher Hall." She stepped across to the fireplace and rang a small electrical buzzer under the lip of the great mantlepiece.

When Dodson entered, after a polite knock at the door, Morag said, "Ah, Dodson, please show Inspector Edwards to his room."

★★★

Morag opened her eyes slowly, aware that the rain had now ceased and a peacefulness had returned to the world outside their bedroom windows. She was wrapped in the arms of her husband, their naked bodies entwined in a beautiful embrace; and she sighed, still feeling his warmth inside her.

Nestled there within his arms, she felt protected and loved. His breath, deep and rhythmic, swept across her shoulder, tingling her nerves and soothing her back to sleep.

It was still dark, with a tiny crack of moonlight flitting across the bedroom from a gap in the curtains. From downstairs came the tick... tick... of the grandfather clock, and occasionally, from somewhere deep within the house, a creak cut through the silence as Frobisher Hall turned in its sleep, troubled by the ghosts of its chequered past.

Though drowsy, Morag couldn't find that peaceful descent back into slumber and so lay next to Harry, her mind spinning with endless thoughts and different interpretations of the previous day's events. She was also keenly aware of her experience in the bath; something she'd not spoken to Harry about. Her own reasoning was that she'd fallen asleep and woken in a panic; but why was the door to the bathroom closed when she'd left it open?

And then there was Harry himself.

Ever since their meeting with Canon Trebarwith after they'd left Bodmin Police Station, he'd been subdued to the point of morose. She knew his eyes had been irritating him lately, and she decided that, in the morning, she'd discuss the option of consulting with a specialist. She also knew he was concerned about the events unfolding around them, as she was herself; but he felt it acutely, his apparent inability to protect her from whatever was stalking them.

Canon Trebarwith had been his usual charming self and had wholeheartedly agreed to hold a small service of remembrance by the Walter Raleigh Gilbert Monument on Sunday after the morning service at church. She'd been impressed by the photographs on his study wall – memories of his work as an army chaplain during the war – the letters of thanks he'd received from both soldiers and the families of those he'd personally written to informing them of the death of a loved one.

Sometimes they came to me and all I could do was hold their hand and comfort them as they drifted away...

She recalled his words and nestled further into Harry's outstretched arms, closing her eyes and desperately trying to banish the terrible images that came to her.

It was then that she heard it – a distant sound that came from somewhere deep within the house. At first, she thought she'd finally drifted off and was pleasantly dreaming, until she realised she was wide awake and staring across the bedroom to that flicker of moonlight that had captivated her attention.

It was the sound of music, beautiful and familiar.

She eased herself from Harry's embrace and raised her head.

It was now more distinct, coming from the hallway.

Straining her ears, Morag moved to the side of the bed until she was seated, and brushed her hair back from her face. The music was certainly familiar, but through her sleepiness she just couldn't place it.

It did not, though, take her long to realise that the sound was coming from the polyphon in the hallway. She'd once asked Harry why it wasn't situated in the lounge, or somewhere more comfortable, for them to enjoy. He'd replied that it had been a gift to his mother from a visiting prince from Austria, who'd had it shipped over from Germany as a thank you for her hospitality on his tour of England. It had been the prince who'd suggested it be positioned in the hallway, so the whole of Frobisher Hall could enjoy its beautiful music.

Morag had learnt how to operate it from Harry's verbal instructions and so knew of the large collection of discs neatly stacked in a cupboard to one side. Though she'd played many of them, she couldn't remember playing this one…

And then it came to her…

It was playing the overture from Mozart's *Don Giovanni*.

At this sudden realisation, she stood up, grabbed her gown and slipped it on, pausing briefly to consider waking Harry. Thinking better of it, and not waiting to pull on her slippers, she walked quickly to the door and inched it open.

It came to her now, strangely sinister yet equally soothing.

Peering out into the passageway, she wondered if one of the staff might have been cleaning it, but immediately banished the thought. Easing herself out into the hallway, she gently closed the door and made her way to the top of the staircase, hoping she might bump into Edwards along the way.

Pausing at the top of the stairs, she glanced nervously around, scanning the hallway below her for any signs of movement. The music was quite distinct now, with musical notes fluttering up around her like delicate butterflies. Not wanting to call out, for fear of waking others in the house, Morag descended the stairs quickly and stealthily, ready to challenge the person responsible for this idiotic caper.

There was no one to be seen.

She dashed across to the lounge and opened the door.

Nothing – just three empty glasses on the table, testament to the presence of herself and her companions the previous evening.

Walking back to the polyphon, she eyed it suspiciously, watching as the metal disc inside worked its way relentlessly round, wound up by someone who would live to regret they'd ever thought this might be a humorous trick to pull. Flicking her hair back, she felt anger and frustration compete for control of her emotions, though she also knew they were quickly losing out to intrigue and a hint of fear. Why should anyone want to do this? Maybe the disc had been left in there and not run itself out the last time someone had played it.

She yawned and turned to the grandfather clock.

It was approaching 3am.

A door creaked behind her, immediately arresting her attention.

The sound came from the library, and Morag instinctively called out, "Who is it?"

Her initial thought was that it might be Edwards and that he was following a line of investigation; maybe in a second his face would peer around the doorway.

There was no such friendly encounter.

The hallway was dark, with small pockets of natural light spilling in from rooms where the doors had been left open. As she approached the library door, the darkness increased, and she looked around for a candle and holder, immediately spying one left on top of the cabinet next to the door.

Striking a match, she lit the candle and tentatively entered.

Even in daylight the library stood imposing and intimidating, with rows of rare and ancient editions lining the countless shelves that reached from floor to ceiling. But at night, in the gloom and darkened shadows that enveloped her in their dreadful embrace, the room reminded her of something out of one of those Edgar Allan Poe stories she sometimes read to Harry.

Moving the candle from side to side, Morag held her breath as shapes flickered and materialised around her. The floor beneath her bare feet felt cold, until she moved to the centre of the room and stepped on a large rug that brought instant relief.

Listening, she turned slowly around.

The false door amongst the rows of books was open.

For what seemed an eternity, Morag stood staring at it, trying to hold her nerves in place and understand why it should be like this when she'd ordered it be nailed shut the previous year. But the more she stared at it, the more it stood mocking her, inviting her to enter the darkness beyond. As though to prompt her, beguiling her to take those tentative steps forward, the false door creaked a little on its hinges.

Holding the candle further away, she noticed her hand was shaking, causing little drops of wax to splatter onto her wrist. Though she saw this, Morag felt nothing, only a familiar fear growing inside of her, a recognition of the tormented world in which she'd once existed and the terrible realisation that the genesis of that nightmare was probably waiting for her within that darkened secret passage.

Feebly she shook her head, feeling tears begin to well up.

"Morag..." The voice was warm and inviting. "Dearest Morag... I'm waiting for you..." It drifted from the secret passageway like some ghoulish voice from a crypt.

As though caught in a trance she was powerless to resist, Morag felt herself pulled inexorably towards the voice, that strange voice that seemed so peaceful... and yet so...

Oblivious to the chairs and table she bumped into, she stepped slowly towards the darkness, towards that padded cell and the straitjacket. With no thought of anything else in her life, she moved towards that place called Amble Lodge, that place where his cold hands had touched her and his foul breath had swept across her face...

As she reached the door, she paused, hearing a voice, a beautiful voice that was loving and sincere. It called to her from somewhere in the house, shining a light to guide her home...

She reached her free hand into the passageway, illuminating the darkness with the candle. As she did so, a face appeared, hideously disfigured and staring at her with such hatred she started to feel herself pitch forward in a daze. Her senses were filled with the pungent smell of stagnant air, as though a coffin had been opened.

"Morag?" The voice grew louder, nearer... "Morag? Where are you?" There was fear and concern set deep in the words. Though it was hesitant and uncertain, it was also familiar; it was the voice of the man she loved.

"Harry..." Morag stuttered. "Harry..."

She heard Harry enter the library and stumble frantically towards her. For one brief moment she saw the hideous features of Morgan Treave snarl with evil intent before withdrawing into the darkness. As she closed the false door, Morag turned and slumped back, jamming it shut and holding out her arms.

"I'm here, Harry..." she cried. "I'm here... in front of you."

When he finally caught her in his arms, she felt her tears roll freely down her cheeks.

14

Saturday 23rd May…

Inspector Edwards eyed the front of Rose Cottage and stifled a yawn. He'd slept heavily during the night, finding the bed in the guest bedroom at Frobisher Hall utterly relaxing and without the slightest imperfection. Unashamedly ostentatious and more suited to a visiting member of the Royal Family, it had wrapped itself around him and soothed him into immediate slumber. When he'd closed his eyes, he'd listened to the house creak and groan; like himself, it settled and relaxed, holding him within its embrace.

So deep was his sleep, it was as though the very atmosphere in the house had drugged him, whispering words spoken by unseen figures that hovered by his bed, studying him and running invisible fingers across his troubled face.

He'd missed breakfast, choosing instead to visit Susan and Lawrence's cottage. After a brief exchange of pleasantries, and a comment about learning to ride a horse, he'd left them both to enjoy their own breakfast and sought the small Austin Twenty, which he found parked in the garage between the Daimler and the Rolls Royce. The keys were hung on the wall, and he'd driven the car around to the front of the house and left it there, engine running, whilst he quickly made his way back inside to find Morag and Harry.

It was Dodson who informed him that Lord and Lady Frobisher were still in bed.

Knowing he was already running late, and that he had much to complete in Bodmin before the piano recital, he'd asked Dodson to pass on his regards to his hosts and to tell them he would meet them later, before he climbed back into the car and drove into town.

Parking the car over at the police station, he'd found Sergeant Cadan filling in reports from the night before, and he nodded his acquiesce when Edwards asked if he knew the way to Rose Cottage.

Now, standing before the cottage, he was filled with memories of a similar place in a small coastal town, not far from Dundee. He'd spent his honeymoon there with Elisha and dreamed one day that they might settle there. They'd walked barefoot upon the golden sands and watched the sun set...

The most beautiful woman he'd ever known... and a love he knew would never die...

Edwards forced the memories from his mind before they became too painful. Glancing around he noticed faces peering out from neighbouring cottages and the occasional car slow down as it passed by, the driver peering across at him with an inquisitive expression. He tipped his Fedora hat a little further down, aware of the rising sun catching his eyes. The recent storm had heralded a beautiful cloudless sky and a warming breeze that blew fragrant aromas of jasmine and honeysuckle across his face.

His jacket, as usual, was double-breasted, and in the lapel was pinned a small golden cricket bat given to him by his wife.

Taking his watch from his jacket pocket, he looked at the time.

10.37am.

He began to walk briskly towards Rose Cottage…

★★★

Annette Myers answered the door and peered at the identity card Edwards held out in front of him.

"Yes? What can I do for you?" Her words were cold and dismissive.

She was dressed in a simple grey and peach skirt with a plain cream blouse. Her hair was tied neatly back and her face looked almost false under the make-up she'd applied that morning.

The first thing Inspector Edwards noticed were the nervous glances she made over his shoulder, as if she expected someone else to be following him.

"Mrs Annette Myers?" he asked casually.

She nodded.

"My name is Inspector Edwards. I'm down here from Scotland Yard, investigating a murder, and was wondering if I might ask you some questions?"

He'd lost count of how many times he'd used those very same lines to introduce himself, and smiled inwardly as he tried to work out how many of these introductions had led to the other person dangling at the end of the hangman's rope.

"I've heard of you… Weren't you the chap who…?" Annette Myers narrowed her eyes and stepped back a little.

"Yes, quite…" Edwards smiled. "May I come in?"

The door led directly into the kitchen, and he could detect the faint aroma of bacon and eggs, which reminded him of his missed breakfast. From the kitchen he could see directly through the lounge and into the garden. The low ceiling and wooden beams would have knocked his hat from his head if he hadn't removed it upon entering.

"I'm not sure how I can help you, Inspector." Annette Myers walked round the kitchen table after shutting the door behind him. She beckoned him to a chair and added, "I've heard the gossip in town, but other than that…"

"It's just routine questions, Mrs Myers." Edwards sat down, his eyes darting around the room, studying, scrutinising. "It is *Mrs* Myers?" he added as an afterthought.

"Yes," she replied, a little gloomily.

"May I ask where your husband is?"

"My husband died in the war." Annette Myers fumbled with some plates stacked on the sideboard.

"Oh, I'm sorry."

Edwards felt it wasn't the best start to an interview, though it had been an all-too-familiar response these past few years, since the Armistice. His eyes caught sight of the sideboard behind her and of two photographs. Even from where he was sitting he could clearly see the images.

Two boys, one slightly older than the other.

Both holding toys.

One holding a small boat and the other a fine-looking cavalry officer on horseback.

The photographs captivated him and drew his attention deep within their images. It was the look in their eyes, so innocent and lost. He wondered what it might have been like to have experienced the love of children with Elisha, and he coughed slightly, trying to draw his attention away from their eyes.

"Are you from these parts originally?" It wasn't a prepared question but one Edwards needed to ask simply to draw his focus back to the woman before him.

"No, I'm not from Bodmin… I came down here to live when my husband died." Annette Myers rubbed her hands together and stared at the tabletop.

"Bodmin seems a strange place to move to," Edwards reflected. "Do you have friends down here, or relatives?"

She shook her head and remained silent.

Edwards contemplated pursuing the line of questioning, more out of curiosity than anything else. Her mannerisms struck just about every inquisitive nerve in his body, and his mind raced a little ahead of him regarding how he should approach his next move.

Like a chess player observing his opponent, he eyed her intently.

"It's the death of an army officer not far from here that's the main focus of my investigation." He glanced again at the two photographs, desperately trying to fathom what is was about them that intrigued him so much.

It was then that he saw the same toys in the images, now sitting beside the two photographs looking charred and battered. Upon realising what they were, he was filled with an immediate feeling of loss and sadness, as though a grey veil had descended around him, covering his eyes and enveloping his heart.

So much hurt, he found himself thinking... *So much sadness... Good God...*

Catching his breath, Edwards regained his composure and said, "There are just a few questions I'd like to put to you, Mrs Myers, to clear up a few loose ends, so to speak."

"As I said, Inspector, I'm not sure how I might be able to help you." Annette Myers glanced nervously at him before dropping her gaze.

"Well," he said, pulling out his notebook and a small pencil, "you could tell me how long you've known Captain Grant."

Annette Myers raised her head, widening her eyes. "I... I don't know who you're talking about."

"Well, that's strange, Mrs Myers. We have a witness who observed you leaving 13 Creek Lane yesterday morning, around the time we believe Captain Grant was murdered." Edwards waited for his words to sink in, wishing she would raise her head so he could look into her eyes. "Mrs Myers?"

"I... don't... please... I don't..."

Edwards took a deep breath, ready to continue his questioning, then paused as he found himself reluctantly drawn again to the two photographs.

Mother... please... help us...

It was a familiar feeling, the sensation of someone calling to him from another room. He could hear the sound of children crying, and wondered if they might be calling from a bedroom upstairs. Their cries were so tormented and anguished, he thought he might ask her to respond to them...

Staring around the kitchen, Edwards strained his ears.

Silence.

Turning his attention back to the woman before him he continued, "Captain Grant was murdered in the kitchen of 13 Creek Lane, a place with an already dubious reputation. I need to ascertain why he was there in the first place. Did he arrange to meet you, Mrs Myers?"

She nodded meekly.

"Why was that?" he prompted impatiently.

She remained staring blankly at the table.

"Mrs Myers!" Edwards called softly but firmly.

She raised her head, responding to his voice.

"Why did he want to meet with you?"

"He left a note here, asking me to visit him at Creek Lane," she mumbled, her eyes reddening.

"Yes, but why?" Edwards saw how close she was to bursting into tears and so gently lowered his voice. This was going to easier than he'd first thought; it was all there; she just needed the right questions.

"We... once knew each other," her voice stumbled and lurched from one emotional extreme to the other.

"How—?" Edwards stopped abruptly, the sound of children screaming now reverberating through his head. For some strange reason he thought of Old Solomon and the night he'd come to him.

Since then the sounds had continued to echo in his mind.

People whispering… voices calling…

He noticed Annette Myers staring up at him, her expression one of confusion.

Standing up, he dropped his pencil and gazed around the kitchen, marvelling at the tidiness and regimented storage of everyday items such as plates and cooking utensils.

As he moved towards the photographs, the sound of crying increased. When he reached the sideboard and picked up the charred boat, he grimaced, feeling an electrical bolt shoot through his body.

"What was your relationship to Captain Grant?" Edwards remained staring at the boat.

"We were lovers," Annette Myers choked.

He nodded, still staring at the boat in his hand. "And these were your two sons?"

"Yes…" she sniffed, breathing heavily, "they were my two sons."

"How did they die?" Edwards heard the words but couldn't believe he was speaking them. It was as though he'd somehow transcended his body and was watching himself following a line of questioning that reached into another world.

He turned to face her.

"Oh, God… Oh, dear God… Please… don't…" She wept.

"How did they die, Mrs Myers?" he asked coldly.

"There was a fire… at my house…" Her words jutted through her tears. "I was away visiting Captain Grant… It was our nanny's night off…" Her sobs became heavier, threatening to completely overwhelm her.

Edwards sighed and replaced the boat on the sideboard.

"My husband was away in France... We met... I couldn't stop myself..." She'd pulled a small handkerchief from a drawer and was dabbing her eyes.

"How did you meet?" He returned to his seat.

"By chance... It was in London... I was doing voluntary work... We just... We just fell in love... That night, he sent me a message... begging me to see him at his flat..." Her voice became distant. "I left them in bed... There was fire... The house was completely destroyed..." She buried her head in her hands. "Oh, God... People in this town think I'm so prim and proper..." She stared up at Edwards, her eyes pleading. "My world ended when they died... Shortly afterwards, my husband was killed in action... I had nothing left... Those photographs survived because they were being developed at the time."

"And the toys?" Edwards asked, eyeing her closely.

"Captain Grant retrieved them from the wreckage. Nothing else survived... He kept them until yesterday when I went round to see him."

"Did you kill him, Mrs Myers?" Edwards fiddled with his pencil. He was starting to recover a degree of professionalism, feeling his senses regain some equilibrium. The voices had died down, as though now content with the confession of their mother.

"I went around to Creek Lane yesterday morning..." She took several deep breaths. "You see, I wrote to him via his old regiment. They must have passed the letter on to him... I wanted to see him again... I knew he had the toys and I wanted them back..." She reached into another drawer, pulled out a cigarette and lit it. "When I got there the front door was already open. He was sitting in the kitchen... I thought he'd committed suicide... Why do you think it was murder?"

Edwards remained silent.

"Anyway, I stood staring at him for a while and then searched the house for the toys... They were upstairs... I left him there." She flicked the ash onto the stone floor.

Edwards looked at her coldly. "Go on," he said.

"I didn't even close his eyes," she added affectionately. "He looked so peaceful." She finally fell silent.

Edwards pulled his pipe from his jacket pocket, reached across to the box of matches she'd just used and lit it, drawing heavily, deep in thought. How long he sat there he couldn't work out. Time passed, as though the world was moving forward, leaving the two of them seated in its wake.

"Did you see anyone else when you arrived or when you left?" he finally asked.

"No one," she answered.

"Did you visit anyone else?"

"I… I went to see Canon Trebarwith at the church." She finished the cigarette, drew another from the packet and lit it from the dying embers of the old. "I needed to confess my sins… You see, Inspector, all these years I've been living here, devoting myself to the church… I suppose I've been trying to atone for what I did… Canon Trebarwith recently proposed marriage to me…" Again, her voice trailed off.

"You say confess your sins, Mrs Myers… What exactly did you say to him?" Edwards leaned forward and gently prised the old cigarette butt from her hand. Glancing around, he found an ashtray and stubbed it out.

"I had to tell him. The poor man was waiting on my reply to his proposal. I told him that I'd been involved in an adulterous affair with Captain Grant… I told him about the fire and the deaths of my sons."

"Did you say anything else?"

"I don't know… maybe… I was too upset."

"What did he say?"

"He listened… as a man of God would… He prayed with me for forgiveness. But there was a sadness in his eyes…" She sighed with a wretched resignation. "I don't think any man would want to marry a woman who's done the things I have…"

Staring around the kitchen, Edwards contemplated extending his curiosity to the rest of the cottage. But that would take time, and time was not on his side. He said, "Do you own a revolver, Mrs Myers?"

"A revolver...?" Annette Myers stared indignantly at Edwards. "You think I killed Captain Grant?"

"I'm just asking you if you own a revolver?" he replied flatly.

"The answer to that question is no, Inspector. What would I want with a gun?"

Drawing on his pipe, Edwards reflected upon her own question before adding, "You see, Mrs Myers, talking to you now, after what you've just said about your family and Canon Trebarwith's proposal of marriage to you, I find it hard to believe that you calmly walked into 13 Creek Lane, saw the dead body of your former lover, then simply searched the cottage for those two toys..." He pointed across the room. "You then find them and simply walk away from the cottage."

"It really doesn't matter what you think, Inspector, I've told you the truth. Captain Grant was dead when I arrived." Anette Myers shuffled uneasily in her seat and drew another cigarette from the packet in front of her. "Why would I want to kill him?"

"Why indeed, Mrs Myers?" Edwards asked coldly. He added, "Did you still love him?"

"Yes..." She lit the cigarette and sat back in her chair, eyeing the detective curiously. "Do you love anyone, Inspector?"

Edwards ignored the question. Drawing on his pipe, he asked suddenly, "Mrs Myers, have you ever heard of The Nest of Rooks?"

"No." Her answer was final and resolute.

Edwards considered questioning her further, before noticing her staring at his wedding ring.

"Do you love your wife, Inspector?" Annette Myers smiled.

"Yes, Mrs Myers, I love my wife very deeply."

"Then never stop telling her… Tell her how much you love her when you return home."

Inspector Edwards smiled and with a heavy heart closed his notebook.

★★★

"Harry, I wasn't dreaming." Morag finished her coffee and pushed her plate away. Harry was sitting to her right and she noticed he hadn't touched his bacon and eggs; his head was bent forward, and she could tell he was in deep concentration. "Someone must have wound up the polyphon; that thing doesn't just play itself. I heard the noise and came down."

"But we checked it first thing this morning," Harry replied, raising his head and inclining it towards her. "There wasn't a disc in there. It was empty."

"Then someone removed it!" Morag pushed her chair away and stood up. Glancing across the room she saw Dodson standing discreetly by the door and nodded towards him. "Besides…" she turned to Harry, "why was the false door in the library open? Lawrence nailed it shut, along with the rest of them, last November."

Harry shook his head. "I don't know."

"I saw him, Harry. As plain as I see you… He's here in this house."

Morag moved towards the open doors and the terrace. The warm morning breeze soothed her, and the clear skies above helped raise her spirits.

"If he is," Harry replied, "then we can trap him… I'll get Sergeant Cadan to bring some of his men over here at once."

"Which will achieve nothing," Morag responded sharply. "Like you said, he's too slippery… Evil bastard… Who the Hell does he think he is?" She saw Harry's shoulders slump forward, and walked across to him. "Harry, if he's here, then I have to confront him. It's me he wants… I suppose his twisted mind has convinced him that he can take me back to Amble Lodge." She ran her fingers across his face. He hadn't shaved and she felt bristles slide across her skin… Though rough to feel, she wondered what it might be like if he grew a beard, then considered the scars that streaked across his face. Burying those thoughts, she added, "If he's been here a while, then he's had ample opportunity to harm us."

"You think he's playing games with us?" Harry reached out and grasped her hand.

"Yes," she replied. "He's using the house in the same way I did… The passageways are endless; some of them reach out into the forest. You could bring over the entire Bodmin police force and never find him."

"Then what do you suggest?"

Morag squeezed his hand. "When I was hiding out here last year, I only used a few of the passageways to move around the house. As I said, some of them are endless – even I couldn't trust myself to use them. That's why I stayed in the tower. If he's using them, then he has a more detailed knowledge of them than I did."

"You say there may be other entrances in the house? Other secret doors?" Harry leaned back in his chair.

"I'm certain of it. Neither you nor William knew where they were. I only found some of them… But there's another thing…" Morag sighed and turned to lean on the table. She now faced the open doors to the terrace. In the distance, a gardener worked his way methodically through a rose bed, weeding and generally tidying up. "Cyril told us about Edwina Baker having a sister – a sister who mysteriously disappeared after Edwina hanged herself."

"What about her?" Harry asked.

"What if she's working here, Harry?" Morag whispered, staring at the door. "What if she's helping Morgan Treave to live like I did, hidden away in the secret passageways?"

"Like—"

"Yes, like Edith Travers did for me... Helping him, bringing him food..." Morag glanced nervously around.

"But..." Harry spoke carefully, recollecting his thoughts, "that day when Inspector Edwards left on the train... before he came back for the inquest..."

"Aye, I know. You said you felt the presence of Morgan Treave on the train. But what if he came back...? What if Nurse Baker's sister is helping him...? Cyril said that nobody knows what she looks like."

"But that would mean..." Harry was about to continue, when Dodson walked into the dining room.

"Will there be anything else?" Dodson bowed slightly.

Morag eyed him carefully before asking, "Do you know if Inspector Edwards will be joining us for breakfast?"

Dodson looked slightly bemused, before replying, "Inspector Edwards left for town some time ago. He took the Austin... Said he would join you later." He hesitated, seemingly unsure if to collect the remaining plates or wait for another question.

"Thank you, Dodson," Morag smiled, "that will be all."

Morag watched him load the cups and plates onto a large tray, systematically working his way from Harry's seat around to Morag's. When he reached Morag he paused, staring at the revolver in Morag's hand.

"That will be all, Dodson... Thank you," Morag repeated, her voice heavy and cold. She watched as he collected the last of the breakfast plates and accompaniments and made his way slowly to the door and out into the corridor. With her back to the terrace, Morag pondered Dodson's departure with an air of fleeting curiosity, aware that she should have waited until he'd completed clearing the table before talking about such things. "I was hoping to speak to Cyril before he left," she said, a little dejectedly.

219

"I expect we'll see him at the recital," Harry replied encouragingly.

"What do you think about informing the staff of our suspicions?" Morag asked, still staring at the doorway and corridor and hearing the distant clanging of doors.

"I think they already suspect." Susan's voice came as almost a hushed whisper from the terrace doorway; her words carried a chilling weariness about them.

Morag swung round, feeling her heart miss a beat. She initially felt compelled to comment about listening in to private conversations, but then she saw the vacant look in Susan's eyes.

"Susan...! You startled me..." Moving back a step and smiling, she beckoned their housekeeper into the dining room. "What was that you said about the staff already suspecting?"

Susan stepped into the dining room and smiled affectionately at Harry and Morag. She wasn't wearing her usual skirt and jacket, but had opted for a tweed skirt with a pullover. "They already suspect something is wrong, Lady Frobisher."

"Please, Susan, you know you can call me Morag..." Morag eased a chair away from the table and added, "Please, sit down."

"No, I'm fine, thank you, Morag." Susan recovered some of her composure. "I wanted to see you both and knew you'd be taking breakfast here... Inspector Edwards paid us a visit this morning. He was concerned about Lawrence and his fall yesterday."

"Yes," said Harry, "how is Lawrence?"

"Oh, he's fine, sir. Just a little bruised. He dislocated his shoulder... the one where he was shot." Susan stared at the table, and Morag guessed she had something important to say. "His fall wasn't an accident... Someone startled his horse."

"Who?" Harry asked.

"Larry described him, but I don't think he realised at first who he was... Then, later on, when we were looking for him..." Susan's voice faltered.

"Yes, Susan?" Morag prompted.

Susan remained silent.

"You saw him, didn't you?" Harry's voice was thick with apprehension.

"Yes," Susan whispered. "I joined Dodson and Kenick, trying to look for Larry. We all became lost. I was alone... He was there, standing behind me."

"Morgan Treave?" Morag's words were barely audible.

Susan nodded. "It's you he wants, Morag."

"I know..." Morag reached behind her and found Harry's hand. "You say the staff are suspicious?"

Again, Susan nodded. "Both Kenick and Dodson thought they saw a man in the house. Being new they thought he was the Head Butler or someone. Dodson described him... the grey beard, patch over one eye, face heavily scarred... He thought he might have been injured during the war... They're bound to talk."

"That's all we need," Harry reflected solemnly, "staff leaving us when we've only just replaced the previous lot... If this gets around Bodmin, nobody will want to come and work here... It's a bad show."

"Did Kenick and Dodson see him in the forest?" Morag asked.

"I don't think so..." Susan's face tightened into a fearful expression. "I had Larry's revolver... I could have shot him." She looked at the revolver in Morag's hand.

Morag placed the weapon on the table, the clunk of metal reverberating around the dining room. "I'll speak personally to Kenick and Dodson. They seem reasonable enough; not the kind of people to lose their nerve." Morag stared out onto the terrace. Turning to Susan she asked, "Did Lawrence tell you exactly who helped him?"

"It was a woman living in one of the estate cottages," Susan replied. "Sunrise Cottage, he said... Said her name was—"

"Ellen Carfax." Harry scratched his chin and nodded.

"He said she had someone living there with her… a mute… fought in the war… She thinks he might have deserted and made his way back here for some reason." Susan glanced out onto the terrace. "Lawrence said there was something strange about her… something familiar… She set his shoulder back into place and let him rest a while. This other man helped him back onto the main path and walked with him until they were near the house… That was when he saw me…" Her voice drifted off.

"Could Lawrence possibly give me directions to this cottage?" Morag asked. "I know he has maps of the estate; maybe he could—"

"Sunrise Cottage isn't marked on any map," Harry cut in.

"Why ever not?" Morag countered.

"It just isn't…"

"Well, what does this Ellen Carfax do?" Morag asked hesitantly.

"We don't know, Morag," Susan said cautiously. "Lawrence has compiled a list of all the estate buildings and farms. He's also listed names of all the estate workers… Many of them haven't been paid for months and are living solely off their own means. You say that Sunrise Cottage isn't on any maps… Well, you're mistaken, Lord Frobisher. Larry found Sunrise Cottage marked on an old map dating back to the 1890s. From then on, all subsequent maps erased any reference to it."

"But why do that?" Morag finally sat down on the chair she'd pulled out for Susan. Looking across at Harry she said, "Do you know why, Harry?"

Harry fiddled with his stick and eased himself round in his chair. "All I know is that, when we were boys, our father absolutely forbade us to ever visit Sunrise Cottage. He burnt all the old maps of the estate and had new ones printed; the map Larry found must have been one he missed. When William and

I were older, we asked him about the place, and he made us swear never to try and find Sunrise Cottage and never to ask him about it again."

Morag digested his words, nodding her head and narrowing her eyes. After a while, a wry grin appeared on her face and she said, "But you didn't stay away, did you?"

Harry chuckled and tapped his stick on the stone floor.

"No, not you, Harry Frobisher." Morag smiled.

"William and I knew the estate like the back of our hands. We'd ride out on our horses and find the shortcuts out onto the moors or into Bodmin... One day I was returning from town on my own – I'd taken a longer route back to the house – and I found Sunrise Cottage quite by chance. It's down past Templers Copse and well off the main path."

"And you met this Ellen Carfax?"

"Yes..."

"And?" Morag asked patiently.

"She became my friend. She seemed to understand me... I couldn't actually work out why she was there, living alone in such an isolated place. But for a young boy growing up, unable sometimes to talk to his parents, Ellen Carfax would just sit and listen..." Harry sighed heavily. Taking a deep breath, he continued, "On the eve of William and I joining our regiment in France, I saddled my horse and rode out there one morning. It was as though she were waiting for me, standing by the gate. She knew about William and myself going off to war. We talked... I told her how scared I was..." Harry shook his head. "Can you believe that? I actually told her my true feelings. Something I'd not been able to do with my parents. When I left her, she gave me a small Bible, which I kept with me when I was in France..." Harry's voice faltered.

Morag eased herself forward, pushing the revolver out of the way and grasping his hands. She recognised the signs, knowing the flashbacks would be thrusting their way through his mind like red-hot pokers. She felt his breathing become heavier.

"Harry," she whispered, "don't..."

"No... it's fine... While I lay in that hospital, drifting in and out of consciousness, I heard a voice... I can't..."

Morag felt his body tremble.

"Someone rummaging through my pockets... Benson..." Harry jerked his head sideways, as though reliving the excruciating pain of blistering hot shrapnel burrowing deep into his eyes. "Someone thrust that Bible into my hand, and I clung hold of it... I thought I was dying... And the only person I could think of was that woman in Sunrise Cottage who had shown me so much kindness."

Morag pulled him close and nestled his head into her shoulder.

15

Saturday mornings usually brought with them a varied day ahead for Canon Trebarwith. From weddings to christenings and funerals, he normally found his time taken up with some ceremony or another that needed to be conducted. Come mornings such as these, when the early summer sun warmed the town and surrounding moors from first light, he would always say a silent prayer of thanks if he was contemplating one of those rare days when he had no ceremony to perform or visits to the sick and elderly.

Usually, on a morning such as this, he would breeze through his sermon for the Sunday morning before taking a brisk walk through town. Lately he'd taken to following the path past Rose Cottage, sometimes waiting by the gate, hoping to catch a glimpse of Annette Myers, and a possible conversation about something he needed talk to her about but could wait until he popped in for a cup of tea and a stroll around her delightful garden.

He had resigned himself to never take that route again.

How was he going to confront her that afternoon? In his capacity as a minister of God, he'd opened his heart to her in the form of a marriage proposal, only for her to confess to an adulterous affair.

Though he'd asked God to forgive her, he found he could not.

His heart had sunk to unfathomable depths, seemingly pulled down into the darkness by a bitter resentment that saw his only chance of love, pure and innocent, snatched from him. In all his years serving God, he'd heard the confessions of murderers, moments before their walk to the scaffold, and of men ready to climb out of their trenches and walk bravely towards certain death during war.

Yet what Annette Myers had confessed both disgusted and alarmed him.

Dear God...

She had come to confess her sins...

It would be difficult meeting her again that afternoon. He supposed he might even see her before, as there were tables to prepare and cakes to help set up. She would be there; such a prominent member of the town hall committee was bound to be helping out and organising.

What would he say to her?

What *could* he say to her?

Hopefully the afternoon would bring some comfort into his life. It would be nice to see his parishioners and to possibly welcome new visitors to his Sunday morning services. He usually enjoyed a large congregation at these services, indeed at most services throughout the week. His relaxed but attentive style went down well with his parishioners. He could happily say that, in the few years he'd been holding services in the local church, he'd been warmly accepted into the community as both a man of God, providing pastoral care, and as a friendly face people would always look towards when walking down Bodmin's high street.

These thoughts raced through his mind as he peddled his bicycle through the streets of Bodmin towards the hospital. The ride was pleasant enough in the early sunshine, though he did feel quite sticky and clammy under his shirt. The streets seemed quiet, as though the town were taking longer than usual to wake up. As he came round a corner, he noticed a stranger, a man smartly dressed in a double-breasted pinstripe jacket with matching trousers and a Fedora hat tilted low over his eyes. He looked familiar, but Trebarwith couldn't fully see his face. He did, though, walk with a slight stoop, as though a sadness bore heavily upon his shoulders.

Trebarwith continued to peddle furiously, pushing his own Panama hat down firmly on his head for fear a sudden rush of wind might send it flying into the road. Nobody had seen him and that pleased him, as he always felt quite conspicuous with his large frame balanced precariously upon the rickety old cycle that had come with the vicarage and parish duties. His sleeves were rolled up and he'd unhitched his dog collar to enable him to unbutton his shirt in readiness for the cycle ride. In a basket perched over the rear wheel, his black jacket lay neatly folded, though a little dusty.

Upon approaching the main hospital building, he eased back on the peddles, just enough to enable him to glide effortlessly along the last fifty yards or so. Catching his breath, he tried to banish all thoughts of Annette Myers from his mind.

By doing so, he invited darker thoughts, that swept in and settled contentedly, ready to tease and torment. He remembered the night he'd visited this very building, to say a prayer over a seemingly deranged young woman...

It took an extreme amount of persuasion to get permission to see her before her incarceration at Amble Lodge.

Through her tear-stained and glazed eyes, he saw a troubled soul, innocent and pleading for help. The prayers he said for her salvation fell on deaf ears, for already the restraints were fitted and the documents signed; the Amble Lodge staff waited, respectfully but coldly, for the signal from Doctor Treave to carry her to her new home – a padded cell, lost within that darkened ward set aside for the criminally insane.

The thought, along with the foreboding image of Bodmin Hospital looming up in front of him, sent a chill down his spine, and a feeling of self-reprimand poured forth from his heart as he remembered just how complicit he was, along with the rest of the community, in their reaction to her false imprisonment.

The truth is, he thought, *none of us knew the true reasons for her committal to Amble Lodge. I suppose this collective outpouring of self-guilt and reproach is all part of the healing process.*

He pulled to a halt by the front steps of the hospital.

The building stood in stark contrast to the bright and sunny morning and reflected the troubled thoughts that swirled in his mind. The gloomy and melancholy exterior, built upon a slight incline that rose behind it, gave the impression of a monstrous entity, rising up, ready to engulf the approaching visitor.

There was speculation around town that it might soon be demolished. Indeed, areas of the building were already in decline and had been shut down, which always made his visits, providing spiritual care for the sick, just that little bit gloomier than he thought they needed to be. But the staff were always on hand to help and he was always greeted with a friendly smile and a cup of tea.

Today, though, standing on the steps to the front door, and after quickly reattaching his dog collar and slipping on his jacket, he felt a strange sense of comfort in the melancholy atmosphere of the place, as though his heart had found a sense of belonging in such a dreadful building.

He thought carefully of his next move, before taking a deep breath and walking purposefully through the already open front doors.

Inside the building, he was immediately met by several nurses, milling around, too absorbed with their daily tasks to take notice of him, though one or two acknowledged his arrival with a smile before scurrying off down corridors. A sister emerged from one of the side rooms and was about to cross into one of the other offices when she caught his presence out of the corner of her eye.

"Canon Trebarwith?" She smiled, extending her hand. "How lovely to see you here this morning."

"Sister Lomax, I'm glad I found you." Trebarwith heard the hesitation in his voice and hoped she hadn't felt it in their handshake. "I'm here, in a way, rather unofficially."

Sister Lomax, a rather thick-set woman approaching middle age, still held his hand and guided him into her office. "Yes, Canon, is it something I can help you with?"

"Well," Trebarwith glanced nervously over her shoulder, "I'm aware of the two deaths that have recently occurred. The poor chap on the train, and I think a Captain Grant, here in town?"

"That's right, Canon. They're down in the mortuary," Sister Lomax replied as she turned to close the door behind her.

They were in a small administrative room, with shelves stacked with box files and ledgers. Though the outside of the window was grimy to the point of blocking out any natural sunlight, the inside of the office was meticulously clean.

"I've come to say prayers over the two deceased, Sister. To think they both died in such a terrible way, and now lie abandoned..." Trebarwith took a deep breath, a lost and forlorn look upon his face. "I think, Sister, whatever their past, we need to commend their souls to God."

"Yes, of course, Canon Trebarwith," Sister Lomax replied quickly. "You know the way to the mortuary?"

"Yes, indeed I do," Trebarwith smiled; "I've had the misfortune to visit there many a time in the past."

Sister Lomax turned, opened the door and stood aside.

"Thank you, Sister. God be with you."

Trebarwith eased himself past her and commenced the long walk down the main corridor to the stairs at the far end. The blue and white walls positively gleamed, yet failed to conceal the dankness and gloom slowly consuming the building. It was as though it was disintegrating from the inside, checked only by the dedication and hard work of the staff who kept it clean and functional, knowing that its final days were approaching.

Standing in front of the door to the mortuary, Trebarwith noticed the figure of a young police constable, looking suitably lost and uneasy, within the shadows of the small passageway that led from the stairs. Down here no attempt had been made to spruce up the general surroundings. The floor was original Cornish stone, and the walls were cold and uninviting.

The young man looked at Trebarwith and smiled as he recognised him.

"Hello," Trebarwith called ahead with a light tone as he approached the constable; he pointed to the door. "If you'll allow me a few minutes, I have prayers to say over the two deceased. By the fact that you're standing here, I would assume they're through there?"

The young man frowned and looked past Trebarwith, as though expecting someone to walk down the stairs at the end of the passageway and join them. The look of unease and confusion on his face was apparent, even before the clergyman finally stood before him.

"I hope you're not going to deny them the right to a Christian prayer." Trebarwith reached into his jacket pocket and pulled out a Book of Common Prayer.

"I've been given... specific orders... not to allow anyone... into the mortuary." The young constable stumbled with his words, gasping nervous breaths. He shifted from one foot to the other.

"Yes, Sergeant Cadan probably wasn't thinking of a minister of the church when he gave you that order," Trebarwith said with a slight hint of irritation. The damp and chilly air in the passageway was a gloomy alternative to the fresh, warm air he'd experienced earlier.

"No, not Sergeant Cadan, sir." The answer came back like a lightning thrust.

"Well, who, then? Sergeant Cadan is the highest-ranking policeman in Bodmin. Who else is here?"

Trebarwith noticed the uncertainty in the young man's eyes. It was as though he had immediately regretted suggesting that his orders had come from anyone other than George Cadan. The more he tried to look at him, the more the young man tried to avert his eyes.

"Well?" Trebarwith prompted.

"Said his name was Standish. Colonel Standish. From London. Showed me his papers." The words tumbled forth, almost like a confession.

But there was an anxiousness within those words, as though he wanted to hurriedly dispel them, that they might be causing him personal discomfort. Trebarwith eyed him closely; he was used to hearing people talk about things in their lives, things they might not speak to anyone else about. Sometimes they needed to be prompted, other times their fears and concerns, regrets and sins, simply poured forth; all he could do was listen.

This man before him seemed afraid.

"What did he want?" Trebarwith asked, a little more sympathetically.

"Said he'd just come down from London and was taking over the investigation. Said Sergeant Cadan knew all about it... Said he wanted to see the two bodies."

"And what did he do?"

"I couldn't tell you that, sir. You see, he asked me to stay outside."

"Was there anyone else with him?" Trebarwith's mind began to whirl with intrigue and speculation.

"No. He was alone... and..."

"Yes?"

"He carried a walking stick, with a silver handle... You

231

know, like the toffs carry." At this the young man seized up, as though he'd said too much. He glanced nervously around.

Trebarwith looked intently at the young man.

Strangers have come to this place, he thought, *and died. Now a stranger arrives to investigate.*

"You say he came down last night?"

"That's right, sir."

"From London?"

"Well… that's the thing, sir." The young man removed his helmet and scratched his head.

"Go on."

"Well, I'm sure I saw him in Bodmin a few days ago… which means he couldn't have come down here yesterday."

"Are you sure it was him you saw?"

The young man smiled, probably the first genuine smile he'd managed all morning. "Bodmin's a small town, sir; strangers do tend to stand out a bit."

"So why would he tell you he'd travelled down here yesterday?" Trebarwith was asking the question more to himself than anyone else, so he wasn't surprised when no answer was forthcoming. "Have you spoken to Sergeant Cadan about him?"

"No, sir. I've not seen him since yesterday morning when we brought the body of Captain Grant here. I was relieved late last night by a colleague and came back here early this morning. We're working six-hour shifts. Didn't particularly fancy the night shift myself." The young man looked around, his face gloomy and suspicious.

Trebarwith pulled out his watch; time was racing and he had several tasks to complete before the afternoon piano recital. "Well, Constable," he placed his watch back into his pocket, "I won't be long—"

"I have my orders, sir—"

"Yes, young man, but I don't think he included myself in

that order. Not only do I have a duty to my congregation, of which I don't remember seeing you, but I also have a duty to provide pastoral care to strangers. These two men were strangers to our community, and they died in a most horrible way. I think I owe it to them to say a prayer over their bodies. Now, are you going to let me through?" Trebarwith stared intently at the young man.

"Yes, well, I suppose a few minutes won't hurt, will it?"

"No, my boy, it won't."

The young constable stood to one side, his hands clasped behind his back. Trebarwith noticed that his uniform was a little too large for him, and so hung heavily from his shoulders.

So young, thought Canon Trebarwith, *like so many I prayed over as they were lowered into the mass graves.*

As he entered the small annex room he was suddenly aware of a distinctive plunge in temperature. The ride over to the hospital, the walk along the corridor and down the stairs had brought about a cold sweat that had dripped from his body and made his shirt clammy against his skin.

This plunge in temperature now made him shake slightly.

He turned to the police constable. "Before I say these prayers, can you let me have a look at their personal belongings?"

"I'm not really sure if I can do that, sir." This time there was an air of defiance in the young man's voice.

"I would like to look at their belongings. There might be an address, or anything; someone I can write to and inform them of what has happened."

This time the young policeman looked directly at Trebarwith. "You'll find their clothes and personal belongings in two bags on the main table. Both of them are in there." With these words, he slipped back out into the passageway.

Canon Trebarwith waited until the door closed before pushing his Book of Common Prayer back into his pocket.

"You're that police inspector." Mabel Tregunnel eyed Inspector Edwards, her face scornful, her words accusing. "You were here last year. We know all about you… Came down here to look for your sister-in-law… They say you saw the ghost of Old Solomon."

Edwards observed the old woman and the mass of papers and files stacked around the room in which he now stood.

The walk from Rose Cottage had revived him after the meeting with Annette Myers, though he still felt melancholy and painfully aware that he'd not taken her in for further questioning. Her answers to his questions had seemed genuine, and her emotional outburst and subsequent explanation about the fire and the deaths of her two sons quite plausible; especially so when he considered the terrible visions he'd experienced whilst talking to her.

But he'd heard convincing alibies before, from people eventually convicted for some of the most hideous crimes he'd ever encountered. Her account of her discovery of Captain Grant had focussed on her desire to retrieve her sons' toys and could have been a ploy to distract his attention from the true reason for her visit to 13 Creek Lane.

When investigating murder, Edwards would always follow the well-trusted principles of means, motive and opportunity; keeping these as the foundations of his theories. And, in that sense, Annette Myers would probably have wanted to murder Captain Grant as an act of retribution for taking her away from her children and leaving them alone to perish in that fire. Maybe she'd written to him with every intention of killing him once she'd retrieved the only two possessions left belonging to her sons. Emotional instability after the death of a child could lead to anything.

He wondered if a more thorough search of Rose Cottage might produce further concrete evidence.

And then, of course, there'd been the question of her knowledge of The Nest of Rooks. She'd been fairly resolute in her answer on that score.

Could Annette Myers be the Fourth Rook?

Her recollections of time spent during the Great War were patchy. A married woman living in London; a husband fighting in France. There was her voluntary work, along with an adulterous affair.

That was not uncommon.

Did her children truly die in a house fire? Well, that would be easy to prove via a short telegram to Scotland Yard. He cast his mind back, trying to recollect. During those four years of conflict, he'd found himself working long hours, mostly away from his home, as a shortage of police officers meant a busier than normal workload. A fire and the deaths of two children, though tragic enough, would have been lost amongst the stories filtering back from the Front.

Considering the fact that he could quite easily prove or disprove her story about the fire, he was inclined to believe her.

But she had been at 13 Creek Lane around the time of Grant's murder. If she'd seen his body and simply ignored it, did anyone else see her leave other than the witness Sergeant Cadan had questioned? Because if she didn't murder him, perhaps she was seen by the real murderer – which now put her life in danger.

"What is it you want?" Mabel Tregunnel spat out the words with a vicious tongue.

"I want to know why you didn't tell the police of Nurse Edwina Baker's connection with 13 Creek Lane, Mrs Tregunnel," Edwards responded flatly, banishing all thoughts of Annette Myers. "You own the place; you rented it to her and her sister. When you found out about the events over at Amble Lodge Asylum, and Nurse Baker's involvement in the false imprisonment of Morag Donaldson, did you not think it wise to inform the authorities?"

"What does it matter?" the old woman hissed. "Edwina chose to pay for her crimes and ended her life there."

"Did you know her well?"

"She was a troubled soul… That man, Doctor Treave, cast some kind of spell over her."

"I asked if you knew her well," Edwards persisted.

"She would visit me here… We'd talk," Mabel Tregunnel sighed, and Edwards detected a slight warming of her attitude.

"Well, it's actually her twin sister I'd like to know more about. Can you describe her? Did you meet her?"

"Nobody ever met her sister. She kept her locked away. Said she was mad." She eyed Edwards closely.

"There seems to be a strange irony there," he said to himself; "Nurse Baker, complicit in keeping a totally sane woman chained up in a padded cell in a lunatic asylum, yet keeps her own deranged sister locked up in her cottage."

He looked around the room, feeling as though he were walking through a valley, with files and ledgers towering above him. He thought about pursuing the question of this old woman's decision not to inform the police of Nurse Baker's connection to 13 Creek Lane, but decided against it. There would be no point, and time was of the essence. He was hardly going to achieve anything by dragging her down to the police station for further interrogation; and, besides, considering the sting in her voice, he didn't want to leave her with some innocent young constable to take a statement.

The question of Nurse Baker's sister was a completely different matter, and he was suddenly aware of an overwhelming desire to find her. "And there's nothing you can tell me about Nurse Baker's sister? Do you have a name for her?"

The blank look in Mabel Tregunnel's eyes shut that particular door in his face.

"I saw her once," the voice of an elderly man croaked from the door behind him.

Edwards swung round.

"Don't listen to him…" the old woman mocked, "he doesn't know what he's talking about."

Edwards raised his hand and she fell silent. "And you are?"

The old man shuffled into the room and looked at Edwards with eyes worn deep from years of scolding and abuse. "Horace Tregunnel… You asked about that woman who lived at 13 Creek Lane with Edwina Baker."

"Did you know her?" Edwards asked crisply.

"What my wife says is true…" he coughed, unaware of drops of spittle landing on his chin. "Nobody ever saw her to speak to… though some caught sight of her looking out of the windows… I saw her once… whilst I was walking down Creek Lane and happened to glance over at the house. She was peering down at me…" He moved closer to Edwards, so close the policeman could see the ravaged and distant stare in those pitiful eyes. "I remember she smiled at me… and I prayed that I would never see that face again."

"Why not?" Edwards whispered.

"It was a terrible sight… Pure evil… I couldn't sleep that night, I can tell you." Horace Tregunnel moved away, as though he were passing through to the next room, but turning round he said, "I showed that young man around the house… That army officer… I knew he was going to die… There was something about him… He might even have known himself."

"How did you know this?" Edwards swallowed, totally hypnotised by the old man.

Horace Tregunnel smiled knowingly, "The same way that you know things."

"I'm not sure I understand?"

"You will if you open your eyes. They say the spirit of Old Solomon came to you that night out on the moor… Helped you reach Frobisher Hall… Have there been other visions…? Other encounters?"

"I... er..." Edwards took a step back, unaware of the books piled high behind him. He tried to fathom the meaning of the old man's words, though deep within his heart a light began to glow. It was the same feeling he'd had that night when Old Solomon pulled him out of the snow.

"You've recently suffered a loss... Somebody very dear to you... Your wife?"

Edwards nodded blankly.

"You loved her dearly, didn't you?" Mabel Tregunnel's voice, warm and comforting, came to him.

"Yes," Edwards choked, swallowing hard and biting his lip.

"Sometimes it's the loss of someone close, a loved one, that can open a door..." Horace Tregunnel said calmly. "You've sought the help of another."

"Yes," he replied, "a woman in London... a psychic."

"And what did she say?" Mabel Tregunnel moved around the room, finally standing next to her husband.

"The same as you... That I should open my mind..." Edwards smiled. He felt suddenly tired and wanted nothing more than to rest his head in Elisha's lap, the way he used to when he came home from dealing with the terrors of the day; he'd sit on the floor at her feet, feeling the gentle touch of her fingers in his hair. Desperately pulling his senses together, he asked, "Were they identical twins?"

"No, Inspector," the old man replied. "From the glimpse I had of her, she had short hair, and her face..." He paused.

"Yes...? Her face...?" Edwards prompted, his pencil hovering over his notebook.

"Drawn and haggard... as if she were a walking corpse... I did wonder if there was something wrong with her, but when she smiled... God forgive me..." The old man slunk back against the desk.

Edwards cast his mind back to the previous November and his encounter with Nurse Baker. The memory of the look in her eyes as she'd mocked him, taunting him as to the fate of the woman with the red hair, threatened to completely absorb him. He remembered trying to assess her age; he'd found it difficult, as she had one of those faces that was quite beguiling.

Drawn and haggard, he reflected, *as if there were something wrong with her…*

"And you don't know her name?" he asked.

The old man leaned against the desk and shook his head.

"I know it." The old woman stepped away from her husband and shuffled towards Edwards. "Edwina mentioned her a couple of times when she came here to pay her rent. Would never stay long, though; and never really had much to say, but I do remember her mentioning her sister's name."

"What was it?" Edwards eyed her closely.

"Locusta… Locusta Baker."

Edwards dropped his notebook and felt his blood run cold.

16

Ellen Carfax carefully observed the liquid boiling and bubbling in the saucepan that sat on her small oven at Sunrise Cottage. The heat from the mixture was intense, and it added to the general warmth of the morning sun. Set so deep within the forest covering much of the Frobisher Estate, Sunrise Cottage never usually enjoyed the warmth of the sun, and Ellen always felt compelled to keep a fire burning even in the height of summer. For some reason, this morning was different. The sun had burst through the canopy of trees overhead, warming her face as she'd taken her morning stroll.

With Branok's ability to find wood and keep a large supply drying out in the rickety old shed behind the house, the cottage never felt cold or damp. Within it beat a heart that was forever warm and inviting, and she always felt it was the beating of that heart that drew Branok to her door so long ago, away from the terrible things he'd seen which had silenced him.

Hovering her hand over the mixture, she assessed the temperature and decided it might be getting too hot; this was not a mixture to overheat, for to do so would mean losing its potency. Her hands were still dirty from picking mushrooms during her stroll. They grew in abundance around the estate, and lately could be found in plentiful supply on the eastern slopes of the main house, in a clearing that offered some of the most beautiful views of the East Tower.

She knew it had been in that particular tower that the woman with the red hair had taken to hiding after her escape from the asylum. Ellen Carfax had admired her bravery and pluck as soon as she'd heard the story that spread like wildfire across the county after the night of the snowstorm... the night that that inspector from Scotland Yard made his heroic trek through the blizzard to Frobisher Hall.

She leaned back in her chair and remembered the first time she'd seen the towers of Frobisher Hall, as a young woman...

... walking slowly towards the main house, her feet bloodied and swollen after her own heroic walk from Launceston. She carried a small bag, with a broken strap that forced her to cover the last mile or so to the house dragging it behind her.

By the time she reached the house, her clothes were practically worn away to rags. She'd crossed the wilderness of Bodmin Moor, resting occasionally under the granite tors and spending the nights huddled in some remote barn or stable.

It was autumn, and the equinox gales had blown relentlessly, chilling her to the bone and leaving her soaked with a rain that seemed to drive right through her. The spirits that haunted the desolate land she found herself in had swept around her, mocking and calling to her.

When she collapsed in a heap, her body numb with exhaustion, her mind tormented by ghostly whisperings that might have been manifestations of the fever consuming her, she heaved herself forward to rest her head upon a small outcrop of rock. It was then that she saw the lights of Frobisher Hall and those splendid towers that rose out of the distant forest, guiding her...

With memories of the workhouse she'd left behind, and a determination that she would either find a better life or die out there on the moors, she staggered forward until she reached the massive iron gates....

"Good Heavens!"

Ellen jumped up, cursing herself for her daydreaming. Grasping the handle of the saucepan, she sighed heavily and moved it a little towards the edge of the oven. Closing the damper beneath the door, she heard the roaring fire inside die down. Lowering her head a little over the mixture, she breathed in the pungent fumes and smiled as she realised it hadn't burnt or caught.

As she sat back in her chair, she allowed herself one last thought of that fateful day...

It was Lord Alfred who saw her, slumped on the gravel driveway. He'd been out riding and had taken a shortcut through the front of the estate, following the old Bodmin Road. As he swung his horse round and into the driveway, he immediately jumped down and knelt beside her...

"So handsome," she whispered, rocking herself gently in her chair, her mind wandering.

Was she seventeen at the time?

"My... so long ago." Her eyelids threatened to close as the memories weighed heavily upon her...

He wiped the tears from her face and picked her up, pulling her close to him, and carried her into the house. His strong arms held her, and she felt a peacefulness and comfort she'd not experienced before. It warmed and revived her. She heard voices around her, smelt the crisp aroma of polish and, most wonderful of all, the smell of burning logs...

There was a doctor... Doctor Mitchell...

She eased herself forward and pulled the saucepan completely away from the oven. The mixture would need time to cool, though the quicker she set about pouring it into a glass jar the easier it would flow.

But these memories, so distant and vague, and so real, refused to release their grip upon her tired and weary mind.

The maid who bathed her soothed her with a soft lullaby, and she slept, soundly and without fear, in one of the grand bedrooms in the west wing. And when she awoke, Lord Alfred was sitting on the bed, holding her hand...

The tears that gathered in her eyes were expected. They always came when she remembered the look in his eyes and his wonderful smile. She wanted to rebuke herself for her weakness in succumbing to these memories; but, as always, she let her emotions have their way, and she pulled her apron up and wept silently into the folds, rocking herself back and forth...

When she'd recovered her senses, she gazed at the saucepan and a small glass jar on the shelf beside her. Now would be the best time to pour it; deadly nightshade always poured easier when still slightly warm...

The label on the jar simply said 'Poison'.

★★★

Annette Myers was waiting for Inspector Edwards by the time he walked through the main doors of Bodmin Police Station. The duty officer, a young constable, had made her sit in the waiting area on an old bench, and Edwards felt compelled to say something to the lad before he realised that, although he outranked everyone there, he was still a visitor.

He'd been looking forward to taking lunch in the St Petroc Hotel but had lost his appetite since his visit to Mabel and Horace Tregunnel. His return to the station had been one of aimlessly walking through a world that was both alien and hostile; and though he heard the occasional mumbled greeting from someone passing by, he just couldn't find it in himself to respond.

Locusta Baker... Every fibre in his body recoiled at the name.

Annette Myers stood up and nodded her head.

As he guided her into the side office, he ordered two cups of tea and glared menacingly at the young constable.

When he closed the door, he said, "Please, Mrs Myers, take a seat. I'm sorry there's nowhere more comfortable around here... We could take tea at the St Petroc..."

"No, Inspector," she said abruptly, sliding a chair away from the table and sitting down, "I need to speak with you... I should have said something back at the cottage."

Edwards eased himself into the chair facing her and laid his Fedora hat on the desk. She was wearing the same clothes as earlier, though now with the addition of a flannel jacket with a small brooch on the lapel. Her hair was tied back under a scarf, and her eyes, though still red and swollen from their previous meeting, had been made less so by the heavy application of make-up.

"You..." She took several deep breaths and stared around the room, as though searching for something that might make her next words easier to convey.

Edwards followed her gaze, patiently waiting for her to choose the right moment. His own mind kept lapsing into different worlds: the psychic reference to his wife, and the mention of Locusta Baker... *Good God*, he thought... *Locusta Baker... Could it really be true...?* He'd need to get a telegram to Scotland Yard, and fast. Of course, it might only be a coincidence... But God... what if it wasn't?

"You asked me, Inspector?"

"I'm sorry?" Edwards shook his head, hearing her voice amongst the many that seemed to be whispering around him.

"The Nest of Rooks?"

"Er... yes, I asked if you'd heard of the name?" He gathered his thoughts and set himself back on track.

Annette Myers slumped back in her chair and eyed him wistfully. "I misled you, Inspector, when I told you about how I spent my time during the war. I suppose a respectable wife of an officer serving in France, filling her time doing voluntary work, was an easy ruse to play. It was the ideal cover story..."

"A cover for what, Mrs Myers?" Edwards leaned forward and studied her intently.

"I didn't kill Captain Grant, Inspector."

"I didn't ask if you did."

He looked deep into her eyes, noticing how empty they now looked. Maybe she was looking for redemption and needed to find the right way to receive it, or maybe she was looking to guide him away from the truth, to muddy the waters and frustrate his investigation.

He felt his stomach rumble and wished she'd get to the point.

"My association with Captain Grant went beyond that of mere lovers." She gazed anxiously around, as though she suspected others to be present and listening.

"An associate?"

"Yes…" The words were barely audible.

"In what way?"

"In the worst possible way. We both worked for Military Intelligence. He was my contact over in England… in London."

"The Nest of Rooks?" Edwards opened his notebook and drew out his pencil.

She smiled weakly. "Yes, that's what we were called. I suppose it sounds all very intriguing and melodramatic."

Edwards eyed her blankly, though expectation raged within him.

She continued, "We weren't ever meant to know our fellow operatives. There'd been leaks and covers blown. Some of our colleagues had been arrested behind the German lines, and many of our secret communications had fallen into enemy hands. Captain Grant was supposed to be my ghost contact, which meant we would leave each other messages but never meet."

"But you did…"

"I was nothing more than a whore… working for the Government. My job was to socialise with Government officials and high-ranking foreign officers, even to sleep with them if the need arose. The agents I worked with were based mainly in France and Belgium, but I stayed in London. It was easy, you see, what with my husband being away all the time, and the ease of employing the services of a nanny. We met quite by chance really, in the rain, outside his club in London. We became lovers instantly. He kept an apartment in Kensington, not far from my house. We would meet, anywhere; it didn't matter. He knew what I was but didn't care... Maybe I was his whore as well."

Edwards was about to say something when there was a knock at the door. It opened, quite abruptly, and the young constable from the front desk entered trying to balance a tray with two cups of tea and a plate of biscuits on it. When he placed it on the desk, Edwards said flatly, "Thank you, Constable." He stared at the biscuits on the plate and inwardly groaned at the realisation that there were just two, and they weren't shortbread.

"Anything else, sir?" The young constable's tone of voice was equally flat and emotionless.

"No, Constable, that will be all..." He was about to speak further to Annette Myers when he was suddenly struck by a thought. "Oh, er... Constable? Can you find Sergeant Cadan and tell him I'll need to see him before this afternoon's piano recital?"

"Certainly, sir." The young man slipped quietly from the office.

"Yes," pondered Annette Myers, "I need to help out with setting up the teas and cakes. I've made a sponge cake..." She peered around the room again.

"So, you were both lovers and associates in a spy network called The Nest of Rooks?" Edwards scratched his chin.

"Yes, Inspector."

"But you never travelled to the Continent?"

"Never. I'd been recruited by an old colleague of my husband's. They wanted someone to infiltrate social gatherings in this country... As I said, to sleep with foreign officials."

"But why spy on our Allies?" Edwards hastily pencilled in some rough notes.

"Inspector, some of our friends in the French and Belgium armies were the worst offenders for spying for our enemy..." She paused and lowered her head. "I'm not proud of what I did. At first, I thought it might actually be fun... There was even a patriotic reason buried in there somewhere. But a woman who sleeps with another man solely for money or information is a whore, nonetheless."

"And your husband?"

"He never suspected. As the war progressed, his nerves became more jaded. He should have been repatriated back to Britain long before he was killed..." She reached into her handbag and pulled out a packet of cigarettes. Lighting one, she drew on it heavily, her hand visibly shaking. She reached out and grasped the cup of tea, which she sipped with a slight raising of her little finger.

Edwards took one of the biscuits, reaching across and dipping it into his tea before quickly plunging it into his mouth.

"When my contact died, I was stranded. I had no one to communicate with or take orders from. Then, one day, a stranger sat next to me whilst I was with my two sons in Green Park in London. He said he worked for Military Intelligence and knew everything about me. He asked if I would be prepared to work under his direction for a small group of spies called The Nest of Rooks."

"And you'd never seen him before?" Edwards finished his biscuit and eyed the remaining one thoughtfully.

"No," Annette Myers replied.

"Could you describe him?"

"It was winter. He was buttoned up with a scarf around him." She shuddered, obviously recalling the incident. "Besides, the way he spoke to me... I think he was just a messenger."

"Why did you agree to his request, if you were having doubts about the morals of what you were doing?"

"Because…" Annette Myers paused, and again drew deeply on her cigarette. She tapped her fingers against the table. "Because… he said that there were many people who would be interested in my activities… including my husband." She stopped tapping the table and wiped her hand nervously across her eyes.

"And so you joined The Nest of Rooks?" Edwards asked solemnly.

"Yes… I knew there were four of us; though I only actually knew Captain Grant, and that was through our own discussions when we were together… It wasn't hard to work out who he was: letters that came to me; communications; things he said; where he was on certain times…" She smiled and flicked cigarette ash into a large ashtray in the middle of the table. "Knowing each other, who we really were, made everything so much easier."

"In what way?" Edwards prompted.

"Because there were no secrets between us. We trusted each other implicitly. He knew what I was doing, my sordid existence, but he never cared." She stubbed out her cigarette, though still some way from finishing it, and lit another. "About a week or so before the fire that killed my children, he said that something was terribly wrong… that there was a double agent working alongside us… We knew it must be one of the other two; he suspected it was the Fourth Rook – that was the person who commanded us. They knew who we were, but we didn't know their identity."

Edwards sighed heavily and cleared his throat. Not waiting to ask, he reached forward and grasped the remaining biscuit and devoured it within a couple of bites. He sat silently, digesting both the biscuit and her story. Finally, he said, "Mrs Myers, we may have one of the Rooks over in the mortuary, in addition to Captain Grant."

"The man on the train?"

"Yes, that's right. I'd like to take you over there to see if you might be able to identify him."

"But I never met the other two members." Annette Myers began tapping her fingers again on the table, now with an irregular and agitated motion.

"Yes, but you won't know that for certain until you see him, will you?" Edwards reasoned.

"But I'm setting up the cake stall for this afternoon's concert." She turned her gaze towards him, her eyes pleading. "And there's the piano to be tuned; Mr Freeman said he'd come over to the town hall and tune it last night, but I don't think he did. And I need to go home and pick up my sponge cake—"

"Mrs Myers…" Edwards reached across and placed his hand over her tapping fingers.

"And I expect I'll see Canon Trebarwith…" Visibly faltering, she looked at him. "What am I going to say to him? The only man who might have given me spiritual succour… who might have one day shared my life and accepted me for what I am… How am I ever going to face him…? And we were going to make tea and coffee for everyone in the break…"

Edwards gently squeezed her hand. "Mrs Myers, if what you say is true, your life might be in danger. The man over in the mortuary was called Archie Cummings… Does that name mean anything to you?"

She shook her head.

"He was a member of a criminal gang which specialises in contract killings…"

She gazed back at him with blank and indifferent eyes.

"Although he may not have been one your colleagues, he might have been hired to come down here and kill you…" Edwards felt he was walking on thin ice and wondered if he should be pursuing this line of questioning. The inescapable fact was that Archie Cummings could not have killed Captain Grant.

He was drawing a completely different conclusion as to the purpose of Cummings' presence on the train, and that was cause for a different concern.

"During the war, did you ever meet Captain Harry Frobisher?" He pulled his hand back and reached into his jacket pocket.

Annette Myers shook her head. "No, Inspector. The first time I heard of Captain Frobisher was when I moved down here. But he was still away in France... And then there was that incident up at the Hall when he came back."

Edwards produced his pipe and began to tap out the remnants of his last smoke into the ashtray. This was a procedure he used to great effect when questioning a suspect. The process of clearing his pipe and reloading it gave him ample time to reflect upon what had been said, and carefully plan his next question. He also knew it would sometimes lull a suspect into a false sense of security, as they carefully watched the seemingly innocent process unfold before them.

Was there any point in dragging her over to the mortuary?

He was almost certain there wasn't.

But there was the question of either believing her or continuing to treat her as a suspect. She had come over to the police station, unprompted, to tell him her story. Maybe she'd done so to control his line of questioning and deflect suspicion from herself.

If she did murder Captain Grant, who was her next target?

Harry Frobisher immediately sprang to mind, and he whistled softly as he produced his tobacco pouch and began the delicate task of filling his pipe. The office had grown hot and oppressive; the very air around him hung heavy with anticipation, not only of the question of her innocence or guilt, but also of his next move.

The room had also become thick with tobacco smoke from the endless cigarettes she was smoking. Her short, gasping puffs had all the hallmarks of someone desperately trying to hold down their nerves. Her eyes darted continually around the room, and he wondered, if he'd actually poured her a glass of whisky, whether she would have drained it in one gulp.

He eyed her intently.

There was certainly a beauty about her, through the aging lines that criss-crossed her face and the smears of make-up that were becoming more apparent as she fought the tears threatening to erupt. Why she'd done the things she had, he could only speculate; like the burden of grief she so obviously carried, it manifested itself in a strange aura that hung around her, heavy and wretched.

As he finally lit his pipe, Inspector Edwards looked at Annette Myers and said softly, "My dear woman, go and help set up the cake stands and fetch your own sponge cake as well. I'll see you later at the recital." Drawing deep breaths of aromatic pipe smoke, he added, "I'll look forward to a cup of tea and a slice of your cake."

As though in a trance, Annette Myers rose from her chair, stubbed her latest cigarette out in the ashtray and gazed questionably around her. When her eyes finally descended upon Edwards, she smiled wanly, as though trying to acknowledge the gentleness of his statement. Drawing her handbag up to her chest, she unclipped it and reached inside. "Earlier you asked me if I owned a revolver…"

For some strange reason Inspector Edwards was not surprised when she drew out a small revolver and placed it on the desk next to his hat.

"I'm sorry, Inspector, I lied." She lowered her head.

"And was this the weapon used to kill Captain Grant?" he asked, though he already knew the answer; the gun was smaller, and probably more suited to a woman. The thought made him inwardly smile, as he treated both men and women with equal respect in terms of their ability to hold a gun of any size and shoot someone; but, from an initial assessment of the weapon, he could see that it hadn't been used to kill Captain Grant.

"All those years working for Military Intelligence, Inspector, gave me an appreciation of the dark world of murder and espionage… Do you honestly believe this gun killed Captain Grant?"

Edwards smiled and gently pushed it back across the desk towards her. "Give me some credit, Mrs Myers… If you are innocent, then I think you might be needing this."

"Thank you, Inspector, but there's been enough killing. I hope I might one day marry Canon Trebarwith and that he might forgive me for what I've done. I'd rather walk out of your office and leave that symbol of my past with you." Adjusting her scarf, she walked slowly to the door.

As she was about to leave, Edwards called out, "Mrs Myers?"

She turned and said vacantly, "Yes, Inspector?"

"You said a Mr Freeman was going to tune the piano?"

"Yes, he's due to play this afternoon. He's a very good pianist. But he never turned up at the town hall to tune the piano…" She paused and stared at the floor.

Edwards narrowed his eyes, recalling the events of last November. "You are referring to Mr Peran Freeman of Freeman Solicitors?"

"Yes, Inspector." Annette Myers walked out of the room and closed the door.

★★★

Doctor Mitchell had grown tired and frustrated with the modern world around him. When he'd first opened his practice in Bodmin thirty-five years ago, he'd taken a small cottage in the centre of town, only a short walk from his surgery, and had only ever seen horses, or the occasional horse and cart, pass by his window. Happy for it to remain that way, he'd never been tempted to move into the larger cities with their faster pace of life, and watch the arrival of the automobiles.

When he'd agreed to become the Frobisher family physician, he'd done so with a degree of trepidation, knowing that, once summoned, he would need to saddle his horse and ride out of town and across the moors to reach them. Lord Alfred had been happy with this arrangement, knowing that Mitchell was probably the best doctor in Bodmin and also the nearest.

Even when the coughing and spluttering sound of the first automobiles clanked and shuddered their way through the town, Mitchell, who was usually inspired by any new scientific breakthrough, chose to ignore their arrival with a disdainful look and a shrug of his shoulders.

He always carried his slight frame with an ease of movement, as though he could glide casually from one event in his life to the next without ever raising an eyebrow from either himself or his patients. As he'd grown older, his frame had become leaner and sharper, as though age were preparing him for a more stoic approach to later life.

And it had been.

When the Great War came, he'd been asked to work at one of the hospitals in London, leading a team of specialist doctors treating men coming back from France and Belgium with some of the most horrific injuries he'd ever seen.

His time had been spent mostly in Woolwich, close enough to London to hear the distant chimes of Big Ben when the wind blew in the right direction, but further enough away to breathe the cleaner air of the London suburbs. He'd treated just about every injury a man could suffer, and remembered with both horror and deep affection the night they'd brought in a badly wounded officer who'd suffered massive injuries to both his eyes...

The man's tattered clothing and bloodied face belied his true identity. But the Bible he still clutched in his hand, as he lay drifting in and out of consciousness, sparked a flame of recognition that drew tears to his eyes.

When he gently prised the Bible away from Harry Frobisher's bloodied hand, he opened the inside cover and read the inscription with eager anticipation...

'My dearest Harry, God Bless you and keep you safe'

As his fellow officers began to closely examine the shattered and ruined remains of Harry's eyes, Mitchell pushed the Bible back into his hand and gently closed his fingers around it. When he lowered his ear to Harry's face, he heard him calling for his brother, William, though his words were almost incoherent.

There were shrapnel wounds to his leg, but his eyes had taken the full force of the explosion.

He'd heard, through various sources, that no anaesthetic had initially been administered, and so a piece of wood had been shoved into Harry's mouth whilst medics had tried to dig out the countless pieces of metal from his body...

He thought about the other night, and smiled as he remembered the invitation he'd received from Harry and Morag to celebrate their return from honeymoon. The ride over to the Hall had been utterly delightful, with the warm evening lifting his spirits. Not that he needed encouragement. He'd heard about the adventures of Harry and Morag and had wanted to meet this strange woman with the red hair ever since he'd overheard his staff gossiping about her.

The evening had been convivial, with just himself, Canon Trebarwith and Lord and Lady Frobisher. If he was honest, he'd fallen slightly in love with the beautiful wife of Lord Frobisher; with her flowing red hair and Scottish accent, he'd marvelled at the freckles radiating across her face, her high cheekbones accentuated by the light in the dining room, and the beautiful curvature of her body...

He shook his head and dug in his heels, momentarily startling his horse.

The famous Frobisher wine had loosened his tongue and banished his inhibitions. The next day he'd regretted his comment about Ellen Carfax and hoped it wouldn't be a cause of discussion between Harry and Morag.

As he cantered along, approaching the outskirts of town, he pulled his watch from his pocket and checked the time.

Experience told him he'd probably be hitching his horse outside the St Petroc Hotel around lunchtime. Now, that would be perfect, as he could enjoy lunch and complete his business with Peran Freeman fairly quickly. He would be away from Bodmin well before people gathered for the afternoon's piano recital.

As he approached the main road that could either take him left, towards the Frobisher Estate, or right, into town, he drew his horse to a halt and peered across the tree tops to the twin towers looming magnificently towards the clear blue sky.

To dine with the new Lord and Lady Frobisher that night had been magical, beyond his wildest dreams.

He remembered the night he'd delivered Harry into this world; it had been a few days before Christmas, during one of the coldest winters he'd ever known. The cold had been so intense he'd wrapped Harry in his own coat for added warmth; and when he'd eventually handed him across to Lady Margaret, she'd received him with a cold indifference that had concerned him deeply.

Yes, it had been a wonderful evening.

As Lady Frobisher had talked about her beloved sister, Elisha, and her parents in Scotland, and Canon Trebarwith had slowly succumbed to the effects of the wine, Doctor Mitchell had gazed at Harry and inwardly wept – with relief that he'd survived both the war and the terrible experiences of last November, and with sadness as he watched Morag reach across and cut the meat from his chicken bone.

He thought again of the business he needed to conclude at Peran Freeman's, and kicked his heels, turning his horse towards Bodmin. His face was solemn and grey.

17

Harry Frobisher was stretched out on the sofa in the lounge when the thunderous roar of someone banging the great brass knocker on the front door reverberated throughout the house. Over the years he'd grown accustomed to its angry and intrusive sound and had promised himself he would change it for something a little gentler on the ear. He supposed his blindness didn't help, as his hearing was now sharper than ever, and even the tiniest of sounds, anywhere in the house, would come to him quite clearly.

That was how he'd heard Morag the previous night, as she'd bumped into something in the study. Though he'd not initially heard the polyphon, he'd heard her subsequent movements in the library.

The great brass door knocker clanged menacingly against the door twice more, louder, demanding attention.

As he raised his head, he realised he'd been sleeping, as his mind tried to comprehend the familiar feeling of sudden confusion that still gripped him when he awoke in his world of darkness.

"Morag...?" he called softly, expecting to hear her voice from across the room. She'd been sitting at a small table by the window, writing letters.

There was no answer, only the sound of footsteps scurrying across the hallway towards the main door.

He heaved himself into a sitting position, peering into the darkness around him, trying to gather his thoughts. Even now, after all this time coming to terms with his blindness, he still struggled with those first few seconds of waking, when he still hoped to see a bright and vibrant world around him, fully defined images and the face of the woman he loved.

It was probably Morag who'd hurried off to answer the door. He clipped open the glass front of his watch and gently pressed his fingertip onto the hands. The time was approaching 11.15am. The ferocity of the pounding on the door troubled him. Visitors usually tapped gently, after giving the household plenty of notice of their arrival.

Standing up, Harry groped for his stick, sliding his hands along the front of the seat cushions before moving to the top of the small table; he inwardly swore as he realised it could be anywhere in the room. The stupid thing, he considered, was that he would normally feel confident enough to navigate his way around the lounge and into the hall without his stick, as he'd fast become quite self-assured in his endeavours to find his way to any part of the house without his stick or Morag's supportive arm.

The panic of knowing he was about to receive strangers started to stir within him. The realisation that he'd soon be trying to ascertain their reason for calling, arranging tea and guiding them into either the library or lounge, bore down on him like a heavy burden that was, lately, becoming almost intolerable. The days of him calling out orders to his men, proudly standing before them on parade and knowing how much he commanded their affection and unstinting loyalty, had faded to a distant memory. The thought of now finding himself in such a position filled him with dread.

"For God's sake." He blundered into one of the other chairs, lost his balance and tried to steady himself. Wearing a pair of light flannel trousers, a shirt and a sweater without a cravat, he felt totally unprepared to receive visitors and hoped they might be patient enough to wait for him to hurry to his room to dress properly.

He heard the front door opening, muffled voices, and the sound of footsteps approaching the lounge. In his desperation to put distance between himself and the person approaching the door, he staggered back against the side of the fireplace and felt the poker jab him in the leg. As he reached down, fumbling with a hand that now shook with fear and frustration, he heard the door open and a familiar voice.

"Lord Frobisher." Dodson's voice, stoic and reassuring, came to him through the darkness from the other side of the room. "A Colonel Charles Standish to see you, sir."

Harry raised his head, trying to clear his mind and push back the angry tide of fear and anxiety that threatened to wash over him. For some reason, he couldn't quite gather why, he was holding the poker in his hand.

"Lord Frobisher?" This time there was a flicker of concern in Dodson's voice.

"Thank you, Dodson. Please take him through to the library and arrange for tea." Harry began to feel the natural rhythm of his breathing return; maybe it was the reassuring voice of Dodson, or the fact that the panic was now receding.

"Yes, sir. There are other men in attendance."

"Do you know who?" Harry slipped the poker back into place and inched his way towards where he thought the nearest chair might be.

"Altogether, there are three gentlemen in army uniform."

"Okay, Dodson, show them through. I'll receive them in here…" He paused before adding, "Do you know where Lady Frobisher is?"

"I saw Lady Frobisher ride out a short while ago with Mr Matthews, sir. I can't say for sure where they were going," Dodson replied.

"I see."

Harry found the chair and positioned himself so he was leaning nonchalantly against the back. He knew that from here, if he stayed the way he was, he would immediately face whoever walked into the room. He also knew that the drinks' cabinet was directly behind him. His mind whirled with past memories of how the room was laid out: the tables and chairs, along with vases that stood precariously upon marble bases. He remembered them as a sighted person, though now feared their locality as a person moving in eternal darkness.

Morag had once laughingly told him never to go into the lounge if he had overdone the whisky...

He just wished...

"Sir?" Dodson's voice was closer now, supportive and gentle. "Here... You might want this?"

Harry felt his stick ease gently into his hand.

"Thank you, Dodson." Harry's relief was almost palpable. From where he was standing, a gentle breeze blew into the lounge and warmed the perspiration on his forehead.

Taking a couple of deep breaths, he brushed himself down and tried to secure the top button of his shirt – an act that quickly became more desperate as he heard the approach of several footsteps and the sound of leather boots squeaking.

"Colonel Charles Standish, Lord Frobisher," Dodson announced flatly.

"Thank you, Dodson. If my wife happens to return, please ask her to join us." Harry took a tentative step forward, tapping lightly from side to side with his stick.

For God's sake, man, he thought, *get a grip of yourself. You know your way around this room.*

"Colonel Standish, forgive me for not dressing appropriately; we weren't expecting you." Taking a couple of nervous steps forward, he held out his hand.

"Captain Frobisher. I'm here on official business, I'm afraid.

These gentlemen here beside me are Captain Little and Captain Hemmings."

Harry lowered his hand and swallowed deeply. Licking his lips, he tried to ascertain his distance from the men standing before him. The fact that his offer of a handshake had been so flatly declined filled him with cold trepidation. His mind, though, began to churn quickly as the names of his visitors began to register.

Remembering the conversation the previous evening with Inspector Edwards, and the latter's recollections of his meeting with Colonel Standish in London, Harry felt suddenly very alone and extremely anxious. Knowing that these men could quite easily overpower him made his blood run cold, and he wondered if he'd ever felt so frightened as to what was going to happen next. The cold and detached tone of Colonel Standish's voice did nothing to arrest his fears.

He sensed something threatening, rolling towards him in his darkened world. It made no sound and gave no warning. Relentlessly it bore down upon him and there was nothing he could do…

A sparkle of friendly recognition briefly shone in his mind.

Though he didn't recognise Captain Little's name, he certainly felt a wave of memories, distant and vague, begin to wash over him as he repeated the name of Hemmings in his mind. He smiled slightly and gripped his stick.

"Captain Hemmings…? John Hemmings?"

"Yes, Lord Frobisher. Captain John Hemmings… Though you'll remember me as Lieutenant Hemmings, when we went over the top that third day during the Somme."

"My God… John…" Harry whispered, shaking his head.

"It's good to see you again, Lord Frobisher." Hemmings' voice carried a deep West Country drawl.

Harry immediately recalled their time together, though wondered if it might have all been a terrible dream.

"You stayed with me when I took that bullet in the leg…" Hemmings continued, "Until the medics arrived… I was never able to thank you for what you did."

Harry held out his hand, this time aware that he was reaching out to a former friend and comrade, spanning the years and sweeping away the terrible memories they both shared.

Hemmings grasped his hand and whispered under his breath, "I'm sorry about this."

Harry wanted to reply, but his mind was confused. Why this man, who had once stood resolutely beside him, should now stand beside a man such as Standish confused him. The purpose of their visit had not yet been made clear, though the very atmosphere in the lounge had become heavy with dreaded anticipation the moment the Colonel had entered.

He inclined his head a little towards Captain Little. "I'm afraid I don't recall your name, Captain Little."

"You won't, sir. Although I served in the same regiment as yourself, I never actually got to meet you." The voice of Peter Little was nervous and hesitant. "But I'm honoured to meet you now… and just wish it were under more pleasant conditions."

"Yes," Colonel Standish snarled. "I couldn't get anyone from your regiment to volunteer to come here… not when I told them the purpose of my visit. It seems they all regard you with the highest level of admiration and respect… I had to order Captains Hemmings and Little to accompany me here."

There was a dark and foreboding silence that settled like a cold hand upon Harry's shoulder.

Standish continued, "We are here on official business, one of deep importance to the security of the country."

Harry released his grip on his stick and stepped back. "Then you'd better get to the point, Colonel. What is it you want?"

"Captain Frobisher," commenced Standish, "I am arresting you on a charge of high treason. These two gentlemen have orders to accompany you to the regimental barracks in Bodmin and hold you there until transport can be arranged for your eventual removal to London."

Harry staggered back, as though an invisible force had pummelled into him. By doing so, he dropped his stick and instinctively bent down to find it.

"I… I'm not sure…" he stuttered, frantically searching for his stick, desperate for Morag's hand.

"Captain Hemmings!!" Standish's voice thundered across the room. "Leave Captain Frobisher's stick where it is. He won't need it where he's going."

Harry tried to raise himself, aware of a dizziness seizing him. He heard the words, but couldn't define their meaning. "Are you joking…?"

"Not at all, Captain Frobisher," Standish replied, his words falling like lead weights. "I intend to prove that you were the Fourth Rook, a double agent working for our enemies during the war; that you fed useless information to Military Intelligence, whilst supplying top secret information to the Germans using the three agents you controlled as dupes in your endeavours."

"That's rubbish. Complete rubbish." Harry staggered to his feet, thought briefly of grasping the poker, then thought better of it as he decided it would probably take him forever to find the bloody thing.

"We know you held clandestine meetings with Captain Grant and that he shared secrets with you. It is my opinion that you were controlling both him and the other two members of your team." Standish's voice was nearer, much nearer, and Harry desperately tried to back away, fearful of restraining hands suddenly grasping him. "Even after you were blinded and brought back to London, it is my belief that you still sent messages through an outside associate, someone I have yet to track down."

"It's not true," Harry muttered, struggling to speak. He turned his head, staring through his sightless eyes at the darkness that surrounded him, mocking and accusing. "I was injured... Morag... Where's Morag?"

"Your wife can't help you," Standish said with contemptuous venom. "The next time she'll see you is when you stand trial... Though... of course... it will be a military trial. And if that's the case, she may never see you again, Captain Frobisher. If you're found guilty you will be hanged at a military garrison—"

"But why...?" Harry asked feebly. "Why are you doing this?" Though he spoke the words, he had no idea where he was in relation to the other three men in the room and so couldn't direct them at anyone. He held out his hand and began to step awkwardly around the room. "Morag...?"

"Captain Frobisher. Please come quietly, or I will order these men to handcuff you," Standish jeered.

"Morag, please... don't leave me..." Harry whispered, feeling his nerves begin to finally break. "Where are you?"

"I really don't have time for this... I need to go into Bodmin. Gentlemen," Standish called to Little and Hemmings, "restrain Captain Frobisher and—"

"What on earth is going on here?" The words cut through the room, stunning everyone into silence.

Harry recognised the voice. It came to him like a lifeline thrown to a drowning man. Eagerly he grasped it and clung hold, drawing immediate strength; he felt as though he might take a moment's respite and gather his thoughts. He called across the room, "Susan?"

"I'm here, Lord Frobisher," she replied, before adding with a razor-sharp tone, "Who are you gentlemen?"

"And who might you be, young lady?" Standish taunted.

"Mrs Matthews, the Housekeeper."

Harry heard footsteps hurrying towards him, then a warm hand grasp his. "Here you are, sir..." He felt the hand open his fingers and close them around his stick. "Are you okay, sir?"

"Susan… Where's Morag?" Harry leaned a little on her and let her guide him towards a chair.

"Lady Frobisher rode out to Sunrise Cottage earlier with Lawrence. She wanted him to show her exactly where the place was," Susan explained. "You were sleeping, and she left me a message to tell you when you awoke."

Harry felt his knee brush against the side of the chair, and he groped desperately for the armrest to get his bearings. In his mind he grappled with images that shot through his brain like lightning bolts…

Recollections of Captain Grant… of Sergeant Benson carrying him from a terrible dream… And that voice… That blessed voice that spoke to him in the Red Cross tent… talking… beguiling… hands searching through his pockets…

Susan's voice dragged him back from one nightmare into another. "I couldn't tell you earlier…" she lowered her voice, "but we've been looking for Gregson… She's disappeared."

"Gentlemen, please do as I say and restrain Captain Frobisher," Standish commanded.

"Stay away from him… Can't you see he's ill…?" There was a savagery in Susan's voice that made Harry recoil. In these last few months, since he'd held the dead body of his brother at the foot of the stairs, he'd sworn he would never raise a hand in anger again; it had been a promise easily made when he'd slipped the wedding ring onto Morag's finger and felt the love of not only the woman beside him, but of an entire town, enclose around him.

"Young lady, stand aside. Otherwise I will arrest you for obstructing the law," Standish spat.

Harry felt Susan shudder then move herself around, as if to shield to him.

"Harry, he has a gun," she whispered.

"Colonel Standish, I must protest," Captain Hemmings' voice echoed, concerned and worried.

"If you don't move aside I'll shoot you where you stand."

"Please, Colonel—" Hemmings objected.

"Shut up! Of course. You're the little maid who married Constable Matthews, the hero of that night... Yes... I've read the reports..." Standish's voice now moved from one of arrogance to one of cold bitterness.

"Please, Susan, stand aside," Harry whispered into her ear.

"I'm not leaving you, Harry." Susan pushed her small frame against him, forcing him back into the chair. "Morag will be home soon."

Harry felt a momentary spark of hope ignite, then fizzle out as he felt the muzzle of a revolver jab violently into his forehead, and heard a firing pin click back.

"Captain Frobisher, tell this young lady to step aside, or I will splatter your brains all over this beautiful lounge." Colonel Standish's voice was neither arrogant nor cold.

It was as empty as a bottomless pit.

★★★

Morag eyed the paintings of Frobisher Hall in the small hallway of Sunrise Cottage and held her breath. Every emotion she'd ever felt since the day she'd arrived at the Hall, so long ago now it seemed like a dream, was wrapped up in their beautifully created images. Their angles and shades literally breathed and pulsated with a love that drove deep into the heart of the house with each painting telling a different story to the next.

One, an autumn view of the rear of the house, with the towers slightly shaded and not so prominent, suggested a more personal engagement with the building, as though the viewer might feel as though they were part of the estate.

The same couldn't be said about the next; this one was painted as though the artist were sat just within the borderline of trees and staring across the open lawns. To have moved closer, to maybe gain a better perspective, might have been an infringement too far; so they'd painted the terrace, with the doors to the dining room open and the curtains flapping as a small breeze swept through.

Morag moved slowly along the hall.

"You like my paintings?" Ellen Carfax had removed her apron. She wore an old skirt and a light cardigan. Her long hair was tied back, in a similar fashion to Morag's, and her eyes, wide and inquisitive, followed Morag's every movement.

"Aye… I think they're beautiful."

Morag paused at the last one before they entered the dining room. It was of a winter scene, with snow and grey light suggesting a late afternoon, as the sun, already low in the sky, began its lamented descent. The view of the house was from the front and to the side, and was mostly obscured by the high Victorian wall that skirted around to the eastern slopes; it reminded her of that day she'd stood peering out of the East Tower and noticed Harry speaking privately with Edith Travers. But what caught her eye, almost immediately, was the huge Victorian wall that blotted out any reasonable view of the house or anything else. It was as though there were a beautiful image to behold, if only that high, red and grey brick wall didn't obscure it.

And then it came to her.

Standing back a little she gazed at the paintings as a collective, narrowing her eyes and feeling Ellen Carfax staring at her with eager anticipation. "It's almost as if…"

"Yes?" Ellen whispered.

"It's almost as if the artist belongs to Frobisher Hall, but yet doesn't…"

"In what way?"

"I'm not sure…" Morag felt resolved to stand there for an eternity, so determined was she to fathom the mystery that was slowly consuming her. "I feel there's a sense of being an outcast, as though someone who should belong at the house cannot gain entry... yet the images have been painted with such love and tenderness... They're quite remarkable."

"And she painted them herself," Lawrence Matthews called through from the dining room. "You should sell them in town, Miss Carfax."

"I'm afraid," Ellen Carfax smiled, "I could never sell these paintings; they're much too dear to me. Each one has a place in my heart."

"You painted the one in the lounge at Frobisher Hall, didn't you?" Morag turned and looked at her; instantly feeling a bond, that might have existed for ages, draw them a little closer.

"Is it still there?" Ellen laughed, and finally moved into the dining room. "It was the only time I ever dared enter the house after..." Her smile waned and a sadness filled her eyes. "I actually removed the old painting – I forget which one it was – and hung that one up instead. I was so scared I might be discovered."

"And you've painted them ever since you came to live here?" Morag followed her into the dining room.

Lawrence stood up respectfully.

"That's right... And that must be nearly thirty years ago." Ellen lifted the teapot and turned to Lawrence. "Constable Matthews, please help yourself to another biscuit... Eat them now before Branok comes back. He's checking the traps; I'm hoping to make a rabbit stew tonight. It's his favourite." She paused before adding, "How's the shoulder?"

"Coming along fine, Miss Carfax," Lawrence replied, before shoving a large gingerbread biscuit into his mouth.

"That was some fall you had." Ellen poured three cups of nettle tea. "I'm surprised that young wife of yours actually let you ride out here again."

"Well, it was the fact that Lady Frobisher was with me, and she's an experienced rider." Lawrence gratefully received his cup of tea. Looking at Morag, he said, "Try it... You'll be surprised."

"Ellen Carfax," Morag muttered the words to herself, though loud enough for her two companions to hear. She looked at her host. "There's no mention of you in the list of estate workers or house staff. The maps of the estate have no reference to this cottage... and yet there's an old map which does."

"Ah... so one map escaped Lord Alfred's attention." Ellen sat down and sipped her tea.

Morag followed her lead and sat opposite her.

The dining room, like the rest of the cottage, was sparsely furnished, with old and tatty furniture that carried with it no reference to any style or fashion, as though it had been bought from second-hand shops in town.

Morag was of the opinion that neighbouring cottages and farmhouses had possibly played a charitable hand by gifting items to her, but she couldn't think why she had that particular notion.

Again, there were several paintings hung upon the walls; she tried to give them a cursory glance, immediately finding she couldn't. Each one demanded her attention, as though casting its spell upon her and toying with her emotions. She found herself thinking of her own home in Edinburgh and of the parents she'd shunned. Though these were images and reflections of the Frobisher Estate, her mind was whisked away to her childhood in Scotland... of walks in the hills and fishing with her father in the lochs... and of the time she'd visited that beautiful little town on the Firth of Tay not far from Dundee, where she'd walked as a young girl on golden sands and dreamed of the man she might one day fall in love with.

That he had been an Englishman would have made her friends laugh.

As if reading her thoughts, Ellen said, "Tell me about your family in Scotland."

Morag lifted her cup and wrinkled her nose at the strange smell. "You mean the family I ran away from, for no other reason than to find adventure? What's there to tell…? Other than the terrible anguish my parents suffered, losing one of their daughters to Spanish flu and the other to her own selfish pride and obstinate nature… Harry's always telling me to write to them, to invite them to Frobisher Hall."

"He sounds like a very perceptive young man, this Harry Frobisher." Ellen reached out and laid her hand across Morag's.

"He's everything a woman could wish for." Morag felt her eyes well up. She glanced across at Lawrence.

Lawrence Matthews returned her gaze and narrowed his eyes. For what seemed like an eternity he sat blankly looking at her before the flash of realisation illuminated his eyes and he blurted out, "Oh, er… yes… Think I'll take a walk outside… Might find Branok and help him with his traps…" He stood up and made his way to the door. Turning round, he said, "Lovely tea, Miss Carfax."

Morag smiled as he walked into the kitchen and eventually out into the garden.

"He did a brave thing last year…" Ellen watched him leave, then added, "as you yourself did."

"I did what needed to be done." Morag sighed and sipped her tea, staring into the green contents and instantly finding its taste satisfying beyond anything she'd ever tasted before.

"You saved the lives of both Harry and that inspector… and ultimately many other people." Ellen squeezed Morag's hand.

"I know… I…" A single tear found its way onto Morag's cheek. "But William was his brother… and I killed him…" Morag lowered her head and began to weep silently, feeling emotions, pent up and ignored for too long, burst upon her. "I killed him…"

Ellen eased herself forward and wrapped her arm around Morag's shoulders, pulling her close and gently kissing her forehead. "William was a very sick man," she soothed. "The war affected all of us, Morag…" Her voice trembled, as though she were fighting to shore up her own emotional dam. "Here…" She pulled out an old handkerchief and offered it to Morag.

Morag dabbed her eyes and tried to compose herself. "It doesn't make it any easier… He was Lady Margaret's son, and I always feel her staring down at me in the lounge… accusing me." She forced a smile and stared at Ellen.

"Like you said," Ellen Carfax said sadly, "you did what you had to do…" She pulled away from Morag and sat down in her chair. "Morag, the love between a parent and their child knows no boundaries; it doesn't recognise class or title. You are now Lady Frobisher and have a wonderful man as your husband… Your parents are just as much a part of your life with Harry as Frobisher Hall and everything you see around you." She reached forward and wiped a tear from Morag's face. "I've only known you since you arrived earlier, yet I see so much of myself in you…"

Morag drew a deep breath; now free of their constraints, her emotions splashed violently around her mind, washing up repressed fears and anxieties onto the shores of her subconscious, leaving them there like broken and jagged objects protruding from the sand. "We're in danger," she muttered.

"Morgan Treave?" Ellen said quietly.

Morag nodded, then added, "And something else… Something from Harry's past… You know my brother-in-law?"

"Ah… the eminent Inspector Edwards…" Ellen smiled and leaned back in her chair. "That man is in danger of becoming part of Cornish folklore."

"Yes, Harry and I would certainly agree with you." Morag straightened herself up and cleared her mind. She felt a strange confidence consume her, as though she had better control over events now that she could see the obstacles in the sand before her. "Cyril's come back to Frobisher Hall to investigate Harry's possible involvement with a network of spies during the war… A man was found dead on the train that brought us back to Bodmin; he was a hired killer... There was a fight... Cyril killed him..."

"Inspector Edwards?" Ellen stiffened up. "Good grief!"

"Aye..." Morag wasn't too sure on how to elaborate on that particular piece of information. She knew her brother-in-law's military background and the dangers he now faced on a continual basis as a policeman. She continued, "Harry received a letter from a Captain Grant, warning him and asking to meet him in Bodmin... but he was murdered before we could get to him... We think someone wants to kill these so-called Rooks – the codenames of these spies." Her mind was certainly clearing, as she now found the confidence to talk freely about the events of the past few days.

"Do you think Harry has had anything to do with this organisation... or even these deaths?" Ellen eyed Morag closely.

"Good God, no..." Morag responded. "I know Harry. I trust him. After what we went through last year... You see..." she desperately searched for the right words, "there's a bond between us... It goes beyond mere love; it's something almost spiritual."

"And Inspector Edwards? What does he think?"

Morag smiled proudly. "He thinks it's nonsense... There's no evidence."

Ellen Carfax nodded and spoke slowly, accentuating every word, "My dear child, you must fight to protect Harry and the home you have together. I know he carries the physical and mental scars of his time during the war..." She reached forward and grasped Morag's hand again, though this time with a strength that made Morag wince. "Promise me you'll look after him and protect him."

Morag nodded and felt Ellen release her grip.

As if to alleviate the tension, she turned her gaze towards the paintings, feeling Ellen Carfax follow her line of sight, as though sharing her thoughts.

271

Her attention settled on a small painting situated near the door to the kitchen. It was a view of a small glade in summertime, with the tops of the Frobisher Hall chimneys just in sight above the lush canopy of trees that framed the image.

Morag rose slightly from her chair.

There was a ray of sunlight cascading through the kitchen, reflecting off something she couldn't see. The light splashed into the dining room and illuminated the painting before her. Moving closer, she set down her cup of tea, aware that she was in danger of letting it spill over.

What she saw filled her with both happiness and a sense of loss.

In the middle of the glade were two small boys, of about seven and five, in shorts and white shirts, cheerfully playing; maybe they were chasing each other, maybe they were running towards the woman who sat amongst the long grass, a bonnet tilted low over her face and with her back to the observer.

Morag knew immediately that they were brothers; the eldest had a familiarity about his young face that filled her heart with so much love she couldn't resist the urge to reach her fingers forward and gently touch his face. "Harry…" she whispered.

Morag, where are you? Harry's voice came to her, frightened and desperate.

She turned to Ellen Carfax and saw the same look of fear spread across her face.

18

Annette Myers began to feel the first numbing effects of the poison that was working its way through her body, and she felt a strange sense of relief that her ordeal in this life was almost at an end. She eyed the person opposite her and tried to reach out as they moved swiftly past her towards the kitchen door.

They paused before opening the door and looked back with eyes that were empty and cold. As if changing their mind about leaving, they moved a little closer to the kitchen table until they were close enough to whisper to her.

"Poison hemlock, Annette Myers... You'll die slowly... Paralysis will consume you, spreading throughout your body until you lose the ability to breathe... You might even have trouble hearing and seeing me now..."

"Please..." Annette stretched out her hand towards the two photographs. "My boys..."

"No, I think it best you die without the comfort of holding them close... Now, please excuse me... I have one last Rook to dispose of..." The figure slunk back towards the kitchen door, opened it quietly, then slipped out into a beautiful summer's day.

She could feel a numbness working up from her feet, and her left hand was totally useless. To swallow took an inestimable amount of effort, and she realised it was only a matter of time before Death enveloped her and drew her into that twilight world where she believed her two sons were waiting for her. If only she might make it out onto the street, find someone, give them a name. She might then die knowing she'd finally exposed the identity of the Fourth Rook.

But therein lay her dilemma.

To stay where she was meant the poison taking more time to work its way through her body.

To try and move meant exhausting her already tired and rapidly failing body. She might not even make it to the door.

Gazing at the cup of tea she'd completely consumed gave her some idea of how much of the poison she'd ingested, though how much had actually been added she couldn't work out.

She thought about the piano recital that was due to start later that afternoon. It would have been so nice to have heard Peran Freeman play Beethoven, though she found herself slightly concerned as to why he hadn't been there to tune the piano the previous evening. He was such a nice man, so full of dignity and…

For God's sake, Annette… make some kind of effort!

A voice in her head screamed and instantly blew her idle thoughts away. With an initial effort that was surprisingly easy, considering her predicament, she heaved herself out of the chair and steadied herself against the table, trying to compensate for the lack of feeling in her feet. As she lurched towards the door, she pitched forward and slumped against it, aware of a strange sensation of floating on air.

Pushing herself up, she caught the handle with her good hand and lowered it until the door eased open. As she slid through the gap, the first thing she became aware of was her inability to smell the honeysuckle outside her door. With this realisation that she was approaching the end of her life, she groaned a little, hoping that someone might hear her.

From somewhere across the road, children played with a small ball, bouncing it against the side of a neighbouring house. As she stumbled along her pathway, she tried to draw their attention, but could only gurgle a string of incoherent words. When she reached the pavement, she noticed they'd moved out of sight.

Were they even there in the first place?

Her mind, like her body, was slowly shutting down, turning out the lights that illuminated her conscious thinking and causing her to see things that weren't there...

Or were they?

She turned, knowing a small path to her left would eventually take her into the main high street. There were bound to be people there. There had to be.... She prayed to God for the strength to find someone... anyone...

It was then she noticed a rook, shiny and regal, sitting on a nearby post and staring at her with mocking contempt. For some reason she thought it might be an avenging angel, sent to refuse her entry into Heaven and consigning her to Hell as punishment for all her sins. When she tried to scare it away, it sat silent and defiant, grinning at her staggering steps and rambling speech.

She thought again of Peran Freeman.

He'd listen to her.

He'd always listened to her. Of all the men in Bodmin, he was the most dependable, the most astute and reliable. If she could possibly make it to his office, she might actually catch him before he left for the town hall. She smiled as she realised that the path she was now taking would eventually bring her out onto the main high street and directly opposite his office.

But the path was agonisingly uphill, and she was fast losing the feeling in her legs. The day was also warm, and she found herself losing the ability to control her body temperature; she gasped and spluttered as she felt herself drifting from extreme cold to a torturous heat that threatened to burn away what little breath she had left.

And then she saw them.

More rooks had fluttered down and were now settled upon random posts and gates, creating a terrible guard of honour, as though she were walking her final steps to the very gates of oblivion. As she passed each one, they flapped their wings and cried out to her, scornful, accusing...

The end of her life was nearing.

The high street was tantalisingly close. She knew that when she emerged onto the main pavement, the office of Peran Freeman would be directly opposite. But there would be steps... and a long pathway to his front door. And what if he wasn't there...? He might already have made his way over to the town hall...

These thoughts compelled her forward, staggering and tumbling as she slowly lost control of her body. She needed to atone for her actions, to make peace with God and pray that her sons, wherever they were, might actually find it in themselves to forgive her.

As she staggered onto the main high street, several local people stopped and watched with a strange interest as she fell into the road, pulled herself up and raised a hand just as a large and shiny Daimler screeched to a halt not two feet from her.

★★★

Inspector Edwards looked up sharply as the door to his office opened, his eyes widening and his mouth opening in disbelief as he watched Colonel Standish walk briskly into the room. Resisting the urge to tell the army officer to go back out and knock, he said quietly, "Well, this is a turn-up for the books."

"Good afternoon, Inspector. I was hoping to catch you." Standish stood on the other side of the desk and let his eyes slowly peruse the room. When they finally settled back on Edwards, he added, "If you would be so good as to stand up and move around here… I'm used to sitting in the main chair; and seeing as I outrank just about everyone in this station, I think we should start as we intend to go on." He started to tap his fingers on the desk.

Edwards nonchalantly closed his notebook, along with a large folder that contained several pieces of paper, one of which was the letter from Captain Grant to Harry Frobisher. He'd been studying its contents for the past ten minutes, knowing he was missing something but damned if he could figure out what. He was surprised at the relaxed way in which he received Standish, and that he hadn't stood up and thrown him out in light of his last statement.

He looked at the clock.

1.35pm.

His stomach had eagerly digested the two biscuits he'd consumed whilst talking to Annette Myers earlier that morning, and now his stomach roared its disapproval at the lack of lunch.

"Well?" Standish demanded impatiently.

"Well, what?" asked Edwards, finding his pipe in his pocket and striking a light. He eyed Standish curiously.

"Are you going to vacate that chair?"

"No." Edwards puffed several times on his pipe and blew the smoke towards Standish.

"No matter." Standish stepped back, coughing disdainfully. "You will do after I tell you why I'm here."

Edwards narrowed his eyes and tried to think quickly; something told him that events were about to take a sudden turn and he'd need to respond appropriately. He remembered the telegram from his colleagues at Scotland Yard and its indication that Standish had probably taken an earlier train down to Bodmin. If this were true, then why hadn't he announced his arrival before now?

He yawned and said, "Well, then, you'd better get on with it."

Standish chuckled, took off his cap and tossed it onto the desk; it bounced off Edwards' Fedora before coming to rest on the latter's notebook and folder. The police inspector gently picked it up and placed it precariously near the edge of the desk closest to Standish; if either of them so much as coughed, it would fall to the floor.

"The first thing I need to tell you is that you are now officially off this case," Standish sneered. "You were acting under my orders, and now I want you to hand over all your notes and interview statements. Do you understand?"

Edwards said nothing.

"Do you under—"

"You said that was the first thing…" Edwards replied calmly.

"What?"

"You said that was the first thing. Which implies there's a second thing?" Edwards smiled.

"Okay, Inspector…" Standish stepped forward and pushed his cap a little further back onto the desk. "I have arrested Captain Frobisher on a charge of high treason and he's now in the cells in his regimental barracks up the road." He stepped back and eyed Edwards with contempt. "I told you he was our main suspect, and you came down here and did nothing about it… And now Captain Grant is dead… And I've heard about your little caper on the train; you'll be finding yourself answering questions about that, I would imagine."

Edwards remained motionless, his face stern and deeply set. It was, though, a beguiling façade, as his heart had plummeted and his blood run cold at this sudden announcement. Though the room was warm to the degree of stifling, he found it hard to suppress the shiver that ran through his body as a morbid feeling of gloom took hold of him.

"Have you anything to say?" Standish moved forward and pushed his cap back into the middle of the desk, this time pushing Edwards' notebook and folder back towards the opposite edge.

Edwards brushed his moustache right... then paused... "Where have you been these last couple of days?"

The question seemed to knock Standish slightly off balance. "What do you mean?"

Edwards lowered his hand and placed it on the desk next to Standish's cap. "What I have just asked... Where have you been these last couple of days?"

"Where I've been has absolutely nothing to do with you," Standish replied indignantly.

"It has everything to do with me." Edwards picked up the cap, eyed it for a moment, then threw it spinning onto a side table. "You see, when I left your office in Whitehall on Wednesday, I immediately had you followed. You're not the only one who has friends in Whitehall... Seems they were only too pleased to help me... Which says a lot about you, doesn't it?"

"You can't speak to me like that," Standish blustered, his face reddening.

Edwards nonchalantly raised his hand.

Standish fell silent.

"You see, Colonel, I couldn't initially understand why you sent me down here... Yes, I know all about your suspicions about Lord Frobisher—"

"When they hang him," Standish snarled, "he'll be plain Harry Frobisher. They'll strip him of his rank and title." He grinned triumphantly.

"Yes, quite..." Edwards's expression and tone of voice were deadpan. "But there's the issue... You've convinced yourself of his guilt and yet cannot produce a single scrap of evidence. When we spoke on Wednesday morning you supplied me with various assumptions and conjectures, but no real proof—"

"That will come out at his trial," Standish interrupted.

"Maybe… maybe not. But you sent me down here to find out about Lord Frobisher's possible involvement with The Nest of Rooks. I was even tempted to give you the benefit of the doubt. If anything, it was an excuse to come down and visit the only family I have left in my life… and to visit a town I've come to love. But personal feelings aside, I end up confronting a hired killer on the train that brings Lord and Lady Frobisher back from their honeymoon and then find Captain Grant shot dead."

"He committed suicide!" Standish stammered, then stepped back a little.

Edwards leaned forward and smiled. "Who told you that?" he asked.

"It was in the report the commanding officer has over at the barracks!"

"That's what I deliberately told them."

"Why?" Standish glanced across at his cap and walked over to the side table.

"Because if this Fourth Rook were actually still in Bodmin…" Edwards watched him carefully, "… chances are they would be staying up at the regimental garrison; probably using their military connections to fabricate a cover story. Strangers in a place like Bodmin tend to stick out. But apart from Captain Grant, there've been no reports of visitors or strangers in town. You see, I wanted to give them time to relax and think that their plan to make it look as though Captain Grant had taken his own life had succeeded."

Standish picked up his cap and looked at Edwards' desk.

"Colonel Standish, if you place that bloody thing on my desk it'll disappear out of this window." Edwards relit his pipe.

"My God…" Standish sneered, "the wonderful Inspector Edwards… The hero of Frobisher Hall… For all I know you're probably involved in this plot, along with your friend Captain

Frobisher... That would make sense. I can see it was a mistake getting you involved in the first place. I thought you were a man to be trusted."

"I'm afraid I was involved well before I sat down in your office on Wednesday, Colonel. You see, I had Lord and Lady Frobisher tailed throughout their honeymoon, though not all the time they were abroad. You see, after that particular incident last year, when William Frobisher was killed, there was some unfinished business to take care of. He had an accomplice, a man called Morgan Treave, the former governor of Amble Lodge Asylum; he, in turn, also had an accomplice, one Edwina Baker, a nurse at Amble Lodge. It was the two of them who falsely imprisoned Morag. Treave found Morag hiding out in the East Tower. There was a fight; she thought she'd killed him, and left him for dead. When my men eventually searched the place, he was gone. So, without their knowledge, I arranged to have Morag and Harry Frobisher followed, in the hope that we might be able to trap Morgan Treave if he decided to exact some kind of revenge whilst they were away from Cornwall."

"So, what has this to do with Captain Frobisher?" Standish moved across to one of the old wooden chairs and sat down.

"Well, everything, really." Edwards smiled. "You see, if Lord Frobisher had been up to no good, meeting with hired assassins, scheming and planning the death of Captain Grant, I would have got to know about it. He did nothing of the sort." He flicked his finger across his moustache. "Apart from speculation as to Lord Frobisher's actions in the months leading up to his injury, and the time he spent on the Continent seeking a cure for his blindness, you have absolutely nothing to justify holding him... Unless *you* are hiding something..." He scratched his chin. "Can *you* account for your actions since you arrived in Bodmin?"

"I've told you," Standish replied coldly, "I don't have to explain anything to you... As I said, you've been taken off the case. I don't even have to sit here talking to you—"

"Colonel Standish." Edwards leaned forward and tapped his pipe in the ashtray. Leaving it there, he clasped his hands together and said very softly and slowly, "Lord Frobisher is a very close friend of mine. I'll also remind you that he is blind. You say you're holding him in a cell over at the regimental barracks… If any harm comes to him, anything at all, I will hold you personally responsible. And by that, be under no illusion, I will hunt you down and make you pay dearly for this wonton act of cruelty and spite…"

"How dare you!" Standish went to say more but stopped when he heard Edwards continue.

"I am looking for a cold-hearted, sadistic killer… As of now, Colonel, you are at the top of my list of suspects."

★★★

"I'm so sorry, Lady Frobisher," sobbed Susan. "I tried to stop them…"

Morag stood in the lounge and ran her hand across Harry's favourite chair, imagining him sitting there, dozing before the log fire as she read to him.

From the hallway the grandfather clock chimed midday, but Morag neither heard nor cared. Her mind was trying to contend with the feeling of utter despair that had settled in her heart. She noticed his pipe on the table and the small pocketknife he used to clean it. The despair had spread to her arms and legs and she felt powerless to move, as though shock rooted her to the floor and she'd be unable to move again until she saw him walk through the door.

"They…" Susan sniffed, then announced, "Colonel Standish didn't even let Harry take his stick with him." With a trembling hand she presented Harry's favourite stick to Morag, who received it with a sad resignation.

"Thank you, Susan." Morag held it tightly against her face and closed her eyes. He would be frightened and disorientated, she thought. He always was when he found himself in unfamiliar surroundings. He had called to her and she hadn't been there for him. For that one thing alone, she could have openly wept.

She couldn't bear to think of him alone.

"He pointed a gun at him… threatened to shoot him… He said he was a traitor, that he's committed high treason." Susan had composed herself and was now reciting the events as though ticking them off a list. "There were two other officers with him. Harry seemed to know one of them: a Captain Hemmings. I don't think they wanted to be there."

"And you say they've taken him to the garrison in Bodmin?" Morag opened her eyes and took a deep breath.

"Yes, the two officers took him… Colonel Standish drove off in another car; he said he had business in town."

Morag moved around Harry's chair and sat down. Her blank expression belied the conflict raging inside her, as a fury like no other ignited and began to take hold, fed by the kindle of her initial shock and indignation of what this man had dared to do. The feeling of utter hatred against him, for thinking he could come into their house and take from her someone so precious, was beyond comprehension.

It didn't frighten or trouble her.

If Colonel Standish had been standing in the room at that moment, she could quite easily have shot him dead.

Her mind wandered aimlessly along this road of revenge and retribution until the voice of reason drew her onto another path. As usual, it soothed and justified, gently and carefully, knowing her natural Celtic temper could quickly overpower it and drive her to do something she might later regret.

If they hurt him… If they…

Her mind entangled itself with notions and speculations as to how they might be treating him. He'd never spoken openly of his links to his old regiment; to do so usually brought instant memories of the war, so she'd steered him away from such thoughts.

After the events of last November, she'd sat with him to go through some outstanding correspondence and had come across an invitation to a regimental reunion. When she'd read it to him, he'd shaken his head and reached out his hand to her. The only two people she associated with his time in the army, William and Benson, were both dead. The world was now moving forward, though sadly leaving the survivors of that conflict to face their nightmares alone.

If she drove over to the garrison now, chances are she'd not be allowed to see him. She didn't know anyone, or have any influence over the commanding officer in charge. She would be reduced to ranting and raving at the main gates, and probably end up being arrested herself.

Her only hope was Cyril Edwards.

"Morag?" Susan's voice came to her from somewhere in the room.

Morag lay Harry's stick on the small table next to his pipe and stared at it whilst her mind grappled with another option. Once all the dust from her anger had settled, and she'd poured out her heart to her brother-in-law, the underlying problem would still be there.

Harry needed legal advice.

Whatever charge they'd laid against him, they could not deny him access to legal representation. She wasn't sure just how it all worked in the army; she supposed they might appoint an officer to give Harry some degree of council, but that in itself might be useless if there were darker forces driving this affair.

The face of Peran Freeman appeared to her, coldly professional and loyal to the end. She remembered the day she'd entered his office, frightened and lonely, the previous year and handed her letter to him. He'd received her with respect and understanding, and had listened to her as she'd told her story.

It had been his unbiased attitude and that look in his eyes, not judgemental or clouded, that had filled her with hope during those terrible months at Amble Lodge.

For some strange reason she was gripped by a fear that he would already be making his way over to the town hall, probably to start preparing for his recital that afternoon. If she moved fast, she might catch him at his lodgings behind his office before he left.

The anger that threatened to consume her and drive her to confront the might of the British Army stationed in Bodmin began to dissipate. As it did so, a light shone through the dense and dark forest of her mind. It glowed through the trees, guiding and comforting her.

It was time to pay another call on Peran Freeman.

"Morag…" Susan slipped her arm around her shoulders, "what are we going to do?"

Morag reached her hand up and clasped Susan's. "I'm going to bring Harry home."

19

Lawrence Matthews gazed around him at the trees and marvelled at just how dense the forest was in this particular part of the estate. Considering he was so close to his cottage, and therefore not so far from Frobisher Hall, he found it difficult to see both buildings through the thick foliage that surrounded him. His eyes followed the path that ultimately led through the forest and out towards the estate boundary; it had been just a couple of hundred yards down there and into a small copse where they'd found the body of Reginald Travers the previous November.

If he turned round and followed the path in the other direction, he knew it would eventually take him back to his cottage. But it was the partially covered path now situated behind him that most intrigued him, being the one he'd found on his return to Frobisher Hall after Ellen Carfax had informed him of Morag's sudden decision to return home. Earlier, when he'd left Morag and Ellen together, he'd spent some time helping Branok cut logs; he'd found helping to set the logs upon a small stump a useful exercise for his shoulder, and he'd stood well clear as the big man had brought his axe smashing down. He thought they'd formed a strange sort of friendship, with Branok smiling at Lawrence's struggle to position even the smallest of logs before him, and pretending to swing the axe down in mock anger.

Lawrence had spoken about his wound, and of the night he'd felt as though a cannon shell had exploded in his shoulder... He'd told Branok how he'd thought he was going to die, and how unfair it had all seemed, considering he'd just met Susan. He'd spoken of his loyalty and affection for Inspector Edwards and how he missed working with him.

And Branok had listened with kindness and understanding.

He assumed that Morag hadn't had time to tell him of her decision to return to Frobisher Hall due to him and Branok working out of sight of the cottage. He'd heard Ellen calling out to him, but by the time he'd returned to the cottage, Morag was gone.

His next decision eventually led to this most interesting of discoveries.

Climbing onto his horse, he had politely refused Branok's muted offer of help and quickly made his way after Morag, only to become lost as he'd attempted to negotiate the endless crisscrossing of paths and dirt tracks. Afraid of ending up as he had done the previous day, and maybe not being discovered this time, he'd climbed down from his horse and led her through the thickening undergrowth.

When it became painfully and worryingly obvious that he was lost, he'd stood silently, trying to block his mind of all the forest noises that echoed around, along with the sound of his own heavy breathing.

All he needed was the sound of a voice, maybe Susan's voice, and he frowned as he remembered meeting her the previous day, and her subsequent scolding words.

It was then that he heard it.

The sound of the Daimler... Yes, it was distinctly the sound of the Daimler being driven off at high speed, its wheels thundering across the gravel driveway. If it had been a singular noise, the echo of its sound reverberating around the forest would have simply confused him further.

But it was the deep thrum of the engine starting up, and the noise as it drove off, that gave him an immediate clue as to the location of Frobisher Hall, and he turned and followed the sound, stepping through the dense undergrowth.

He'd been walking for about five minutes, studiously searching through the trees for sight of his cottage, when his foot caught on something metallic, and he pitched forward, catching his leg on a metal handle that jutted up through the wild grass, jarring his shoulder as he hit the ground. As he lay on his back, he realised he was still holding the reins with his good hand, and he stared up at his horse, who peered down at him with a strange curiosity.

Climbing back to his feet, he kicked and thrashed at the undergrowth and was surprised to find it coming away from the ground with ease, eventually revealing a metal latch that was part of a large door. Upon prising it open, he saw steps leading down into a darkened tunnel. His first thought was to climb down and take a better look, but common sense got the better of him; he knew he wouldn't get far without some form of light. The steps were Cornish stone and quite slippery, and he guessed their condition wouldn't improve the further into the tunnel he progressed. He also didn't wish to take another tumble in a place he might never be found.

Closing the lid back down, he eventually found his way to the rear courtyard of Frobisher Hall, unsaddled his horse and left her munching on a pile of hay in the stables.

Upon entering the cottage, he found it empty. He thought about going into the Hall to find Susan, before finally letting curiosity get the better of him and deciding to look for a paraffin lamp and matches.

Now, as he stood with the metal door prised open, he scanned the trees around him, conscious of what he was about to do, and slightly anxious that someone might step out of the undergrowth after he'd entered the tunnel and entomb him underground forever.

He reminded himself to tell Lord Frobisher to stop reciting those tales from his beloved Edgar Allan Poe.

Lighting the lamp, Lawrence took a deep breath and descended the steps, feeling the reassuring warmth of a summer's day turn to a cold and dank dampness that seeped into his lungs with every breath and step he took. When he eventually reached the bottom, he held the lamp out in front of him and stared into the murk and gloom.

A tunnel stretched out before him, and he was immediately aware that it followed a line directly towards Frobisher Hall. It looked surprisingly solid, with arched brickwork that glistened with moisture. There was probably just enough room for a person to scamper through, as long as they were hunched down. With his lanky frame, Lawrence was already hunched over and crouching.

He started forward, assessing just how far he needed to crouch down as his fingers scraped along the brickwork, while in his other hand he held the lamp out in front of him. The darkness swallowed him, and the only light he saw was from the flickering flame from the lamp that lit up a small area around him. Cobwebs wrapped themselves around him and something scurried along the ground, brushing against his shoe. He was already convinced that it was a tunnel leading to and from the Hall, which had probably been used in earnest many years ago when the family were involved in the dubious affairs of the local smugglers.

He had learnt a little of the family's past from Harry.

Lawrence also considered the fact that if it did lead back to the Hall it was a fairly long way, and he was already out of sight of the little shaft of light that illuminated the entrance. He was making steady progress, even though his back was beginning to ache and his knees were grumbling with abject misery at the strain they were having to endure.

His mind drifted back to the other day, when he'd seen the figure of somebody disappear into the woods. It obviously wasn't a surprise that he'd lost sight of them so quickly, and he guessed they must have disappeared down this particular passageway. He wondered if there might be others, and he hoped there wasn't a network of tunnels leading to God knows where... like a maze, entrapping him, sending him on endless pursuits until his lamp finally burnt itself out.

He stopped and considered turning round.

There'd been no other passages other than the one he was following, so it would be a simple journey back to the entrance in the forest. But something kept nagging at him, compelling him to move forward – a feeling that the house was drawing him nearer, beckoning to him, pulling him inexorably towards some terrible secret Frobisher Hall held within its heart and so desperately wanted to share.

The light flickered a couple of times as a draft swept through the tunnel. Lawrence quickly shielded the lamp, forgetting that the flame was protected inside a glass casing.

A breeze could only mean one thing: there was a flow of air between the entrance and exit. He'd found the entrance; he now just needed to find the exit.

He was at a point where the temperature was at its coldest, and he shivered violently as the cold air sunk into his chest. With this sudden chill came an agonising ache in his shoulder, and he paused, leaning against the brickwork, trying to steady his breathing. *I must be practically there*, he thought, *at least maybe under the rear courtyard*. Straining his eyes, he caught a slight glimpse of a light flickering another twenty yards or so in front of him. Being so dark, and unable to assess exactly what was creating the light, Lawrence couldn't accurately tell how far ahead the light was.

And if there was a light, with someone holding it, then maybe they were now observing his progress.

He thought what Inspector Edwards might say to him now. Probably, *Don't turn back; get to the bottom of the problem. Go forward, Matthews.* He could hear that crisp London accent thunder. But then the inspector wasn't there; and what if someone were waiting for him with a knife? If he were attacked, he'd struggle to defend himself with his shoulder playing up. He would certainly never be found, and Susan would never know of his fate.

He thought again of Inspector Edwards, sighed, and started to move forward towards the light.

As he closed the gap between himself and the distant light, the brickwork around him began to change, merging into more solid foundations. Spaces opened up around him; darkened recesses and alcoves appeared beside him, menacingly, so he feared hands might reach out at any moment. The light wasn't so distant now. As it grew bigger, it split into smaller lights. Lawrence had the feeling he was certainly beneath the main structure, and the lights that guided him seemed to illuminate the very heart of Frobisher Hall.

When he finally came to the end of the tunnel, he found himself staring into a large room, with more candles than he cared to count adorning the floor and shelves that bordered the room.

With a relief that made him groan with delight, he pulled his large frame through the entrance and practically fell into the room, collapsing onto his knees, and stretching and arching his back, desperate to get some circulation back into his cramped limbs. He lowered the lamp and gently sat it upon the floor, not thinking to extinguish the flame. As his back creaked in painful displeasure, he stretched out his arms, feeling instant relief.

How far he was below the house he couldn't work out.

It was still cold, but there was no longer a damp atmosphere.

In the furthest corner, a flight of steps worked their way up through the ceiling, finally to disappear in the shadows. In another corner, an old mattress lay on the floor with some old blankets.

Lawrence finally stood up, feeling the aches and pains of his journey recede into dull moans that he knew would eventually die out. He blinked a couple of times, trying to focus his eyes on the walls around him. They seemed alive, full of images beautifully drawn. With the sudden intensity of light, compared to his small lamp in the tunnel, he'd been temporally blinded by the glare.

As his eyes became accustomed to the brightness, the images became more defined… more dreadfully defined…

"Oh my God," he whispered, his mouth staying open.

Illustrations of Morag adorned the walls, carefully drawn in charcoal and coloured chalk. In each one, her hair had been coloured the most vibrant red, and the freckles on her body seemed so lifelike that Lawrence felt compelled to reach out and touch them. Some of the images were of just her face, with her eyes mesmerising and seductive, her lips invitingly parted and her hair tumbling down around her. In others, she was lying naked on a bed, her hands and ankles tied to the bedposts, her face frightened, her eyes pleading. As he continued to turn his body around, Lawrence gazed in morbid fascination at the nightmare unfolding around him.

He stared with growing disgust and anger at an image of her chained on a bed and restrained in a straitjacket. In another, she lay naked on her front, her thighs parted and her head turned towards the observer.

They were both shocking and obscene, and a name drifted from his lips, "Morgan Treave…"

★★★

292

Morag slammed hard on the brakes, feeling the Daimler grind to a screeching halt. In front of her, a woman had staggered out into the road, deathly white and sweating profusely. At the sight of the Daimler bearing down upon her, she'd stumbled to a halt and meekly raised one of her hands.

Morag sat silently for what seemed like an eternity, aware that she was actually opposite the building of Freeman Solicitors. *Funny*, she thought, *I could have driven right by the place…* Her mind had been so consumed with fearful speculation as to the fate of her husband, she'd not even been aware of the drive from Frobisher Hall. If this woman hadn't staggered out in front of her, she might well have driven right through the town and into the surrounding countryside.

She applied the handbrake and turned off the engine.

Noticing the woman was no longer in view, she climbed out and made her way to the front of the car. The woman had collapsed and was gurgling something that rattled from deep within her lungs. Upon seeing Morag kneeling before her, she tried to smile and raise her hand, as if to tenderly stroke Morag's cheek. There was a surprised look of recognition on her face that seemed helpless and forlorn.

"Are you okay?" Morag grasped her hand and gazed at the dreadful lines of paralysis etching their way across the face before her. Glancing at a woman standing on the pavement, staring blankly at her, she called, "Please… call a doctor… This lady's ill."

"My dear…" Annette Myers croaked.

Morag lowered her head, aware of whispered words trying to reach her.

"My dear… Lady Frobisher… God protect you and your husband…" Looking past Morag, her eyes became glazed and distant. The faint flicker of a smile spread across her face as she murmured, "Dear God, forgive me for what I have done…"

Morag went to say something, then paused.

Annette Myers was dead.

Harry Frobisher sat at a desk he imagined to be approximately three foot by four. Running his fingers along the edge, he found that if he stretched both arms out he could feel the end of the lip before it ran at right angles away from him. It was old and chipped, and smelt of polish. In fact, the whole room smelt of polish, and it had the familiar feeling of military prowess, as though whoever sat within its walls was constantly under the glare of something brash and intimidating.

He was certain it wasn't one of the cells, as he remembered them from his days with the regiment, accompanying the commanding officer during inspection visits. They were situated outside, near the main gate, and looked and felt cold even during the summer. In stark contrast, the room in which he was now sat was quite warm.

From the moment the car that took him from the Hall had pulled up outside the main garrison gates, Harry had tried to clear his mind and imagine himself walking through and into the main compound. By doing so, he thought he might find some comfort in an awareness of where he was. This had been easier said than done; without his stick, and being handcuffed, he'd stumbled several times and landed heavily on some stone slabs, jarring the air from his lungs. Hands had roughly hauled him back on to his feet and pushed him forward into a darkness that was both hostile and frightening.

After his third or fourth fall, he'd given up hope on tracing his steps from previous walks through the buildings, concentrating only on quelling the rising tide of panic that threatened to rear up from the pit of his stomach.

When he'd finally reached this room, huge hands, with a vice-like grip, had slammed him into the chair in which he now sat, and taken off his handcuffs.

Now, Harry tried to fight the trembling sensation spreading through his body. He wished Morag had woken him before she'd left, but he understood why she hadn't. He wasn't surprised at her decision to ride out to Sunrise Cottage; knowing her the way he did, it was inevitable that she did so eventually. If curiosity were ever going to get the better of someone, it was going to be her; though he wished he'd been able to ride out with her, knowing that a visit to that strange little cottage hidden deep within the estate was well overdue.

Throughout the events that followed his homecoming in the November, he'd not given it any consideration, so wrapped up was he with the mystery slowly unfolding around him. To think that Ellen Carfax had been there whilst his parents were murdered, and when he'd met Morag, seemed utterly amazing, and yet so obvious.

He wished he had his Bible with him now.

The room had to be one of the small offices in the part of the main building set aside for administrative duties. He guessed his arrest would have been hushed up and kept from the general ranks, and so he would have been bundled quickly out of sight.

Maybe, he thought, *that was why they were so forceful in getting me from the car to this office.*

He coughed, a contrived effort meant only to help his senses try and ascertain the dimensions of the room by the echo. He'd long been aware of an inbuilt ability to gauge his surroundings by the echo of his voice.

Nothing seemed to reverberate around him.

He tapped his fingers and took a deep breath. "Hello...?"

Silence.

"I know someone is standing there, as I just heard you swallow."

From somewhere in the building a door slammed and a voice barked out an order that was inaudible.

Harry listened intently. He thought the room was about nine foot by twelve, with a door to his rear and maybe several wooden cupboards and bookshelves around the walls. He guessed this, as the echo from his voice seemed to partially resonant around him, suggesting furnishings absorbing his words.

"Please say something."

Silence.

He thought further attempts at communication would be a waste of time. In the eyes of whoever was guarding him, he was a traitor, a dangerous enemy of the state who hopefully would end his days dangling at the end of a rope. The thought also occurred to him that if the person was the one with the huge hands, he didn't want to goad them into striking out. For to receive a blow to his face from those fists, with no warning, would probably break his jaw.

As always, when his mind began to feel the onset of panic, he thought of his wife. Morag would probably grab one of the shotguns and drive straight here. She might well be approaching the main gates now, and his mind pleaded with her not to do so. His only hope was Inspector Edwards, knowing the connections he had at higher levels.

When the door opened suddenly, Harry jumped and held his breath. Raising his right hand, he tentatively reached out into the darkness, desperate to fend off the expected assailant.

There were muffled whispers and the sound of someone shuffling out of the room. Whilst the door was open, he felt a breeze sweep through and was suddenly aware of just how clammy he was. When the door slammed shut, he sighed and turned his head nervously around.

"Harry?" The voice was familiar and, for once, reassuring.

"John Hemmings?" Harry thrust his hand out, waving it in the air.

"Here, old friend, right here..." A hand grasped Harry's and held it tightly. "I haven't got much time. Colonel Standish has gone into town to see Inspector Edwards. He's taking him off the case before coming back here to arrange transport for you back to London. Some of us are going to delay that order… Harry, if you go to London you'll be lost for good."

"For God's sake, John, why? I'm innocent." Harry loosened his grip as he felt his visitor move round to the opposite side of the table.

"That's as maybe, Harry. But I overheard Standish speaking to one of the guards, ordering him to shoot you if you made any attempt to escape."

"Escape?" Harry laughed, though he cringed at just how manic he sounded. "In my state?"

"It doesn't matter. If you're taken from here, I'm afraid he might arrange for something to happen. He can't do it down here; too many people know and respect you. The two guards who brought you from the car are replacements, transfers from Plymouth."

"John," Harry fought to control his breathing, "you know I'm innocent… I'd rather kill myself than betray my country."

"I know that, Harry. The one thing you have on your side is the loyalty of the men around here. Many of these men fought alongside you and don't believe any of this rubbish."

"And what about the man who was standing in this room?" Harry asked sardonically. "He might have said something… even if it was to tell me to shut up."

Captain Hemmings chuckled. "I'm afraid he's one of the many men who were brought in to bolster our numbers at the end of the war. He doesn't know you, and there are others like him. He'll probably inform Colonel Standish of my visit."

"And then what?"

"And then I'll probably be court-martialled for disobeying orders."

"Then why help me?" Harry's voice had dwindled to a pitiful whisper.

"Because you were there for me once… You could have left me to bleed to death in that crater, but you didn't. I remember lying there scared out of my wits; you were calm and in charge. When I was stretchered back, the medical officer stitched me up and told me that if it wasn't for you I would have died, or had to live with only one leg… You're a hero to everyone who holds this regiment dear in their hearts."

Harry lowered his head, unable to contain his emotions. His shoulders shook as he began to sob quietly, unashamed of where he was or whose company he was in. The thought of dying had never really occurred to him before now – not that it actually worried him much.

It was the thought of never holding Morag again that frightened him.

"Come on, Harry. You have a lot of friends in this place… Standish will give the order for you to be transported to London to the commanding officer, who'll pass it to either myself or Captain Little. We'll delay it… probably say there's some administrative error that needs correcting. I'm going to drive over to Frobisher Hall later tonight to see Her Ladyship…" Hemmings squeezed Harry's arm. "Is there a message you'd like me to give her?"

Harry nodded and tried to compose himself. Taking several short breaths, he drew himself up in his seat and said, "Thank you, John. That's very kind of you. Have you got something to write on?"

"Yes," Hemmings replied, "I have a piece of paper and a pencil… I'll write it down and deliver it to her."

"It might embarrass you," Harry heard himself say.

"No matter. No one will see it other than your wife."

"Okay…" Harry smiled, arranging his thoughts, desperate to say the right things and knowing that they had so little time. How was he ever going to say in a few words what raged within his heart; or tell her of the lifetime of love he'd known in the precious months since she'd first come into his life?

Sighing deeply, he said…

'My darling Morag,

If this letter should be the last thing you ever receive from me, I want you to know that my love for you will never die. I came home last year a broken man, believing there was no hope left in this awful world. Then one morning you reached out to me and drove the nightmares away. You've been my strength and my love, and for that alone I owe you so much. Please be strong and know that this man loves you more than life itself.

Harry'

★★★

"I should have seen this coming." Inspector Edwards glanced down at the lifeless body of Annette Myers, still lying where she'd fallen in the middle of the road. Morag's Daimler was still where she'd left it and was blocking any attempt by other traffic to pass through the high street. He tilted his Fedora hat to one side. "I warned her; I told her quite clearly that her life was in danger." Kneeling beside her he glanced at the gathering crowd, eyeing them closely, aware of the look of recognition in their eyes.

He'd come at once, alerted by the constable on the front desk, who had himself been notified by a young boy who'd witnessed Annette's final moments as he'd passed by on his bicycle.

His mind had still been clouded by dark and avenging thoughts, that had scattered bitter seeds in his mind as he'd watched Colonel Standish walk smugly from his office. The announcement of a woman collapsing in the road had partially shaken him from his thoughts, and he'd needed the brief walk from the police station up to Morag's Daimler to fully clear his head.

A cursory search of Annette Myers' body revealed no signs of violence, though her distorted features and discoloured face suggested something just as sinister. She carried no handbag, or anything else to suggest a motive for her journey. She was still wearing the same clothes she'd had on earlier, though without the scarf.

No scarf or coat…

He looked again at the crowd and noticed they'd fallen silent, as though thoroughly engrossed in the drama unfolding before them. Their faces were a mixture of young and old, rich and poor, and all held that same look of interest and awe. He began to scrutinise their features, assessing, gauging, determining who might actually be the killer. Several times in the past he'd known killers return to the scene of their crime and mingle with onlookers to glean some kind of understanding of which direction the investigation might take.

But he knew it was a pointless exercise; whoever had murdered Captain Grant, and now Annette Myers, was too clever and shrewd to make such a mistake.

"She came out from nowhere and walked right in front of me," Morag sounded dazed.

"From which direction?" Edwards scanned the pavement to his left, then right.

"Er… that way." Morag pointed to the pavement and a row of shops set back a little… and a small alleyway that cut down between them.

"That would lead down to her home, Rose Cottage."

Edwards recognised the voice and swung around. Sergeant Cadan was standing staring at the alleyway, his notebook in hand. He looked drawn and haggard, a mere shadow of his former self, yet Edwards was glad to see him there. "Which means…" He turned to look in the opposite direction and immediately read the sign above the familiar granite building:

He remembered the last time he'd stood facing that sign and of the meeting he'd had with the little solicitor. Could it be that Annette Myers was trying to get to him? That she'd been poisoned he had no doubt; her collapsed features, discoloured lips and dilated pupils were consistent with her ingesting some form of poison.

But where had she been poisoned?

Probably in her home, and by someone she trusted enough to invite in. But if she'd made it this far, it had taken longer than expected for her to die. Poisons could be instantly fatal if the correct dose was administered. A lesser dose would probably mean a slow and prolonged death. She could have taken it at home and staggered this far in an effort to...

He stared at the solicitor's office.

Of course, there would be the post-mortem and toxicology reports, but they would take a long time; and time wasn't on his side.

He noticed that someone had brought out a blanket and was about to cover the body. He stepped forward and raised his hand, halting their endeavours.

"Sergeant, clear this area; we don't want this to become a public spectacle." He knelt down and tried to turn the head.

She was stone cold.

He averaged the time it had taken to alert him and his subsequent response time. On top of that he considered the time of day and the warmth of the sun; the road was fairly open, with little shade to hasten the onset of loss of body temperature. Still, the question of what poison had killed her would be one to consider, along with a host of other questions.

Strychnine was quite common and was used in many households as a standard poison, and he thought painfully of Lord Alfred and his wife. The rapid decline in body temperature could possibly suggest hemlock, but that alone wasn't conclusive.

He said to Morag, "When you saw her, just before she died, did she say anything? Was there any noticeable muscle spasm?"

Morag shook her head. "She was very weak... She just muttered, 'God forgive me for what I have done.'" She looked down at Annette's face. "It's strange... It was as though she recognised me and was glad to see me..." She looked away. "You think she was poisoned?"

Edwards looked at her but didn't reply. He was beginning to get that familiar feeling: when ideas, once hovering, tantalisingly out of reach, then descended around him. He was having to formulate different thoughts into one coherent idea; he now had to speculate on her final movements to try and put together some kind of hypothesis that might support the picture building in his mind.

Poison...

That usually required some degree of knowledge in such matters. He pondered his options and considered the idea of a doctor. People who dabbled in poisons were sometimes connected to the medical profession. He would get Sergeant Cadan to compile a list of all doctors within the Bodmin area and also request an inventory of poisons over at the hospital. The hardest thing was going to be checking the unofficial use of poison within the community – substances that might be kept for pest control.

He pondered over the question of just how much poison the murderer had.

The person who'd poisoned Annette Myers had probably used a small dose, running the risk of her staying alive long enough to speak to someone. Not very professional... Unless they only had a small amount of poison to use, and needed the rest of it to dispose of the Third Rook.

He nodded to the woman who lay the blanket over Mrs Myers.

Moving towards Morag, he gently took her arm and whispered, "I take it you're in Bodmin because of Harry?"

She nodded blankly. "They have him over at the garrison... I came here to visit Peran Freeman; he helped me out last year when he held that letter for you in case anything happened to me."

Edwards smiled, remembering it clearly.

"What's going on, Cyril?" She swallowed and looked at him with the same despairing and questioning look he'd seen on Elisha's face as her body had finally succumbed to Death's icy embrace.

Edwards tried to think where to start.

To talk like this, in the middle of the main thoroughfare, seemed inappropriate. But he needed to talk to somebody, to try and articulate his thoughts into words and gain their perspective. At this moment in time, he was pleased and grateful to be in Morag's company.

He said, "It was my original idea that the murder of Captain Grant was planned and carried out by one individual, who must have followed him down to Bodmin. But then Annette Myers told me she'd written to Captain Grant, asking him to return something very precious to her. You see, they were both lovers during the war. One night, when they met in his flat in London, a fire broke out in her house and killed her two sons. It had been their nanny's night off, and she'd left them alone."

"My God..." Morag muttered.

"I initially thought she might have visited him at Creek Lane and shot him. That was until I interviewed her this morning..." He recollected the images of her two sons and the charred remains of their toys. "She confessed to being one of the Rooks and briefly explained her role within the overall organisation... It all comes down to that letter Captain Grant wrote to Harry..."

"But there's nothing in there," Morag shook her head; "it just mentions that the Rooks have flown and then it ends abruptly."

"But think, Morag. Over in France during the height of the war, Captain Grant tells Harry that he thinks he knows who the traitor is. He gives Harry a letter, a form of insurance, which Harry keeps with him for fear of losing it or having it stolen. That day in the trench, when William throws that grenade at him and he's blinded... someone takes it."

"The murderer?"

"Possibly... And if so, they would have the letter. They'd probably think they were safe for a while, and need only silence Captain Grant. But then they find him elusive and hard to track down..."

"He comes to Bodmin," Morag continued, "responding to a request from Annette Myers. When he realises Harry lives nearby, he writes to him. In the letter, he refers to the Rooks having flown... meaning they're threatened?"

Edwards nodded in agreement. "He knows Annette Myers is one of the Rooks, as that secret came to light during their affair, but what if the Fourth Rook either followed him down to Bodmin or was here already?" He glanced again at the dispersing crowd. "Morag, is there any way Harry could possibly be the Third Rook?"

She stepped back a little, as though trying to comprehend what she'd just heard.

He continued, unflinchingly, "I know it would mean he's been lying to you, but it would make sense."

"How could you say that, Cyril? Harry would never lie to me..." She shook her head. "No, he isn't the Third Rook... I'd swear to it." Her voice trembled.

There was a sternness in her eyes that again reminded him of his wife, and he knew not to pursue the subject. But the thought had settled in his mind and refused to budge. The less he tried to consider it, the more it made sense. And the more it made sense, the more he began to consider Colonel Standish. It was one of those moments of comprehension that made the biggest noise in his head, when everything seemed to fall into place unexpectedly. Standish had been in Bodmin longer than he'd led Edwards to believe. He'd had time to murder both Grant and Myers, and now he had the perfect opportunity to let the hangman finish his work by dispatching Harry.

The motive was there... By God, the motive was there...

But when it came to proof...

And then the notion came to him.

He looked again at Morag and said, "What I want to know is why Grant wrote that letter to Harry. If it was to warn him, then a cleverer detective than myself would assume he was warning a fellow member of the organisation... but there is the other option, one that could be just as credible... If Grant was of the mind to write down his suspicions in a letter to Harry for insurance all those years ago, then why not do the same when he arrived here?" He glanced around, fearful of even the policemen who were milling around Annette's body.

"But why warn Harry again when he'd already given him that letter during the war?" Morag asked.

"That was a long time ago. Maybe something happened since then that prompted him to repeat his warning. Remember, if Grant was tracking this person, and then realised they were still at large after all these years, then I suppose he would warn Harry." He pulled her closer. "He didn't want to write down the name of the traitor in case the letter never made it to Frobisher Hall. Although he paid one of the local boys to deliver it, how could he be sure it actually was delivered? No... If you or I were visiting a strange place and knew no one, and certainly didn't trust anyone, and you wanted to leave such a letter with somebody... who would you approach?"

"You'd do what I did last year." Morag shook her head and held her hand over her mouth.

They both looked across towards the office of Peran Freeman.

20

Susan watched the outside door to the kitchen open and smiled as she saw Lawrence standing in the doorway, dusting off cobwebs and thick dust from his clothes. He was holding a paraffin lamp, and she wondered exactly where he'd been to get in such a state. She'd been concerned about him: Morag had hastily returned, leaving him to come home alone.

The cottage had been cold and melancholy without him, and she'd sat at the kitchen table staring at the door since her own return from the Hall thirty minutes before.

Harry's arrest and removal from Frobisher Hall had left her reeling and severely shaken. When Colonel Standish had threatened to shoot him, he'd savagely pushed her to one side in his endeavours to thrust the muzzle of his revolver into Harry's face. There had been a manic look in his eyes that had scared her – not so much for her own life but for Harry's.

His look of frightened vulnerability hadn't lasted long, and had been quickly replaced by one of agonising despair.

She also remembered Colonel Standish's departing words, as he'd walked behind Harry and the two accompanying officers through the main hall and towards the doors. He'd called out, as though addressing the entire house, "I don't think you'll ever return here, Captain Frobisher."

It had been a chilling moment that had stunned those gathered around to watch the drama unfold.

As the sound of their cars had roared off into the distance, she'd suddenly become aware that she was holding Harry's stick.

"Larry," she said relieved, "I'm glad your home…"

"What's happened?" He dropped the lamp onto the table and crossed over to the sink. Running cold water into his hands, he splashed his face several times, before groping around for a towel.

"Here." Susan quickly rose from her chair, opened a cupboard and handed him a clean towel. She watched him wipe his face before saying softly, "Harry's been arrested."

"What?" Lawrence turned and dropped the towel onto the table. "What do you mean, arrested? What for?"

"A Colonel Standish came whilst you and Morag were away. He accused Harry of high treason… Something to do with the war. He had two men with him. They've taken him to the barracks in Bodmin." She felt herself succumbing to the emotions of the morning, and fought the urge to burst into tears. "He looked so helpless, Larry. They took him away and didn't even let him take his stick."

"High treason?" Lawrence pulled a chair back and sat down, eyeing Susan and shaking his head. "Morag came back here early. She left me behind… I was with Branok and she couldn't find me. She must have known something was wrong."

"She seems to have a sixth sense when it comes to Harry." Susan worked her way round the table and sat down on the chair next to Lawrence. "She's gone into Bodmin to visit Peran Freeman, the solicitor. He helped her out last year when she was arrested for the murders of Harry's parents."

"I know…" Lawrence replied. "Something to do with a letter she'd written outlining her suspicions, and he kept it safe in the event of anything happening to her. Inspector Edwards told me."

"I hope he can help Harry. That man, Colonel Standish…"
Her voice trailed off.

"What about him?" Lawrence reached across and caressed her cheek.

"He's evil, Larry, pure evil… The things he said… spiteful, terrible things…"

The touch of his hand was reassuring, instantly warming her and brightening her world. She thought of their cottage and the happiness she'd found with him. It seemed such a stark contrast to the world she'd come from: a grocer's daughter with little or no expectations in life. Whenever she looked into his eyes, she always marvelled at their brightness and radiance. Lawrence had a lust for life that she could sometimes find overwhelming, a desire to never give up and certainly not to buckle under at the first tribulation to appear over the horizon. So now, even though his touch felt wonderful, she was aware of a concern in his voice and a strange doubt in his eyes.

"We should get word to Inspector Edwards," he said calmly.

"I think Morag will try and find him as well…" She paused, before adding, "Gregson's disappeared."

"Gregson?" Lawrence pulled his hand back and looked at her closely. "When was this?"

"I don't know, Larry." Susan lowered her voice, staring at the open door, "The strangest thing is, I'm not sure who actually employed her, or even what she looked like. She just seemed to appear whilst Harry and Morag were on their honeymoon. I thought Morag had employed her… but now I'm not so sure. And when I spoke to the rest of the staff, nobody could actually remember her." Susan narrowed her eyes, aligning her thoughts and sorting them into some kind of order. "Come to think of it, people would mention her name, but nobody actually saw her… Yesterday, when I was looking for Dodson and Kendrick, I thought I saw her enter Morag and Harry's bedroom. But when I went in there, she was gone… And that's not the first time; I've seen glimpses of her around the house, but when I go to speak to her she's not there..."

"You sure she's real?" Lawrence eyed her suspiciously.

"You know, Larry, normally I would laugh at what you're suggesting, but after everything that's happened in that house..." Susan shook her head.

"What about her room?"

"Good question," replied Susan. "Other members of staff say they've never actually seen her enter or leave her room. I had a brief look around there and I don't think the bed has been slept in."

Lawrence took a deep breath, and Susan shivered as she saw how withdrawn he'd become, as though he were considering something so devastating he feared sharing his thoughts with her. He glanced across towards Frobisher Hall then turned and peered out through the kitchen door, towards the forest.

"What is it, Larry?" she whispered.

"Something's wrong, Susan; something is terribly wrong."

"I know..." She stood up and walked across to stand beside him. "Dodson and some of the other staff have told me about a strange man they've seen walking around the house. Dodson thought he was the head butler... He said he had a patch over one eye."

Lawrence slowly shook his head and whispered, "Morgan Treave..."

"I saw him yesterday, in the forest." Susan felt a strange sense of relief wash over her as the terrible reality of their predicament became clear.

Lawrence nodded.

"It's strange, Larry; when I checked Gregson's room, there was nothing in there to suggest she ever existed. No personal belongings or anything... Nothing except..." She reached across the table and grasped the piece of paper she'd been holding when he'd walked into the kitchen. As she carefully unfolded it, she glanced at him. "This was in her top drawer. I imagine she must have drawn it herself."

She stared down at the image, as did Lawrence.

It was a portrait of Morag, drawn in pencil, and one of the most beautiful and accurate images of anyone she'd ever seen. From the freckles on her face, to her thick, cascading hair that framed her features; every detail reflected not just a perfect representation of her, but captured the very essence of her wild and passionate persona. She was naked, and spread seductively across a bed, her legs slightly parted, her mouth open and her eyes...

"Good God," Lawrence muttered, "I think it's beginning to make sense."

"I'm assuming she must have drawn it, as I don't know anyone else who could have done this." She stared at Lawrence and held her breath.

The usual confident and rational look in his eyes had been replaced by a grey cloud of doubt. It both alarmed and intrigued her. But there was something else, something she'd never seen before in his eyes.

Fear.

"What is it, Larry?" she asked.

He picked up the drawing and examined it closely. "I think Morag is in grave danger, Susan."

★★★

Inspector Edwards stared, momentarily transfixed and shocked, at the battered remains of Peran Freeman. Standing in the doorway to the solicitor's office, he studied the body professionally, positioning it in relation to the furniture and searching for a possible murder weapon. Peran was lying on his back, his arms flayed out to his sides, with his head tilted to one side and resting against the open door of his large safe positioned against the wall and away from the desk.

Edwards had seen the safe before, but never open. It stood approximately four feet tall and was of a Victorian design, in cast iron, with a key mechanism. He was of a mind to sift through the documents that lay scattered around the body, several soaked in congealed blood.

But that would come later.

He took several deep breaths, trying to calm his nerves, holding his handkerchief to his mouth to block the sickly sweet smell of a rapidly decomposing body. Peran Freeman's face was horribly bloated, and with the number of flies buzzing around the room, Edwards estimated he had been murdered sometime the previous day. With the air hanging heavy with death, and the curtains closed, the room resembled nothing less than a ghastly charnel house.

Edwards glanced at the curtains and noticed a tiny ray of sunlight slanting through a small gap. He followed its line across the room and shook his head in astonishment as it finally fell upon the opposite wall, lighting up the print of the Walter Raleigh Gilbert Monument. Normally it would induce nothing more than a curious representation of a local landmark; but right at that moment, towering over such a terrible scene of carnage, it seemed to mock and jeer at his inability to prevent such a monstrous act of slaughter.

He became aware of Morag standing just behind him, peering into the room. How long she'd been standing there he didn't know; she'd been silent even as they'd entered the building and worked their way along the hall and into the main office. Inching a little back, he grabbed her arm.

"Morag, this is no place for you." He tried to ease her away from the door. "I need Sergeant Cadan in here. Could you go and find...?" He paused, catching her line of sight. She wasn't looking at the body of Peran Freeman, nor staring blankly with the tell-tale signs of shock at the scene before her; she was staring at the figure of Doctor Mitchell sat slumped in a chair facing the solicitor's desk.

Edwards gasped, scolding himself for missing something so obvious.

From where he was standing, he couldn't deduce if he was alive or dead, and so lurched quickly forward, stepping over scattered legal documents in his endeavour to negotiate his way around the desk.

Kneeling before the doctor, he realised very quickly that he didn't have to search for signs of life. Doctor Mitchel sat silently staring ahead, his face ashen, his eyes cold and empty, yet blinking intermittingly, as though desperately trying to dispel the awful thing they'd just witnessed. Reaching forward, Edwards touched his face; it was cold and clammy.

"Can you hear me?" He grasped Mitchell's hand, which tightly gripped the edge of the chair.

"It's Doctor Mitchell. He's the family's doctor," Morag whispered.

"Doctor?" Edwards thundered. "Can you hear me?"

Mitchell stared blankly ahead.

"He's in shock…" Edwards stood up and quickly removed his jacket before covering the doctor's shoulders. "If we don't act fast, he'll die." He reached forward and pushed his finger against the doctor's neck. "His heartbeat's racing." He looked at Morag. "We need to get him to a hospital."

"I have the Daimler," Morag responded.

"Good, go and get Sergeant Cadan and a couple of his men and bring them here." Edwards leaned forward, aware that Mitchell's lips were moving.

"Do you think…?" Morag finally stared across towards the body of Peran Freeman.

"I'm not sure… I wouldn't have thought so… He's been dead for a while. The problem is, in the heat in this room, the body will rapidly deteriorate. Hence the flies. I need time to get a pathologist here, and time isn't on our side." Edwards remained kneeling beside the seated doctor. "Quick, Morag."

Morag staggered back and into the hall, and he heard her footsteps racing towards the front door.

"Doctor Mitchell… Can you hear me?" Edwards leaned forward again and tried to listen for a response. "My name is Inspector Edwards. You've obviously had a shock… Can you tell me what happened here?"

Mitchell's lips moved but no words were uttered.

Edwards began to speculate. "Did you find the body of Mr Freeman?"

Mitchell's eyes moved fractionally and glanced at him.

"Did you come here and find the body?" He glanced at Mitchell's hands, searching for any signs of blood.

His lips parted and moved slightly.

"We're going to get you to a hospital." Edwards glanced frantically around, now conscious of voices approaching the main door. Anything, any possible explanation as to the identity of the murderer, would be invaluable. It could even be Mitchell himself. It was not uncommon, in Edwards' experience, for a murderer to succumb to shock and remain beside the body of their victim.

But Peran Freeman had been dead for a while, probably since Friday. Would Mitchell have remained seated here for all that time before either coming to his senses or dying of shock?

He saw what he was looking for – on a cabinet, a small decanter of either whisky or brandy was proudly positioned on a silver tray, along with two small glasses. Obviously refreshments for those clients needing a little more sustenance than a cup of tea. As the sound of footsteps approached the office door, he hurried across to the cabinet and poured a small amount of what he thought was whisky into a glass. As Sergeant Cadan appeared at the door, Edwards returned to Mitchell and raised the glass to his lips, letting the initial surge of liquid gently lap against his closed mouth.

Mitchell licked his lips.

"Sergeant, you need to get Doctor Mitchell here over to the hospital. He's in deep shock. Stay with him and note down anything he says." He tipped the glass again, this time watching the liquid penetrate further into the doctor's mouth.

Mitchell gagged and coughed a little.

"Easy… Easy…" Edwards soothed.

Mitchell moved his mouth and tried to speak.

"What happened here, Doctor?"

"I… I… should have told… Harry." Mitchell whispered the words so quietly that Edwards had to lean forward, his ear practically pressed again his mouth.

"What…? What should you have told him?" Edwards pulled back and looked deep into Mitchell's eyes.

"Should have told Harry…" There was despair and regret in his voice.

"Cyril…" Morag's voice called from the doorway, "I've started the Daimler. I'll drive him over to the hospital." Her voice was calm, authoritative and utterly reassuring.

"Okay." He stepped back and watched as Sergeant Cadan directed two men to support Doctor Mitchell into a standing position before guiding him out through the door. "Sergeant Cadan?" He called out before the policeman disappeared into the hall, "One moment, please."

Sergeant Cadan issued some muffled orders to the two policemen, before stepping back into the office. "Yes, sir?" he asked calmly.

"Sergeant, when you get Doctor Mitchell over to the hospital, have two men stay with him. I don't want him left on his own for one moment. Is that clear?"

Cadan nodded.

Edwards continued, "Put one of your more experienced men by his bedside and ask him to note down anything he might say… Oh, and could you tell Lady Frobisher to go back to Frobisher Hall? I'll meet her there. Under no circumstances

314

is she to try and get to her husband… I don't want any further bloodshed."

"Very good, sir. Anything else?" Sergeant Cadan started to make his way out of the office.

"Yes, please send in one of your constables; I want this entire building searched." He looked around the room. "I'll find whoever did this, Sergeant. I can promise you that much."

Cadan smiled and said, "I know you will, sir." He turned and disappeared into the hall.

"One more thing, Sergeant," Edwards called out.

The big sergeant peered around the doorframe. "Yes, sir?"

"You'd better pop into the town hall and tell them the piano recital is cancelled for today… but don't go into detail."

"Very good, sir."

Edwards studied the room before finally letting his eyes fall on the body of Peran Freeman. He allowed himself the smallest of indulgences as he affectionately recalled their meeting the previous November and how the little solicitor had welcomed him with such professionalism and concern for the welfare of Morag.

His face was hardly recognisable. The attack had been frenzied and brutal to the end; and Edwards sighed heavily at the thought of the pain and suffering Mr Freeman had most certainly endured.

Edwards moved across and knelt beside the body.

With a deep groan he raised the dead man's left hand; each finger had been broken. Looking across to the right hand, he noticed the same; each finger had been wrenched and snapped like a twig.

Looking around the office, Edwards saw only rudimentary furnishings. Everything had a purpose – from the desk to the safe, along with the cupboards and filing cabinets. The only two items which stood out to him as doubtful in having any professional purpose were the print on the wall behind the desk and the whisky decanter on top of the cupboard. And even then, he gave the whisky decanter the benefit of the doubt.

Looking at the body he saw the eyes staring lifelessly towards the ceiling along with a dreadful look of fear on the face. *In murder, there is always a motive*, he thought. *Grant and Myers are dead because of their connection with The Nest of Rooks*. But Freeman, he assumed, wasn't a member. However, his death had to be connected in some way; and the only connection that sprang to mind was the possibility that he knew, or held within his possession, something of value.

It had to be some form of letter, something containing information the murderer was desperate to find. Why else would they have tortured him?

Looking around at the scattered documents, he thought that the killer had possibly found what they were looking for. He visualised them rummaging through the safe after torturing Peran Freeman for the key.

Or *had* they found what they came for?

Someone searching through paperwork held in a safe, and not finding what they were looking for, would probably become desperate. They might have had only a small window of opportunity to complete their task; perhaps they would have been missed by others… maybe worried at being discovered in this office.

He considered the idea further, picturing them becoming frantic, tossing papers around the room in a desperate attempt to find…

It had to be a letter… a letter hidden in the safe. And if it had been hidden there, then it was almost certainly gone. He stared again at Freeman's broken fingers, finding the very notion of his torture utterly despicable. He'd confronted such violence in London and many other cities; but for it to have happened here, in this quiet and unassuming town, was certainly a surprise.

Edwards cast his mind further back, now visualising the solicitor's last moments, allowing his mind to run freely as it registered the facts, before digesting them and slotting them into place. As he did so, he turned his head, following the events as they appeared in his mind. It was like watching one of those cinema screens he'd recently seen for the first time, marvelling at the flickering images unfolding before him.

"Sir?" a voice called out from the doorway.

Startled, Edwards swung round. A young constable stood to attention and regarded him with an obvious sense of awe. He was tall, with jet black hair, and Edwards was instantly reminded of a certain Constable Matthews. "Ah, good. Your name?" he asked abruptly.

"Smith," the young man replied hesitantly

"Okay, Constable Smith, I need you to carry out a preliminary search of the secretary's office next door and Mr Freeman's personal lodgings upstairs and to the rear of the premises. I want you to check carefully for any signs of forced entry, anything that might have been tampered with... as if someone were looking for something."

"Right you are, sir." Constable Smith stepped back.

"Oh, and Smith?" Edwards called after him.

"Sir?"

"If you find the body of Mr Freeman's secretary, give me shout."

Constable Smith swallowed and mumbled, "Yes, sir."

Edwards returned his attention to the scene around him.

Freeman would have been killed after he'd closed for business, certainly on the Friday evening, otherwise the secretary would have still been there. He quickly assessed the chances of the young constable finding her dead as well, then shook the thought from his head.

There'd obviously been a struggle, with Freeman threatened with violence unless he opened the safe; upon doing so, the murderer emptied the contents. Maybe the little man tried to resist. Maybe the murderer couldn't find the letter… Edwards shook his head… It had to be a letter, or some form of document incriminating the Fourth Rook…

This was where his imagination opened the door to some dreadful thoughts.

The murderer couldn't find the letter, he pondered, and so they tortured Peran Freeman, breaking his fingers and beating him relentlessly in a frenzied attack, until he died. Compared to the swift and clinical way Grant and Myers had been murdered, this was positively savage, as though the murderer had plunged to the very depths of their own base animal instinct.

"This wasn't planned like the others," Edwards whispered. "This was an act of sheer desperation."

Something caught his eye.

It was a small leather book on the middle shelf of the safe, pushed just far enough back to be hidden in the recess. Reaching in, he caught hold of it and pulled it out. It looked like a journal of some kind, not particularly big and rather tatty. He flicked it open, randomly selecting a page and nodding as he realised his assumptions were correct. There were entries, next to dates which showed only the day and the month. Flicking the pages back, he found the front page and narrowed his eyes as he read the inscription on the inside page:

Journal of Lady Margaret Frobisher 1891-95

Why on earth had this not ended up on the floor?

And what was it doing in Peran Freeman's safe?

Edwards concluded that the murderer had either missed it or thought it bore no resemblance to what they were looking for. But then a letter could have been hidden within its pages.

He flicked through the entire journal.

No letter.

He stood up, moved across to the curtains and pulled them open, blinking slightly as bright sunlight spilled into the room.

With another cursory look around, to check for anything he might have missed in the darkness, he made his way to the desk and sat down in Peran Freeman's rather mundane and not very comfortable chair. He peered almost reverently at the book, before turning some of the pages and reading the entries. The handwriting was utterly beautiful, both neat and stylish in its flair. The passages were fairly short, and he found himself running an eye over one entry before flicking forward and reading another.

After about five minutes, he found one entry that he read, and re-read, before muttering, "Good God…"

★★★

Ellen Carfax drew her horse to a halt and stared blankly at Branok as he took the reins from her hand and reached up to help her down. She was tired, and it was all she could do to muster a smile and a word of thanks as she took the big man's hand and leaned on him as she felt him guide her towards the ground. He held her tenderly, that familiar look of concern etched deep within his scarred face. She noticed that his right hand was bruised and slightly inflamed, and wondered if he might have caught it whilst cutting wood. His strength, as always, both scared and reassured her; knowing he could probably kill a man in seconds with his vice-like grip filled her with dread. Yet to feel his colossal strength work its way through to a touch so delicate and supportive made her very thankful she had his companionship in her life.

Drawing away from him, she felt for her small leather bag over her shoulder and started to move wearily towards the cottage. The sun had long since passed its zenith and, like her, was easing tiredly towards the end of the day. When she entered the back door and made her way into the pantry, she glanced over her shoulder and saw Branok walking round to the other side of the cottage.

With a deep sigh, she pulled her bag from her shoulder and laid it on the table. Opening it up, she rummaged through some old jars before pulling out one marked 'Poison'.

With a wry smile, she placed the empty jar back on the shelf.

21

Morag stood waiting in the lounge, staring with idle curiosity at the painting of Frobisher Hall nestled between the two huge portraits of Lord Alfred and Lady Margaret. The grandfather clock in the hall had just chimed 8pm, and she listened to the footsteps of Mrs Chambers recede purposefully down the corridor to the kitchen.

After telling the cook she was adamant she wasn't going to eat dinner until she could do so with Harry, Morag had stood silently whilst the cook remonstrated with her, until she'd smiled and asked her to return to the kitchen to ensure the staff were fed. With her enforced abstinence from food, the house seemed to settle around her in a deep melancholy, as though the spirits of Harry's ancestors were airing their disapproval at her decision.

The atmosphere in the house had become heavy and leaden, as though every effort by members of staff to complete even the most mundane of tasks was contrived and filled with a deeply entrenched gloom. It felt like a house in mourning, as though it sadly bore the memories of Harry Frobisher and the love he'd once shared with a beautiful Scottish woman with red hair.

Listening to the kitchen door slam in the distance, she thought only of the man she loved, and looked sadly at his stick resting against his favourite chair. After driving Doctor Mitchell across to the hospital, she'd reluctantly adhered to the instructions of Inspector Edwards and driven herself home. Since then, she'd walked the corridors of Frobisher Hall and seen Harry in every room. It was in here, though, in the lounge, where she missed his presence acutely; she saw him sitting in his chair, or on the floor with his head resting against her knee whilst she read his favourite Edgar Allan Poe stories. In this room she felt the depth of her spiritual bonding, not just with Harry, but with the legacy of the Frobisher family, for both the past and for what she might contribute to future generations.

She thought of what it might be like to see their children running through these rooms, in a world without war and hate. The thought of losing Harry seemed almost absurd, as though he might, at any moment, walk through the door and call out to her. They would embrace, she might cry, and he would hold her tightly.

He had to come back to her.

She smiled and placed her hand on her stomach.

From across the hallway, towards the study, the sound of the telephone rattled until a member of staff answered it. There was the sound of muffled voices, before Dodson appeared, professional and dependable, announcing a call from Canon Trebarwith.

"Your Ladyship," Canon Trebarwith announced on the phone, "I've just heard the news about your husband… Is there anything I can do?"

"No, Canon," she replied as if in a dream. "Maybe… if you think of Harry in your prayers." She thought of how selfish that sounded, considering Captain Grant, Annette Myers and Peran Freeman were now lying in the morgue alongside a complete stranger.

She shuddered.

"My dear, I already have…" He paused, before adding, "I know you wanted to hold a short service of remembrance for Edith Travers at the Walter Raleigh Gilbert Monument tomorrow afternoon… I thought we might hold the service tomorrow morning… I have a young curate who would be happy to take the Sunday morning service, which would allow me to meet up with you at the monument?"

Morag was initially of a mind to refuse the request in its entirety and postpone it until Harry was home. She felt reluctant to do anything without him, so empty was her world. The cold and clamminess that caressed her made her feel uncomfortable and on edge. Her rational mind fought a losing battle against her nervous state, trying to tell her that she was suffering not just from the shock of these recent deaths, but from the brutal and violent way in which Harry had been taken from her.

She felt an anger rise within her that seemed suddenly real and tangible as she spoke to this man of God; maybe it was his calm and steady voice that drew this bitterness out of her. He was a man of God; wasn't he supposed to have all the answers?

So much evil, she thought; *so much evil.*

It seemed quite inconceivable that a person could commit murder in this way, so coldly and clinically. The world had witnessed the most brutal and savage war in history and here was someone who felt compelled to continue that ruthless legacy.

Additionally, there was the question of Morgan Treave.

His face, that terrible face, that haunted her subconscious, now, it seemed, was just as much a part of the very heart of Frobisher Hall as the portraits of Harry's ancestors that hung in every room she entered. She was in no doubt that he had set the polyphon in motion the previous night, knowing it would draw her to him. He'd played a fairly safe hand, knowing the staff were asleep in their quarters at the furthest end of the house, and that Harry would pose no challenge if he were to hear the sound and choose to investigate on his own.

Morgan Treave was playing with her, as he had done so before when she was locked up and restrained under his authority. Maybe the game was drawing to a conclusion; if so, she felt as though she were losing... badly... With Harry gone, her very soul had sunk into a mire of despair and self-pity. She thought of what her father had told her through the years, to be strong and grasp the challenges of life with a firm hand. And this was where her self-pity turned to guilt and regret, knowing that she'd left her parents so coldly, choosing to follow her own impulsive nature and break free from the constraints of their expectations.

But it was the thought of losing Harry that finally brought tears to her eyes and the realisation that now, more than ever, she needed him in her life.

"Lady Frobisher...?" Canon Trebarwith's voice came to her through the darkness surrounding her.

Wiping her tears, she coughed, clearing her throat. "I'm sorry, Canon... Yes... I think that would be nice... I'll inform Inspector Edwards; I know he wanted to attend the service. It was he who..." She desperately wanted to continue but found her words stifled by the emotions that clogged her ability to communicate.

"I know..." His voice seemed so peaceful and forgiving.

"I just want this to end..." she said sadly. "I want the killing to stop."

"My dear, I've prayed every day since Captain Grant committed suicide... And now these other poor souls... Good will prevail over evil as it did during that terrible war."

"What..." Morag sniffed and drew a deep breath, "What time shall we meet you tomorrow at the monument?"

"Shall we say 10am? Would that be convenient for you?"

"Yes, Canon. That would be fine..."

"I will see you both then. God bless you, Lady Frobisher, and please... please do not despair."

Morag muttered something and slowly replaced the earpiece.

In front of her, on the desk, one of Harry's pipes lay forlornly, resting against an empty whisky glass. She decided she'd speak with her brother-in-law later that evening, as he would probably be returning to Frobisher Hall to spend the night. No doubt he would be eager to head back into town early in the morning to continue his investigation, so she felt that a 10am meeting with Canon Trebarwith would fit in comfortably with his plans.

She wondered how Harry might be feeling, if he was lonely or afraid. He bore the emotional weight of his blindness with a dignity and an acceptance that sometimes beguiled her into believing his mind was totally resigned to his world of darkness. But there were times, especially at night, when he would reach for her and she would feel his hand shaking, and she would hold him tightly, resolved never to let go.

Yet tonight they would be facing their first night apart since that night in his room last November. To even think of sleeping in their bed without him left her feeling sick, and she decided she would sit and wait for him in the lounge.

Turning round, she stopped abruptly, startled by the presence of Susan and Lawrence standing in the hallway, facing the study, waiting for her. Their faces were set with an air of deep concentration, and it was obvious they had news to impart. Feeling her resolve start to finally crumble to nothing, she closed her eyes and tried desperately to draw strength from Canon Trebarwith's words…

Please do not despair…

Opening her eyes, she took a deep breath and walked out into the hallway.

"Susan, Lawrence…" She smiled.

"Lady Frobisher…" Lawrence respectfully replied.

"Have you any news?" The desperation in Morag's voice was pitiful.

"We need to speak to you," Susan said hurriedly, glancing nervously around.

"About Harry?" Morag choked.

"Not exactly…" This time it was Lawrence's turn to peer anxiously around. He moved forward until he was close enough to whisper, "We need to speak to you, but away from the house…"

★★★

Harry Frobisher sniffed weakly, feeling a small trickle of blood ease its way down his nostril and onto his moustache. It was warm, and he was aware of every little drip that eventually splashed off his lip and onto the table. He tried to raise his hand, with every intention of wiping his face, but found he was shaking too much. Also, to stave off the onset of panic, he'd settled both hands on top of the table, knowing that its presence gave him some degree of security and focus as his immediate world around him crumbled and disintegrated into a nightmare of someone screaming at him… and a hand slapping his face.

His only consolation was knowing that the voice was that of Colonel Standish, and it was probably his hand that had slapped him across the face, the last one cutting across his nose and sending a stream of blood cascading down. He smiled at the relief he felt at being struck by Standish and not that almighty brute of a hand belonging to whoever had initially dragged him into the room. With each question Standish aimed at him, Harry instinctively recoiled, expecting the sharp sting of his hand across his face.

"I could keep this up all night, Captain… And, believe me, it's getting late," Standish said calmly.

"Then you might as well give up and return to whatever rathole you emerged from." Not usually one for losing his temper, Harry fought desperately to retain some semblance

326

of a level mind and self-restraint. He knew he was completely helpless and at the mercy of this man on the other side of the desk.

Colonel Standish...

Harry tried to recall the name, as he'd done when Edwards had initially mentioned him. But nothing came to mind. That he was a colonel meant very little to him, as he would have been a lower rank during the war. Maybe he'd been a captain like himself; if so, he wanted to know to which regiment he'd been attached, or which particular theatre of the war he'd served in.

"Captain Frobisher, be under no illusion as to what lies ahead of you if you don't cooperate." Standish's words flicked across Harry like a lizard's tongue. "You were part of The Nest of Rooks—"

"Prove it," Harry snarled, before collapsing back under the thunderous crash of Standish's hand.

"It doesn't work like that, Captain Frobisher...You'll find it a lot easier if you just follow the simple rule of me asking the questions and you answering." Again, that cold and dehumanised voice jabbed into Harry, like a lethal injection, spreading its vile venom through his body.

Feeling the left side of his face contort into spasm, Harry tried to quell the inevitable scream that was going to erupt from his lips. That last slap had caught his left eye, and the resultant pain was like a thousand red-hot needles plunging into his brain. At best, he managed to stifle it to a mere groan, pitiful and wretched.

"Please stop hitting me," he mumbled. "If you have any ounce of common decency within you... I can't even see you to defend myself." The pain in his eye subsided, but his face raged like a furnace.

"You see, Captain Frobisher, it's too much of a coincidence... Captain Grant travels down to Bodmin to meet with Annette Myers; now they're dead; you live over in Frobisher Hall; Grant knew you during the war... Now, I'll ask you again, how did you arrange the murders of Captain Grant and Annette Myers?"

"I've told you... I don't know what you're talking about," Harry muttered, beginning to lose control of any rational thinking. He was tired and thirsty. When he'd asked for a glass of water he'd been slapped across the face and told to remain silent.

"You do know, Captain Frobisher." Standish had moved across the table and was now only inches from Harry's face.

Harry cried out and tried to move his head back.

"You know, if you confess to these charges, I might be able to ensure you live... If you don't, then you'll hang for sure... but that will only be the beginning." Standish raised his hand and pushed his fingertip gently into Harry's left eye.

Harry screamed out as the broken and fractured remnants of nerves erupted in a terrible cacophony of pain and agony. "Please... no more," he whimpered.

"You know something, Captain Frobisher? People like you make me sick. Born with a silver spoon in your mouth and a superior attitude to the rest of society. I thought the war might have ended all that. Maybe I'll be doing the rest of the world a favour by ensuring you hang."

Harry, trembling and resisting the urge to fling himself across the table at his tormentor, raised his hand and held it against his eye. Feeling a slight relief from the agonising pain that had exploded only moments ago, he breathed deeply and tried to rally his thoughts. "I've been selfish," he said quietly.

"What?" Standish spat.

"I've been extremely selfish."

"Explain yourself," Standish drew nearer.

"I have wallowed in my own self-pity since coming back from the war last year. I have sought the comfort and support of others and not faced up to the reality of my life as it is now. If I get out of this alive – and by the sound of your voice, Colonel

Standish, I don't think the odds are on my side – I'm going to do two things… First, I'm going to tell my wife how much I love her… And second, I'm going to learn to read Braille. One day I'm going to read Edgar Allan Poe to my wife for a change." Harry held his head up and lowered his hand. Gripping his fists, he continued, "And if you strike me again, I swear to God I'll rip your bastard head off."

"Brave words, Captain, very brave words. And we'll see just how brave you can be when they lead you to the scaffold. As I said," Standish settled back in his chair, "that would be the end of your torment but only the beginning of an even bigger torment for your wife."

Harry only vaguely heard the words, as the nightmare had taken a completely new turn with the horrendous pain pulsating in his eye.

"I will ensure that your wife is found to be complicit in your treacherous activities…" Standish flicked his words across the table. "I'll ensure she spends a long time in prison. And the Frobisher name will always be synonymous with scandal and corruption. Don't think I can't do it. Don't think I won't do it… Now, would you like to bring that misfortune upon the woman you love?"

★★★

"Morag…?" Edwards soothed. "Wake up." He eased back from the chair as she flickered her eyes before finally opening them.

"Cyril…? I'm sorry… I…" Morag's eyes searched frantically around the room before coming to rest sadly upon her brother-in-law. "I thought…"

"Harry?" Edwards stood up and stepped back, leaning against the fireplace. "No news as yet." He decided to wait until she'd fully come round.

He noticed she was still wearing the same outfit as earlier; though, as usual, wore nothing on her feet. Her eyes were puffy and bloodshot, and there was a pallor to her face that was troubling. "Mrs Chambers tells me you haven't eaten."

"I'm not hungry," she replied, yawning and stretching.

"Hungry or not, I've asked Mrs Chambers to bring us both some soup and bread." He drew his pipe from his pocket, then noticed Harry's on the small table next to Morag. He discreetly placed his back in his pocket. "I've just come back to see how you are."

"A Captain Hemmings called by earlier." She straightened herself up in the chair.

"Captain Hemmings?"

"Yes, he was one of the officers who accompanied Colonel Standish to arrest Harry."

"What did he want?" Edwards asked suspiciously.

"He brought a letter from Harry." She ran her hand down the side of her cardigan and squeezed a tiny bulge in her pocket. "Hemmings wrote it down for him."

"Is he okay?"

"I'm not sure… His letter makes no mention of his health and Captain Hemmings just said he was being held in a room in the main building and not a cell."

"May I read the letter?" Edwards asked carefully.

Morag thought for a moment, then drew the letter from her pocket. It was a small piece of paper folded in half. "You're the only person I would show this to, Cyril," she said, handing it over.

"I know, Morag, thank you." He took the note, unfolded it and quickly read its contents. "Of course," he said slowly, "this could be a ruse… There's nothing to prove that Harry did actually dictate this."

"Those are Harry's words," Morag replied, nodding her head. "I know him… It's what he would say."

"Well, if that's the case, this Captain Hemmings certainly took a chance going to all this trouble to get this to you…" He looked again at the words and sighed deeply at their emotional outpouring of despair. "He must have visited Harry whilst Standish was with me at the police station… Did he say anything else?"

"Only that Harry had once saved his life in France and that he and many of the men over in the garrison don't think Harry could ever commit such a crime as treason."

Edwards handed the letter back and watched Morag tenderly fold it and return it to her pocket.

"He said Standish is planning to take Harry back to London, and he's worried about his safety if this happens… He thinks something will happen…" Her voice trailed off, and for a moment she seemed lost in a twilight world where reality and dreams entwined in some bewildering dance.

"What will happen?" Edwards prompted, fearing her lapse of concentration might be a prelude to some kind of descent into a state of deep depression.

"I don't know, Cyril… He seems to think Harry will never make it to London."

"Maybe I should try and speak to this Captain Hemmings," Edwards reflected.

Silence descended; familiar sounds, reassuring and warming, of staff going about their business, came from all corners of the house. Morag knew that, no matter how bad things might get, she still had a house and an estate to look after.

But surely not without Harry.

"There is something I do need to tell you, Morag." Edwards fiddled in his pocket, looking for his pipe, though resigned not to light it in her presence. "This morning I telegrammed a message to Whitehall, asking them to check with Somerset House the names of three of your new members of staff… Dodson, Kenick and Gregson. I advised them of the urgency of my request and they came back to me this morning, which was impressive to say the least, considering what day it is. Anyway, Dodson and Kenick are who they claim to be; the Register of Births and Deaths confirm their identities."

"What about Gregson?" Morag prompted.

Edwards tapped his pipe into the palm of his hand. "It also confirms Gregson… but, more accurately, her full name. She is one Locusta Gregson Baker, twin sister of Edwina Baker, former assistant to Morgan Treave over at Amble Lodge Asylum."

"Nurse Baker?" Morag climbed out of her chair and staggered back. "Are you sure?"

"This morning I spoke with Mabel and Horace Tregunnel, who own 13 Creek Lane. It seems Nurse Baker lived there with her twin sister. From all accounts she was a recluse and hardly ever seen. Mabel Tregunnel only ever got to hear her full name occasionally when in conversation with Nurse Baker."

"But why come here?" Morag had regained her composure, and perched herself on the armrest.

"I think she may be in cahoots with Morgan Treave. When her sister hanged herself, she knew she had to leave. Somehow she found her way into your household."

With a distant look in her eyes, Morag said, "It's strange… I've never seen her to talk to, just heard others making reference to her… and I always make a point of meeting new staff. When I asked Susan about her, she thought I had employed her."

"There's something else you should know," Edwards paused before taking a deep breath. "I've been hunting Locusta Baker ever since she poisoned her family a couple of years ago. Since then she's been complicit in the murders of several other unfortunate victims. Twice I've cornered her, and twice she's escaped… I would like to think she's completely mad, but that would be a mistake. She's evil, pure evil… and very clever… very manipulative. Several times she's written to me at Scotland Yard, taunting me and my colleagues. I was investigating her when I came down here last November… To think she was actually related to Nurse Baker…" Edwards shook his head. "Incredible… She must have used 13 Creek Lane as a place to hide. Why the connection with Edwina Baker never came to light in our initial investigations, I'll never know. She was an art student in London before she abruptly left. No one saw or heard anything of her until those first murders. It was her husband and two children. We found sketches in the house of their dead bodies. We also found sketches at the homes of her other victims; it seems she takes great pleasure in sketching her victims as they're dying."

"Do you think she has anything to do with The Rooks?" Morag asked.

"I think it unlikely," replied Edwards. "I'm of the opinion that her presence here opens up another line of investigation; well, a continuation of one already open."

"Susan told me she's disappeared – packed her things and left. Her bed wasn't even slept in last night, and none of the other staff have seen her since yesterday evening."

"She might have left the house, but she could still be a threat to yourself and Harry," Edwards reflected. "It might be an idea to ring through to Sergeant Cadan and ask for an armed constable to stay with you tonight."

"That won't be necessary, Cyril."

"Why do you say that?" Edwards narrowed his eyes.

"Please, Cyril, just take my word for it. That won't be necessary." Morag's words were almost chilling.

The stoic determination and cold resignation in her voice told Edwards not to pursue the matter.

He did, though, share the following thought. "Interestingly, though, history tells us that there was a woman called Locusta who lived during Ancient Rome. She made a living out of concocting poisons, and sold them to whoever was of the mind to commit murder. They say she even had a hand in dispatching

Emperor Nero... A strange coincidence, but nevertheless quite deadly. The details of our suspect are all correct: Locusta Gregson Baker." He regarded his pipe thoughtfully.

"I don't know what to say." Morag pushed her hair back from her face.

"Are you sure you never met her? Think, Morag..."

Morag turned her head away and stared across towards the doors leading out onto the terrace. "It couldn't be," she whispered.

"Who?" Edwards watched her closely.

"A woman... Lives out on the estate... Her cottage is full of the most beautiful paintings I've ever seen of Frobisher Hall and the estate... And I saw something else today when I was visiting her..."

"Go on."

"It was a bottle marked 'Poison' on the shelf in her dining room."

"Where is this cottage?" Edwards pulled out his notebook and pencil.

Morag shook her head. "No... it can't be her... And, besides, she wouldn't make it so obvious, would she?"

Edwards sighed, noticing the troubled look in her eyes. She appeared to be drifting away, deep in thought and grappling with questions, yet struggling to find the answers. This was where she was different to her sister. Elisha had had that wonderful ability to weigh up a situation and let clear, rational thinking prevail. He also knew that Morag was desperately holding back a tidal wave of emotion since Harry's arrest; if he pushed the issue of Locusta Baker too far, she might withdraw from him completely.

Placing his pipe back into his jacket pocket, he caught the outline of Lady Margaret's journal. Locusta Baker would have to wait. If Morag was walking a fine line between cool rational thought and despairing panic, he feared her reaction to what he was about to do.

"How is Doctor Mitchell?" Morag looked up, completely changing the mood and topic of conversation.

"He'll pull through…" Edwards almost welcomed the question. "I think he was visiting Peran Freeman and came across the body. The shock would have probably killed him if we hadn't found him. He kept muttering…" He paused as the door to the lounge opened and Mrs Chambers walked in, with Dodson and Kenick following in her wake. Each bore a tray which they balanced with professional ease as they approached Morag and Edwards.

"Here you are, Your Ladyship…" Mrs Chambers announced cheerfully, "a nice broth for you both and my freshly baked bread." She stood aside as Kenick and Dodson settled their trays of bread, along with a pot of tea and accompaniments, on the table.

"Mrs Chambers, I really don't think—" Morag stared at the food before her.

"Rubbish, Morag," Edwards said sternly. "You're not going to be of any use to Harry sitting here wasting away." He felt his own stomach rumbling and realised it had been a long time since he'd eaten. Stepping forward, he picked up a slice of bread and dipped it into one of the soup bowls.

"If you require anything else, please ring." Mrs Chambers turned and ushered Dodson and Kenick from the room.

When they'd left, Morag said, "Canon Trebarwith phoned earlier… I've said we'll meet him at ten tomorrow morning up at the monument for a small service of remembrance for Edith Travers and her husband Reginald."

"Yes, I think that would be a good idea, Morag." Edwards watched as she sipped a little of her broth. "I also want to lay flowers on her grave whilst I'm down here…" He looked towards the window and the slowly diminishing light. "I still feel responsible for her death."

"You can't blame yourself, Cyril." Morag dabbed some bread into her soup. "It's the same with everything now. It all seems so pointless... What can we do? What's to stop this Colonel Standish taking Harry away from us for good?" She lowered her head.

They finished their soup in silence, and drank their tea in quiet contemplation of the events of the day. Finally, as the grandfather clock in the hallway chimed 10pm, Edwards stood up and crossed over to the drinks' cabinet. Pouring a large rum, he returned to Morag and handed it to her.

"Morag, last year I promised Elisha, before she died, that I would find you. Well, as it turned out, you found Harry and a happiness I remember once with your sister. I have nothing left in this world except her memory and the companionship of you both, and I'll do everything in my power to prevent Harry coming to any harm. I'm going to stay over at the garrison tonight and hopefully meet with the commanding officer. Also, by being there, I might actually get to see Harry."

"Thank you, Cyril." She regarded the glass before gently placing it on the small table. "It's so empty without him... And I feel so helpless."

Edwards observed her carefully, aware of what he was about to do. There had been occasions, in both his professional and private life, when he'd been faced with decisions that were to have momentous consequences for himself and, sometimes, those around him. Reaching into his jacket pocket, he pulled out Lady Margaret's journal and found himself having to draw on a level of courage he thought had never existed within him. "Morag, it's getting late, and I need to drive back into Bodmin. I'll meet you tomorrow morning at the police station..." He handed the journal across to her. "I found this in Peran Freeman's safe. Everything else had been scattered around the room. I think they were after a letter written by Captain Grant that named the Fourth Rook..."

Morag reached out and took the journal from him.

"It's Lady Margaret's journal," he said, "and I think you should read it…" He bent forward, kissed her on the cheek, turned and walked slowly from the lounge.

22

Morgan Treave had never realised before how much he loved Morag Donaldson.

In his mind he repeated her name and swore undying love for her, a love that, one day, he knew she would willingly consummate. It would happen, of that he was sure, upon the dank and squalid mattress he now lay upon, in the room that had become her shrine, amongst the numerous candles that illuminated those wonderful drawings on the walls.

On the floor, next to the mattress, lay scattered the things she would wear for him, the objects of his love and her desire: the straitjacket that had once constrained her whilst she'd been carried, drugged and subdued to her room at Amble Lodge; the ropes that had bound her ankles to the bedpost; and the very syringe he'd desperately tried to drive into her arm that fateful day in the East Tower. She'd had no right to do what she'd done to his face; but he had forgiven her, knowing it had been a necessary act on her part to test his eternal love for her.

He now had to find it in himself to forgive her those endless nights she'd given herself to Harry Frobisher, and he feared to what depth of bitterness and anger her cavorting with his blind and mentally crippled love rival might drive him. He hoped her interest in Harry Frobisher was just a passing fancy, and that she'd succumb to her desires and join him in eternal bliss, hidden away in the vast underground chambers and secret passageways beneath Frobisher Hall.

Maybe Lord Frobisher would spend the rest of his life wandering blindly around the house, searching and calling for her. And they would be together, laughing at his pitiful voice... pleading... crying...

He thought of Locusta and smiled with delight at her wonderful artistic talents. Each image of Morag had been drawn by her, whilst he'd sat on his mattress gazing reverently at the way her fingers had sketched and shaded, coloured and portrayed the most beautiful woman to have ever walked upon the face of this pathetic and corrupt world.

But now Locusta was gone, and Morgan Treave knew there would be no more drawings, no tenderness during those awful nights when the woman he wanted was locked in the arms of another man.

He wanted so desperately to have Morag back, to fill the void in his life she'd left when she'd done that terrible thing to him in the East Tower. Locusta had understood, like her sister Edwina. From the day she'd found her hanging from the rafters in 13 Creek Lane and made her way to Frobisher Hall, she'd always understood.

He sighed, listening to the distant sounds of the polyphon tinkering out the strains of Mozart's *Don Giovanni*. Such a wonderful example of modern inventions, and how perceptive of Morag to have the metal disc of his favourite opera slotted in the adjoining cupboard with the other discs.

That would bring her to him.

As it did the other night.

And now that pathetic husband of hers wasn't around to spoil their inevitable union. Tonight, he would take her hand, guide her down the darkened passageway to this very room and remove the nightgown she'd been wearing the previous evening; the night her husband had stumbled into the library.

He thought about those nights at Amble Lodge when he'd visited her...

Her eyes, though closed, were so inviting, so enticing, he fought to control his heartbeat as his hand massaged her leg before sliding between her thighs.

"Come to me, dear Morag," he whispered, and reached across for the syringe.

★★★

Morag tossed and turned in her sleep, reaching out for Harry but finding only a cold and dispassionate armrest that rebuked the touch of her fingers. As sleep released its hold, she felt a numbness in her arm and a fierce spasm tighten her neck muscles, and she realised, painfully, that she'd fallen asleep in Harry's chair in the lounge. So desperate was she to see her husband that she raised her head and surveyed the room, fully expecting to hear the sound of his soothing voice.

But there was no Harry to bring her comfort, no words or the touch of his hand. The urge to simply burst into tears was so overwhelming she collapsed back into the chair and let the pain in her neck and the realisation of her loneliness totally consume her.

Through this terrible mist in which she had awoken came a familiar sound, something she'd heard before but couldn't quite fathom. As she sat up properly, she felt something fall to the floor and realised it was Lady Margaret's journal. The realisation that she must have fallen asleep whilst reading its contents filled her with a sense of shame and foreboding at the legacy of what Inspector Edwards had passed on to her.

She shook her head, sighing deeply at his decision to present her with the journal before beating a hasty retreat from Frobisher Hall. And how could she have fallen asleep after reading its contents? For God's sake, what was she to do…?

The caressive strains of *Don Giovanni* drifted through to the lounge.

It was the same as last night, hypnotic and entrancing, every note floating through the house, calling her… She remembered attending a performance of *Don Giovanni* in Edinburgh with her parents and Elisha, many years ago. It was the first time she'd ever attended an opera, and she'd fallen in love with the costumes, the radiant scenery on stage and, of course, the music, that beautifully crafted story of the infamous Don, habitual lover and seducer of women. At the end of the performance they'd hired a carriage to take them back to their home, a large Victorian granite house set high above the city. Later, she'd lain in bed, gazing out of her window, thinking of that handsome and seductive scoundrel who had reached deep into her soul and beckoned her into his sordid and corrupt life…

The music did likewise, like a hand summoning her; she knew who was calling to her and realised she had no option but to follow.

She climbed out of the chair and walked slowly towards the library door. When she entered the hall, she gazed casually at the polyphon before glancing across at the grandfather clock.

The time was 2.47am.

Around her, Frobisher Hall slept fitfully, with the occasional sleepy creak and moan as ghostly shadows flitted through the rooms and passageways; memories of past generations scurrying to warn this beautiful woman with red hair who crept slowly through the hallway towards the library and a terrible assignation.

Dreamily, she entered the library and walked towards the false door beside the fireplace. She had once slipped through this very door and seen Harry dozing in his chair, the day Susan had entered…

The false door began to open, inching back into the darkness within. Realising she didn't have a light of any kind, she paused, shuddering slightly as an icy chill settled around her. There was a familiar dank and musty smell, yet Morag seemed oblivious to its rotten and pungent odour.

She reached her hand into the darkness.

A hand, cold and sinewy, wrapped itself around hers, and a voice whispered, "I knew you'd come to me, my dear…"

Morag stepped into the darkness and gazed briefly at the passageway that led to the East Tower. She thought she might visit her room again, but knew that that nightmare had ended… or maybe it hadn't. Maybe it had simply stepped aside as one far greater, and certainly more real, now enticed her into its lurid and dreadful domain.

The hand eased and guided her away from the familiar passageway, the steps Harry had once climbed when she'd called to him. She stepped into another small entrance, dirty and matted with old cobwebs that laced themselves across her face. Something scurried across her bare feet, and she flinched as she trod upon pieces of brick and mortar, before finally feeling the floor give way to some old rickety wooden steps that led down further into a narrower passageway.

"Take your time, my dear. I don't want you to fall and hurt yourself…"

The voice came to her more clearly, and Morag found herself remembering how he'd said those very same words the night they'd dragged her, struggling weakly against the straitjacket confining her and the drugs clouding her mind and judgement, into the very depths of Amble Lodge…

"Not far now, my dear. I'll make you comfortable again…"

Morag stumbled slightly as she reached the bottom of the steps. Looking ahead, she found herself gazing through drugged eyes at a kaleidoscopic world of hallucinatory figures, glaring faces and white suits… The smell of disinfectant came to her, wave after wave, assailing her senses, only to then recede and be replaced by the smell of stagnant urine...

Yet that beautiful music, so haunting and delightful, seemed to make everything right...

She knew she was beneath the house, in the darkened chambers Harry's father had once told her about, the places where his ancestors had hidden vast amounts of illegal contraband from the Customs and Excise men.

Or was she in Amble Lodge?

Her mind whirled with recollections and memories too monstrous to comprehend.

Finally, as a door opened before her, illuminating her world with seemingly thousands of candles, she beheld the face of Morgan Treave, grinning through a mouth that was contorted and twisted, smirking with an evil look in the one eye that peered deep into her, mentally undressing her and running its gaze across her breasts. As his scarred face narrowed into a hideous visage of lust and wanton desire, the gaping black hole that had once held his other eye opened and closed.

She thought she might still be holding the broken bottle that had ripped his face apart, and that she might be able to finish the job. And maybe she would have done so had it not been for the drawings etched upon the walls, that drew her attention and finally pulled her away from the nightmare of Amble Lodge and into the reality of this dungeon shrine.

Once Morag was in the middle of the room, Morgan Treave let go of her hand. He stepped reverently back, and she gazed at him with a feeling of revulsion and fascination. He was thinner than she remembered and certainly more stooped and hunched in his movements. The grey beard, that might once have been a distinguishing feature, was now matted and scraggly, its former neatness now ripped apart with the scars that criss-crossed his face.

Morag looked away and at the drawings of herself, those numerous drawings of her staring down triumphantly, as though her alter ego were now laughing at her presence in this dreadful place. The more she stared, the more her mind cleared itself of the hypnotic sounds of that beautiful melody, and she gazed around with both revulsion and fascination.

Standing before her, Morgan Treave regarded her as though he'd just carried his bride into their honeymoon suite.

Strewn across the dirt floor lay empty bottles of wine and the remnants of half-eaten meals. In a corner, a filthy mattress had been set slightly away from the wall, with space enough to drive a metal stake into the ground at each corner. From these hung heavy chains, with leg clamps at the bottom and wrist constraints at the top.

But it was the item lying on the mattress that filled Morag with horror. A straitjacket, neatly folded, was positioned at its centre.

"Your nightdress, my dear. It'll be like it was when we were together at Amble Lodge." Morgan Treave approached her and ran his hand across her shoulder. "You'll get used to the chains... I'll wash you, feed you... You'll never want for anything..." He paused, grinning.

Morag shook her head, marvelling the accuracy of the drawings. It was as though she had posed for every single drawing, and could even remember doing so.

"You like my drawings, Morag?" Treave stepped back and away, smiling... admiring... "I'm afraid I can't take credit for any of them; they were drawn by my dear friend Locusta. Do you know her?"

As Morag continued to stare at the drawings, realisation began to dawn. The images of just her face, with her hair cascading around her shoulders, were reminiscent of how she would sit on the bed, gazing lovingly at Harry as he slept. And the sketches of her lying seductively naked and on her back... *My dear God*, she thought... showed her lying in eager anticipation, waiting for Harry to ease himself into her.

She frantically moved her gaze to another, and then to another...

The one where she was on her front, her thighs parted... Harry liked to...

"She..." Morag tried to speak but couldn't find the words.

"You know her as Gregson. The delightful maid, so sweet and innocent..." His words dripped menace. "Her sister was Nurse Baker, that gentle soul who looked after you at Amble Lodge. When she found her sister hanging, she came here with every intention of murdering you and your husband... and she would have done so... But she arrived whilst you were on your honeymoon, and I gave her shelter down here. At first, she was of a mind to kill you whilst you slept, but she had always loved you – as her sister and I have done since that night you came to join us at Amble Lodge..." Treave gazed at the drawings, letting his eyes drift leisurely over their sensuous suggestions. He paused at the images of her chained to a bed. "She'd visit you in your room whilst you were sleeping and then completed these purely from memory. The rest..." He swung his hand above his head, pivoting around. "She liked to draw you... Watching you and sketching... And then she'd come down here to copy her drawings onto the walls... just as I asked her to," he chuckled.

"But how...?" Morag looked upon the images of her chained and wrapped within the straitjacket's loving embrace.

"My dear... you never knew, did you...? The secret door that leads into your bedroom... She sketched you whilst peering through a crack in the opening... When you slept, undressed, bathed, and when you gave yourself to your husband... She watched and sketched everything... Alas, I do not have her skill, and so could only watch...It was she who sat beside you as you dozed in the bath; she wanted to touch you... We both wanted to touch you..."

"I swear to God..." Morag caught her breath and turned to face her tormentor. "I swear to God I'll break every bone in your perverted, twisted body." A thought entered her mind and she heard herself say, "The body on the train, in the carriage next to ours..."

"Hmm, Archie Cummings... I spent some of my time, after you saw fit to rearrange my face, hiding out in London's docklands. A surgeon, specialising in patching up criminals wounded in gangland fights, took pity on me and finally removed what was left of my eye and tried to reset my face. Whilst I was there, I got talking to a couple of members of The Laggers, a rather intriguing and shadowy gang which specialises in assassinations." Treave licked his twisted lip, snorting as he did so. "I paid Mr Cummings to kill your husband. You weren't to be harmed. I left the time and place for his choosing, and eventually travelled back to Cornwall. The next thing I heard, a body had been found on the same train as yourselves... And then I heard the staff talking about Inspector Edwards and how he'd killed him... Then I overheard you and your husband talking in your bedroom and the name of Archie Cummings mentioned." Treave shook his head. "That man cost me a lot of money..."

Morag felt the small flame in her stomach erupt into a raging furnace. Her hatred for this man was pure and unsullied; it knew no boundaries and respected no conventionalities. When she spoke, her voice echoed with a deep desire for vengeance and retribution. "I'm going to make you regret the day you ever decided to come back into our lives." She clenched her fists.

Morgan Treave sighed and shook his head. "I thought that would be the case." He walked across to a pile of clothes on the floor and heaved them to one side, revealing an old leather bag. Opening it up, he pulled out a syringe – one that Morag had seen before. It was already full, and he turned to her, smiling.

"Come near me with that and I'll kill you," Morag snarled.

Treave chuckled and reached into his pocket, pulling out a small revolver.

"What exactly do you plan to kill me with, my dear?" He pointed the revolver at her and added, "If I can't have you, then nobody ever will. From what I hear, your husband has enough trouble and might never return home. Personally, I hope they do hang him for these murders… Oh, don't look at me like that; I had nothing to do with them. Strange, though, how all this unfolded around him since your return from honeymoon…" He moved to the centre of the room.

Morag stepped back towards the door.

"All I'm asking for is your eternal love." Treave held the revolver steady in one hand, the syringe in the other. "We can live together down here… You ran away from me once; you mustn't do that again."

"You're going to pay for murdering those people, Treave," Morag said calmly. For the first time since she could remember, her mind was clear enough to see a shining light at the end of this awful nightmare. "Martha Smith, Edith and Reginald Travers… You're going to rot in Hell." Stepping to one side, she peered over his shoulder and smiled.

A look of confusion spread across Morgan Treave's twisted and warped face. It quickly turned to one of rage as he swung round, instantly raising the revolver but realising he was too late.

Susan Matthews stood defiantly at the entrance to the passageway leading out into the forest; she held a Webley revolver aimed directly at Treave's face. Its colossal size seemed to dwarf her small hand, but that was where any question of her ability to handle such a weapon ended. Her face was expressionless, her eyes set firmly upon the target before her.

With no hint of emotion or flicker of mercy, she squeezed the trigger, instantly filling the room with a blinding flash and a thunderous roar.

Morgan Treave staggered back and slumped dead upon the mattress, a bullet hole set neatly in his forehead.

Susan stepped forward, keeping the gun pointed at his head.

As she did so, Lawrence Matthews appeared at the entrance to the passageway and peered into the room. When Susan and Morag looked across at him, he smiled and nodded his head.

23

Sunday 24th May

Sunday morning dawned grey and heavy with a familiar Cornish mist that spread itself like a veil across the town of Bodmin. It settled deep within the valleys and obscured the tops of the hills in the surrounding countryside. It left those who ventured out feeling damp and dreary, aggravating coughs and leaving an air of despondency in its wake.

From the railway terminus, a small engine chuffed and clattered as it shunted empty wagons, stained with clay, into position, grouping them ready for transport back to the main line. The men working on the footplate looked solemnly towards the grey clouds before staring at the regimental garrison across the road. There'd been an increase in activity, something not seen since the days of war, when their time had been taken up with the endless transportation of men back and forth to the mainline. Since the end of hostilities, life had quietened down; and during the blessed years of peace that followed, the soldiers stationed at the barracks had withdrawn into the normal routine of army life.

But this morning that peace had been shattered, and they stared across in amazement at the figure of an officer shouting and screaming orders at a guard standing to attention outside the main gates.

"I want Captain Frobisher brought here immediately!" Colonel Standish roared as a deep feeling of desperation began to surface within him.

"I'm sorry, sir, but I can't leave my position." The young private pushed out his chest and stared directly ahead. "You must ask the sergeant of the guard."

"I don't need to ask anyone, Private," Standish snarled. "But I can put you on a charge for disobeying orders…" He stared at the young man's face. "Never mind, I'll get him myself. One of your men is bringing a car around for me." He stormed past the young man and disappeared into the guardhouse. Within a couple of minutes, he reappeared with a set of keys and walked to the first of a line of cells outside.

Clanking open the door he yelled, "Captain Frobisher, come with me!"

The clock tower chimed the hour of ten, and the young private breathed a sigh of relief as he realised he'd be relieved in a matter of minutes and could quickly scurry back to his barracks.

Harry Frobisher lay on his back, his hand groping desperately in front of his face as Standish caught him by the scruff of his collar and heaved him from his makeshift bed.

"You're coming with me now, Captain Frobisher. I am personally going to drive you back to London…" He pushed Harry's flailing hands down, pulled out his revolver and pushed the muzzle into his face. "If you resist, I will shoot you. Do you understand?" Spittle ran down his chin and splattered across Harry's face.

Then came the sound of muffled voices outside and footsteps approaching. Standish quickly pushed the revolver back into its holder and turned to face the door, his face contorted into a mask of fury. He drew a deep breath, ready to scream his defiance at anyone who dared to challenge his actions.

Captain Hemmings appeared at the door, braced himself and saluted.

"What do you want, Captain Hemmings?" Standish relaxed his grip on Harry and curbed his rising anger back to a growl.

"I want to know where you're taking Captain Frobisher, Colonel Standish," Hemmings replied curtly.

"As an officer in Military Intelligence, I have authority over this man. As you know, he's suspected of committing treason against this country, and I have every right to take him into custody and transport him back to London to face trial." Standish pushed Harry back before adding, "And if you obstruct me in any way, Captain, if you hinder my attempts to take him from this garrison, I will order your immediate arrest and court martial. I'll ensure you spend the rest of your time here cleaning the latrines—"

Captain Hemmings called across to Harry, "Captain Frobisher? Are you okay?"

"I've felt better, John," Harry muttered. His lips were swollen and his face was terribly bruised. Around his eyes, the skin was inflamed, with old scar tissue now bloody and torn.

"My God, Harry, did he do this to you?" Hemmings took a step forward.

"Do not speak to the prisoner, Captain Hemmings," Standish said nonchalantly, clenching his walking stick and turning the serpent's head towards Hemmings. "Now, I have a car being driven round to the front, and I want—"

"Until I authorise his release into your custody, Lord Frobisher is still a prisoner of this garrison," Hemmings interrupted, "And, as such, I'm responsible for his welfare."

"What?" Standish glared contemptuously.

"Under military law, a prisoner cannot be released until the proper procedures have been followed. The officer of the guard will need to formally authorise his release." Hemmings kept his eyes fixed on Standish.

The clock tower chimed the quarter hour past ten.

From somewhere in the distance, the sound of a car heading in the direction of the garrison cut through the mist like an approaching angel of vengeance, a terrible harbinger of doom.

Hemmings stepped back a little and turned his gaze towards the approaching car as it pulled off the main road and turned towards the garrison. As it drew nearer, he narrowed his eyes and smiled.

Standish suddenly appeared beside him and walked out into the small courtyard. As the car drew to a halt, he muttered, "Good Lord…"

★★★

Inspector Edwards drew his watch from his pocket and glanced at the time: 9.45am.

He steadied himself as Morag lurched the Daimler from one side to the other as she negotiated the road leading out of Bodmin, the engine roaring its disapproval at the steep gradient it was trying to climb. He'd travelled this route before, but it had been dark and extremely cold. It had also been a night of murder, cold-blooded murder that had chilled him to the bone.

"I've asked Sergeant Cadan to personally supervise the removal of Morgan Treave's body. He'll be taken to Bodmin Gaol and kept there until somebody decides to arrange his burial." Edwards braced himself as Morag turned onto a dirt track, driving carefully as she worked the big car around the numerous rocks and stones ahead of her. "Whatever the three of you planned, it certainly worked out." He smiled.

"Lawrence found it… He accidently located the entrance to the tunnel out in the forest. It was a room the family used years ago to keep contraband away from the Customs and Excise men. Treave must have found it and made his home there…"

"Like a rat," Edwards mused.

"Aye, like a rat. Lawrence told Susan about it and they both came to see me. The previous night he'd set the polyphon playing and I'd gone downstairs to investigate. I caught a glimpse of him, and I knew it wouldn't end until he was dead."

Morag eased the car to a halt opposite a gate leading into a field.

Above them loomed the towering presence of the Walter Raleigh Gilbert Monument, its peak lost within the grey mist that embraced the surrounding countryside.

"The plan was for Susan to make her way through the tunnel and wait for him to draw me down into the room. It had to be Susan, as she was small enough to work her way through the passageway without being heard…" Morag turned off the engine. "Even though we planned it, he still managed to…" She shook her head. "I just felt as though I were under his spell. It was disgusting… Drawings of me…"

"Morag," Edwards took her hand and squeezed it, "the man's dead, and that's an end to it. He deserved everything he got… I think it might be an idea to fill in that tunnel and properly seal off any remaining passages in the house."

"Aye, Cyril, I've already spoken to Lawrence and he said he'd sort it out."

"And leave the report to me. The inquest will be a formality. Susan won't even be called to give evidence." There was an air of finality in his voice. He did, however, nod his head in genuine respect before adding, "No wonder you didn't want one of Sergeant Cadan's men with you last night."

They both climbed down from the car and stared up at the monument.

"I never thought I'd ever want to return to this place after what happened last year," he said as they began to walk up the slight incline. The grass beneath their feet was luscious and damp, the air moist and heavy. He wanted to ask if Morag had read Lady Margaret's journal, but the morning's news of Morgan Treave's death had dominated any discussions between them.

As they approached the structure, Canon Trebarwith appeared from behind the base and said, "Ah, Lady Frobisher... Inspector Edwards..." He shook their hands. "I thought some prayers, and then if—"

Edwards held his hand up, bringing the proceedings to a sudden halt.

He was eyeing the plaque positioned on the side of the base, and reading the name over and over again in his mind.

Sir Walter Raleigh Gilbert...

The monument...

Taking a deep breath, he cleared his mind and fought to control the mental lightning bolt that speared him to the ground.

Think, man, think...

Behind the...

The letter to Harry... Look for the Fourth Rook behind...

WRG...

Wilbur Richard Grant...

"Everything okay, Inspector?" Canon Trebarwith's voice came to him from somewhere...

"Don't you see?" Edwards shook his head.

"See what, Cyril?" Morag stared blankly at him.

"The letter Captain Grant sent to Harry... Those weren't his initials at the end; he was telling Harry something... My God... How could I have missed it?" Edwards moved closer and touched the side of the granite structure.

It felt moist and cold.

"He knew his life was in danger. He wrote two letters; one to Harry and the other to be opened in the event of his death. That second letter he gave to Peran Freeman and asked him to keep it safe. Old Mr Freeman must have laughed at the irony." Edwards was finding it hard to control both the excitement rising within him and the despairing thought of what might be happening to Harry. "You see, Canon, when Morag became suspicious of a plot to murder the former Lord and Lady Frobisher last year, she wrote a letter and did the same thing. When she was committed to Amble Lodge, Mr Freeman sent that letter to me at Scotland Yard. When I came down here to investigate her disappearance, I visited him and thanked him for doing so. I remember commenting on his choice of hiding places, and I looked at his safe, but he just smiled and shook his head... because he'd hidden it somewhere else, in case William Frobisher should come looking for it..."

"I think I follow you, Cyril," Morag frowned.

Canon Trebarwith looked completely dumbfounded.

"Morag," continued Edwards, "the letter you read to Harry mentioned something about looking for the Fourth Rook behind the WRG... Don't you see? The *Walter Raleigh Gilbert* Monument; the print in his office, for Heaven's sakes..."

Morag whispered, "Oh, God..."

"The letters WRG were not Grant's initials. He was referring to Walter Raleigh Gilbert. We need to get back down to Peran Freeman's office and check behind that print... Quickly!"

Edwards grabbed Morag's hand.

"I say," Canon Trebarwith called out, "may I come as well?"

"Yes, of course, Canon, but we need to hurry." Edwards was already leading Morag down the hill towards the Daimler.

By the time Canon Trebarwith reached the car, Morag had started the engine and was waiting patiently for him to climb into the back.

As she reversed the car down the hill and onto the main road, Edwards said, "The murderer tortured Peran Freeman and got nothing out of him. I expect he delayed his killer long enough and eventually gave him the key to the safe, knowing they'd waste further time searching in vain... And all this time the letter was behind the print."

Morag drove down the hill before skidding onto the main high street. Parishioners walking to church scattered and a horse reared up, threatening to throw its rider.

"Loyal to the end," Edwards muttered to himself; "to die like that rather than betray the trust of a complete stranger like Grant..."

Morag screeched to a halt outside the solicitor's office.

"Quickly now." Edwards climbed out and raced up the steps. Ahead of him, a young policeman stood guard next to the door and stared anxiously as Edwards bore down on him.

"Step aside, Constable!" He opened the door.

The smell of death still lingered, but the sickly pungent smell of decomposing flesh had thankfully receded.

Racing into the office, he grabbed the print and pulled hard. As it ripped free, a small envelope fluttered down and landed at his feet. Glancing round, he saw Morag and Canon Trebarwith rush into the room and stare at him in bewilderment.

Placing the print on the desk, Edwards knelt down and picked up the envelope. Running his finger along the edge, he ripped it open and pulled out a letter, which he duly unfolded.

With unrestrained eagerness he gazed at the writing several times before staring across at Morag. "Harry was the Third Rook..." he whispered, "Standish is the Fourth Rook... We need to get Harry out of there!"

The small clock on the mantlepiece read 10.10am.

***

Ellen Carfax sat gently on the hospital bed, leaned across and softly ran her hand across Doctor Mitchell's forehead. He still felt clammy, and she guessed his body temperature was still battling against the effects of the shock that had done so much damage the day before. The room was spacious, and he was the sole occupant. The other beds had recently been removed, as rumours of the hospital's impending closure moved closer to reality.

His eyes flickered, then opened. They were weak and took time to focus.

"Hello," she whispered. "I was worried about you."

He forced a smile and tried to raise a hand.

"No… don't try to move. You've been ill… Inspector Edwards found you and brought you here." She stroked his cheek.

He looked so frail under the single blanket that covered him, and Ellen feared he might be too cold. Reaching down, she grasped his hand and watched his fragile smile grow stronger the more she squeezed it. His face was gaunt, and his skin held a yellow tinge and lay tightly over his cheekbones.

He moved his lips and she lowered her head.

"I'm so sorry…" he croaked. "I… should have…" He sighed and rolled his eyes.

"You have nothing to be sorry for; you did what you had to do."

"I wanted you to have… I thought Mr Freeman…" Doctor Mitchell looked sadly away, and Ellen saw the look of despair in his eyes.

The window was open, and a dampness was permeating its way through the room. The walls were grey and flaked, with waterpipes running down the corners and into the floor. Hot water pipes, turned off during the month of March, ran along the furthest wall and disappeared through into the next room.

Ellen glanced around the room and found herself wishing she could take him home and look after him there. Looking towards the door, she saw the massive outline of Branok hovering, watching and protecting.

"Don't do this to yourself..." she soothed; "you've done nothing wrong."

"The journal..." he whispered. "You should have it... It belongs to you... I've lived with this lie for too long..."

Ellen leaned forward, kissed him on the forehead and said, "I owe you everything... everything... Sleep now, my dear friend."

★★★

Morag drew the Daimler to a halt and gazed across the small courtyard to where Captain Hemmings was standing. She thought she caught a hint of a smile, genuine and full of relief. The grey foreboding building behind him might have intimidated others of a more sensitive nature. There might even have been a time, many years ago, when Morag would have heeded her father's advice and been tempted to show a cautious respect for such an establishment; if there was, she couldn't remember. And besides, she now had nothing but contempt for an institution that bred people like Colonel Standish and placed them in charge of ordinary men like Harry and the millions of others who'd responded so heroically to their country's call.

As she approached Captain Hemmings, she saw him nod in both admiration and respect, his features softening into a smile that was completely alluring. He carried himself with such noble dignity yet modest bearing that he immediately reminded her of Harry. Though she stared back, Morag didn't acknowledge him, choosing instead to turn her attention to a rather pompous-looking, red-cheeked man dressed in the uniform of a high-ranking army officer who'd just emerged from one of the cells in the courtyard.

358

The look of smug arrogance was set deep in his eyes, and Morag walked across to him, aware of Inspector Edwards and Canon Trebarwith pausing a little way behind.

"You must be Colonel Standish." Her voice was balanced on a razor edge. Out of the corner of her eye she noticed figures begin to appear, emerging from open doors, materialising from barracks across the parade ground, all eager to observe the sudden drama unfolding before them. She saw several men hastily dressing, pulling boots and jackets on, oblivious to the damp mist settling around them. Within a couple of minutes, a crowd had gathered, eyeing her with a combination of intrigue and amazement.

"And you, no doubt, are the formidable Lady Frobisher," Standish sneered.

"Aye...that I am." Her first feeling was one of relief, knowing that he'd not been able to commence his journey back to London with Harry. The thought made her take a deep breath and silently thank God she wasn't too late. For that alone, she might go some way to forgiving him.

Glaring at him, she watched him take a nervous step back, lowering his head and coughing abruptly, as though her presence caused him an embarrassment he couldn't shrug off. She turned to the cell door and peered into the gloom, covering her mouth and moaning as she saw Harry's bruised and battered face.

"Harry...?" she whispered.

Harry was sitting on the bed, staring blindly ahead. At the sound of her voice, he turned and feebly muttered, "Morag...?"

Turning to face Standish, Morag took a step forward.

There was no warning.

All the hate and bitterness, fear and loathing she'd suppressed since Harry had been taken from her erupted into a fiery explosion of rage. As if in slow motion, she felt her body turn slightly as she brought her fist round and into the side of Standish's jaw, sending him crashing to the ground.

As he rolled drunkenly, trying to regain his senses, she considered striking him again, but stopped as she heard Harry call her name. With one final look of scorn at the man lying dazed at her feet, she turned and stared triumphantly at the crowd of men, who stared back at her, utterly astonished. She scanned their faces, defiance and spite blazing in her eyes.

But her anger was soon quelled as she felt the hatred in her heart give way to conciliation, and the malice in her soul disintegrate around her. For as she stared deep into their eyes, she saw respect and admiration, along with a feeling of reverence, that warmed her and stayed the violence she had threatened.

Allowing the merest of smiles, slight and cautious, drift across her face, she entered Harry's cell. As she knelt down in front of him, she reached forward and took his hand.

"It's time to go home, my darling," she whispered.

Outside the cell, Inspector Edwards made his way towards the prostrate figure of Colonel Standish. Staring down at the crumpled heap, he said dryly, "I see you've finally met Lady Frobisher." Glancing across at Captain Hemmings, he nodded and let the mere flicker of a smile flash across his face. In a moment it was gone, quickly replaced by a look of hardened resolve. Looking down at Standish, who had regained some degree of comprehension, he said, "Colonel Charles Standish, I am arresting you for the murders of Captain Grant, Annette Myers and Peran Freeman. Anything you say will be taken down and used in evidence." He looked across at Hemmings. "Captain Hemmings, please take Colonel Standish under armed guard to Bodmin Gaol. See that he's given one of the older cells… one of those set deep underground."

Hemmings smiled. "It will be my pleasure, Inspector."

24

By mid-afternoon the mist had turned to a fine drizzle, with no prospect of a let-up in the greyness that had descended upon the Cornish countryside. Through the streets of Bodmin, people hurried home from visiting friends and family; out in the fields, labourers ploughed, guiding horses with a supporting shout, keen to plant late crops.

Overhead, rooks fluttered and swooped.

Canon Trebarwith sat in the back of the Daimler, still shaken from his experiences earlier that morning, and peered at the countryside as it sped by. The journey from the vicarage to Frobisher Hall was one he could have made himself, either on his cycle or in his Austin, but Lady Frobisher had been adamant in her request for him to meet with her and her husband at the family chapel for Holy Communion and for Lawrence Matthews to drive him over.

She'd told him she was worried in case he was still in shock over the incident at the barracks, and her behaviour, which, she assured him, was totally out of character. He recollected the punch she'd thrown, so quick and powerful he wondered if it might not have been the first time she'd sent someone crashing to the ground.

But he had been shaken, and he now sat pondering the arrest of Colonel Standish...

Dear me, he thought, *Colonel Standish… The Fourth Rook…*

He closed his eyes and thought about Captain Grant, Annette Myers and Peran Freeman. Their faces came to him, troubled and sad. But it was the face of Annette Myers that truly upset him. He wished he'd found it in himself to forgive her sins; he feared that he might, in some way, have denied her a place in Heaven. Of course, it wasn't up to him where somebody's soul resided after they departed this life, but he always felt a sense of responsibility in guiding them to God in the best way he could.

The truth was, she would have been an ideal wife.

Why did she have to tell me of her past…?

Dear me, he thought, *Harry Frobisher… The Third Rook…*

He liked Lord Frobisher, especially his warmth and sincerity. He was a man to be trusted, a man who would stay beside a wounded comrade… A man who could keep a secret.

"Mr Matthews," he called across to Lawrence, "have you thought about attending my Sunday morning services? You and your wife would be very welcome."

Lawrence eased the car off the main Bodmin Road, towards Frobisher Hall. He was already driving through the estate, and slowed down as he approached someone riding a horse alongside the road. Staring through the drizzle, he noticed Ellen Carfax making her way from the direction of Bodmin.

Canon Trebarwith also noticed the figure of Ellen Carfax but didn't recognise her.

"I suppose we're usually quite busy here on the estate, Canon," Lawrence answered, peering over his shoulder, "but I think it would be nice to find the time to go to church." He finally swung into the main driveway and started to make his way up towards the house.

"My word…" Canon Trebarwith gasped, "what a beautiful house. So very… so very noble and beautiful."

The twin towers rose up, their peaks lost in the mist and drizzle, the battlements silhouetted in the afternoon gloom. With no sun to sparkle off the windows, the house sat leaden and downcast, unable to open an eyelid or raise a smile for such a distinguished man of God. Someone had lit a fire, and smoke belched intermittently from one of the many decoratively bricked chimneys.

Lawrence Matthews turned right, moving slowly past the Victorian walled garden. As he made his way round to the east side of the house, he slowed right down as he caught sight of his cottage, before finally driving into the rear courtyard, with the fountain in the middle and the estate office situated ahead of him.

He pulled to a halt near a footpath that led into the woods, past the stables.

"Lord and Lady Frobisher are already in the family chapel, Canon." Lawrence climbed out, quickly skirted round the car and opened the door. "Will you need a hand to carry anything?"

Canon Trebarwith hauled himself clumsily out of the car and pulled out a small wicker basket. "No, thank you, young man. I have everything here in my basket." He placed his Panama hat on his head and smiled.

"The family chapel is just a short walk down there." Lawrence pointed towards the path beside the stables. "You can't miss it. I have work to do in the house."

They shook hands, and Trebarwith watched as he scurried off towards the main house. He then turned and started to descend the path into the forest.

The Frobisher Chapel was set to one side of the path that led down from the rear courtyard. Early Gothic, its true origins were as mysterious as Frobisher Hall itself; local estate workers said it had stood for over eight hundred years, yet many had never walked its stone floors or knelt in prayer under its roof. Its stained-glass windows had become so grimy and covered with moss that no sunlight penetrated within. It stood, lonely and miserable, a testament to the broken faith of the Frobisher family, and Canon Trebarwith breathed a sigh of relief when he considered the fact that the current Lord and Lady Frobisher were now ready to find their peace with God within its desolate walls.

The small cemetery was overgrown with weeds and wild flowers. Nettles and thorns had long since covered the mounds, and now only the broken and jagged gravestones remained, their inscriptions long since faded, as was the memory of those who lay buried beneath, decayed and forgotten.

He paused.

It was a dreadful place, a lonely and forlorn corner of the Frobisher Estate that seemed devoid of any Divine presence. It was as though God had passed by these gates and ignored the sad cries of the souls within.

As he went to move forward, a lone rook fluttered down and perched itself upon one of the gravestones, eyeing him suspiciously.

Pushing open the large oak door, he immediately noticed two figures sitting silently together in the family pew, facing the altar. As he walked along the nave, he passed three wooden crosses leaning against the stone wall to one side; beneath them, flowers, long since dead, lay scattered upon the floor. Upon each respective cross, the following names were inscribed:

Lord Alfred Peter Frobisher
Lady Margaret Linda Frobisher
William Frank Frobisher

On the walls, commemorative plaques with delicately inscribed Latin text bore witness to the lives of the Frobishers who'd lived and died and whose bodies were now dust and bones buried deep beneath the chapel and surrounding graveyard. Family standards, tattered and threadbare, hung from the rafters, alongside dusty cobwebs.

His footsteps echoed in the small church and a chill settled upon all who gathered within.

Ahead of him, the altar loomed cold and unassuming, flanked by two large red curtains he assumed covered entrances to the crypt or the sacristy.

When he finally approached the altar, Canon Trebarwith bowed in humble penitence before turning to face Harry and Morag.

"Lord and Lady Frobisher," he said softly.

"Canon, thank you for agreeing to come here today." Morag smiled. She was wearing a simple grey dress with her favourite tartan scarf around her neck. Her eyes were heavy and tired, yet her face still seemed so radiant, with her long red hair tied respectfully back.

She was holding Harry's hand.

"I pray that today the Lord will bless you and your house, and that these terrible events that have weighed so heavily upon you both will be swept aside by His love."

Harry nodded weakly, his head lowered and his shoulders hunched. His whole demeanour was of someone broken and bowed. Though his face had been cleaned, he was terribly cut and bruised.

Canon Trebarwith set his Book of Common Prayer to one side, broke and silently blessed two small pieces of bread, and poured communion wine into a silver chalice.

"I thought I might say prayers for the souls of those taken from us so violently, and pray also for God's forgiveness for the man now standing accused of their murder."

Morag pulled Harry closer and gently kissed his cheek. He lay his head meekly against her shoulder.

"Merciful Father, hold close the souls of those dear departed, taken from us so violently... Captain Wilbur Grant, Annette

Myers and Peran Freeman… May they rest in eternal peace. We also ask for your forgiveness for Colonel Charles Standish, who now stands accused of their murders… May the law be fair and his punishment swift… We ask this in your name… Amen."

Turning to a large marble cross standing high above the altar, Canon Trebarwith began to read the service of Holy Communion, before finally turning to Harry and Morag to join them in the Lord's Prayer.

After this, he picked up the two pieces of bread and watched as Morag shuffled forward onto her knees, before turning to Harry and guiding him forward to a wooden rail, on which they now leaned, their hands cupped before them…

"The Body of Christ…" He dropped a piece of bread first into Morag's hand and then into Harry's.

Turning back to the altar, he picked up the chalice, held it high, turned and offered it to Morag, who drew it to her lips.

"The Blood of Christ…" Taking it from her, he gently wiped the rim and offered it to Harry, who tentatively reached forward, before receiving it and also drawing it to his lips.

Taking the chalice back from Harry, Canon Trebarwith returned to the altar and lowered his head in prayer. Above them in the rafters, a dove fluttered, alarmed by the proceedings below.

He wanted so desperately to speak to God… to find forgiveness… He searched his heart… his soul…

But God wasn't there…

"I remember your voice, Canon Trebarwith," Harry's voice, hoarse and distant, echoed in the church.

Trebarwith turned round.

"I remember your voice now…" Harry continued. "The day I lay wounded in that hospital tent… That grenade had taken my sight and I thought I was going to die… You spoke to me… said a prayer for me… You searched through my pockets and gave me my Bible… and you also took the letter Captain Grant had given to me. I suppose you were looking for something that might identify me..." Harry shuffled back onto his seat, helped by Morag, who sat quietly beside him.

"I shouldn't worry about the things I've done, Lord Frobisher... The poison you have both just drunk from this chalice will start to take effect in a couple of minutes..." Trebarwith stepped forward and stood mockingly before them. "Before she vanished, Locusta mixed a rather lethal mixture. Death won't take too long, I hope."

"Why?" muttered Morag, weakly.

"Why...?" Canon Trebarwith smiled. "Because Captain Grant got it wrong; Captain Frobisher was never one of the Rooks. It was Captain Grant, Annette Myers, Colonel Standish... and I was the Fourth Rook... It was so easy... Why should anyone suspect a man of God? Someone who brought comfort to the wounded and dying during those terrible years? You see, I had the freedom to move around the Continent... to complete my work for the good of Germany—"

"Treacherous bastard," Harry groaned.

"That's right, Captain Frobisher... A rise in blood pressure will hasten the flow of poison through your body."

"You didn't have to murder..." Harry whispered.

"Oh, but I did... You see, Captain Grant suspected me... I knew he was a friend of yours. Yes, you are right. The day they brought you into that hospital tent, I initially didn't recognise you. When I searched you, I heard you call your brother's name... William... and then I found the letter. I was going to end your life there and then: a simple pressure over the mouth and nostrils; you were too weak to have resisted. And then your companion, Benson, came back with some bandages... But at least I had the letter, which I duly burned... Are your legs and arms beginning to feel heavy?"

Harry nodded weakly.

"And so I settled in Bodmin," Trebarwith continued, "as far away from the world as I could. And then Annette Myers came down here to live… I knew of her misfortune; the death of her husband and children, though I never knew the circumstances surrounding the deaths of her two boys. I assumed they had died in an air raid… She became a member of my congregation. She would clean the church, and we would pray together. I knew she bore a tremendous guilt, but she never found it in herself to tell me about it. That was until the other morning…" He moved closer, eyeing Harry intently. "You'll soon be unable to speak. Try to relax… The numbness will slowly consume your lungs… Death will follow…"

Harry raised his head.

Trebarwith leaned forward. "Yes, Lord Frobisher?"

"Murderer," Harry whispered.

"Yes, I suppose I am. But therein lies the fantastic irony of all this: military justice will dispose of Colonel Standish, and your joint suicides will tie up any loose ends quite nicely." He looked across at Morag.

Her eyes were closed.

"Poor Charles Standish; he was utterly convinced you were the Fourth Rook," he said, turning his attention back to Harry. "I suppose that was the good thing about knowing the identities of the three Rooks, remaining anonymous myself." He stood up, his face hardening, his lips curling into a snarl. "And then Annette Myers invited Captain Grant to Bodmin, to confront him and ask him to return the only two things that survived that dreadful fire: the charred remains of a boat and a soldier on horseback. And that was when I saw him, walking down the road beside the vicarage…" Turning to Morag, he gently pushed her shoulder.

She didn't move.

Turning to Harry, he did the same.

Harry sat motionless, his head slumped against Morag's shoulder.

"How lucky could I be…? Poor Captain Grant got it wrong."

"But Captain Grant didn't get it wrong." The voice came from behind one of the red curtains beside the altar. It was calm, relaxed, yet resolute and sure.

Inspector Edwards emerged slowly, dressed immaculately in his double-breasted suit and holding his beloved Fedora hat by his side. As he appeared, the curtain to the other side was swept aside and Sergeant Cadan materialised, holding a small revolver which he aimed directly at Trebarwith's head.

For a moment, the clergyman said nothing, as realisation and incomprehension fought for control of his senses.

"I must say, Lord and Lady Frobisher, you might want to brighten this place up." Edwards moved across the altar until he stood gazing down at Trebarwith on the lower step. Shaking his head, he said, "In all my years as a police inspector, I have never met such a devious and evil individual as yourself, Canon Trebarwith… other than a certain person I have yet to hunt down."

Trebarwith opened his mouth to say something, before closing it and dumbly shaking his head. Turning back to Harry and Morag, he stared blankly as they rose tentatively from their pews and inched slowly away from him.

"Don't worry too much if you've lost your voice," comforted Edwards. "When you drop through the trap door, the hangman's noose will snap your neck and clear any obstructions."

"But…" Trebarwith eyed the chalice on the altar.

Edwards looked across at Morag and Harry. "I take it you didn't eat or drink anything?"

Morag opened her hand and let two small pieces of bread drop to the floor. "No," she whispered, looking across towards the chalice, "we did as you said and raised it to our lips, but that was it…" She wrapped her arm around Harry and guided him across the nave. She didn't stop until they were standing next to Sergeant Cadan.

The big policeman smiled and winked at her.

"But the letter accused Colonel Standish...?" Trebarwith's face moved from one of confused disbelief to one of intrigue.

"No, Canon, it accused you. But a letter on its own would never have stood up in a court of law, whereas the contents of that chalice will. Captain Grant named the three Rooks as himself, Annette Myers and Colonel Standish." He pulled a letter from his jacket pocket and handed it across to Trebarwith. "Here it is, Canon."

Trebarwith took it from him and unfolded it.

"As you can see, he names you as the Fourth Rook and has written the word 'traitor' beside your name..." Edwards held out his hand and Trebarwith handed it back. "So, this morning, in Peran Freeman's office, I had to move fast. Naming Colonel Standish as the Fourth Rook and Lord Frobisher as the Third Rook did two things: it drew suspicion away from yourself and it presented an ideal opportunity to teach Colonel Standish a lengthy lesson in humility." Edwards stared across at Harry's bruised face. "They do say Bodmin Gaol is haunted..."

"But why this...?" Trebarwith peered across at Sergeant Cadan, before staring helplessly at Morag and Harry. "Why this subterfuge?"

"Because leaving Lord and Lady Frobisher alive was always going to be... How did you so cheerily put it...? A loose end?" Edwards shook his head. "You see, Lord Frobisher would one day remember who it was who spoke to him in that hospital tent, and he would confront you... so what better opportunity might you have than being asked to come here to perform a quiet ceremony of Holy Communion. You poison them both, then appear at the door of Frobisher Hall, shocked and traumatised after finding their bodies; obviously a suicide pact. I expect you would have given evidence at the inquest telling the coroner that they'd been to see you and that they were finding it difficult to live with the scandal of Lord Frobisher's involvement with The Nest of Rooks."

Trebarwith raised his hands and stared at them.

"Morag?" Edwards called across the nave.

"Yes?" she replied, momentarily moving across Cadan's line of vision.

"Could you please open the door and wave across to the main path? There are several police constables waiting for my signal to enter." Edwards turned back to Trebarwith, his smile fading.

Trebarwith was holding the chalice in both hands. "A public trial is something I couldn't face…" He stared into the cup. "Socrates chose hemlock as his preferred way of dying."

"Socrates didn't murder three innocent people and betray his country," Edwards said coldly.

Morag had moved towards the door, but now she paused, watching intently for someone to make the next move. She glanced briefly at the door before turning her gaze back to the altar.

"I don't think we're going to need the services of those constables, Morag." Edwards' eyes remained cold, fixed rigidly on Trebarwith. "However, there are a few questions I would like to put to you before you depart this world."

"Go ahead, Inspector." The clergyman sighed deeply.

"Thank you. First, you say you saw Captain Grant walking down past the vicarage. How did you find out where he was staying?"

"When Annette Myers left me that afternoon, I followed his route down the path and into Creek Lane. I waited a while and caught sight of him leaving the cottage. I had my Panama hat on and tilted forward, so he never recognised me. I followed him the next day and watched him enter Peran Freeman's office. I never trusted Captain Grant, too clever for his own good. I guessed he was onto me, but couldn't work out why he was down here. I knew he was one of the Rooks, but then so was Annette Myers. I needed to know what his intentions were. So, early on Friday morning, I paid him a visit; with the obvious consequences."

"How did you manage to relieve Captain Grant of his revolver before using it to shoot him? I couldn't see any signs of a struggle." Edwards mentally assessed the distance between himself and Trebarwith. If he or Sergeant Cadan sprang forward they would never get anywhere near the clergyman before he drained the contents of the chalice.

"It was early. The door to 13 Creek Lane wasn't locked. I knew what had happened there and the stories local people told about the place being haunted. I found Captain Grant asleep in the kitchen, his revolver on the table. I decided then that he had to die. You see, I just couldn't take the risk of him exposing me. I took the gun, pointed it at his temple. That was when he opened his eyes and stared at me." Trebarwith gazed dreamily into the chalice. "He wasn't frightened. He just stared with a quiet resignation, almost an acceptance that he was going to find an end to his torment." Looking across at Edwards he added, "You weren't fooled by the fake suicide."

"Captain Grant was left handed. You shot him in the right temple and put the gun in his right hand," Morag said coldly.

"Ah… An easy mistake, but one I could be forgiven for making." Trebarwith smiled.

"And so, Annette Myers had to die," Edwards prompted.

"That wasn't my plan," Trebarwith's face took on a more pitiful and dejected countenance. "She came to me later that morning and told me that she had visited Captain Grant and found him dead. She then confessed her adulterous affair with him. I'd known her identity from the first time I saw her in Bodmin. It was pure coincidence that she came here to live. Remember, Inspector, I knew the identity of all the Rooks, but they never knew mine. Captain Grant was the only one who suspected. I had proposed marriage to her which she was considering. I would have married her and kept my true identity secret. But after her confession, and the fear she might one day find out who I was… well, that was a chance I couldn't take."

"So you poisoned her." Morag's words sliced through the musty atmosphere.

"I had befriended Locusta Baker, and given her shelter from the police when they were hunting down her sister, Edwina. She told me who she was and the murders she had committed. I think she thought the game was up, and wanted to find some kind of atonement for her crimes. Knowing that my past might one day catch up with me, I used her skills and knowledge in concocting poisons and made a pact with her that we could both look after each other. She supplied the poison that I used to lace Annette Myers' cup of tea yesterday afternoon. She's also responsible for this little mixture." Trebarwith eyed the liquid in the chalice and sniffed hesitantly. "It was my idea that she make her way to Frobisher Hall and assume the role of a member of staff. She was clever, I give her that. From what I hear, she was quite elusive, almost ghostly in her comings and goings." Turning to Morag he taunted, "You don't even know who I'm talking about, do you?"

"Gregson, the maid…" Morag muttered.

"Yes, but describe her, Lady Frobisher. Provide a description for the intrepid Inspector Edwards here."

Morag stared blankly ahead.

Inspector Edwards sighed heavily. "How were you planning to kill Colonel Standish?"

Trebarwith chuckled, "Up until now, standing in this chapel, I thought you might have seen to that…"

"My God, all this, just because you turned traitor and feared discovery by the spy network you controlled." Edwards shook his head.

Trebarwith casually shrugged his shoulders.

"Why kill Peran Freeman?" Morag stepped forward.

"I'd seen Captain Grant enter his office holding some kind of letter. Later, when he left, he didn't have the letter with him. I knew it would only be a matter of time before Peran Freeman found out about the death of Grant, and by then it would be too late to act. I couldn't do anything during the day because of his secretary being there in the office. But later... when she had gone home... I'm sorry, I lost control... If he'd just given me the letter, I'd have let him live."

"No you wouldn't," Edwards cut in. "You were going to kill Peran Freeman from the moment you walked into his office."

"You monster. I hope you rot in Hell," Morag hissed, before moving across to Harry and sliding her arm protectively around him. "All that hate and spite."

"It wasn't easy," Trebarwith shrugged, "But a necessity."

Harry stepped forward, tapping his stick against the stone floor. "I remember someone else who once said that to me." He leaned heavily on his stick, as though overcome with painful memories. "I suppose some people are only in this world to hurt others."

Trebarwith ignored the comment and turned to Inspector Edwards.

Edwards spoke slowly, his words heavy with emotion. "Do what you will, Canon Trebarwith. I'll not stop you."

"Thank you, Inspector." Trebarwith turned and stared sadly at the crucifix towering over him. Raising the chalice to his mouth, he gulped down the contents before lowering himself upon the altar steps.

Epilogue

'I saw Ellen Carfax for the last time today. William doesn't have Harry's natural beauty. He looks sad, even for someone so young and innocent. I took him from her and heard her wretched crying as I rode back to Frobisher Hall...'

Journal of Lady Margaret Frobisher

Morag stared at the bottle of poison on the table in Ellen Carfax's dining room before picking it up and delicately unscrewing the lid. The thick brown gooey liquid inside had a slightly pungent smell and Morag wrinkled her nose before quickly replacing the lid. Around her, on numerous shelves, bottles of herbs, ointments and an assortment of different coloured jars stared down at her; a bewildering array of medicines and herbal remedies.

The word 'poison' made her blood run cold.

She continued to stare at the word, pencilled upon a white strip of paper that had been roughly glued to the glass, as she pulled a chair away from the table and sat down. Her mind was still consumed with the recent events that had led to the death of Canon Trebarwith in the family chapel, and she found it hard to believe that two whole days had passed since then. Life had begun to settle down on the Frobisher Estate, with staff in the house going about their daily work with an air of relaxation and ease. Meals had been taken on an informal basis, and Morag had insisted that Susan and Lawrence join both herself and Harry this coming evening as Inspector Edwards would be spending his final night there before travelling to London in the morning.

Morag had asked why he needed to get back to London so quickly, but he'd just smiled and lit his pipe.

She was both surprised and delighted to see Doctor Mitchell sitting in one of the more comfortable chairs positioned by the fireplace in the dining room. He looked up and smiled as she entered, before returning his gaze to the roaring fire. Morag thought he looked tired and gaunt, but certainly much better than when she'd last seen him in Peran Freeman's office. He had a small blanket wrapped around him and a cup of herbal tea in his hand.

"It's good to see you again, Doctor." Morag smiled at him. "Are you feeling better?"

"I am, Lady Frobisher, thank you for asking." He stared across the room, the glow from the fire flickering in his eyes.

"And he'll get better staying here with me for a few days, won't you?" Ellen Carfax appeared at the door with two cups of her magical tea. Turning to Morag she added, "Does Harry's leg give him much trouble?"

"I think they did more damage trying to cut out the pieces of shrapnel. But, yes, it does play him up occasionally."

"Well," Ellen observed the jar in Morag's hand, "rub a tiny amount around the scars, and he should find it a little easier."

Morag glanced suspiciously at the jar.

Ellen smiled, "Deadly nightshade has been used for centuries for many purposes other than killing people. I generally mix small amounts with gin and sell it to local folk. It's very good for bad backs and general muscle pain."

"I was hoping you'd say something like that." Morag breathed a sigh of relief. The room was warm, mostly due to the fire raging in the grate; and the warmth seemed to enhance the smell of herbs that drifted around her.

Ellen sat down and slid one of the cups of tea across to Morag. "Who would have thought it? Canon Trebarwith? And Susan shooting dead that scoundrel Treave."

"Aye," replied Morag, lifting the cup and sipping her tea.

"What will you both do now?" said Doctor Mitchell, turning to look at her.

"Harry's nerves are shattered, Doctor," Morag sighed; "I need to take him away somewhere peaceful and quiet."

"Do they know what the poison was in the chalice?" Ellen sipped her tea.

"Inspector Edwards sent what was left in the chalice over to Plymouth to be tested. He thinks it was hemlock, hence Canon Trebarwith's reference to Socrates." Morag looked around the room, feeling herself relax but knowing there was a purpose to her visit, one that caused an uncomfortable silence to settle between the three of them.

The only relief came from the intermittent crackle of a burning log in the fireplace.

From outside came the harsh sound of an axe cutting through wood. Morag had seen Branok cutting logs as she'd walked down the path, pausing to catch his eye, before smiling and nodding her head in friendly recognition.

She'd thought of the terrible shock he'd suffered that had muted his voice, and remembered her own experiences at Amble Lodge. At that moment she'd said a silent prayer for him.

Placing her cup down, she reached into her cardigan pocket and drew out Lady Margaret's journal. Contemplating it, as though the next decision she made would define and shape her future life with Harry, she hesitated before saying, "I thought I would give this to you, Ellen."

She laid it on the table before Ellen Carfax.

As she pushed it across the table, the atmosphere in the room grew noticeably heavier. It was as though something was about to happen and the three of them were utterly powerless to stop it. Doctor Mitchell glanced at the book before staring back at the fire, his eyes sad and vacant. Ellen Carfax reached forward and drew the book towards her, flicking it open as she did so.

"Was this what you wanted from Mr Freeman?" Morag asked gently, looking across to Mitchell.

"Yes," he said dolefully. "I knew Lady Margaret had given it to Mr Freeman for safekeeping. She told me the day Harry and William went off to war... I think she didn't want to destroy it, but she also knew that what she'd written in there could possibly destroy her sons."

"And you kept this secret for all these years?" Morag tried to adopt a reproachful sting to her words, but one look at Mitchell's eyes weakened her resolve.

"I asked him to." Ellen looked up from the journal and smiled sympathetically at the doctor.

"And you don't think Harry deserves to know?" Morag asked, unable this time to restrain her accusing tone.

"What...?" replied Ellen Carfax. "That I'm his mother...? That I gave birth to both Harry and William and then gave them up to Lord and Lady Frobisher?" She sniffed.

"Ellen..." Doctor Mitchell soothed, reaching out his hand, "don't... You've done nothing wrong..."

"Nothing wrong? Nothing wrong?" Ellen stared at Morag, then back at Mitchell. Finally, she gazed through the door, to a place beyond her cottage.

Morag followed her gaze and knew she was looking towards Frobisher Hall.

"I gave them up..." She began to sob, clutching the journal to her breast. "I gave up my sons... And when they needed me, I wasn't there."

Doctor Mitchell hauled himself painfully out of his chair and knelt beside her.

"Ellen, do not reproach yourself." Looking towards Morag he said, "Don't judge her, Lady Frobisher. Please, I beg of you, don't judge her… You see, Lady Margaret couldn't conceive; I was the family doctor for years, and tried to help. Lord Alfred became embittered; he feared the family name dying out."

"Then I appeared," Ellen sobbed. "I'd left the workhouse near Launceston and crossed Bodmin Moor… By the time I reached Frobisher Hall, I was near death. Lord Alfred found me and carried me to safety. I remember looking up into his eyes… I had never seen such kindness and love…"

"Ellen was taken in and given employment within the house," Doctor Mitchell continued, "but Lord Alfred… You see—"

"I became his lover," Ellen choked, wiping her eyes. "Lady Margaret knew… She wanted to dismiss me, but he wouldn't hear of it…" Her voice trailed off and her eyes stared distantly, lost deep within her memories.

"Anyway, she soon fell pregnant." Doctor Mitchell kissed her hand and looked lovingly into her eyes. "She was forced to live alone here at Sunrise Cottage because it was lost deep within the forest and nobody ever had cause to visit. You see, the other members of staff would have immediately recognised a scandal, and the family couldn't face that; so they were told that she'd left and taken up employment elsewhere…" He smiled at Ellen and squeezed her hand. "I delivered Harry into this world over there in that bedroom." He nodded towards the room in which Lawrence Matthews had recovered after his fall. "And that was when Lord and Lady Frobisher approached me and informed me of their plan."

"At first I said no." Ellen's strength began to crumble.

Morag felt tears begin to well up in her eyes, tears she had no hesitation in letting fall. She'd left Harry sleeping in their bedroom and knew that both Susan and Lawrence were in the house keeping a watchful eye over him. Sitting there, at that moment, she just wanted to be with him, to soothe and caress him, to tell him she'd never let anyone harm him again.

"But then I thought of the life he would have… The heir to Frobisher Hall… the estate, the name…" She finally broke down, her sobbing becoming uncontrollable. "What… What could I have given him compared to that?"

Morag wiped her own tears and took a deep breath. "Come back with me to Frobisher Hall," she said gently, reaching across and grasping Ellen's hand. "Come back with me and tell Harry… He should know."

Ellen leaned forward and pulled Morag's hand to her lips. "I remember Harry would visit me… He knew I liked to paint, and so he brought brushes and paints… He would walk with me and help set up my easel, though I always insisted that I paint from somewhere I couldn't be seen from the Hall… From a young boy he would ride his horse out here and sit exactly where you are, Lady Frobisher… I would talk to him about his school… the books he liked… He once found a book written by Edgar Allan Poe, and read one of the stories: *The Fall of the House of Usher*. He always liked the ghost stories." She smiled and chuckled. "Although Harry was happy to spend time with me, William never visited. It was always Harry… I never knew if he suspected… Then, on the eve of his leaving to fight in France, he came to me and held me tightly; he wouldn't let me go… I knew he was frightened, and I wanted to hide him. I said I would hide him up the chimney, and I remember he laughed… But he was frightened, absolutely terrified… I gave him a Bible, which I signed, and he rode off back to Frobisher Hall."

"Harry's a wonderful man, Ellen, a truly wonderful man. You should be so proud of him." Morag drew a small handkerchief from her cardigan pocket and wiped her eyes. Sniffling, she added, "When I went to the garrison in town to bring him home, the men of his regiment formed a guard of honour as I walked him back to our car. They absolutely adore him." She steadied her nerves and nodded to Doctor Mitchell, who returned to his chair. "Please come back with me… You should see him… He's suffered greatly; but I know him, he'll pull through… He needs you, Ellen."

Ellen Carfax kissed Morag's hand and said, "In time I will, when he's recovered. But now he needs you, Morag. Promise me you'll look after my son. Promise me you'll love him and give him hope… Will you do that?"

Morag stood up, walked round the table and knelt before her. Tears were running freely down her cheeks. Grasping both her hands, she said, "I already have… I'm carrying his child."

★★★

"Your Ladyship," Susan called across the table, "Lawrence and I are so pleased to hear of your news." There was a depth of love and admiration in her words that touched Inspector Edwards immensely.

"Thank you, Susan." Morag glanced across at Lawrence. "And thank you both for what you did."

"Hear, hear," Harry muttered.

"When did you know?" Edwards asked.

"Actually, it was during our honeymoon in London," Morag replied; "I saw a specialist in Harley Street a few days before we came down here."

Edwards wanted to say so much, but the words couldn't break through the wall of emotions he felt as he remembered Elisha. She would have made a wonderful mother, so full of life and an inspiration to everyone who ever met her. He tried, but couldn't stop his heart weighing heavily as he considered the life they might have had. That Morag would make a loving mother, he had no doubt.

But the emotions cut deep, and the memory of Elisha was an open wound he felt would never heal. He looked across at Morag and smiled, seeing the love of his wife reflected in her eyes.

She gazed back at him.

"I think Colonel Standish might have learnt his lesson." Edwards sipped his coffee. "When Captain Hemmings authorised his release from Bodmin Gaol, and went down there to transport him back to the barracks, they found him gibbering about seeing ghosts… Said he'd seen the ghost of a young woman holding a baby."

"I think you might have been a little harsh on him." Harry frowned, lighting his pipe. "I think I would have been terrified."

"Harry," Morag said, smiling and shaking her head, "that's what I love so much about you. After what that brute did to you, you've never shown him any malice."

"My dear," Harry countered, "I saw enough hatred in those four years in France to last a lifetime. I hope and pray we never have to go through it again."

There were the mumblings of agreement from Lawrence and Susan.

Dinner was a sumptuous affair, with meat-stuffed olives followed by grilled lemon and garlic bass with cranberry walnut salad, and finished off with large helpings of Harry's favourite, apple pie, and Mrs Chambers' speciality custard.

At Morag's instruction, enough had been prepared to feed the staff, along with several bottles of the famous Frobisher wine.

While Harry sipped his whisky, she settled for lemonade.

"Anyway," continued Edwards, "I think seeing ghosts whilst locked away in Bodmin Gaol is going to be the least of Colonel Standish's problems. He's been summoned back to Whitehall to face an inquiry into the whole business of The Nest of Rooks. He certainly exceeded his authority on several occasions, especially when questioning you, Lord Frobisher."

"Exceeded his authority?" Morag thundered.

"Yes, I know, what he did was unforgivable; but, believe me, he was a frightened man. First Captain Grant, then Annette Myers. He truly believed Harry was coordinating the murders via another person. As one of the Rooks working on the Continent during the war, he knew he was one of four within the network, but apart from the instructions he received, and the orders he followed, he had no idea as to the identity of his companions. Then he was promoted, quite swiftly really, and found himself privy to information he'd not had access to before. He found out about Captain Grant and his suspicions, and his friendship with Lord Frobisher. What could he do? He knew that one of the four, the Fourth Rook, was a traitor; but he couldn't prove anything. He heavily suspected Harry, but then Harry was blinded and brought back to England." Edwards paused and looked around him. It was as though the entire household were hanging on his every word. "Before he could do anything, Harry disappeared, travelling across Europe in a desperate attempt to find a cure for his blindness." He smiled across at Harry, remembering his first night in this very room. "But whilst he couldn't find Harry, he could watch closely the activities of Captain Grant, wondering if *he* knew the identity of the traitor – which he did. When Harry reappeared last November, Standish held back, content to see whether Captain Grant made contact with him; and he did, after travelling down to Bodmin in response to a request from his former lover and fellow Rook, Annette Myers. Though Standish ordered me to travel down here and find proof of your guilt, Lord Frobisher, he felt he couldn't afford to stay in London, so came down on the same train as yourselves."

"And then of course there was Archie Cummings," whispered Morag.

"Yes," replied Edwards, "good old Archie Cummings, hired killer sent to murder Lord Frobisher on the orders of Morgan Treave... By Jove, didn't he create a red herring. He

383

caused all manner of confusion, both for myself and Colonel Standish, who probably wondered if he was one of the Rooks, or maybe a killer sent by Harry to kill Captain Grant and the rest. That confusion was settled when we found Captain Grant dead, obviously killed after I'd seen off Archie Cummings. But when Captain Grant was murdered, Standish became terrified; was he going to be next? Hence his rough treatment of Harry."

"It still didn't give him the right to treat Harry like that," Morag said sharply, reaching across and grasping her husband's hand.

"I agree. And you might be happy to hear that when Captain Hemmings saw him this morning, his face was still heavily bruised…" Edwards took another sip of his coffee before staring across at the whisky decanter. "Lord Frobisher, you might want to stay clear of your wife's right hook."

The general laughter came as a blessed relief as Edwards realised that Frobisher Hall hadn't heard the sound for a long time. It was good to hear, and the atmosphere in the dining room lifted considerably.

"What about Locusta Baker?" asked Lawrence, swiping away the feeling of light-hearted relief. "She is still a threat."

"Ah yes, Locusta Baker…" Edwards frowned and tapped his fingers on the table. "Wanted for mass murder and now on the run. With Treave dead and his lair discovered, she'll be hiding under a rock somewhere, which will make my task of hunting her down difficult. But I've issued a rough description of her, taken from members of your staff here and Susan, and circulated it across several local constabularies. Sergeant Cadan has men patrolling the Frobisher Estate, but I have the distinct feeling she's long gone."

"And to think she was here… in Frobisher Hall," Morag whispered.

The grandfather clock struck the hour of 10pm.

Edwards was about to say something about the meal but stopped abruptly as the door to the dining room swung open. Looking up, he noticed one of the parlour maids walking in with a silver tray, upon which lay a small envelope. She walked across to him and handed him the envelope.

Turning to Morag she announced, "I'm sorry to interrupt, Your Ladyship; this letter was just found inside the main doors. We don't know how long it was there or who delivered it."

"Thank you, Lucy." Morag nodded.

Intrigued, Edwards held the envelope up to examine it. Obviously low-grade and fairly inexpensive; probably available from a general stationer. He peered at his name written in ink across the front. There was no address or postage stamp.

Opening it, he pulled out a small letter, written also in ink; and, like the envelope, on fairly low-quality paper.

He read the contents to himself several times:

Inspector Edwards
  We both know your wife never died of Spanish flu.
  Look for me in the eternal nightmare that is about to descend upon you and those you love.
  Locusta Baker

Edwards folded the letter and pushed it back into the envelope.

"Everything okay, old boy?" Harry asked.

"It seems," Edwards replied solemnly, "that my return to London can't come soon enough."

He glanced across at Morag and smiled.

Author's Notes

When Ellen Carfax recalls her final meeting with Harry before he went off to war, she mentions hiding him in the chimney. This was a story told by my mother-in-law, of her uncle, Ernest Kempthorne, who fought with the Duke of Cornwall's Light Infantry during the First World War. One day, when he was home on leave, he was so shell-shocked and traumatised that he begged his mother to hide him up the chimney so he wouldn't have to go back. Of course, like many others, he did. He was killed at the Battle of Cambrai in 1917.

Bodmin Gaol is referred to in both this book and *The Woman with the Red Hair*. An impressive historic building in the heart of Bodmin, I remember as a child visiting my friend who actually lived in part of the building. We used to play in his bedroom, which had once been a cell. When Colonel Standish is forced to spend time locked within the gaol's deepest cell, he claims to have seen the ghost of a young woman holding a baby. This refers to the story of Selina Wadge, who was convicted of murdering one of her two children and was hanged at Bodmin Gaol in 1878.

The Walter Raleigh Gilbert Monument actually exists and is an historic landmark overlooking the town of Bodmin. As a young boy I would walk my dog around the surrounding fields.

When Harry Frobisher remembers a time, as a lad, when he stood beneath its towering structure and thought about writing a book about Bodmin, that is based upon my own experiences all those years ago.